Praise for
The Native Star

"M. K. Hobson dazzles! *The Native Star* is an awe-some mash-up of magic and steam-age technology—call it witchpunk. This debut novel puts a new shine on the Gilded Age."
—C. C. FINLAY

"Splendid! In *The Native Star*, M. K. Hobson gives us a Reconstruction-era America, beautifully drawn and filled with the energy of a young nation—and magic! Her heroine, Emily Edwards, is outspoken, brash, loving, and true; a delight to spend time with. Could there be a sequel, please?"
—MADELEINE ROBINS

BY M. K. HOBSON

The Hidden Goddess
The Native Star

The
HIDDEN
GODDESS

M. K. HOBSON

SPECTRA

BALLANTINE BOOKS • NEW YORK

A Spectra Mass Market Original

Copyright © 2011 by Mary Hobson

Published in the United States by Spectra, an imprint of The Random House Publishing Group, a division of Random House, Inc., New York.

SPECTRA and the portrayal of a boxed "s" are trademarks of Random House, Inc.

978-0-553-59266-5

Printed in the United States of America

www.ballantinebooks.com

9 8 7 6 5 4 3 2 1

Spectra mass market edition: May 2011

For Dan

ACKNOWLEDGMENTS

To everyone who helped make this book a reality (and you know who you are), I offer my humblest gratitude. Special thanks go to Sara Mueller, a brilliant writer and good friend, whose ideas about the mechanics of earth magic inspired many of Emily's magical experiences.

Prologue

Sunday, June 15, 1876
Mexico City

Naked, Lieutenant Utisz stood on a frost-rimed block of black obsidian before two tall doors made of intricately arranged human bones. A red-robed Temple acolyte knelt before him, washing his bare abdomen with a flaccid sponge, dipping it in ice water that smelled of blood.

It will be an honor to serve my country.

Utisz tried to conjure the conviction with which he'd spoken these words to General Blotgate, and willed himself not to shiver.

The lieutenant was in a small anteroom that echoed with the sound of water rushing through deep unseen channels. *The Purification Crypt,* it had been called by the attendant who had escorted him from the steamy heat of jungle summer into the frigid depths of this cavernous necropolis. The attendant had explained that all who would enter the Calendar Chamber must be ritually cleansed then anointed with bitter oils. And then the attendant had relieved him of his uniform, from epaulettes to skivvies.

Utisz clenched his jaw. Apprehension beat against his neologism—the magical ward behind which his emotions were locked. He regarded his own fear with dispassionate distance, as if listening to the far-off screams of a woman being chased by men who would brutalize her. Dissecting it, he decided that it was attributable merely to the coldness of the sponge (now passing over his genitals, damn it!), the disorientation of having been led into this place blindfolded, and a lingering fear of the dark—gained at the orphanage—that he'd never been able to entirely root from his psyche. None of it was pertinent to the task at hand.

The task at hand lay behind the two tall doors of polished bone. In the Calendar Chamber, where she waited—Itztlacoliuhqui, the Black Glass Goddess, the Goddess of Obsidian Knives.

Lieutenant Utisz closed his eyes, ignoring the servile hands traveling (less disturbingly, now) over his calves.

I am sure you have heard rumors about the recent . . . unpleasantness . . . at the credomancers' Institute in New York?

He remembered the words, spoken by General Oppenheimer Blotgate, Director of the Erebus Academy—the highest-ranking magical practitioner in the United States military. A man rarely seen and never spoken to. This in itself had been enough to make an invitation to his rosewood-paneled office unsettling. But adding to Utisz' disquiet had been his inability to imagine any professional matter on which the General might conceivably summon him. He'd only just graduated as a second lieutenant, and hadn't even received a posting yet. Utisz had been left to conclude that he was being called to discuss matters of a more *personal* nature. Word around the barracks was that the General had never once taken exception to his wife's serial indiscretions with much younger men—she had a renowned fondness for cadets—but it would be just his luck if he was the first to be called on the carpet.

So when the General had commenced the interview by asking about unpleasantness and credomancers, Utisz had been extremely relieved, if no less puzzled.

"I heard that Captain John Caul was killed" had been his crisp response. Back ramrod straight, eyes unwaveringly forward. "Murdered, sir."

"A profound tragedy," General Blotgate confirmed solemnly, light catching on the thick-seamed scar that ran from his ear to his shoulder. His voice was a low, crackling rasp. "He was extremely well regarded by the President. Grant kept trying to promote him, and Caul kept convincing him not to. He could have had the command of all the Army's magical divisions—but Caul was a soldier. A man of action. He preferred to operate independently, with a small hand-picked unit of the finest Maelstroms."

"His murder will be avenged," the lieutenant said, guessing that was the ultimate aim of the General's impromptu eulogy. But if it was, the General didn't notice the young officer's cleverness.

"Captain Caul was a true patriot," he continued. "Sadly, there is a fine line between patriotism and paranoia."

Blotgate reached into a carved box on his desk and withdrew a cigar. He did not hurry in lighting it, but rather left Utisz standing while he pierced it, clipped it, and lit it with snapped fingers and a guttural command summoning flame.

"Son, have you ever heard of the Temple of Itztlacoliuhqui?"

"A sect devoted to the worship of an Aztec goddess, sir. It is said that they seek to destroy the world in a great blood-apocalypse called *temamauhti*."

"Nothing could be further from the truth." Blotgate waved the cigar dismissively. "Why would anyone want to destroy the world? A misapprehension spread—with the best of intentions, no doubt—by Captain Caul. The truth is, the Temple seeks to *remake* the world, with themselves and a select group of allies in positions of leadership. We intend that the United States play a key role in that future leadership."

He tapped ash.

"Captain Caul's death has provided me with the opportunity to instruct the President on the *true* nature of the Temple's intentions. I must say, it took some doing to dislodge the misinformation Caul had hammered into Grant's thick old skull." Blotgate paused, half smiling, as if recalling a pleasant memory. It made Utisz wonder just how much convincing the President had required, and how precisely Blotgate had gone about it. "In any case, I am pleased to say that the President has finally relinquished his stubbornness. I have been given approval to proceed with a course of action I have advocated since before the war—a formal military alliance with the Temple of Itztlacoliuhqui."

The General took in a mouthful of smoke and rolled it over his tongue. It was as if he was waiting for a round of applause. But his air of self-satisfaction dispersed as quickly as the smoke, replaced with a bitter frown.

"Of course, we should have embarked on this course a decade ago," he said. "The delay has given our enemies time to work against us."

"Enemies, sir?"

"Captain Caul was not the only opponent of the Temple's plans for the great remaking," Blotgate said. "There is also a group of Russian scientists called the Sini Mira. They have created a poison called Volos' Anodyne. Our intelligence indicates that it is a truly monstrous and inelegant weapon, designed to pollute the global mantic well at its very source, rendering the working of such an immense magic—indeed, of any magic at all—utterly impossible." The General peered at Utisz through a veil of haze. "I am sure you agree that such arrogant foreign interference in our national destiny, and in the magical destiny of all mankind, must be swiftly and thoroughly curtailed."

"Yes, sir!"

"I kind of thought you would," the General said. "And to do that, we have to get the acorn."

"*Acorn,* sir?"

"Of course it's not the acorn we want, rather the redskin Witch inside it." The General leaned back in his chair, savoring the lieutenant's confusion. "The formula for the poison was hidden long ago, and we believe she knows where it is. But for some blasted reason the stupid squaw shed her human body and transferred her spirit into an acorn. And now she and the acorn are under the protection of the credomancers at their Institute in New York."

"*Credomancers.*" Utisz frowned. "A mongrel horde of Jews and foreigners and other undesirables. Why their tampering with the minds of patriotic Americans continues to be allowed by our elected officials, I shall never understand." Utisz, realizing suddenly that he had not been given permission to speak freely, reddened slightly. "Sir."

"Indeed," Blotgate allowed. "There are many things I do

not understand either, Lieutenant. But as men of magic—and officers of the United States Army—sometimes we must accept what we cannot understand." General Blotgate rolled the cigar between thumb and forefinger, contemplating it.

"But what I will *not* accept, Lieutenant"—the General released each word as if he were dropping it into a pond, letting it fall to the murky bottom—"is that a project that has the capacity to shift the balance of global power, and thrust this great country into the position of world dominance that it is destined to occupy, should be threatened by an *Indian* in a *nut.*"

He emphatically ground his cigar into a large brass ashtray.

"Before his death, Captain Caul was overseeing a secret project to stockpile huge amounts of chrysohaeme. He had convinced the President that this arsenal of refined magic was necessary to defend the United States against *temamauhti*. Now that the President has come to recognize how he was misguided, he has agreed that the arsenal should be put to a far more important use. It will be delivered to the Temple to aid them in their great work."

After this, the General did not speak again for a long time. Instead, he rested his elbows on his desk, clasped his hands together, and stared at Utisz. He stared so long that the lieutenant began to feel very uncomfortable. Heat crept up under his collar. He felt, strangely, as if he should fall to his knees and beg for mercy. He did not know why.

"It is my understanding that you have not received a posting yet, Lieutenant," the General finally said.

"I have not, sir," Utisz managed, his throat bone dry.

"Then it's your lucky day," the General said. "I am appointing you Army liaison to the Temple of Itztlacoliuhqui. You will be given command of a squadron. You and your men will deliver the chrysohaeme Caul stockpiled—as well as the bulk of the Army's reserves of Black Exunge—to the Temple. Once the delivery has been made, you will stay to serve the Black Glass Goddess in whatever capacity she requires. Do you understand the vital importance of this mission?"

"Yes, sir!"

"And do you accept it?"

"Yes, sir!" Utisz had ignored the soft, predatory tone of the question. He had lifted his chin resolutely. "It will be an honor to serve my country."

An honor to serve my country.

Lieutenant Utisz shivered with remembered pride, and from the feather-light touch of the Temple acolyte. He recognized the places where the bitter oil was being touched to his ice-washed skin: The brachial arteries along the inside of his arms. The femoral arteries along the inside of his legs. And finally on his throat, the *carotis communis.* The bleeding places.

"She will receive you now," the attendant said, after the Temple servant had silently gathered his things and bowed his way backward into the shadows. The doors of bone grated open; there was only gaping blackness beyond.

The attendant escorted Utisz through a close unlit corridor into an enormous room that seemed to expand around them as they entered it. It was like emerging into a winter night of deepest stillness and chill, all the stars blotted out by an angry hand.

The floor was deeply channeled in an intricate circular design that Utisz recognized as the ancient Aztec calendar for which the room was named. Black Exunge ran in these deep channels, outlining the vast pattern in bubbling stink. Mold-frosted leaves of diviners' sage smoldered over white-glowing charcoal in a hundred brazen tripods, thickening the air with narcotic clouds of smoke. Light from a high aperture in the domed ceiling sliced downward through the blue-silver haze, illuminating a deep, bowl-shaped pit in the calendar's great center.

The pit was deep and unlined. Thick hairy roots extended from the crumbling soil of its sides, piercing the surface of a whale-size reddish-brown lump that glistened like clotted blood. Half submerged in a bitter soup of Exunge, the thing shuddered and spasmed irregularly, making obscene plopping noises.

Lieutenant Utisz could not take his eyes off it. It was so arresting, indeed, that he hardly noticed the approach of a very fat man, his hands extended in jocular welcome.

"The High Priest of her sacred splendor," the attendant whispered in Utisz' ear. Only the hissing sibilance allowed the lieutenant to tear his gaze away from the mound of throbbing flesh. "Her *tonalpoulque,* keeper of her consecrated calendar."

The High Priest wore a plain, ill-fitting black suit—a shoddy background to the lavish ceremonial torque he wore around his neck. It was an extravagant, gaudy ornament; beads of gold and jade big as walnuts were strung through with brilliant, iridescent plumes. Twelve pendants were spaced along the necklace's length, each pendant a golden cage—and in each cage, a bit of dried human flesh. Most of the bits were utterly indistinguishable, but Utisz recognized some of them—a shriveled section of leathery intestine, a whole desiccated brain (which rattled in its golden cage like a little nut), and a small, hard heart.

"Thank you for coming, Lieutenant." The High Priest caught Utisz' hand, pumping it with gusto. "I am Selig Heusler. I trust your journey was comfortable?"

Utisz appreciated plain speaking and plain dealing. The words, spoken to him rather than above him, made him take an immediate liking to the High Priest, feathers and flesh-bits notwithstanding. "Yes, sir, th-thank you. I would p-present you with my papers, but . . ." Utisz clenched his teeth to stop their chattering, and spread his hands to highlight his nakedness.

"No need. Your men have already been hard at work unloading your government's tribute of chrysohaeme and Black Exunge." Here, Heusler leaned in close to murmur in Utisz' ear, "They'll all have to be killed, I'm afraid. They cannot be allowed to leave; with *temamauhti* so close, the Temple's location must remain a closely guarded secret."

Utisz blinked once or twice. But before he could even form words of protest, Heusler laid a hand on his arm to guide him toward a pyramid at the far end of the room. It was constructed entirely of human skulls, and blanketed in heavy, sparkling frost. "Come, let us make haste, for she is expecting you . . ."

As they passed the huge lump of flesh spasming in the pit, Utisz slowed for a closer look.

"The *Liver*," Heusler said, seeing the direction of the young man's gaze. "Incredible, isn't it? That, Lieutenant, is the engine that will power the Remaking. If the Indian in the nut doesn't stop us first."

"I have come with a plan," Lieutenant Utisz said, the words tumbling out on a silvery cloud. "The acorn—I know how we can retrieve it."

Heusler lifted his eyebrows in astonishment. "Do you? How quickly you work! You shall distinguish yourself in her service, I can see."

"Dreadnought Stanton is the key," Utisz said.

"Dreadnought Stanton?" Heusler's brow knit suspiciously. "Whatever do you mean?"

"Surely you've heard he is to be made Sophos—Master of the credomancers' Institute. He will be Invested on Midsummer's Eve. Once Stanton assumes formal control of the Institute, the Indian in the nut will be under his protection."

"Believe me, young man," the High Priest said with something like relief, "Stanton would *never* help us."

"Not willingly, perhaps." Utisz dropped his voice. "But love can encourage a man to compromise. He is engaged to be wed, the poor fool—"

Doest thou know, tonalpoulque, *that the Chinese believe that the liver contains the ethereal spirit?* The words rang through Utisz' head with an odd reverberance that made it seem his skull was carved of brass. *And the Egyptians, when someone is greatly beloved of them, say that person has a piece of their liver.*

"Then you must be very greatly loved, Mistress," Heusler said loudly, his voice ringing against the unseen walls, "for the piece you have is so very large." Heusler hurried the lieutenant toward the pyramid. "She stirs. It is time. Save your plans for her, my boy. Though I warn you, it has been my experience that the most carefully crafted plans of mortal men are no match for the whims of a goddess."

The pyramid was surmounted by an altar stone, and on the icy block a woman's body lay beneath a translucent veil of white silk. But she was not dead, Utisz saw; her breath made the thin silk tremble, and he could sense a pulse at the wrist of the slender dark-skinned arm. Utisz stared at the mask that had been placed over the woman's face. It was a hideous contorted sneer of carved ebony, dominated by curving fangs of amber-smoked ivory. Long braids—sliced from the scalps of long-forgotten victims—mixed with the woman's own glossy black hair, twining down over her smooth bared breasts, brushing caramel-hued nipples.

"Her vessel waits atop the sacred teocalli," Heusler said. "Just a local girl from one of the villages, but we do try to find the best. Her Divinity burns through a new one every time she awakens, and if we don't get her a pretty one she pouts."

"Very . . . pretty," Utisz mumbled, trying to imagine how a goddess might pout.

"Now, if you'll excuse me, she must be fed."

The High Priest scaled the steep teocalli, and was puffing hard by the time he reached the altar stone. He removed his coat and then his shirt, revealing plush rolls of white flesh intricately decorated with writhing black tattoos. The inked designs covered him from throat to wrists to belly, vanishing below his belt like dancing snakes.

Lifting his hands, Heusler began to speak in low, resonant tones:

"Rise, ancient powers of blood."

The words shuddered off the walls of glass, making the Exunge in its channels vibrate, slicing through the thick smoke like flying knives. Crackling tendrils of chain lightning danced over the surfaces of the room—flashes of brightness, viscid translucent cobwebs of bruise blue and bacterial yellow. The smell of ozone and charred bone layered itself over bitter incense and the reek of bile.

A rising light, cutting through the gloom, caught Utisz' attention. The Liver, in its pit of Black Exunge, was starting to . . . *glow.* It was transforming the slick tarry Exunge around itself into a luminous golden substance—chrysohaeme. The golden blood of the earth, magical power in its rawest form. Utisz could barely breathe for astonishment. This . . . *thing* could transform Black Exunge into chrysohaeme? No wonder Blotgate had wanted to ally with a goddess who had such power. And no wonder Caul had wanted to destroy her.

The glow spread outward from the Liver, and the Black Exunge in the channels that outlined the great calendar luminesced as if it had been touched with a torch. The glowing streams flowed toward the teocalli, snaking up the pyramid of skulls to the altar stone. Like sharp golden needles, they pierced the dusky flesh of the Goddess' vessel.

"Feed, Blade of Obsidian."

Far beneath the floor, the rocks of the earth churned. The woman's body on the altar stone spasmed wildly. The covering of white silk fell aside, revealing the woman's jerking limbs, bound by twining ropes of chrysohaeme—unwitting prey caught in a nest of vipers.

"Awaken, Dread Mistress."

At the words, the ropes of power jerked together at once, flaring to a supernatural brilliance. Utisz winced, shielding his eyes. When he brought his arm down, the light was gone utterly, replaced by a blackness as dark as the light had been bright.

The Goddess stood before the altar stone, looking down at him.

She was no longer a woman, that much was clear. All the feminine softness of her vessel was gone. She was a pillar of glossy black hardness, her form molded of smooth black glass, her fingers edged like flint-chipped blades. Utisz watched the High Priest carefully lift the ceremonial torque from around his neck and place it over the Goddess' head, arranging it around her frosty throat. She tenderly stroked one of the golden cages as she glided down the teocalli, vitrine feet barely brushing the skulls.

Utisz' legs buckled beneath him. He fell to his knees without conscious thought. He could not take his eyes off her.

In a moment she was standing before him, huge and black, her edges indistinct. Waves of bitterest cold swirled around her, but Utisz could not even summon the will to shiver. She ran long sharp fingers through his dark hair, tilting his head up, seizing his gaze with hers. Her eyes were shifting traps, ancient abominations, the screams of a thousand generations of massacred innocents.

Such a tender young man.

Utisz was bare before her. He was nothing before her eyes—eyes that were the march of brutal history, oppression, and apocalypse. The light of torches glowed through her, flickering small as if smothered by her mass. She placed a bladed hand on either side of his head.

You have come to be initiated into our service, the Goddess said. *For this, the ward that binds your emotions must be released.* She did not need to ask his neologism, for she already knew it; she knew all. She leaned down and softly whispered it in his ear. His brain exploded, emotions surging through him like a hurricane flood—fear, hate, regret, remorse, terror. And at the crest of each wave rode terrible visions—visions of beauty and power:

The earth seen in a smoking mirror, twisted and tortured and transformed. Black slime gushing up from deep cracks in the earth's crust . . . every living thing withered, frostblackened, destroyed . . . winter-blasted air choked with the screams of the dying . . .

Itztlacoliuhqui, the Goddess of Obsidian Knives, enthroned atop a pyramid of skulls as high as the moon; rivers of blood cascading from her feet, gory rushing torrents . . . and at her side, a High Priest in feathers and jade, with a hand-shaped mark over his heart.

The world become ice and blood, as terrible in its beauty as the Goddess herself.

Temamauhti.

The Remaking.

With his last ounce of free will, Utisz lifted his hands to his throat in defense. Blotgate couldn't have meant this. This went beyond national destiny, beyond *human* destiny . . . this was the end of all of that. This was the end of the world. But the Temple attendants had taken his alembic, his only source of magical protection. All he could do was scream as the Goddess' voice caressed his mind.

Dear child, do not resist us. The fortunes of a little country, a fleeting thought in the infinite dream, do not matter. Our true aim is greater. It will be your honor to help us achieve it.

The Goddess lifted her free hand and held it out as if an invisible maidservant were placing a bracelet around her wrist.

Die for us, child.

The brilliant magic that hummed in the air coalesced around her outstretched hand, becoming a gleaming Obsidian Blade, long and slender. She closed her fingers around it delicately.

Her eyes held his, and Lieutenant Utisz knew that he would die for her. He knew that he would die, and that it had always been his place to die, and that it would be the greatest pleasure he had ever known.

Heusler missed the moment when her blade slashed downward, opening Lieutenant Utisz' throat at the seventh cervical vertebra. He felt rather disappointed that he had missed that, but waking the Goddess always left him drained. Leaning heavily on the altar stone, it was all he could do to remain standing.

The young officer's trachea gaped as blood fountained from the two huge arteries that ran along it. Blood showered the Goddess as she watched the body struggle, then falter, then fall. She was bathed in the lieutenant's blood, drenched in it; steam from its warmth rose up in clouds from her body. The mask's ivory fangs were stained red, as if she'd been rooting in the belly of a corpse. She stroked a finger along one of the tusks, then licked it, savoring the taste with great thoughtfulness.

Poor lost orphan, she said, as if replying to some silent supplication. *Be joyful. In our service, your blood will have its revenge on the blood that abandoned it.*

The Goddess made a small movement with her sharp fingers and, slowly, the lieutenant's slashed throat began to close. Tiny stitches of magic darted along the lips of the wound, pulling them together. When nothing remained but a white-seamed scar, she lifted a negligent hand.

Arise, newborn. Receive the blessing of your Goddess.

The young man's body rose from the ground, upright but

slack, a puppet on invisible strings. Leaning forward, holding his face in her hands, she pressed icy black lips to his forehead. His eyes flew open. He gulped air deep, gasping like a drowned man pulled from the ocean's depths. When she released him, he sank to his knees, whimpering and moaning in a mix of terror, heartbreak, and ecstasy.

The Goddess' kiss had been tender, but even from atop the teocalli, Heusler could see the mark it left—a violent bruise, an oblong mark right between the young lieutenant's eyes, as if he'd been struck by a hammer.

We have taken your life, and given it back, she said. *Do our will faithfully, and you shall be rewarded.*

Turning from him, she did not watch as red-robed acolytes swarmed from unseen alcoves to carry the lieutenant away. She moved toward the center of the Calendar Chamber, her cold black feet gliding over the inscribed channels of Black Exunge. She stopped at the railing that surrounded the pit. She stared down longingly at the trembling mound of glossy flesh. Its glow had faded, and once again it swam in bitter, slimy black. Her gilded nails hammered against the silver rail like tiny smiths.

Heusler carefully made his way down from the teocalli to where she stood.

He lowered himself to the ground (an indelicate and undignified maneuver) and stretched his arms out before himself.

"Does he please you, My Divine? He will make a fine servant. The debt he is owed is powerful. In asserting his claim, he will be able to unlock doors that would not open before."

There was a long silence, in which Heusler furtively watched her for a response. Finally, the Goddess shrugged indifferently. Never once did she take her eyes from the Liver.

He is not who we want, she said softly.

Heusler despised the pathos in her tone. This ancient manifestation of the darkest of powers, the Killing Frost, the Obsidian Blade, feared and adored . . . mooning over a lost love. For all that she was a goddess, Heusler thought, it was still greatly disappointing that she was nothing more than a *female.*

He had served her faithfully for more than three hundred

years—his life preserved by its proximity to her divine magnificence. But it was impossible to remain so long in the company of a female, even a divine one, without suffering some form of disillusionment. He knew her shameful secret—her sordid feet of clay. It was not for the exaltation of her own magnificence that she pursued the great work of *temamauhti;* no, it was for the resurrection of one man—one miserable human man! Xiuhunel, the Aztec High Priest who had perfected the blood-soaked magical ritual that allowed the Goddess to manifest herself within a mortal body. Her time upon the earth was always fleeting; her vast power would destroy the fragile vessels she inhabited within a few short hours. But those hours had been enough. He had taught her the pleasures of incarnate existence—killing-frost thawed by the warmth of a living embrace; razor-edges blunted by desire. She had fallen in love with him.

In his idle hours, Heusler sometimes amused himself by trying to conceive of a crime a mortal man could commit that was more monstrous than making a goddess fall in love with him. He had never succeeded.

When Xiuhunel had died upon a Spanish blade during the fall of Tenochtitlán, the savage rites to incarnate the Goddess had ceased, and Itztlacoliuhqui was left to brood and pine in her own incorporeal eternal realm. Why did he not send for her? She did not learn of his death until many years later, when Heusler—then a mercenary Warlock in service to the Spanish crown's ambitions in the New World—had come across a description of Xiuhunel's great rite in a war-tattered codex. He had decided to give it a try.

Heusler shuddered at the memory.

She had never quite forgiven him for that first time, when she had woken in a new vessel, only to find that Xiuhunel was gone, lost forever. She had grieved on a divine scale, wreaking her awful vengeance on the city that had once been the capital of the great Aztec Empire. She massacred two thousand Spanish in one magnificent night, their bodies slashed into unrecognizable ribbons of flesh. Soaking the ruins of Tenochtitlán in the blood of usurpers sanctified her great vow—that she and Xiuhunel would be reunited, their bodies whole and undying, even if the entire world had to be torn to shreds to do so.

It frequently astonished the High Priest that something as seemingly simple as the former should require the unthinkable profligacy of the latter.

Love. Such a lot of damn fuss.

But he discarded these thoughts quickly. She could so easily read his mind if she chose. It would not do to annoy her with such impertinence—not after decade upon decade of exacting preparation. Not now, with the final culmination so near. Before the moon was new, the calendar would ripen in its most powerful configuration in fifty-two years. In a year governed by the Jeweled Fowl, the year of greatest sorcerous potency, she would come into her greatest strength on 1-Cuetzpalin—the first of thirteen days that she ruled, the trecena of her ultimate apotheosis.

June 30.

The last day of the month. The last day of the world.

We have heard, Keeper of the Calendar, that humans deem June an auspicious month to wed.

The strange question startled Heusler out of his reverie. His legs and feet had gone all pins-and-needles from kneeling so long, and he suddenly realized just how long her silence had been.

"Indeed, My Divine. By the debased mortal calendar, June is the month for weddings."

Is what the initiate said true, tonalpoulque?

Heusler wasn't quite sure what she meant, but he sensed danger in the question.

"He said many things," he said cautiously.

Is Dreadnought Stanton to be wed?

Heusler wiggled his sleeping toes. So she liked the young lieutenant's idea, did she? Of course, he could see why she might find it satisfying—on many levels. "There is a girl from California. A Witch. She was at the Grand Symposium."

Is she pretty?

Heusler frowned. Certainly, he had found the girl toothsome, but he wasn't about to tell *her* that.

"How can I answer, My Divine?" he said. "When I am in your presence, your beauty makes it impossible for my weak mortal mind even to conceive the face of another."

She laughed, a deep chiming sound that started in her throat and expanded as it spread downward, making the earth beneath her feet shudder. One of the smoking braziers toppled with a resounding clang.

Flatterer, she said. *You have never even seen our true face.*

"I have seen it in my dreams."

And the Witch's name, tonalpoulque?

"Emily Edwards," Heusler said.

CHAPTER ONE

The Message in the Steam

Wednesday, June 18, 1876
New York City

Emily Edwards sat in her future mother-in-law's front parlor, sweating in a stiff dress of lilac-colored taffeta and contemplating death.

Could one die from boredom, she wondered? From complete, oppressive, crushing, unmitigated boredom, the likes of which made all other boredom seem like ecstasy's sweet thrilling embrace? And in such a case, if one happened to have a life insurance policy, would it pay?

The room was stifling. None of the windows were open, even though it was eighty degrees out and muggy as the inside of a dead badger. The room's carved mahogany paneling sweated the sharp pungent smell of old lacquer. The wallpaper above it—a profusion of gilded leaves and obsessively wrought peonies in shades of plum and peach—seemed to glisten humidly. A pair of cherubs, frolicking blissfully naked atop a gilt mantel clock, were almost certainly laughing at her.

There were six women in the room, waiting for tea that would be served piping hot. It was herself, Mrs. Stanton, Mrs. Stanton's three daughters (Euphemia, Ophidia, and Hortense), and Miss Jesczenka. They had decided it would be pleasant to read a selection from Wordsworth. Or rather, Mrs. Stanton had decided that it would be pleasant, and as seemed to be the case in all things pertaining to the precise ordering of Mrs. Stanton's world, no one had dared contradict her.

This, apparently, was how people amused themselves in New York.

Or, Emily reflected, perhaps the Wordsworth was just a gloss, and all the women were really having fun placing secret mental wagers on who was going to faint first. Indeed, that dubious mental exercise—and her idle musings about life insurance—were the only things keeping Emily upright.

That, and indignation. What kind of freakish constitution did these New York women have, anyway? Mrs. Stanton looked as if mechanically chilled ice water were being piped into her through a special arrangement of plumbing in her red-velvet chair—and the perfect rigidity of her carriage gave Emily a pleasantly unpleasant idea as to how the piping was plumbed. The elegant Miss Jesczenka—Emily's Institute-assigned chaperone—sat placidly, hands folded in her crisp lap, not a hair out of place, not a trickle of sweat upon her smooth brow.

Ophidia and Euphemia were even worse. Ophidia, staring out from under heavy-lidded eyes, had a fat orange cat spilling over her lap like an ill-tempered carriage blanket, and Euphemia—good Lord!—clutched a woolen shawl around her shoulders.

Only red-faced Hortense posed Emily any kind of challenge in the arena of heat prostration, and that was because she was going through such extravagant oratorical convulsions over Wordsworth:

> *"Ethereal minstrel!*
> *Pilgrim of the sky!*
> *Dost thou despise the earth where cares abound?"*

Hortense's voice trembled with emotion. Emily could not recall ever having seen a skylark, but she assumed it must be a jewel-encrusted wonder-bird from the praise being heaped upon its fool head, earth-despising or otherwise.

Mrs. Stanton, however, was listening closely, making small nods at places where she seemed to especially approve of Mr. Wordsworth's take on skylarks. And since Mrs. Stanton was the mother of Dreadnought Stanton, the man Emily was engaged to marry, Emily could hardly follow her natural inclination, which was to snatch the book from Hortense's hands and hit her bucktoothed future sister-in-law over the head with it.

Emily licked her lips and let her eyes wander over the mahogany paneling, wallpaper, and the goddamn naked cherubs for the hundredth time. The clock read 2:30. Miss Jesczenka had drummed it into her that the proper length of this type of call was precisely one hour—no more, no less. That meant a full half hour more of skylarks, airlessness, and piercing looks from Mrs. Stanton to slog through. Emily sighed silently.

With an impulse of bold rebellion, she let her eyes tiptoe over the carved mahogany side table, on which lay a folded copy of *The New York Times*.

"Unprecedented Earthquakes Along the Pacific Coast. Hundreds Killed from Mexico City to San Francisco. Aberrancies Running Rampant."

Emily's brow wrinkled. She squinted harder, trying to make out the type beneath the headline without turning her head. She'd been so busy since she'd come to New York, she hadn't had a moment to wonder what was going on at home in California. She craned her neck a little further, and was rewarded with the subhead:

"Warlock Experts Attribute Disastrous Happenings to Mysterious Expulsions of Black Exunge. Citizens Are Strongly Advised to Avoid Toxic Earth Substance at All Costs."

Emily hardly noticed when Hortense paused after a final thrilling stanza. Miss Jesczenka drew an appreciative breath.

"Such genius!" she said, as simultaneously, with one slender hand, she pushed the newspaper out of the range of Emily's searching gaze. When Emily's eyes came up, Miss Jesczenka gave her a frosty look of rebuke. "Don't you agree, Miss Edwards?"

Emily returned Miss Jesczenka's look with a scalding glare of her own. For the umpteenth time, Emily found herself missing Penelope Pendennis. Emily felt certain that the big opinionated woman could have offered many clever and useful tricks for getting out of Wordsworth readings. But Miss Pendennis was off on a worldwide lecture tour, and the Institute had provided Miss Jesczenka as Emily's social duenna. And whatever the Institute wanted, it got.

"Oh sure," Emily said finally. "Genius."

Mrs. Stanton was not so caught up in skylarks that she did not notice the subtle misbehavior. She frowned, and Emily quickly adopted her most angelic look (which, she reflected, was much akin to the look she put on when it profited her to look incredibly stupid) and cast her eyes to the ground in a fashion that she assumed was maidenly.

"You must be worried about things at *home.*" Mrs. Stanton spoke the last word with the kind of delicate revulsion she might have used with any other four-letter word. "Such terrible reports one reads."

"I hadn't heard," Emily said.

Mrs. Stanton raised an inquiring eyebrow. "You can *read,* can't you?"

That Emily Edwards was from California was considered extremely unfortunate by Mrs. Stanton. In Mrs. Stanton's rigidly ordered mind, the larger concept "California" contained only three subclassifications: gold, cattle, and whores. Emily was pretty sure which of the three subclassifications Mrs. Stanton put her into. And it wasn't gold.

The Stantons, on the other hand, were pure gold—twenty-four-karat gold with gold handles and some gold leaf smacked on top. Mrs. Stanton came from a very old family, and her husband was the senior Senator from the State of New York. Such people did not have daughters-in-law from California. Oranges for their breakfast table, maybe. But not daughters-in-law.

"Of course I can read," Emily muttered, before adding democratically: "Not as nicely as Hortense, though." She was determined not to spoil the progress—small as it was—that she'd made with her future mother-in-law. Over the past few weeks, Mrs. Stanton's physical revulsion had tempered into smoldering distaste. Despite occasional barbed sallies on the topics of California, Emily's table manners, and her tendency to scrunch her nose unattractively, the old woman had apparently come to accept that her ungrateful son was going to marry Emily despite his mother's noble exertions to the contrary. The battle-ax had even offered to host a lunch in Emily's honor, scheduled two days hence, to which many prominent city women had been invited. It was a start, and Emily was determined to make the most of it.

Her determination was so great, as a matter of fact, that despite her inclination to bite her tongue off rather than say it, she meekly suggested: "Perhaps we could have another poem?"

Mrs. Stanton did not smile, but neither did she frown. Another small victory.

"Certainly," Mrs. Stanton said, glancing at Hortense. "Let's have a nice *long* one."

Miss Jesczenka, who was always pleased when Emily did something socially acceptable, rewarded her with a smile. It did not make Emily feel any better.

"'To the Cuckoo'!" Hortense announced the poem, then cleared her throat.

> *"O blithe newcomer!*
> *I have heard, I hear thee and rejoice:*
> *O Cuckoo! shall I call thee bird,*
> *Or but a wandering Voice?"*

Emily closed her eyes to keep from rolling them. The things she put up with for Dreadnought Stanton were *appalling.*

Thinking of her fiancé made Emily scrunch her nose in the unattractive way Mrs. Stanton so frequently commented upon. But the nose scrunching—which, Mrs. Stanton said, made her look as though she were climbing over a trench of raw sewage—was not an expression of distaste. Rather, it was a physical representation of her evergreen astonishment that someone like her would have ended up falling in love with someone like him. The New York Warlock was extraordinarily provoking. Annoying, even. And Emily was often surprised that falling in love with him had done nothing to mitigate that opinion. It was as if annoyance had moved aside to allow a larger emotion to sit beside it, like a fat woman in stays squeezing in next to a wiry sister.

The adventures that had thrown them together—adventures in which magical pieces of glowing rock, blood sorcery, and the ancient consciousness that dwelled far beneath the earth's surface featured prominently—had been written up in pulp novels and dispatched into the hot greedy hands of every man, woman, and child who could read at a third-grade level and had a dime to spare.

Emily let the fingers of her living hand trail over the smooth ivory of her prosthetic hand—the hand that replaced the one cut off by a U.S. Army blood sorcerer named Caul.

For his part in the adventures, Stanton had been offered the directorship of the Institute—the most prestigious seat of credomantic education in the country, if not the entire world— and the great and powerful title of Sophos to go with it. For *her* part, she had ended up with one less hand, in a hot parlor, subjected to more Wordsworth than anyone should be required to endure, and envying the gilt cherubs their nakedness. Somehow, it didn't seem quite *fair.*

Her thoughts were disturbed by a soft knock on the door. The butler, a tall and distinguished-looking man with graying temples, entered silently, carrying a large silver tray with tea and refreshments. His name, Emily recalled, was Broward. On her first visit to the Stanton house, Emily had assumed he was one of Stanton's relatives. She'd been quickly and curtly disabused of that notion.

His arrival filled Emily with relief. At least the tea would provide some distraction. But as she watched him move quietly across the carpeted floor, a strange feeling came over her—slight nausea mingled with anticipation and dread. Everything took on a peculiar clarity. Broward was suddenly moving very slowly, and Hortense's voice, describing the "thrice-welcome darling of the spring" had become a molasses-thick garble.

Oh no, Emily thought. *Not now.* She leaned forward

slightly, pressing her hand against her corseted stomach. This
was no time for a Cassandra.

She could not take her eyes off the silver tray in Broward's
hands. It gleamed, smooth and polished. Steam curled up
from the spout of the bone china teapot, and as Broward's
small movements made the vapor swirl, it formed two small
words.

Go home.

Emily shuddered, a cat-walking-on-her-grave chill tickling
her back. The steam twisted like a living thing, sinuous and
sinister.

Go home . . .

And then the vision took her, knife pains in her belly and
the bitter taste of gall in her mouth. She felt the ground shaking beneath her, rumbling her from side to side. There was
the sound of far-off screaming and something thundering
and slavering. Then a terrible chomping noise. And there was
a horrible smell. Fresh blood, and hair smoke, and something else—something rotten and black, greasy and sticky.
It was the unmistakable smell of earth's toxic poison, Black
Exunge—the foul sorcerous waste that destroyed and disfigured any living thing it touched. She knew that smell.

The steam curled around Broward's hands as he bent, ex-
cruciatingly slowly, to place the tea tray on the table before
Mrs. Stanton. Emily squeezed her eyes shut, but she could
not block the images flashing behind her eyes, brilliant and
sharp. *Fire. Black crushing maws. Earth cracked and sundered.*

She had to get home to Lost Pine. The certainty of it surged
through her like something remembered. Something terrible
had happened, or would happen. She thought about her adoptive father, blind and aged, a rampaging monstrosity tearing
him apart . . .

"Miss Edwards?" The words made Emily jump. Her knee
hit the tea table, setting the china and silver rattling loudly.
Mrs. Stanton was peering closely at her.

"Miss Edwards? Are you all right?"

Emily clapped her hand over her mouth, certain that she
was going to vomit. She stood, hoping that the movement

would settle the queasy shuddering that was rising beneath her breastbone. It did not. She put out a hand to steady herself, and her hand fell on the newspaper on the side table. She looked down at her hand, at the newspaper, at the terrible headlines.

"No," Emily answered, as she snatched *The New York Times* from the table and crumpled it against her chest. "I'm sorry. Not at all."

And she ran from the room.

"That was a creative way to get out of Wordsworth."

Miss Jesczenka's voice came from behind her as Emily stood on the sidewalk, absorbing the information in the newspaper. Her eyes sped over the same words over and over again. *Destruction. Chaos. Terror. Death.*

San Francisco in a state of panic.

According to the reports, San Francisco had been suffering from earthquakes of varying sizes almost every day for the past fortnight. The earthquakes were opening deep cracks in the earth, belching Black Exunge that turned anything it touched into an Aberrancy. It was the Aberrancies that were the true source of panic in the city. Horse-size rats and other vermin terrorized the gaslit streets, brutally mauling unwary passersby. Worse, since Exunge was extremely flammable, if one of the transmogrified creatures encountered an open flame—a streetlamp or lantern, for instance—the otherworldly conflagration could set a whole block alight. The city had turned off the gas wherever possible, but there simply weren't enough engines to deal with all the fires. With so much horror to be reported on in San Francisco, it was not surprising that there was no news of Lost Pine, the tiny settlement high in the Sierra Nevadas where Emily had grown up.

"You're not really ill, are you?" Miss Jesczenka raised a cool hand to Emily's forehead. Emily pulled away from her touch, repressing an urge to snarl.

"Nobody told me about this!" Emily snapped the paper in her face. Her blood turned to ice at the thought of her adoptive father, spinning ineffectual spells against monstrosities he could not see. "What about Pap? What if he can't protect himself?"

"Lost Pine is almost two hundred miles from San Francisco," Miss Jesczenka said. "There's no reason to think it's in any danger. And even if it were, the Army's Warlocks would address the problem, just as they are doing in San Francisco." She tilted her head at a birdlike angle. "What good would it have done you to know?"

It was a cold question, but a fair one. Emily had fought Aberrancies before, and the experience had left her with no particular confidence in her ability to fight them again. But the Cassandra had told her that she had to go home, and Cassandras like that didn't just pop up, making one nauseated and socially inept for no reason whatsoever. There had to be something important behind the message. She might not know as much about magic as these fancy New York Witches and Warlocks, but she knew that one ignored a Cassandra at one's peril.

Their carriage, lacquered in shiny black with the Institute's golden seal on the door, pulled up at the curb. They climbed in, and Emily settled herself into the deep red velvet upholstery.

"I need to go to California," she blurted as soon as the door was closed behind them.

Miss Jesczenka stared at her before answering.

"But Miss Edwards," she said finally, "Midsummer's Eve is only three days away."

As if Emily could forget. Stanton's formal Investment ceremony as Sophos of the Institute was to be held on Midsummer's Eve. It would be (if the number of florists, caterers, and photographers running around the Institute were any indication) an extravagantly grand affair, temporally surrounded by many smaller gatherings, fetes, and soirees—of which Mrs. Stanton's forthcoming lunch was one.

"And Mrs. Stanton's lunch is on Friday." Miss Jesczenka intuited the drift of Emily's thoughts precisely. "Can you imagine what would happen if you were to miss it?"

Emily said nothing. Some things were better left unimagined.

"Besides which, you still have a number of dress fittings and—"

"Yes, I know." Emily pressed her lips together, staring out the window of the carriage as they traveled along Thirty-fourth Street. The remembered smell of blood and Exunge was still in her nose, and again she thought of Pap, the gentle old man who'd raised her from orphaned girlhood.

"Miss Edwards," Miss Jesczenka prompted softly. "Please, you must tell me what's troubling you."

Emily said nothing. She stared past Miss Jesczenka, chewing her lip. She had long since decided to tell no one at the Institute about her Cassandras. Ever since she'd made a direct magical connection to Ososolyeh—the entity the Indians revered as the great consciousness of the earth—the visions came to her at odd times: strange omens appearing in the movement of grasses, in the swirling of dust in a sunbeam, in the movements of ants.

But if the Institute knew about the Cassandras, they would never cease to annoy her about them. The connection Emily had with Ososolyeh was unprecedented and powerful, and the Institute had a habit of wanting to accrue unprecedented and powerful things unto itself. This she knew from experience. So she'd kept the whole matter quiet—even from Stanton.

If only she could speak to him! He'd be sure to have distinct opinions, the majority of which she'd probably disagree with. But she hadn't even seen him in a week. He was in some kind of ritual seclusion before his Investment, probably learning secret handshakes and drinking beverages out of skulls.

She shook her head to clear the troublesome thoughts. Skulls and secret handshakes were of no use to her at the moment, and even Stanton might not be able to help her with the conundrum she faced. She couldn't go home, but she had to. She stared out the window of the carriage resolutely, as if the answer might be found there.

While the answer was not to be found along Thirty-fourth Street, or even any of the avenues going uptown, Emily knew what she had to do by the time they arrived back at the Institute. She followed Miss Jesczenka placidly as they climbed to the suite of rooms Emily had been given on the fourth floor, on the corner overlooking the back gardens and the ornate crystal-paned conservatory. The rooms had deep bay windows and paneling of polished black walnut. Rich Anhalt carpets and gilt mirrors and Chinese enameled pots with palms in them gleamed luxuriously. Miss Jesczenka threw open the windows in the hopes of catching a breeze.

"How hot it is this afternoon." Miss Jesczenka frowned when no breeze presented itself for capture. "You seem quite tired, Miss Edwards. I'm sure you'll feel better after some rest." She paused. "Everything will be fine. You really mustn't worry."

Emily nodded, and after Miss Jesczenka left, she did lie down.

She lay on top of the silken covers, fully clothed, staring at the ceiling for a full five minutes, thoughtfully stroking the ivory of her prosthetic hand, feeling the cool smoothness of the carved fingers. She lay that way until she heard Miss Jesczenka's feet move silently away from her door.

Then she jumped up, threw on boots and a bowler hat, and left for California.

CHAPTER TWO

An Unexpected Gift

Haälbeck doors were really the most convenient thing ever created, Emily thought as she snuck out of a butter-yellow house that sat atop Nob Hill. There were only two of the magical portals in San Francisco, but since one terminated in the butter-yellow house—which was owned by the Institute—it had been the work of an instant to slip through it to San Francisco. And since Mrs. Quincy—the head of the Institute's San Francisco office who'd once resided in the house—had been dismissed in disgrace over gambling debts and other sundry malfeasances, Emily didn't have to worry much about being seen.

The Institute's door in New York, which was kept in a lavishly appointed room on the mansion's second floor, was customarily kept locked. But Stanton had shown her the secret of opening it on one of the rare, pleasant days they'd been able to spend together.

"You never know when it might come in handy," Stanton had said as he pressed hot kisses beneath her left ear. At the time, their visit to the Haälbeck Room had more to do with its convenient seclusion than its employment for practical tutelage. But Stanton never could pass by an opportunity to be pedantic, and that did come in handy sometimes.

Emily pulled the battered old bowler down over her eyes, glad that her hair was still short enough to pass for a man's. She had changed into a sack suit that she always kept hidden at the bottom of her trunk—she'd purchased it in New York when it had become obvious that people generally took exception to young ladies wandering around the streets on their own. Police officers could get downright huffy about it, so she'd adopted the ruse that had served her so well in the past. Disguised as a young man, she could move with ease and anonymity, and without every fool in the world thinking it necessary to fold down steps, open doors, or press her with annoying questions about what she was doing out alone.

It was still early in San Francisco, just after lunchtime, but the sky was heavy with overcast clouds and a choking smell like burning tar. Pausing at the top of Clay Street, she shaded her eyes and looked down over the city. She could see smoke rising from distant fires, and there was the sound of hand-cranked sirens and the occasional echoing pop of rifle shots.

Drawing a deep breath, she headed down Clay Street toward Market. Emily knew next to nothing about San Francisco, but she knew that if she could get to Market Street she could find Third Street, and if she could find Third Street she could find the Southern Pacific Depot. She stuffed her hands into her pockets and kept her head low, walking fast.

Getting to San Francisco had been the easy part; getting to Lost Pine would be harder. The little timber camp didn't have a train station, much less a Haälbeck door, and it was almost 200 miles from San Francisco. But if she walked fast, she could make it to the depot in time to catch the evening east-bound. That would get her as far as Dutch Flat, which was less than twenty miles from Lost Pine; there she could rent a nag from one of the stables and be at Pap's side by morning.

Walking through the streets, she was even more aware of the pronounced change in the atmosphere of the city. The streets were deserted, windows dark. Clusters of tired-looking soldiers in faded blue stood watchfully near crates of ammunition—marked "99% Pure Silver"—and shining pyramids of rifles, neatly stacked.

At Kearny Street, she came to a small park, shaded by tall maples and fenced with intricately wrought iron. Within the park, a huge bonfire was burning and stinking, sending billows of oily smoke into the already-overcast sky. Emily brought her sleeve to her nose against the horrible stench. They were burning dead Aberrancies. A half dozen military wagons were lined up along Kearny Street, each one piled high with the bodies of slimy black dead things—creatures that had once been ants, insects, earthworms. Someone's pet cat—now the size of a rowboat—took up one whole wagon. It lay stiff and slimy, red eyes glazed and limbs twisted.

Under the watch of a small detachment of soldiers, strong men in black-streaked overalls leaned on shovels, grimly tending the unnaturally colored blaze; a few women with handkerchiefs over their mouths watched through narrowed eyes. The flames leapt and spat, tinged purple and blue and sulphur-yellow.

"Your folks know you're out, son?" Emily jumped as a heavy hand fell on her shoulder. The words were spoken by a kind-looking older man with long gray whiskers, wearing a blue Army frock coat and sash. From the crossed swords on his slouched hat, she could tell he was a captain of the U.S. Cavalry, but his uniform didn't bear the special insignia of one of the Army's Warlock divisions. *So much the better,* Emily thought; she didn't have much use for the Army's Warlock divisions. She gave him what she hoped was a boyish grin.

"I'm on my way to the Southern Pacific Depot," Emily said, then turned to continue down Clay Street, hoping to forestall further questioning.

"Well, you're going the wrong way!"

Emily scratched the back of her head sheepishly. "I am?"

"Yep. Nothin' down that way but Aberrancies. I wouldn't take another step along Clay without a rifle and a couple hundred rounds of silver. Now, you carry on along Kearny until you get to Market Street. Cross Market to Third, then go right along until you hit Townsend." He paused. "You gettin' out of the city?"

Emily nodded. She'd learned, when inhabiting men's clothing, that the success of her impersonation hinged upon speaking as little as possible.

"Well, good luck to you." The old soldier shook his head. "The Warlocks in my division say it's going to get worse before it gets better. You watch your step."

Emily tipped her hat to him gratefully and turned down

Kearny Street. It, too, had vastly changed since the last time she'd been there. Then it had been bustling with life and energy, horsecars and carriages and busy people hurrying to fascinating employments. The shop windows had been crammed with wares, and everything had rattled and gleamed. Now the street was deserted, save for the soldiers on every street corner, and devastation reigned. The windows were shuttered or boarded over; she was the only civilian pedestrian. She walked around an overturned wagon that had been smashed to flinders; the traces of black slime on the wood showed the author of its destruction.

As she was crossing Market Street, the earth rolled as if a great serpent were moving beneath it. She managed to make it across the street, tumbling against a telegraph pole for support, wrapping her good arm around it to keep herself upright. The macadam shifted and bucked, and a huge chunk of plaster ornament fell from a tall building nearby, carving a deep gash in the sidewalk, peppering her with sharp bits of rubble. She listened for the cracking sound she'd heard in her Cassandra, expecting next to smell the rotten stench of Black Exunge, but it did not come. That inevitability had been avoided. For now.

When the ground stopped moving and it seemed that all the head-splitting plaster that was going to fall had fallen, Emily hurried toward the depot. When she arrived there, she realized why all the streets had seemed deserted. Every man, woman, and child in San Francisco was here, milling around the station, surrounded by their belongings—trunks and suitcases, cardboard boxes tied with twine, cages with rabbits and chickens. And all of them wanted to go East.

Emily stared at the spectacle, heart sinking.

"You'll never get a ticket." The words, which came from her left, were like a physical manifestation of her own worried thoughts. "They've put on all the cars they have. Everything is sold out."

The voice that spoke was tinged with a thick Russian accent. Emily turned, fixing the stranger with a distrustful gaze. It wasn't fair, but she'd come to distrust Russian accents. But they were common enough in San Francisco, and this man was remarkable in his unremarkableness. A bland early forty-ish, he was of such regular height and build he seemed to have been stamped from a machine. And he was unrelentingly brown—brown hair, a neatly trimmed brown mustache and goatee.

"Do I know you?" she asked, keeping her voice low.

"No, but I believe I can intuit your difficulty. You wish to purchase a ticket. And you will not be able to do so."

Emily frowned, but the man carried on.

"However, I have a solution to the dilemma you are not yet even aware of having. I have a single ticket, which is useless to me. Would you like to have it?"

Narrowing her eyes, Emily employed a phrase she'd just recently learned in New York.

"What's the catch?"

The brown man blinked at her.

"What does it mean?" he asked. "Catch?"

"Why would you let me have your ticket?" She pointed to a well-fed gentleman with a gold watch chain looped across his waistcoat. "That man, for instance, looks like he'd pay you a hundred dollars right now." She turned out her empty pockets—not showing him, of course, the black silk Warlock's purse that she kept tucked safely in the top of her boot. "Do I look like I have a hundred dollars?"

"No," he said. "But you look as though you are in need of help. Take the ticket. You will not get another."

"No, thank you," Emily said. Never mind that she distrusted Russian accents; she distrusted unexpected largesse even more. She quickly made her way into the crowd, putting a thick buffer of human flesh between her and the stranger. What had his game been? Had he seen through her costume and assumed she was some kind of hussy who catered to odd whims? Or maybe he *hadn't* seen through the costume, and thought she was a tender boy who could be bought for the price of passage.

Shocking either way, but never mind. She wasn't going to let herself become indebted to some strange Russian, potentially unclean expectations or not. She pushed her way to the ticket counter, jostling and being jostled mercilessly.

"Just to Dutch Flat!" she called to the harassed ticketing agent, over the din of dozens of other would-be passengers. "I'll ride on the cowcatcher if I have to!"

"Not for days," the harassed ticket agent hollered back. She pleaded with him, told him about her sick father, then added in five starving siblings for good measure. The ticket agent glared at her from underneath his green eyeshade. "Everyone's got a story, kid. *Next!*"

Emily pushed her way back through the crowd toward the front of the station where it was cooler, where she could get a breath of air. The 4:45 train was just pulling into the station, all billowing steam and coal cinders and squealing brakes. She considered sneaking over the fence, climbing surreptitiously onto the caboose, but it seemed that other miscreants had had the idea before her; the fence was guarded by dozens of soldiers in Army blue.

Emily sighed, took her hat off, and ran her good hand through her hair. She should have taken the ticket from the Russian, pervert though he may have been. It was her own evil assumptions that had done her in. She hadn't even considered the third possible explanation for his strange behavior—that he was a perfectly nice man, without an ounce of guile, just trying to be helpful. People helped people in California. Why hadn't she thought of that? She'd only been in New York a few weeks, and already she was turning hard and suspicious.

She sat down on the steps, rubbing a flake of ash from her eye. As she sat, something crinkled in her pocket.

She put her hand there and withdrew a train ticket.

She cast a look around herself, half expecting to see the gleam of the brown man's eyes. Without an ounce of guile indeed. She looked over the ticket for a moment, hardly believing it could be real.

How on earth had he . . .?

The steam-blast whistle and hoarse shout of "All aboard!" jolted her out of her reverie.

"Damn Russians," she muttered, jumping to her feet and breaking into a flat run.

*　*　*

Emily stepped off the platform at Dutch Flat just before midnight, footsore and tired. She'd had to stand the entire way, of course. Wearing the costume of a young man always made her feel sorry for young men. They were always having to surrender their seats, help ladies with improbably heavy bags, hold cages full of squabbling chickens, get kicked in the shins by annoying little brats, and suffer torrents of abuse from sour old geezers who were of the opinion that any able-bodied young man who hadn't stayed behind to protect San Francisco was little more than a lily livered coward, a weakling, a *woman*.

It was a Wednesday night, so there wasn't much doing in Dutch Flat. Emily was reassured by the air of calm and quiet that prevailed. There were no soldiers here, no smell of oily smoke, no screams. By all appearances, everyone was safely asleep in bed. Her heart, which had been thumping like a drum ever since she'd left the Institute, settled a bit. If things were normal here in Dutch Flat, then it was that much more likely that everything in Lost Pine was all right, too.

Still, she'd come this far, and she was looking forward to seeing her pap. Her only chance to get up the mountain before daybreak was to rent a horse, and the livery was shut up tight. The Gold Bucket saloon was well lit, though, and after she'd put down money for a couple of shots of monstrous whiskey, the bartender pointed her in the direction of the livery's proprietor, who was sitting a few stools down. She bought the half-drunk man another couple of glasses of the rotten brew, thus persuading him to provide her with a nag and a saddle, all for the usurious sum of a dollar a day.

Once in the saddle, with the two glasses of monstrous whiskey working to their full effect, Emily felt the fear that had gripped her since her Cassandra in Mrs. Stanton's parlor recede. The night was beautiful and clear, a full moon lighting her way.

She turned the horse up the familiar trail, through sweet-smelling pines with new tips of bright green. Silence enfolded her. The only sounds she could hear were the night calls of birds and the wind rustling the pine boughs far above, and her own horse's feet, crunching on old pinecones and occasionally clopping on a piece of weathered granite.

When she came to the Hanging Oak, spread branches gleaming in the moonlight, Emily pulled her horse to a stop. Beneath it, she'd crafted the Ashes of Amour over a month ago. With everything she'd learned since then, she could hardly believe that she could have been so stupid, so ignorantly cruel. She hadn't been able to remove the love spell she'd put on Dag Hansen—the lumberman she'd hoped to marry for his money—before she left Lost Pine, but she could do it now. She was in a hurry, but the moon was full, and she owed it to Dag. She stripped off her clothes, for such magic had to be performed skyclad. Naked in the sweet summer night air, she knelt before the tree and spoke a very simple incantation.

"Friend, I release you."

It might not do much good. Dag had said he'd loved her before she put the love spell on him, but she hoped with all her heart that it would help.

"Dag, I'm sorry," she whispered, wishing she could say it to his face. But she might never see him again, and it was probably better that way. Now that she understood the power of love, she realized how truly horrible her actions had been.

She dressed as quickly as she could, but her missing hand made it an arduous process. Another part of her life that could never be made whole again, only accepted and compensated for. Pushing the uncomfortable association out of her mind, she climbed back onto her horse and rode on.

By the time she got to Pap's cabin, the sun was rising, drawing a luminous veil of peach and orange over the tops of the tall pines.

The little cabin stood in a wide clearing, with a little crick running behind it, fresh and fast and dark. When she'd left in the spring, only a few tender little plants were peeping shyly up through the dark mud; now everything was a rich riot of tangled green. A few chickens, scrabbling around in the cabin's front yard, clucked welcomingly to her.

Home sweet home, Emily thought, hitching the nag to a

tree. She found that her heart was beating hard again, and she hardly knew why. The cabin's door was open slightly.

"Pap?" She removed her hat as she called inside. "Pap, it's me. Emily."

She had to blink to get her eyes to adjust to the gloom inside. The cabin seemed smaller and closer than she remembered and swelteringly hot as usual, with a huge fire blazing on the hearth. In the light of the fire, she saw a small hunched form, silhouetted in darkness. He was covered in cats, dozens of them, the beloved animals that always surrounded him. They stared at her as she entered, their eyes glowing accusingly.

"Em?" The voice came from the hunched form. Pap's voice was terrible, choked and broken. "Oh, Em, it's you! Blessed be . . . you've come back!"

CHAPTER THREE

Bottle of Memories

Emily rushed to Pap's side, wrapping her arms around him, sending cats scurrying in all directions. Burying her face against his shoulder, she felt his leathery hand reach up to touch her hair, his fingers pressing against her scalp as if to convince himself of her solidity. "Oh, Em, blessed be," he said again.

She knelt before him, looking up into his face, her violet eyes searching his white-rheumed, sightless ones. He looked awful. His face was heavier, older, new-lined with worry. The spiderweb of old scars stood out on his face, pale with tension.

"It's all right, Pap." She reached up for where his hand trembled against her hair. "What's wrong? What's happened? The earthquakes and Aberrancies—have they been here?"

Pap looked at her, his sightless eyes quizzical.

"Earthquakes? Aberrancies? We ain't had none o' them. That's all happening down in San Francisco."

Emily pressed Pap's hand with hers. "Then what's wrong?"

"They came after you, Em. All those men! They meant to kill you, I know they did . . ."

Emily sat back on her heels, releasing a pent-up breath. The Maelstroms—the Army's division of blood sorcerers, led by Captain Caul. Emily had forgotten just how recently they had stormed through Lost Pine, searching for her and Stanton. Was this what she'd come all the way from New York for?

"They won't be coming anymore," Emily explained. "They wanted the stone—you remember, that stone I found up at the Old China Mine? Mr. Stanton and me, we took it to New York and . . . well, we got rid of it. It's gone now."

"But they're *still* looking for you," Pap said, his voice low and urgent. "They was up here just a few days ago, asking questions."

Emily's brow knit. "Who was here?"

"Russians," Pap said softly, his sightless eyes gleaming. "Em, they had so many questions. So many questions about *her* . . ."

At the back of the cabin, there was a sound; the slow creak of the door. Emily tensed, looking up—but it was only Mrs. Lyman, the red-faced mining widow who had taken to keeping house for Pap. When she saw Emily, she dropped an armload of firewood with a resounding crash and clatter. She then burst out in screams of delight, enfolding Emily in a bark-dusty embrace.

"Emily! Why, I can't believe it, you're home! Oh, we read the book!"

She babbled more words as she spun Emily around the small room, but Emily could barely hear them, for Mrs. Lyman was squeezing her so tightly that the blood was beginning to pound in her ears.

"Abby . . ." Pap said. When the words and spinning didn't stop, he barked, *"Abby! Enough!"*

Mrs. Lyman stopped and stared at Pap in surprise.

"Why, Ignatius, I don't—"

Pap made his voice milder. "Could you give Em and me a little while to talk? Then she can tell you all about things later. Over dinner, maybe?"

Mrs. Lyman was silent for a moment, then nodded.

"Why, sure. Dinner! That's a lovely idea. I'll run back over to my place and chop the head off that old hen that's stopped laying. And there's new potatoes from the garden, and half a pie left . . ."

Muttering to herself, Mrs. Lyman bustled out as quickly as she'd bustled in. Emily rubbed her cheek with her hand to see if the old woman's kisses had left bruises.

"Emily, come on over here." Pap reached for Emily's

hands. When she gave them to him, his fingers traveled inquiringly over the smooth ivory of her prosthetic.

"What's this?"

"I lost my hand." Emily always hated saying that. It sounded so careless, as if she'd just misplaced it. But she didn't want to explain what had actually happened—the clang of steel, the smell of blood . . . not to Pap, most of all.

"That's the hand the stone was in," the old man said softly.

"Yes."

Pap said nothing for a moment, letting his calloused thumb play thoughtfully over the intricately carved fingers. Then he let out a long breath.

"But you're all right now, Em? You're not . . . you're all right?"

"I'm all right," Emily said softly. "Tell me what's happened."

Pap was silent for a long time, as if debating something with himself. Then he made a decisive movement.

"Em, you know how you came to me. You were just a little thing, not five years old. Your mother, she came through the pass in the middle of winter with you wrapped in her coat, and then she died without saying a word. That's what I always told you."

"Yes," Emily said warily, not liking the sound of Pap's last sentence.

"I didn't tell you everything, Em. I couldn't. I didn't want you to grow up remembering—" He stopped abruptly. "There was bad things around you, Em. I had to protect you from them. If you could have seen yourself, just a little girl, sweet as could be—you'd understand. You'd forgive me. You'd understand that I couldn't let anything hurt you. And after what she'd done to you—"

"She?" Emily interrupted. "My mother?"

"She was *bad,* Em." Pap's voice became a whisper, as if the very air around them could coalesce into the remembered badness just by speaking of it. "And it wasn't just bad around her, it was bad in her, bad down to her bones. Wicked bad."

"Wicked bad?" Emily echoed softly.

"*Evil,* Em." Pap clenched her hands hard. "I know evil.

I seen it, in the eyes of the men who tried to burn me back in Kentucky, all them years ago."

"I don't understand."

"Your mother, she was on her way to San Francisco. To be with them Russians who come to see me . . . the Sini Mira, they call themselves."

He paused expectantly, waiting for her to make some sound of astonishment. But Emily had already met the Sini Mira—a shadowy group of Russian scientists who had tried to kidnap her on her way to New York. She remembered the iceberg-blue eyes of their leader, a man who called himself Perun, whose white hair and pale skin made him seem to be carved of snow and frost. But he'd said they just wanted the stone, the fragment of the Mantic Anastomosis that had been lodged in her hand. Now that that was gone, what could the Russians possibly want with her?

"I don't know how they found out about her, after all these years." Pap continued hesitantly, through Emily's heavy silence. "They came up here and asked about her—what did she say, and what did she have with her when she died. I told them she didn't have nothing with her, that she didn't leave nothing behind. I wasn't going to tell them about you, Em, honest I wasn't! But they already knew."

"They have ways of knowing things," Emily said. She was thinking suddenly of the brown man, the Russian in San Francisco who'd given her the too-convenient train ticket. Then it had seemed strange. Now it seemed downright sinister.

"Have they been back?"

"No. They rode off, and they ain't been back," Pap said. "But it made me scared, Emily. It made me scared that I ain't told you everything you need to know. Secrets don't die. You can bottle 'em up, but they don't die."

Pap stood, dislodging the last of the grumpy cats, and felt his way to the locked cupboard. Emily knew it well; it was where Pap always kept his most dangerous and precious magical supplies. He fumbled for a key around his throat and unlocked the cupboard. He felt around within it until his fingers found a small bottle. He carried the bottle as if it were a poisonous snake that might bite him.

He gave the bottle to Emily. It was very heavy glass, cobalt blue, with an iron stopper. Around the bottle's throat was tied a card. It was hard to discern in the half-light of the fire, but it was, she realized, a calling card like the ones the ladies in New York traded as a part of their mystifying rituals. On it was engraved four small words in thin, elegant type:

Miss Catherine Kendall. Boston.

"What is it?"

"The card, that was your mother. The bottle . . . that's you. It's you at five years old, Em," Pap said softly. "It's all your memories."

Emily swallowed hard, turning the bottle over and over in her hand.

"It's called a Lethe Draught," Pap said. "It's memories distilled down. The light and sweet ones float to the top. The bitter and dark ones sink to the bottom. It's everything I didn't want you to remember. It's all the nightmares you had, those first few weeks you was here. It's all your fear, and all your misery, and—" He faltered, rubbing his hand across his eyes. "I had to do it, Em. Those memories, they're all so bad. I don't know the half of them and I never wanted to. I just wanted to see you happy. And you were once I took them away and locked them up. Then they couldn't hurt you anymore."

Emily held the bottle away from herself, looking at it with horror.

"I hoped you'd never need them back," Pap continued. "But if these Russians . . . these Sini Mira . . . if they're after you, and looking for you . . . you may have to know, Em. If you don't know, then you might not know how to stay away from them."

"If I drink this, I will get the memories back?"

Pap nodded.

"It was all right, you not knowing, while you was staying here in Lost Pine," he said. "Bad things can't hurt you if they don't know where you are. But now they do. And even if they didn't . . ." He paused. "Well, you ain't back to stay. Are you?"

"I'm going to marry Mr. Stanton," Emily murmured, still staring at the bottle.

Pap smiled. "Decided to fall in love with him, did you?"

"Afraid so," Emily said, and Pap chuckled, nodding. He let his thumb play over the ring she wore on her thumb, the Jefferson Chair ring Stanton had given her.

"Tell me you forgive me, Em," Pap said. "Tell me you don't hate me."

"I couldn't hate you," Emily said. "And there's nothing to forgive. You did what you thought was best."

But as she crouched there before the man who had been the only father she'd ever known, she was painfully aware that doing one's best was never assurance that it wasn't the wrong choice anyway.

CHAPTER FOUR

Dmitri

Mrs. Lyman returned a few hours later with a fresh-plucked chicken and some garden vegetables in a basket. She'd also tucked in half a pie, some biscuit dough in a cloth-covered blue bowl, and a bottle of whiskey. It was clear she meant to make a party of Emily's homecoming.

And indeed, they had a merry afternoon, with the savory smells of the chicken stew on the stove—and Mrs. Lyman's garrulous stream of conversation—filling the warm cabin. The little thimblefuls of whiskey Mrs. Lyman kept pouring out were the chief fuel of her discourse; the chief subject was a pulp novel entitled *The Man Who Saved Magic,* a highly colored recounting of the adventures that had driven Emily from Lost Pine. Emily was astonished that the book had made it back to Lost Pine before she did.

"Heck, everyone in Lost Pine's read the book by now," Mrs. Lyman affirmed as she dipped a string-tied bundle of sage into the chicken stew. "Mrs. Bargett down at the boardinghouse, she raised her prices by a dime just 'cause that stuck-up Dreadnought Stanton stayed in her establishment. Puts the book into the hand of everyone who walks through the door."

Emily flushed, mortification and whiskey reddening in her cheeks. The book, which had been put out by the Institute's publishing arm, Mystic Truth, was an overwrought piece of melodrama designed to thrill readers with precisely calculated measurements of excitement and adventure. The particularly thrilling chromolithographed cover featured lions (though to the best of Emily's recollection, she and Stanton had not encountered a single lion on their trip, much less three leaping with jaws a-froth). It had been carefully crafted to have the maximum impact on the minds of readers like Mrs. Lyman, who dreamed of great adventures and great men to pursue them.

The more powerful people believe we are, the more power we credomancers have, Stanton had once told her.

Books like *The Man Who Saved Magic* were designed to make people believe that little, if anything, was outside the realm of possibility for the type of Warlock who was to be found within its pages.

"But no one understands why you weren't in it!" Mrs. Lyman said indignantly, placing her hands on her hips and glaring at Emily, as if the faults of the book could be laid at her doorstep. "There was just some swooning nitwit named 'Faith Trueheart.' Who's that, I'd like to know? What about good old Emily Edwards, from Lost Pine, California?"

Emily bit her lip to keep from commenting on the particular prejudices of the editors at Mystic Truth. It had been their decision to leave her out of the epic retelling. Given that it was Stanton who would be Invested as Sophos of the Institute, they were more concerned with building his power. Indeed, in their eyes, his contribution to the adventure was the only thing of credomantic worth—given that he was the credomancer, after all. No use diluting his share of the glory to give it to someone who'd have no use for it.

"I guess they left me out for modesty's sake," Emily said finally. "To keep my name from being sullied, or something like that. People in New York have some funny ideas about ladies and names."

Mrs. Lyman crossed her arms disapprovingly. "Well, people in Lost Pine have some funny ideas about girls who run off with traveling Warlocks." She paused. "But since you're going to marry him, I suppose it all turned out for the best."

They enjoyed themselves well into the evening, finishing the bottle of whiskey and the chicken stew, laughing until the coals on the stone hearth glowed orange and Emily could hardly keep her eyes open. How she longed to climb into her old bed up in the loft and fall asleep, her belly full and her head pleasantly addled. But she knew that she couldn't stay even a moment longer. She had to get to Dutch Flat to catch the midnight train back to San Francisco. Mrs. Stanton's lunch was the next day, and even leaving now, she'd be hard-pressed to make it.

"You sure you have to go, Em?" Pap murmured sleepily as Emily banked the fire. "It's so late. I wish you could stay till morning . . ."

"The moon's full, and you know I can get anywhere in these woods even without it." Emily tucked the warm Indian blanket around him in his chair, and scratched a fat old tabby, one of Pap's favorites, between the ears. On the rocker by the fire, Mrs. Lyman snored. Emily lowered her voice to keep from waking the old woman. "I have to get back to New York."

Emily thought about telling Pap about the hideous anticipated lunch with her future mother-in-law, but decided to leave him with a more inspiring image. "Mr. Stanton is being rewarded with a special position at his Institute. There's going to be a big ceremony. He wants me there."

"Oh, well, if *Stanton* wants you . . ." Pap whispered good-naturedly, chucking her under the chin. He was silent a long time. His face became thoughtful, almost the way it looked when he scryed something. "He's a complicated knot, Emily. Be careful how you untie him. You're a hothead. All on the surface. You'll always say too much and at the wrong time, too. But your Mr. Stanton . . . he's all underneath. Like a fish deep underwater. He'll keep secrets."

Emily pressed her lips together, shivering despite the extreme warmth of the room. She'd already found out how closely Stanton could keep secrets. Like failing to tell her that he'd once studied to be a sangrimancer, a blood sorcerer. And when she had found out, he'd refused to speak of it more, as if life could be sectioned into neat post-office boxes that could be closed with finality, at will. Emily knew it wasn't so, but she wondered what it would take to get Stanton to believe it.

"That bottle, Em . . ." Pap's voice broke through her thoughts. "If you do drink it—and I ain't sayin' you should, but if you do—don't drink it all at once. And don't drink it alone. You tell him he has to be there with you. Mr. Stanton. He'll watch over you, and fix it all up if I've got it wrong. You promise?"

"I promise," Emily said.

Emily rode the poor rented nag hard down the mountain, making good time to Dutch Flat. She hitched the tired beast outside the shut-tight livery, then sat on the platform waiting for the midnight train. She tipped her hat down over her eyes, blocking out the yellowish light from the lantern that hung from the platform's wooden rafters.

She drew out the blue bottle from her inside coat pocket. It was heavy and warm from her body. She held it up in her left hand, letting the lantern light shine through it.

She searched backward in her mind as far as she could go. She'd never remembered much from her childhood, but then, she didn't know that people were supposed to. Sometimes flashes of memory would come to her, but they would pass and leave no trace, like a leaf thrown in a running stream. The only things she remembered with any clarity revolved around Pap's cabin: gathering up a handful of pinecones when she was very small, and bringing them to him with great seriousness. She remembered cold winters and brilliant springs, mud on boots and the smell of wood smoke. But before she'd come to Pap's . . . nothing.

She opened her eyes again, and the bottle was still in her hand. It was disappointing, as if a wish she didn't know she'd made hadn't come true. She felt angry—not at Pap, but that such a decision should exist to be made. Angry that she didn't know what to do. She wanted the memories. She wanted to know about her mother, and what had happened to drive her to such desperate straits. But she *didn't* want the memories just exactly as much. Memories changed a person. What if she didn't like the person she became after she drank the contents of that little blue bottle? What if *Stanton* didn't like the person she became?

She dozed during the train ride to San Francisco; there were plenty of empty seats going into the city, so she could put her feet up. Just outside of Sacramento, she heard someone in a seat nearby speaking Russian. She looked up in alarm, eyes searching wildly, but it was only an old woman in a headscarf parceling out a picnic breakfast to a pair of leg-swinging children. Emily relaxed, but only slightly. She laid her head against the glass, watching as dawn stretched pink fingers over the land.

The Sini Mira were Eradicationists who wanted to bring a halt to the use of magic and replace it with the advancements of science. She'd run across the shadowy consortium of Russian scientists once too many times for her liking.

She remembered her encounter with them in Chicago. She particularly remembered their leader, the ice-white man who called himself Perun.

I can tell you where you came from, Miss Lyakhova. Who you really are.

His voice, like exhaled smoke.

The most puzzling thing was that Komé—the Indian Witch who had transferred her spirit into an acorn—had told Emily that she should go with them. But why would Komé want her to go with Eradicationists who had hired a brutal bounty hunter to capture her?

Emily jolted wide awake as the train rattled over some connections. The image of the white-blond man danced behind her retinas. She touched the bottle in her pocket, satisfying herself that it was still there. She needed to speak with Komé. She needed to know what the Holy Woman knew.

But just as Stanton had been commandeered by the Institute, so had Komé—and even more completely. It had been determined that her spirit could not survive long in an acorn, so Emeritus Zeno had the nut placed into a rooting ball—a hermetically sealed device filled with nutrient fluid. It was hoped that the acorn would sprout and grow, and Komé's spirit could survive in a new form.

It seemed an excellent plan—the least they could do for the Witch who had given her body to speak for the consciousness of the earth. But more than once, Emily had found herself wondering whom the actions were truly intended to benefit. Emeritus Zeno now kept the rooting ball on his person at all times and was so zealous in his protection of it that one might suspect that he had ulterior motives—motives other than Komé's future health and happiness.

Oh, surely not, Emily thought. Benedictus Zeno, father of modern credomancy, Emeritus Master of the Institute, having ulterior motives? Impossible!

But as she laid her head back against the cool glass, she recalled the words Professor Mirabilis had always repeated, like a mantra: *Nothing's impossible.*

When Emily reached the depot, the summer sun had risen, washing the buildings of white limestone and red brick with the bright promise of a hot day to come. Emily tried to find a cab to take her to the butter-yellow house, but there were none to be had. She sighed heavily, aware suddenly of just how bone-weary she was. She was sure to be a delight at Mother Stanton's lunch. She'd have to fight to keep from falling facedown into the terrapin soup. Pounding down exhaustion, she started jogging along Third Street.

At Market, she glanced up at the large clock atop the Chronicle building: 8:15 a.m. That meant it was already 11:15 in New York. It would be a tight squeeze, but by heck, she could still make it! Twenty minutes up to the butter-yellow house . . . a half hour from the Institute to Mrs. Stanton's . . . of course, she'd have to change first . . . She looked down at herself. She was smudged with grime and her hair was oily and limp from having been stuffed under a bowler hat for a day and a half. She looked like she'd just stepped out of California. All right, so she'd be a little late to Mrs. Stanton's lunch. *Fashionably late,* she suggested to herself hopefully.

The rumble under her feet started small—small enough that it could be mistaken for one of the hundreds of small temblors that Emily had already grown accustomed to. But it kept shaking, growing in thunderous intensity. This was a big one, Emily realized with sudden dread. The buildings around her seemed to sway; terra-cotta crashed down around her. She hurried to the middle of the street to avoid the falling debris, stumbling as the earth bucked like a wild horse. Then, there it was, the sound from her Cassandra—the horrible tearing, the cracking. The earth was opening up before her, a deep wide fissured gap, cobblestones churning like peas in a stew. The ground fell from beneath her feet, and Emily jumped, landing hard on a ragged jutting outcropping. She scrambled to keep from sliding down into the stinking darkness as Black Exunge flowed up from deep within the earth, covering everything.

Emily screeched and drew up her legs to keep from coming in contact with the foul goo. If any part of her flesh touched the Black Exunge, she would be transmogrified into an Aberrancy—just like the vermin that were blossoming up around her from deep underground. Beetles and centipedes were inflating and expanding with hissing shrieks. As the Exunge deformed them, they expanded to hundreds of times their normal size, otherworldly jaws clattering menacingly.

Of particular and immediate concern were the cockroaches.

They clambered up over the lip of the torn sidewalk, mucus-dripping antennae waving like hairy carriage whips.

Dear Mrs. Stanton, Emily thought, as she looked around herself in a panic for something she could use in her defense, *Miss Edwards deeply regrets missing the lunch you arranged in her honor, but her absence was unavoidable, as she was being eaten by giant cockroaches.*

She seized a cobblestone and heaved it. She was grabbing another one, but thought better of it when she saw that the first cobblestone did little more than attract the attention of the giant cockroach she'd thrown it at. The thing was heading straight for her.

Boom.

A shotgun blast, close enough that she could smell the powder. A man was beside her, a blur of motion. He leveled a short-barreled shotgun at the huge slimy cockroach bearing down on her and pulled the trigger of the second barrel; the creature exploded in a rain of chitinous black parts and slimy mustard-yellow guts. Thrusting the spent shotgun into Emily's good hand, he unslung a rifle from his back and aimed it at another cockroach that was waving greedy grasping mouth parts at them. He blasted a load of silver into what would have been the thing's face, if it had a face, rather than a clattering maw. It collapsed, whistling and keening, hairy black legs twitching.

The man wrapped a hand around Emily's arm, dragged her down the side of the crumbling mound of earth and rock, then pulled her back behind an overturned wagon. He crouched by her side, putting the wood of the wagon bed at his back. Taking the shotgun from her, he reached coolly into his pocket and pulled out two more shells. He chambered these and clacked the weapon shut, thrusting the gun into her hand.

And at that moment, Emily got a good look at his face. She realized suddenly that it was the brown man, the Russian who'd given her the ticket to Lost Pine. Despite the fact that death was approaching them rapidly, she stared at him for a moment.

"Do you just hang around San Francisco waiting for me?" Emily said.

He tipped his hat to her.

"I have been sent to protect you," he said. He dropped a handful of silver-packed shells into her lap. He nodded toward a rat that was sniffing curiously at the edge of a flood of Black Exunge. "Keep your eye on that one. He will go at any moment."

And indeed, the rat did; the moment its pink quivering nose touched the Exunge, the little creature stiffened and began to grow. Steadying the shotgun against her prosthetic forearm, Emily unloaded the first barrel. Silver shot tore the beast's head into a cloud of black and blood.

"You're one of the Russians that was up bothering my pap!" Emily yelled at him. *"Sini Mira."*

"We did not harm him," the brown man said. He lifted the rifle, his bullet somehow finding the eye of an ant the size of a greyhound as it scurried over the top of the wagon. Emily winced as sticky bits spattered her clothing and her face. "We had only a few questions."

"He doesn't have any answers for you," Emily said. "And neither do I."

"As I said, Miss Edwards, I'm just here to protect you. If you will cover me, I have a way to get us out of this terrible predicament."

Emily lifted her shotgun again. An earthworm was whipping and flailing up from the ground; she wasn't quite sure where she should put her shot. Finally, she just blasted the thing in two. She wondered if, like a normal earthworm, the thing would continue to live in two sections. But it had stopped wiggling toward them, at least.

"What does the Sini Mira want with me?" As she struggled to reload, she noticed that he had taken a pineapple-shaped device from his jacket pocket. He pulled a small glass vial from somewhere inside his shirt, pulling out the cork with his teeth. He poured the contents of the vial into the device and screwed the top shut as he spoke.

"I apologize," he said finally, "but that is not for me to answer."

Then, popping up from behind the wagon, he depressed a button on top of the pineapple-thing and threw it into the vast black pool of Exunge that was gathering in the middle of the ruined street.

There was a bright flash as the contraption exploded. A sparkling, glowing mat spread over the Black Exunge. Little glistening bubbles formed, glittering edges rushing out from the center of the pool like a piece of paper burning from the center. The Exunge solidified like cooling magma, turning an ashy-gray color. No more Aberrancies blossomed from within it; those that were still alive slowed, their movements becoming stiff and jerky.

"Aberrant-resistant bacteria," he said. "It neutralizes Black Exunge, then devours it. It is a sadly fumble-handed technology for the battle situation. The bacteria must be kept warm, by the body, until it is ready for use, and then mixed with a high-powered glucose solution at the last minute." He paused. "My name is Dmitri."

Emily gaped at him, trying to think of what she should say to *that* when something slammed against her head, staggering her backward. Everything went blurry. There was a high buzzing sound and the rapid sound of beating wings. She thudded to the ground, her foot catching between two loose stones, twisting her ankle. Pain sparkled up her leg. She was aware of dark hairy parts pawing at her face and chest; she brought up her shotgun to fend the thing off. A flying thing, buzzing and whirring, with a long tubular mouthpart. *A mosquito,* Emily realized, hazily. A giant goddamn mosquito.

She swung the shotgun blindly, trying to beat the thing back, but it was on her, probing and groping, heavy as a small child. Dmitri was trying to pull it off her.

But the needlelike feeding mouth of the thing was feeling for the place of bare skin between her belt and shirt . . .

Then the tube plunged in, and Emily screamed.

"Quiet now. Don't try to move."

A sour liquid was trickling down her throat, spilling over the corners of her mouth. Coughing, she spat it out. Her entire body vibrated and hummed; she felt like a string that had just been plucked. She itched all over.

"Slowly now, Miss Edwards," Dmitri said as he helped her sit up.

Her hand fumbled at her waist, encountering a welting wound that was the size of a dinner plate. It itched like mad. She scratched with momentary frenzy before Dmitri pulled her hand away.

"Don't," he said. "You will make yourself bleed."

Emily looked over. Nearby, the giant mosquito lay dead, its head blown half away, its myriad eyes dull and lifeless. Dmitri had the rifle by his knee. He was putting the cap on a small bottle that he tucked back into his pocket.

"What was that?" she asked suspiciously. Her voice sounded far away in her own buzzing ears.

"A restorative elixir . . . nothing baneful," Dmitri said. "I know you don't trust me, Miss Edwards. But as I have said—"

"Yes, I know. You're here to protect me." Emily blinked thick mucus from her watering eyes. She rubbed her face, trying to will away the terrible itching. Whatever the restorative elixir was, it did seem to be helping. The buzzing in her body was subsiding slowly, leaving only soreness and a faint nausea in its wake. The military had finally arrived, and dozens of soldiers were surveying the damage. They shouted as they clambered over the wreckage of the street.

"Come along," Dmitri said, casting a meaningful glance at

the soldiers. "I don't expect you want to be delayed answering questions."

"Delayed?" Emily started as fresh panic surged through her. How long had she been out?

She looked up at the clock on the top of the Chronicle building. She did a swift terrible calculation.

It was 1:41 p.m. in New York.

Emily closed her eyes. She took a deep breath and let it out.

"Oh . . . fiddlesticks," she muttered.

She climbed to her feet, wincing. Her ankle was badly twisted. She took an experimental step, stumbled; Dmitri caught her. She pushed him away, willing herself to be steady, increasing the weight on her bad ankle slowly. After a bit, she was able to walk—hobblingly—over the broken jumble of brick and cobblestone toward Kearny Street.

Dmitri followed.

"Leave me alone!" she yelled over her shoulder, as if scolding a persistent cat.

"It is a free country, Miss Edwards," Dmitri called back. "I have as much right to walk in this direction as you do."

Emily stopped and waited for Dmitri to catch up with her. When he did, she whirled on him fiercely.

"You tell the Sini Mira that I don't have anything for them." She jabbed a finger at him for emphasis. "If you wanted the stone, that's gone."

"We know," Dmitri said.

"Then there's nothing else to discuss," Emily said, starting along Kearny Street again. "And while I appreciate your help with the cockroaches, I do *not* need your protection."

"Miss Edwards, if you think it pleases me to protect a Witch, you are deeply mistaken," Dmitri said. "But it is the assignment I have been given, and I will do it to the best of my ability, whether you like it or not."

Shaking her head, Emily walked on as quickly as her sore ankle would allow. Dmitri continued to follow in silence. He did not speak again until they'd turned up Clay Street.

"I am sorry you do not trust us," he said finally.

"*Trust* you?" Emily growled. "You people sent a bounty

hunter to capture me . . . a very brutal bounty hunter." She shuddered, remembering how her will had melted like butter under the command of the Manipulator Antonio Grimaldi. Under the bounty hunter's psychic control, she'd handed the knife that murdered Professor Mirabilis into the hands of his assassin without a moment's hesitation.

"It was a matter of necessity," Dmitri said. "Nonetheless, you have our apologies for it."

Emily snorted derisively.

"Not enough," she said, remembering how the knife had cut Mirabilis' still-beating heart from his chest. "Not enough at all."

CHAPTER FIVE

Dreadnought

Emily knocked on the door of the butter-yellow house, leaning heavily against the doorjamb. She felt rather bad for dirtying up the nice clean paint job with all the black slime and insect guts that covered her, but her ankle was throbbing from the steep climb up the hill. Behind her, on the sidewalk below, Dmitri waited silently. She'd given up telling him to shove off; it did no good.

After a few moments, the Haälbeck attendant, a girl named Dinah, opened the front door, staring at Emily in astonishment.

"What the—Miss Edwards?" She looked Emily up and down. "My gracious! Everyone's been looking for you! You missed Mrs. Stanton's lunch."

Emily sighed, pushed herself away from the doorjamb.

"Good day, Miss Edwards," Dmitri's voice called up to her from the street. Emily turned just enough to see the brown man tip his hat before walking briskly away, hands tucked in his pockets. Dinah craned her neck over Emily's shoulder, watching him go. She looked at Emily quizzically.

"Who was he, miss?"

"No one," Emily said, limping into the house. "He was just here to protect me."

"It's lovely to see you, miss!" Emily followed Dinah's crisp black-and-white-clad form through the neatly swept hallway toward the Haälbeck Room. "I can't imagine how you came through earlier without me seeing you."

"Well, I can be extremely sneaky," Emily said.

"Oh, I'm sure you're not," Dinah demurred, hiding a grin behind her hand. "What a thing to say."

They came to the Haälbeck Room, and Emily was once again surprised at how empty it seemed. She remembered standing in this room when it had overflowed with stifling clutter—all of which apparently had gone with Mrs. Quincy when she'd been kicked to the curb. Only one thing remained: an important-looking picture of Emeritus Zeno, its frame decorated with bunting and silver paper. Emily scrutinized it, trying to find the face of the mild-mannered man she'd first known as old Ben in the face of the somewhat crazed-looking young priest. She finally decided that it was Zeno's eyes that were most unchanged; she recognized that spark of single-minded, uncompromising determination. In Zeno as she knew him today, it was easily attributable to wisdom. In the eyes of the young priest, it seemed hardly indistinguishable from insanity.

Looking away from Zeno's eyes, her gaze traveled to the bottom of the picture, where she noticed the date of the picture's execution: 1741. The man in the picture was certainly in his thirties—that would make Zeno 175 years old now! She knew he was old, but she'd never imagined he was *that* old.

Dinah laid a slim hand on the Haälbeck door's frame and unlocked it with a few soft words. She held the door open for Emily. Framed by its edges, Emily could see the Institute's Haälbeck Room on the other side, murky and indistinct.

"Be sure to give Mr. Stanton my congratulations on his recent triumph over the Dark Sorcerer of Trieste," Dinah said as Emily stepped through.

Emily had grown accustomed to making short hops by Haälbeck—there were hundreds of local doors in New York, greatly facilitating interurban travel. But traveling such a long distance by Haälbeck was like being stretched into the finest silken thread. There was a huge rushing and a feeling of speed, as if she were a waterfall tumbling down a million miles . . .

. . . And then she pooled abruptly back into a water-shaped version of herself and stepped out of California and into the Haälbeck Room of the Mirabilis Institute of the Credomantic Arts in New York City.

It was a cozy, richly appointed parlor, filled with marbles and tapestries and the fragrance of blood-red orchids. Emily noticed that it was filled with something else, too.

The foot-tapping form of Miss Jesczenka.

Emily wondered how on earth the woman had known she was coming. She'd hoped to sneak back as quietly as she'd left—but Emily already knew there was going to be hell to pay, and she supposed there was no use allowing it to accrue interest.

"Welcome back, Miss Edwards," Miss Jesczenka said. She held a cut-crystal glass of iced lemon water in her hand, which she offered to Emily immediately. Emily took the glass, draining it in a protracted and unladylike guzzle. The long Haälbeck journey had left her feeling as if she'd just crossed an Arabian desert. Miss Jesczenka poured her another glass from a pitcher on a small side table.

"You missed Mrs. Stanton's lunch," Miss Jesczenka said. Her eyes roamed over Emily, lingering on the chunks of exploded cockroach innards.

Emily smiled brightly. "Did I?"

"Yes," Miss Jesczenka said.

Miss Jesczenka took the glass from Emily after she'd drained it again, and placed it on a marble side table without making the slightest noise.

"Well, I can't imagine she'll mind all that much." Emily attempted bravado. "Just a 'little get-together,' she said."

"She invited a hundred people," Miss Jesczenka said. "And two Astors."

Emily sighed. She took a limping step forward.

"Are you injured?"

"Not in the least," Emily lied again.

Miss Jesczenka was silent for a moment.

"When you did not return, I sent word to Mrs. Stanton that you had been seized with bewildering fits. I implied that you were wildly pounding on death's door, demanding admittance. I had to concoct quite a dire scenario to excuse your absence."

Probably made the old hag's day, Emily thought. But instead of saying this, she smiled. "How clever of you."

Miss Jesczenka did not smile back. "So, are you going to favor me with an explanation of why you went to California dressed in men's clothing and came back covered with intestines?"

Emily was silent. She actually rather wished she could tell Miss Jesczenka about the cockroaches. For some reason, she thought the woman might find it amusing. Or not.

"I'll go to my room and get cleaned up," Emily said.

"That's a very good idea," Miss Jesczenka said, wrinkling her nose. "Mrs. Stanton may come by later to confirm that you're on your deathbed. I trust you will be obliging enough to look three-quarters dead?"

"I shall have no problem playing the part," Emily said, as honestly as if she were swearing on a stack of Bibles.

Once in her room, Emily stripped off her clothes and kicked them into a stinking pile. Someone would have to burn them.

Then she ran herself a well-earned bath. One thing she could say for the Institute—the plumbing was fantastic. The suite she had been given had all the most up-to-date features, including a bathroom with a giant white porcelain tub. She ran water gushing with steam, and as it ran, she unbuckled the straps that held her prosthetic in place, briskly rubbing the red welts where the leather had cut into her flesh. She laid the carved ivory hand on a table, carefully avoiding looking at the puckered stump of her arm.

Sliding into the warm water, she released a moan of pleasure that any well-bred observer would have found positively indecent. The heat felt particularly good on her sore ankle. She explored the abused joint with her fingers. It was still swollen, but with a little rest, it would be fine in a day or two.

It took a long time to get completely clean, for the insect innards had dried to an intractably sticky crust. When she'd finally gotten every bit off her skin and out of her hair, she climbed out of the tub, pulled on fresh cotton underthings, and collapsed onto the wide white bed, feather softness and the smell of honeysuckle enfolding her.

She was snuggling deep into the sweet-smelling sheets when she felt something hard under the pillow. Reaching underneath, her fingers encountered something cool and smooth. Withdrawing it, she discovered that it was a student's slate, the kind a small child would use to learn his alphabet. It was quite new-looking, framed in polished beech and painted with frolicking lambs. It had a little slot carved into the side that held a sharpened pencil. On the slate, in Stanton's jagged cliff-peak handwriting, were the words:

MEET ME IN CENTRAL PARK. 4 P.M. URGENT. BRING THE SLATE.

Emily looked at the clock on the mantel. It was three o'clock.

Groaning, she threw an arm over her eyes.

She hadn't seen Stanton at all during the past week, not even for a minute. And he did say it was urgent. This could be her one opportunity before the Investment to tell him about her visit to California and the bottle of memories Pap had given her.

She lay there, feeling the rise and fall of her own chest. If only she could sleep for a few hours first. She was supposed to be on her deathbed with bewildering fits, after all. And what if Mrs. Stanton came by to gloat? Well, Miss Jesczenka would just have to think of something. Say that death's door had finally opened, and Emily had stepped inside for a cup of tea. The worse the fate, the better Mrs. Stanton would like it.

Emily sat up. It was a feat of miraculous willpower. She took a deep breath and swung her feet out onto the floor.

The things I do for Dreadnought Stanton, she thought once again.

She put herself into a suite of ladies' clothing, certainly not daring to call Miss Jesczenka for help. The outfit was knife-pleat new and much fancier than anything she'd ever owned before; Emily was still trying to get used to the necessity of costuming herself for different social purposes. She'd had fewer dresses in her entire life than she was supposed to have for one season in New York, and having a different one for every quarter of the day seemed ridiculous in the extreme. Still, Emily recognized the need for conformity to fashion's whims, and thus had invested some of the money Mirabilis had paid her on a wardrobe appropriate to decent society.

Fumbling with a long silver buttonhook, Emily got herself fastened—at least buying new clothes had meant she could get them with the buttons up the front. This allowed her to dress herself, despite the handicap presented by her missing hand. It was just too tedious to have to stand around half naked, waiting for someone to do up your buttons.

This dress was of pistachio-green silk, deeply bustled and trimmed with black Dieppe lace and jet-beaded embroidery. It had a matching reticule and sunshade. With the addition of a little veiled hat and a pair of black gloves, Emily felt like an imported doll in a shop window.

Thus appointed, she snuck out of her room, looking back and forth down the hall to make sure Miss Jesczenka wasn't lying in wait. She tiptoed downstairs to the Institute's great entry hall. She'd have to get a carriage; she wasn't going to walk to the park with her aching ankle, and certainly not in this getup. The admissions clerk in the entry hall could get her one of the Institute's carriages discreetly; she'd quietly slipped him a double eagle a few weeks earlier on a similar occasion, and he'd shown himself more than willing to be bought.

Once it was clear that Miss Jesczenka was nowhere in the vicinity, Emily stopped skulking. Straightening her back, she came down one of the broad twin marble stairways and into the rotunda, domed in colored glass. It was designed to be maximally impressive, with thirty-foot ceilings and walls of gold-veined white marble, and everywhere, the fragrant blood-red orchids that were the Institute's signature flower.

The entry hall was in a state of last-minute confusion, as decorators, florists, and caterers buzzed about, making arrangements for the Investment that was to be held the following night. Abandoned ladders rested against the walls, half-hung draperies of gold foil bunting hung drooping and limp. It was going to be quite a gala, Emily thought with some apprehension.

She went to the admissions desk and had a few low words with her well-bribed clerk; he nodded to her cheerfully. He hastened from behind the tall imposing admissions desk to pull out a chair for her, giving the seat an obsequious brush, though Emily had never seen a speck of dust in the Institute. He offered to fetch her some water, which she quietly declined. It was always like this, in clothes like these. Men offered her hands, arms, shoulders to lean on; they opened doors, they extinguished cigars, and always—most annoyingly—they stopped talking. Emily thought she could probably get used to being treated as if her body was a blown eggshell, but she doubted she could ever get used to being treated as if her head was as empty as one.

When all the nonsensical fiddling and showy chivalry had run its course, the carriage called, and the clerk returned to his desk, Emily noticed a group of people sitting in a cluster by the front door, chatting animatedly among themselves. They were a zealous-looking lot—a sallow young man with anarchist eyes and an overbite, an assortment of tightly wound females, and two gentlemen who seemed to be twins. They were under the command of a plump, pretty blond girl who looked once at Emily, then twice.

"Miss Emily?" The blonde's dress was a profusion of ruffles and lace. Her brown eyes narrowed as she came over to where Emily was sitting, squinting to peer through the dark veil that Emily wore. Emily lifted it reluctantly, and the girl's face became joyous. "Oh, it is you! How wonderful to see you up and about. I heard you were at death's door. You missed Mrs. Stanton's lunch!"

"Hello, Rose," Emily said. She was far too tired for Rose's twittering intensity at the moment.

Miss Rose Hibble was the president of the Dreadnought Stanton Admiration League, a group formed immediately after the publication of *The Man Who Saved Magic,* the pulp novel outlining Stanton's astonishing adventures. The same book that Emily was not in, despite the fact that she'd played as large a role in the adventures as anyone. Even Rose herself had played a small part; Stanton had saved her life, and she'd abruptly fixed her tendency for hero worship upon him. In a spasm of veneration, she'd followed him to New York, and used her secretarial degree from the Nevada Women's College to get herself a position at a downtown brokerage. She'd then proceeded to form the Admiration League, which already boasted more than two hundred members, thanks entirely to Rose's tireless organizational efforts.

"Mr. Stanton was supposed to speak to us today," Rose said, a note of distress in her tone. "He was going to tell us how he defeated the Dark Sorcerer of Trieste!" She raised a well-thumbed book at Emily, showing her the brilliant cover of a new pulp novel, one Emily hadn't seen yet. On it, Stanton's idealized form could be seen trampling victoriously over a cringing man in a black cape.

Emily smiled wearily. It had been little more than a month since their actual adventures had been completed, and Stanton had spent every moment of it safely in New York, preparing for his Investment under the guidance of Emeritus Zeno. But on pulp pages squeezed between chromolithographed covers, he'd already reclaimed three mystical artifacts of unparalleled magnificence, defended the Austrian throne against the depredations of a golem, and solved some mystery involving the recently delivered hand of a big French statue they were going to erect in New York Harbor. Emily could hardly keep up.

"I hope he's recovered from the grievous wound the Dark Sorcerer delivered him! Is he feeling well? The Investment is tomorrow, and he's got to be at his best!" Rose's face was taut with worry. "We brought him a card."

"I'm going to see him now," Emily said. She squeezed Rose's hand—a strengthening gesture. While Emily was frequently astonished at Rose's credulity, and was sometimes just slightly jealous at the way the girl's brown eyes lit up when she spoke of Stanton, she was genuinely fond of her. "I'm sure he'll pull through."

"Please give him our best," Rose said. "And would you give him this?" She proffered a large card in an envelope that was printed with brilliantly colored flowers and addressed in a careful, intricate script.

Emily tucked it into her bag, next to the slate with the leaping lambs. "I'll make sure he gets it," she said.

"Oh, thank you!" Rose said, clenching her hands together. "Thank you!"

The afternoon air was sticky and dead calm, and even the thin green silk Emily wore seemed too warm. Little rivulets of sweat trickled down the sides of her forehead as the carriage carried her along a twisting cobblestone path through the park. She found herself missing San Francisco's milder clime. A fresh breeze off the ocean offset a lot of Aberrancies in her book.

Stanton's note had directed her to meet him in Central Park, but had failed to specify exactly *where*. So she went to the place that was her favorite—the park's wild northernmost reaches. It was an easy distance from the Institute's opulent, expansive (and somewhat incongruous) headquarters on Eighty-fifth. Emily had heard it said with some pride that the Institute owned all of the Nineties from the park to the Hudson. Emily supposed that was quite grand, in its way. But given that most of the valuable property in New York City lay below Twenty-third Street, and the Nineties pretty much consisted of squatters' shacks, small farmholdings, and wide dirt roads that turned into mud slogs whenever it rained, Emily didn't quite see what there was to get so excited about.

Because of its remote location, the Institute also maintained an imposing facade downtown, on Lexington Avenue near Gramercy Park, but it was not large enough to house all the Institute's students and activities, so it was little more than an extravagantly splendid shell with a few offices and a Haälbeck door connecting it to the mansion uptown. Emily had found that it was most convenient to travel from the wild reaches uptown to downtown by Haälbeck—as did many others. While primarily an establishment of magical learning, the Mirabilis Institute also had quite a profitable sideline in interurban travel. Mirabilis had cornered the market on Haälbeck timber many years ago, and since only small amounts—hardly more than a sliver—were needed for travel over such short distances, the Institute had built doors all over the city.

For a dollar, businessmen could flash downtown, uptown, and across in a thread-stretched twinkling. Certainly much more convenient than clopping through crowded streets in a cab, or riding on one of the clattering streetcars.

The Institute's carriage let Emily out near the big stretch of water called Harlem Meer. The area surrounding it was rugged, less daintily landscaped than the park's groomed southern reaches. Beyond the Harlem Meer, farms and muddy roads stretched to the northwest. It was like being home; there were jutting outcroppings of gray mica-flecked stone and the good clean smell of trees and grass and water. Downtown always smelled like sewage to her, even though Stanton insisted he couldn't smell it and she must be imagining things. But it did smell; it smelled like things all crowded together and moving too fast.

But here it was quiet, fragrant with good living soil. And there weren't as many people, though she still found herself amidst knots of strollers out enjoying the warm summer afternoon, beautiful children in short white dresses, and nurses pushing prams. Even New York's most deserted places bustled, Emily had found, and she was certain she'd never get used to it.

At that moment, Emily was surprised to hear the sound of a lamb baaing. As if that were not surprising enough, the baaing was coming out of her bag. Exploring further, she discovered that the baaing was, more precisely, coming from the slate. She drew it out curiously.

LOOK IN FRONT OF YOU, the writing in Stanton's angular hand now read.

She looked up, seeing nothing but a swarming mass of pigeons. But then there were hands on her shoulders, and the brush of very warm lips against the bare place on the back of her neck. She shivered pleasantly.

"You missed my mother's lunch," came the voice of the man to whom the warm lips belonged. Pleasure became annoyance with startling rapidity. Emily spun and stomped a foot.

"If people don't quit saying that to me, I'm going to—" Stanton grinned and leaned forward to stop her threat with a kiss—an action that had to be averted at the last minute as a group of loudly conversing German tourists came strolling past. He put his hands behind his back, looking sidelong at the Germans.

"Was your mother furious?"

"She'll get over it," Stanton said. "Perhaps not in this lifetime, but I happen to believe in reincarnation, so there's still hope." From somewhere inside his coat he produced another student slate, the exact match of the one she'd found under her pillow.

"Have you called me here to do sums?" she asked. "I hate math."

"All right, we'll stick to geography," Stanton said, wiping his slate with his sleeve and scribbling something new on it. Emily's slate baaed. She looked at it. Now it read: WHERE WERE YOU, ANYWAY?

Emily laughed with delight.

"Turn around," she said. She steadied the slate against his back with her ivory hand and rubbed out the letters with her good hand. She wrote shakily, for it was her writing hand Caul had taken: CALIFORNIA.

Stanton's slate baaed. After a moment's pause, he looked at her over his shoulder.

"Instead of going to my mother's lunch, you went to *California*?"

"I wanted to see Pap." Emily tucked the slate pencil into its slot. "I'm sorry, Mr. Stanton, really I am. I didn't mean to miss it. Things . . . happened."

"Oh, well. Things happened. How nice to have that cleared up." He lifted an eyebrow. "And by the way, why do you persist in calling me Mr. Stanton? Don't you think that's a bit formal? It hardly matters while we're engaged, but after we're married, it just won't do."

He was right, of course; running around calling him Mr. Stanton after their wedding would make her sound like his sixth Mormon wife. But try as she might, she could not make Stanton's given name sound at all right. It sounded ludicrous coming out of her mouth.

"Dreadnought," she said experimentally. "Dreadnought,"

she tried again, more lightly. She shook her head. "I'm sorry. You'll have to change it."

"What on earth is wrong with my name?"

"You have to admit, it's one fly-killing cannon of a name," Emily said. "Can you imagine what it will be like after we're married? Dreadnought, please pass the toast . . . Dreadnought, please close the window . . . Dreadnought, shall we paint the walls yellow?"

"What an appealing vision of married life," Stanton said drily. "One hopes it will include more intriguing things than toast passing and window closing."

"One hopes," Emily agreed. "Didn't you have a nickname when you were younger?"

"The Senator always called me 'boy.'" Stanton's tone was contemplative. "Mother, on the other hand, would call me 'Not,' as in the adverb used to express negation or prohibition. Or, I suppose, as in 'zero.' Neither interpretation appeals to me very much."

"How about 'knot,' as in something difficult to untangle?" Emily thought suddenly of the discussion she'd had with Pap.

"I hardly think I'm that complex," Stanton said.

Emily bit her lip. "All right, then what's your middle name?"

Stanton paused, then drew himself up. He took on a look of steely resolve. "I won't tell you."

She drew back, blinking surprise at his unexpected vehemence. "But it can hardly be worse than—"

He took her chin in his hand, kissed her quickly to stop her talking, then pulled back before the Germans could see.

"Never mind. Call me whatever you like. 'Dear' will do nicely."

Emily did not much like to be kissed to be shut up, but she did like to be kissed. It sweetened her disposition enough that she decided to refrain from pestering him for his middle name. For the time being, anyway. She filed the pester away for implementation at some convenient future date.

She regarded his long spare frame and gaunt face. He seemed thinner, if such a thing were possible. He was burned—a degenerative blight that made it impossible for him to keep weight on no matter how much he ate. *Ten years to live,* Emily had once been told. Stanton himself had stalwartly refused her the dubious comfort of thinking that it might be longer. *Ten years.* And with the hard work of running the Institute facing him, it might be even less. Fear flickered through Emily's chest, but she damped it down ruthlessly. They had today. Today, his dark green eyes glittered, and today he was alive. Today—and however many todays came after it—was all they would have.

"I'm not the only one who skipped out on my duties," Emily said. "You were supposed to speak to Rose's Admiration League today. You can't always be ducking them."

"Having Rose as the president of my Admiration League—indeed, having an Admiration League at all—is an exercise in patience to which I am not always equal."

"She adores you." Emily smiled up at him. "She'd walk through fire for you."

"Sometimes I wish she would."

"Oh, stop it. You have to take your duties seriously, you know."

"Of course I must," Stanton said, with the exasperation of a man who has heard the same thing a million different times from a million different people—an exasperation Emily was intimately acquainted with herself. "But I hadn't realized exactly how consuming they were going to be. Having to meet you in a public park, as if this were some kind of . . . assignation? Having to resort to a child's toy just to get messages to you?" He glanced at the student slate he was still holding in his hand, then tucked it away inside his coat. "But Zeno maintains I have to stay focused. He's got this odd idea that you distract me."

"Who, me?" Emily said. "My, what you have to go through, just to achieve the zenith of credomantic power."

"I just hope it won't be too much," he said, raising a hand to touch a shining brunette lock that had escaped from beneath her small feathered hat. He pulled the movement up short when a loud exclamation came from behind them; the Germans, who were still lingering nearby, had drawn out a map and were consulting it and conversing loudly among themselves.

"For pity's sake!" he muttered. "Even if they can't find where they're going, can't they at least find their way away from us?"

He went over to the Germans and spoke a few words to them in their own language. They seemed overjoyed at his help and clapped him on the back. When Stanton returned to Emily's side, there was a wicked grin on his face.

"Did you help them find what they were looking for?" she asked, not quite understanding what had transpired as Stanton took her arm and led her away.

"No," Stanton said. "But I did share a closely guarded secret with them. Specifically, that all the city's streetcars may be ridden free of charge if one tells the driver that one's brother-in-law's name is Mickey Doogan."

"Mickey Doogan?" Emily scrunched her nose. "Who's he?"

"No idea," Stanton said. "Made him up whole cloth. I haven't the time to put a bunch of bothersome tourists in their place. The streetcar drivers are better at it anyway. They've practically elevated it to an art form."

Emily looked after the Germans. Having experienced the artful brusqueness of New York's streetcar drivers herself once or twice, she felt a twinge of sympathy for them.

"You're just plain cruel, that's what you are."

"Not as cruel as not being able to kiss you as much as I like, given how pretty you look today. Come on. We're going to find someplace less populated."

Emily tried to match his long strides, but she found herself faltering. In her small boots of tight kid, her ankle was swelling and aching again. He paused, looking down at her foot.

"Did you hurt yourself?"

"I'll tell you about it when we get to that less populated place you promised me." She squeezed his warm arm closer to her, acutely desiring a change of subject. "Just exactly how many languages do you know, anyway?"

"I don't think I've ever counted," Stanton said thoughtfully. "Latin and Greek don't count; anyone with pretensions to know anything should know those. Same with Sanskrit, Sumerian, and the Dravidian languages, though one needs only to be able to read them. As far as speaking, I'm quite good in French, Spanish, Russian, German, Hebrew, and Arabic. I can get around in Turkish and speak enough Hindi to buy dosas and a mango lassi, if required. Then there's bits and pieces of others."

She stared at him for a long moment. She felt as if he'd just hit her over the head with a dictionary.

"You can't be serious," she said.

"Well, I haven't got a stick of Chinese," Stanton said, making the lack sound egregious indeed. "Believe me, the list I just gave you is unimpressive compared to some credomancers you'll meet."

"Where on earth do you put them all?" She tried to imagine knowing thirteen ways to say the word "pickle," never mind that you didn't know how to say it in Chinese.

"My dear, language is the currency of credomantic power," he said. "A spell in English won't do you a sliver of good in Moscow, or Berlin, or Paris. Besides, a credomancer's power derives entirely from local customs and beliefs. One must have the ability to discern and exploit those beliefs."

They turned onto an overgrown path that wound up into the green darkness of a densely wooded, boulder-strewn hillside.

"Will your ankle bear up?" he asked Emily, putting an arm around her waist to support her once the threat of being seen had passed.

"My ankle has been through worse," Emily said, but let herself lean against him nonetheless.

They ascended up the tangled path, pausing every now and again to disengage Emily's garments from snagging branches and roots.

Somehow they managed to outwit the local flora and achieve the objective Stanton had apparently been aiming for: a squat, thick-walled building of irregularly shaped stones. It was a perfect cube, with one very small, rusty door hanging off its hinges. Ivy grew all around the structure; midafternoon light poured down through its shattered roof.

"It's called the blockhouse," Stanton said, taking Emily by the waist and lifting her up over a fallen tree trunk. "It was here long before Central Park was even thought of. My grandfather fought here in the War of 1812. He used to bring me up here to shoot birds." He touched the door, which creaked and showered them with flakes of rust. He peered inside. "It's fallen apart a bit since then."

As Emily stepped inside the large empty fortress, she noticed that there were two small barred casement windows set in each stone wall. While secluded, it was also rather like being in a jail.

"How romantic," Emily said, looking up at the sky through the collapsed roof. Fat, curling tendrils of ivy framed the ceiling of mellow blue. It was like looking up from the bottom of a well.

But Stanton seemed to have no interest in the sky. He gathered her in his arms and pulled her close into his sweltering embrace; he was as warm as a fever victim. He began kissing her—kisses that progressed in duration and intensity until it was clear that for the moment, it was better to stop kissing altogether.

He let his arms rest loosely around her waist, resting his forehead against hers.

"You promised me you'd tell me about your ankle," Stanton murmured. "Have you been chasing Aberrancies again?"

The guess, though playfully intended, was far too close to the truth for Emily's liking, and she found that she didn't want to talk about all that now. She enjoyed the warm glow of Stanton's embrace far too much to risk losing it.

"You first," she said, lifting her chin. "Your note said 'Urgent.' Is anything wrong?"

"Other than you missing my mother's lunch?" Stanton said. "Everything pales in comparison to that, I'm afraid."

Before she could hit him, he pulled a velvet box from his pocket and presented it to her with a flourish. She opened the box, and found that it contained a ring of mellow white gold, set with a huge diamond. The stone didn't just sparkle like other diamonds she'd seen; it blazed fire all around it, blue and red.

"I captured it from the Dark Sorcerer of Trieste," Stanton explained. "Haven't you been reading my books?"

"No."

"It's a meteorite diamond. Incredibly rare, outlandishly expensive." Stanton took the box from her and removed the ring. "I rather wish I *had* captured it from the Dark Sorcerer of Trieste; it wouldn't have set the Institute back quite so much, and we wouldn't have had to go through such paroxysms of secrecy to obtain it." He took her hand and slid the ring on her finger. "It's to be your engagement ring. I was supposed to have given it to you before the lunch you didn't attend, so you could flash it around. Oh well."

"The Institute bought me a big vulgar diamond ring?"

"Well, *I* couldn't afford it," Stanton said. "If it were up to me, you'd keep that one." He gestured to his gold Jefferson Chair ring that Emily had taken to wearing on her thumb. "But Fortissimus says you have to help reinforce the mythology. I supposedly captured this ring from an enemy of exceptional power and villainy. If you're seen wearing it, it heightens the illusion." He tilted her hand up to the light and placed a kiss on each of her fingertips.

"It's grotesque!" Emily said. "Think of the muscles I'll have to grow to carry this thing around. I'll have to have a dress of one size and a sleeve two sizes larger!"

"Now, mustn't overdramatize." Stanton smiled, apparently wholly unaware of the irony. He slid the gold Jefferson Chair ring from her thumb and pocketed it. She swallowed a sound of protest; she'd grown quite fond of the simple gold band.

"So what does this monstrosity do?" Emily tilted her hand back and forth, watching the diamond glitter. "Does it allow me to summon armies of the undead? Levitate on nights with a full moon? Read the hidden motives of the wicked and untrue?"

"It doesn't *do* anything."

Mildly exasperated, she let her hand fall.

"Well, it must have some magical power, otherwise why did you risk your life capturing it from the Dark Sorcerer of Trieste?"

"It wasn't the diamond I risked my life for," Stanton said

quite seriously, despite the fact that his life had been risked only in the most purely fictional sense. "It was an affirmation of the Manichaean principle of Ultimate Good triumphing over Ultimate Evil. Dreadnought Stanton does not battle for material gains, he battles to defeat the forces of darkness. The capturing of treasure is mostly incidental." He sounded heroic—melodramatically so—and she smiled at him patiently until he got ahold of himself.

A sheepish grin curved his lips. "One does tend to start thinking of one's self in the third person," he said more mildly.

"So, no armies of the undead," Emily said.

"Like you said, it's just a big grotesque diamond. It's supposed to sit there and look pretty."

Emily stared mutely at the mostly incidental ring, which carried on blazing ostentatiously in the afternoon sunshine. Obviously, she could learn a lot from such a ring.

Noticing her unexpected shift in mood, Stanton adopted a lighter tone. "Never mind, you'll get used to it. Now . . . your ankle. And an explanation of the injury thereto."

Emily sighed, looking over her shoulder for a place to sit. Speaking about her ankle reminded her of it, and that was enough to set it throbbing. She eased herself onto one of the blockhouse's weathered concrete abutments. She had been so looking forward to talking things over with Stanton, but now she didn't want to. She wanted to forget anything had ever happened. She wanted to forget about the bottle of memories in her pocket, pretend it never existed. But unpleasant things could not just be forgotten, no matter how one wished they could. She drew a deep breath, let it out. The afternoon smelled of warmth and growing plants and sunshine.

"I had a strange talk with Pap," Emily began. "He had a lot of things to tell me." She paused. "He told me that there were things about my mother I never knew. He gave me this." She pulled the heavy blue bottle from her pocket. "It's called a Lethe Draught."

"A Lethe Draught!" Stanton settled himself beside her. He took the bottle between his fingers and held it up to the light. He examined the card that was attached to the neck.

"'Catherine Kendall,'" he read. "'Boston.'"

"It was my mother's card," Emily said softly.

"Unglazed bristol board, excellent engraving. This is the card of a woman of good family." Stanton paused, obviously surprised. "How unexpected."

"Thanks a lot."

"When I can spare a second, I'll take you down to the Institute's library, and we'll look up the name in the Boston Social Register. The Institute has copies of all of them back a hundred years or more."

"I hardly think my mother would be in the Boston Social Register," Emily said.

Stanton did not comment, but continued to peer closely at the contents of the bottle. "Why would he Lethe you?"

"He said my mother was evil."

"Evil?"

"He didn't want to explain," Emily said. "He just said that my memories were so bad that I had to be protected from them."

Stanton frowned. "That *is* the commonly accepted usage of Lethe Draughts—to mitigate the harm of traumatic memories. But it's a pretty drastic step, one that most practitioners don't take lightly."

"I'm sure Pap wouldn't have done it if he didn't have to." Emily felt suddenly cold, and pressed closer to Stanton for warmth. "Well, what do you think? Should I drink it, or what?"

Stanton's response was immediate. "Drink a Lethe Draught decocted by your pap? I think not!"

Then he quickly lifted an ameliorating hand. "Not that he isn't an able Warlock, but they're awfully tricky potions, Emily. Easy to get wrong."

"So I should let my memories of my mother go? Just like that?" Emily said. "Let my history stay dead and bottled up?"

"Sometimes it's better to let sleeping dogs lie," Stanton said. Then he let out a long sigh. "But knowing you, you won't let them. Promise me one thing. If you decide to drink it, don't do it alone. Wait until I can be there with you."

Emily nodded assent, remembering her similar promise to Pap.

"A Lethe Draught!" Stanton shook his head in disbelief. Then, in a darker tone, he added, "He kept a lot from you, didn't he?"

"He did it to protect me," Emily said.

"I wonder if that makes it right," Stanton mused. Then his eyes widened. "But you still haven't explained your ankle!"

"Well, that happened when I ran into the Sini Mira," Emily said. The words had the predicable effect of making Stanton blink twice at her; Emily compressed her lips, but did not smile.

"The Sini Mira sent men to Pap's cabin to ask about my mother," Emily explained. "They are interested in her. They wouldn't tell me why."

"They wouldn't tell . . . you spoke to them?"

"I spoke to one of them. His name was Dmitri."

"He *hurt* you?"

"No . . ." Emily was hesitant to go into all the details of her battle with the Aberrancies; she felt he'd been alarmed enough for one day. "There was an earthquake . . . you know, there've been terrible earthquakes in San Francisco . . . and I twisted my ankle. He was there, he helped me up . . ." She waved an impatient hand, as if to brush aside the strands of her story that didn't hold together. "He had been following me. He said he'd been sent to protect me."

"The Sini Mira is not interested in protecting Witches."

Emily frowned. Dmitri had said as much himself. "Why do they hate us so much?" she asked, inching herself back on the ledge and extending her ankle to rotate it. "Magic is as natural as . . . sunshine! They might as well hate sunshine!"

Stanton lifted her foot and let it rest in the crook of his arm. With his large hand, he began lightly kneading her ankle through the soft kid.

"And how exactly do they think they can stop people using magic, anyway?" Emily added, leaning back and enjoying the warm play of Stanton's fingers on her leg.

"As I understand it, they propose to implement a sort of poison," Stanton said. "A poison, deployed within the Mantic

Anastomosis itself, that would make magic toxic to any practitioner channeling it. The idea was put forth in the fifties by a scientist named Aleksei Morozovich. It sent the magical community into an uproar."

"I can imagine." Emily winced as Stanton's fingers found a particularly sore spot. Then, she asked softly, "How toxic?"

"As Morozovich's research was never disseminated, that's a matter of speculation. Some say that even the smallest charm could leave a practitioner feeling ill . . . and that perhaps, it could be fatal to an individual working a great magic."

"And what about someone like you?" Emily asked. "Someone burned?"

Stanton pressed his lips together and was silent for a long time. His hand played over her ankle gently.

"Being burned means I cannot control the magic that flows through my body," he said eventually. "I have no defenses against it; it flows through me untrammeled. I do not choose to channel magic, and thus I cannot choose *not* to channel magic. If the poison as it has been described were to be implemented, I imagine it would be unpleasant."

"Mildly unpleasant?" Emily ventured hopefully. "Maybe?"

"Fatally unpleasant," Stanton said. "Probably."

Emily let his words hang in the air, hoping the afternoon brightness would blunt them. It didn't.

It was Stanton who finally spoke again.

"The Sini Mira does not care about me, or people like me. They are fanatics, willing to trample innocent bystanders in the pursuit of their goals."

"Great. So I have fanatics following me around. Again."

He looked at her. "Well, the preliminary indications are that they're not after you, per se. They are interested in your mother. And even if they do think that you can help them find something out about her, as long as you stay within the Institute, you'll be completely safe."

The sureness and protectiveness in his voice made her feel like giggling. Emily hated girls who giggled, so she bit her lip and tried to look serious.

"I just wish I knew what they wanted."

"You said your mother was going to the Sini Mira. Whatever business she hoped to transact with them was obviously never completed. What that business could have been . . ." He furrowed his brow quizzically. "A nice young woman from Boston, with a child, crossing the country to get to the Sini Mira in San Francisco." He rested his hand on her ankle, shaking his head. "Whatever the situation, it must have been dire." He gently lowered her foot. "Better?"

"Much." Emily smiled at him. "I need to speak with Komé. I think she knows more about the Sini Mira than she ever told me." She softened her voice. "She wanted me to go with them, back in Chicago. Remember?"

"I remember," Stanton said. "I didn't agree with her then either."

"I'll speak to Emeritus Zeno tonight," Emily said, thinking of the rooting ball with Komé's acorn in it. "He has to let me talk to her."

"It's not getting Zeno to let you speak to Komé, it's getting Fortissimus to let you speak to Zeno," Stanton said. "You know what he's like."

"*Fortissimus.*" Emily grumbled the word like a curse. Yes, she knew exactly what Rex Fortissimus was like. The most prominent presentment arranger in New York, Fortissimus supposedly knew more about credomancy than anyone besides Emeritus Zeno. He had been retained at an extremely handsome rate to arrange the Investment, promote Stanton's public image, and advise him on decisions of importance. He'd been making a nuisance of himself for weeks, mostly by claiming whatever share of Stanton's time was not already claimed by Zeno. "I don't like him."

"Well, like him or not, I need him. It's a big leap for someone in my position to become Sophos." He paused thoughtfully. "Actually, tonight might not be a bad night to get yourself in front of the Emeritus. Fortissimus is throwing a beefsteak for me at Delmonico's, and he won't be around to bother you. Try after nine."

"Then you're not coming back to the Institute?" Emily tried unsuccessfully to hide her disappointment. "I swear, I don't know why I always get left out of things! Why shouldn't

New York see my face once in a while? Is there something wrong with it?"

"There is nothing wrong with your face." Stanton lifted a hand to stroke her cheek. "But it is Fortissimus' considered opinion that it's best to keep you under wraps just at the moment. And even if I were to take you around, it certainly wouldn't be to a beefsteak. There won't be any ladies there, just lots of cigar smoke and politicians and—as one might suppose—beefsteak. Hideous."

"I still don't understand why I have to be kept under wraps, as Fortissimus puts it. Won't it seem strange when you marry some complete unknown out of the clear blue sky?"

"Fortissimus has a plan for that, too," Stanton said. "Ninety-two percent of New York society thinks you're a daughter of one of those eccentric California cattle barons with a fortune in gold."

"And the other eight percent?"

"We're paying them to keep their mouths shut."

Emily drew an outraged breath, but before she could say anything Stanton chucked her under the chin in a way she thought she could grow to dislike. "My dearest beloved darling, you'll be able to go around with me all the time soon enough. After we're married, people will take you as a fait accompli."

Emily didn't know what a fait accompli was, but she was certain she didn't want to be one.

"But even after we're married"—Stanton raised an infuriatingly patrician index finger—"*Especially* after we're married, in fact, I don't intend to take you to a single beefsteak."

"Oh, fine," Emily said. Stanton smiled at her again, as he often did when she was annoyed. Apparently there was something in the set of her nose when annoyed that he found charming.

"Cheer up. The Investment is tomorrow, then all of this nonsense will be over." It was clear that Stanton was looking forward to the end of the nonsense as much as anyone else. "Meanwhile, let's make the best of the time we do have, shall we?" Leaning back on the rough concrete abutment, he drew her against his chest so that her body rested against the length of his. His hands smoothed along her waist, his mouth dipped to the hollow of her throat, lips traversing the curve of her clavicle. Gasping, she brought her head close to his and growled something softly into his ear.

"Miss Edwards!" he scolded, his breath quickening.

"Don't tell me the thought hasn't crossed your mind."

"Yes, I know that there are plenty of nice hotels in New York. And yes, you've made it clear—painfully so—that you might reluctantly consider shedding your virtue prior to the wedding."

"I could be convinced," Emily said, letting her hand wander over parts of his anatomy to accentuate the point.

He captured her hand with desperate quickness and held it tight against his chest. "But the issue, my beloved, is not *your* purity. It's *mine*. It's very important that I remain chaste prior to the Investment. Once I'm Invested, all bets are off. But before the Investment . . ." He let out a heavy sigh. "Well, let's just say there's a reason the Pope is celibate."

Emily stared deeply into his eyes. "Let's leave the Pope out of this," she said.

"Tomorrow," he said. "After tomorrow, everything will be better." He clenched her hand firmly over his heart. "I promise."

"And I'll get to see you once in a while?" she whispered into his throat, closing her eyes and savoring his smell of bay rum and collar starch.

"Anytime you like," Stanton said, his voice soft and rumbling, his breath hot in her ear. He tried to pull her closer, but she slipped nimbly from his grasp—a trick made neater by the fact that she managed to hit him in the face with her hat feather as she did it.

"Until then, Mr. Stanton, let's not drive each other to the madhouse." Emily sat up primly and made a great show of straightening her costume. "It's getting late, and I believe you have a beefsteak to attend."

Stanton looked at her for a long moment. "There's a word for ladies like you," he said.

She grinned at him. "In which language?"

"All of them. And in Chinese, too, I bet," Stanton said.

"Engaged?" she asked, waggling her ring finger at him. The otherworldly diamond glittered like an explosion of stars.

"That wasn't the word I was thinking of," Stanton said, rising swiftly and offering her his arm for the rugged descent back to civilization.

CHAPTER SIX

Treachery

Emily and Stanton went their separate ways in separate carriages. Emily's went one way and Stanton's went the other; hers would carry her back to the Institute, and Stanton's would return him to his family's brownstone on Thirty-fourth Street, where he could change for his beefsteak.

But even if Emily and Stanton had both been returning to the Institute, they would have taken separate carriages in the interest of propriety. Emily was continually amazed at the mealymouthed prissiness of these New Yorkers. Engaged to be married, yet it would be indecent for them to be seen climbing out of a carriage together—as if carriages were rolling dens of iniquity. But then again, the way Stanton's kisses had made her feel, perhaps the New Yorkers did have a point. Oh well. *Tomorrow.* Tomorrow Stanton would be Invested, things would settle down, and all this foolishness would subside. And *then* she could get him up to see her etchings.

She stared out of the window of the hansom. Daughter of a California rancher with a gold fortune! Oh, brother.

When Emily got back to the Institute, she found that the last-minute confusion had intensified. Caterers screeched through the sober marble halls, rolling carts of food to be stored in the Institute's cool cellar kitchens. Dodging a fast-pushed cart, she headed for the stairs. She was looking forward to returning to the comfort of her deathbed just as quickly as possible. She gave the admissions clerk a conspiratorial wink as she ducked under a dangling streamer. The man lifted a finger.

"Miss Jesczenka was looking for you. She said that if I saw you, I was to send you to her immediately." He looked sober, as if Miss Jesczenka had said quite a bit more than that. "She's presenting a class right now, in the tutorial wing. The green lecture hall." The admissions clerk offered her an obsequious arm. "Would you like me to help you there?"

Emily sighed. "I can find it." Reluctantly, she turned her steps toward the tutorial wing. There was still hell to pay for her trip to California, and this tryst with Stanton would surely compound the interest due.

Emily found Miss Jesczenka finishing up a presentation to an advanced group of students. The room was hot; the high windows had been opened to let in whatever coolness the early-evening breeze contained. Even though the air was close and stifling, the young male students all wore dark suit coats, neatly buttoned. The title of the lecture, written on the chalkboard wall behind Miss Jesczenka, was "Appearance Manipulation."

". . . thus, the proper choice of professional name is of vital importance." Miss Jesczenka looked up as Emily took a guilty seat at the back of the room, but did not miss a beat of cadence. "A well-designed professional name will have power both literally and numerically, effective on a variety of levels. It will evoke favorable images in the minds of those who hear it, and those images will only be unconsciously reinforced if it also adds to a propitious numerical value . . ."

Having a notable dislike of lectures, Emily stopped listening almost immediately, concentrating instead on the way Miss Jesczenka spoke, the lustrous timbre of her voice, the elegant movement of her slim white hands. It always puzzled Emily how none of the men in the Institute ever noticed how pretty Miss Jesczenka was. A negligible old maid in tortoiseshell glasses, that's what Emily saw in their eyes when they looked at her. For a bunch of Warlocks who were supposed to be masters of the minds of men, they sure didn't seem to know much about women.

At a pause in Miss Jesczenka's presentation, a hand in the front row shot up.

"Professor, could you inform the class why you've never chosen a more credomantically correct professional name for yourself?" Emily tensed, expecting giggles, but there were none. The students awaited the answer soberly, steel-nibbed pens at the ready.

"Oh, certainly I've *considered* it." Miss Jesczenka's dark eyes sparkled playfully. "Potentia La Grand, perhaps? Madame Dangereuse? Sagacia Maxima de Luxe? I welcome your suggestions, gentlemen; thinking them up is exceptionally good fun."

Miss Jesczenka impaled the young man with her calm, questioning gaze. When he lifted a hand to tug at his collar, she looked away abruptly. "In magic, just as in life, females must play by a different set of rules. When a man is presumptuous or forward, it is taken as a sign of drive and determination. When a woman behaves so, she seems merely ridiculous. As seeming ridiculous is the most perilous situation a credomancer can face, I'm sure you can see how it is to my advantage that I practice under my own name, humble as it is." She looked down at her lectern, released a small sigh. "That's all for today, gentlemen. Thank you."

When everyone had gone, Emily came down the steps to where Miss Jesczenka stood neatly putting her papers in order.

"So that's why so many credomancers have names like Mirabilis and Fortissimus," Emily said.

"The late Sophos Mirabilis' birth name was Japheth Beckenbauer. Hardly propitious in a nation where Jews are still generally reviled."

"And Rex Fortissimus?" Emily leaned in close for an answer.

"Ogilvy Creagh Flannigan," Miss Jesczenka returned in a low voice. She paused. "So. You snuck off to meet Mr. Stanton, didn't you?"

Emily blushed. "We didn't ride in any carriages," she offered, as if to mitigate the misbehavior. "Did Mrs. Stanton come by?"

"I told her you were contagious," Miss Jesczenka said. "It now appears that you have a case of the plague."

Emily frowned. "And how, exactly, am I to get over the plague before the Investment tomorrow?"

"That's *your* concern." Miss Jesczenka picked up her papers and climbed the stairs toward the door. "Come along, let's get you dressed for dinner."

Emily rolled her eyes. Of all the social customs of New York, dressing for dinner was certainly the most preposterous. Change out of a perfectly good dress, into a fancier dress, just to eat dinner? Who came up with this nonsense?

"Oh, not tonight, please." Emily fanned herself with her hand as she followed. "It's too hot to get all dressed up all over again. Honestly."

"Miss Edwards, these things get easier once you get in the habit of them. You can't kick against convention forever. You must get used to swimming with the current."

"I've always gone my own way," Emily said. "There never was any current. So I'm not used to swimming with it."

"Well, there is a very strong current here. And I'd hate for you to find out how dangerous the undertows can be." Miss Jesczenka's voice was surprisingly stern. But after a moment of silence, she gave Emily a sympathetic little smile. "Never mind. If you'd rather not dress tonight, we'll not stand on ceremony. Besides, you'll have your fill of dressing tomorrow."

Emily wasn't sure if that was a promise or a threat.

Miss Jesczenka had arranged to have a table laid in Emily's room. It was spread with crystal and white damask and a full complement of strange-looking forks. Emily sighed. She recognized all the signs of one of Miss Jesczenka's "teaching" dinners.

One of Miss Jesczenka's duties, since Emily's arrival, had been to inculcate Emily in the finer points of using forks, the elegant management of her napkin, and how to drink the right amount from the right glasses. Each of these points had presented a challenge to Emily. The forks were indecipherable, the napkins (always large enough to serve as towels at need) unwieldy, and as for the glasses, Emily drained hers of wine far too quickly for Miss Jesczenka's liking.

Emily looked at the covered plates of food waiting on a wheeled tray, and then at Miss Jesczenka.

"What's it to be tonight, then? Cracked crab? Pâte à choux? Corn on the cob?"

Miss Jesczenka smiled but said nothing. Her teaching dinners often featured strange and exotic foods meant to challenge Emily's developing social skills. How should a banana in caramel sauce be tackled? With a spoon, or with a fork? Emily didn't see why it mattered much, as long as a sufficient quantity of banana and caramel passed one's lips. Miss Jesczenka took a less sanguine view of the matter.

Emily seated herself and waited patiently as Miss Jesczenka lit the candles—hardly necessary, with midsummer brightness streaming in through the windows—and gently lifted the lids from the steaming dishes. She served Emily quietly and deftly. Emily didn't see anything too exotic—roast beef and potatoes and a steamed artichoke. Emily guessed Miss Jesczenka was trying to trip her up with the artichoke, but she couldn't imagine any way to eat it other than taking it apart with her fingers. To her surprise, Miss Jesczenka smiled approvingly, as if she'd been outsmarted.

Emily should have felt proud, but she didn't. In fact, she still felt awfully cross. Miss Jesczenka was pleasant company, but all in all, she'd rather be eating oysters in a chophouse with Stanton. The obsessive rules of etiquette struck Emily as mean-spirited, like the old trick of tying someone's shoelaces together under the table. It was only fun if you liked watching people fall down.

Emily found herself wondering suddenly if her mother had known which forks to use. She thought of the card that was attached to the bottle of memories, her mother's calling card. *Bristol board, elegantly done.* She looked across the flickering candles at Miss Jesczenka, who was delicately cutting a piece of meat.

"Do you know where I could get my hands on a copy of the Boston Social Register?"

Miss Jesczenka lifted an eyebrow. "The Boston Social Register? The Institute's Library has a copy, of course. Who do you need to look up?"

Emily shoved the potatoes around her plate with her fork—the correct fork, in case Miss Jesczenka had anything to say about it. "In Lost Pine, I learned my mother's name, and that she was born in Boston. I doubt she'd be in there, but maybe it's worth a look."

"Perhaps after dinner," Miss Jesczenka said. "Unless you plan to be otherwise occupied?"

No, Emily thought, she didn't plan to be otherwise occupied. She lifted her glass of wine and took a fortifying swallow, then addressed her attentions to the slice of roast beef on her plate. She carefully wedged her fork in the joint of her ivory hand—the narrow place where the thumb met the palm. Carefully, she held the meat while she cut it into small, manageable bites. When she was finished, she laid the knife aside and switched the fork back to her left hand.

"So have you ever heard of a beefsteak?" Emily asked, after savoring a hard-won mouthful. Even the abrupt change in topic couldn't faze the unflappable Miss Jesczenka.

"It's one of those things men get up for themselves," she said. "They generally involve beer and oysters and steaks grilled on shovels and great quantities of cigar smoke. They gather to watch negligible girls sing off-key while showing their legs. Distasteful, but very effective at strengthening credomantic ties between gentlemen."

"Mr. Stanton said there wouldn't be ladies there," Emily said, sitting up straighter at the mention of the negligible girls.

"There won't," Miss Jesczenka said. "But that doesn't mean there won't be any *females*." She lifted an eyebrow. "Does that bother you?"

"Of course it does!" Emily snapped too quickly, then added in a grumbling tone, "A bit," aware that she sounded foolish.

"Well, this *is* to be a teaching dinner, isn't it?" Miss Jesczenka put down her fork, rearranging it and its fellows neatly before her as she spoke. "It's part of the business, Miss Edwards. Men have to bond with their fellows, and this is the manner that suits them best. Even if Mr. Stanton happens not to share their appreciation for such entertainment, he can't hold himself aloof from the people whose support will provide him with his power."

Emily frowned.

"I can promise you, Miss Edwards, as Rex Fortissimus is hosting the event you're referring to, Mr. Stanton won't enjoy a moment of it, no matter how many girls or legs there are."

"Why not?"

"Right now, Rex Fortissimus is unquestionably the most powerful credomancer in New York," Miss Jesczenka said. "The Fortissimus Presentment Arranging Agency is internationally renowned. He made his fortune consulting for Tammany Hall, coming up with creative methods for keeping their subliterate constituency pliable and amused—"

"He didn't seem to be able to do much for Boss Tweed," Emily interjected.

"Fortissimus is no idiot," Miss Jesczenka sniffed. "By the time the graft and corruption got so far out of hand that no amount of creative Presentment would cover up the stink, he had switched sides. As a matter of fact, he helped Tilden to convict Tweed. All those cartoons by that clever Mr. Nast? His idea."

"So when things got tough, Fortissimus not only jumped like a rat from a sinking ship but blew a few extra holes in the boat while it was going down?"

"You could put it that way," Miss Jesczenka said, though it was clear she wished Emily wouldn't. "He worked for Tammany Hall when it was profitable. Now it is profitable to whisper in Tilden's ear, because Tilden has a chance to become the president of the United States, and Boss Tweed is rotting away in a jail in Spain somewhere."

Emily knit her brow. "So what does that have to do with Mr. Stanton?"

"Fortissimus is sure to have packed this beefsteak with his Democratic cronies. Given that the Stanton family is staunch Republican, he will certainly be in tor an evening of . . ." Miss Jesczenka paused, obviously choosing her words carefully. "*Partisan wrangling.* He'll have to be on his guard from the time he walks in to the time, if he's lucky, he passes out from drinking Fortissimus' cheap liquor."

"But I thought Fortissimus was hired to *help* Mr. Stanton!"

"He was," Miss Jesczenka said. "But credomantic power is hierarchical. One gains power only by someone else losing power. Since Mr. Stanton will be assuming the full power of the Institute, it's in Fortissimus' interest to propitiate him—but it's also in his interest to make sure that his own power base remains intact. Fortissimus will take this opportunity to ensure that Mr. Stanton maintains a healthy respect for the considerable extent of his influence."

"Well, why is Mr. Stanton going to his beefsteak at all then?" Emily asked. "Shouldn't he just 'cut him dead'?" She used the term with self-conscious pride; she'd just learned it during their last lesson. But Miss Jesczenka seemed too horrified by the idea to notice her student's dexterity.

"And start a conflict with a vastly more powerful credomantic practitioner?" Miss Jesczenka recoiled. "That wouldn't help anyone, Miss Edwards. Powerful enemies can be valuable, in certain situations, but powerful friends are better. And Mr. Stanton is by no means strong enough to make powerful enemies. Not *real* ones, at least." Miss Jesczenka leaned forward and lowered her voice. "Really, it was a stroke of genius for Emeritus Zeno to invite Fortissimus to participate so closely in Mr. Stanton's Investment. I'm sure that if he hadn't, Fortissimus would have proved extremely obstructive."

Emily shook her head. Of course Zeno had come up with the perfect solution to Fortissimus' potential obstructiveness. Zeno always came up with the perfect solution. The old man was a continual mystery to her. He seemed such a kind and gentle soul—but behind his mellow visage roiled a stormy sea of schemes.

"But I don't understand why being Invested is going to make Mr. Stanton any more powerful," Emily said. "I mean, he is as powerful as he is, isn't he?"

"That might be true if Mr. Stanton specialized in another form of magic," Miss Jesczenka said tactfully, simultaneously referring and not referring to the years Stanton had trained as a blood sorcerer. "But that's not the way it works in credomancy. Mr. Stanton is as powerful as his cultors believe him to be. And right now, strictly speaking, he has no cultors. That is what the Investment is designed to do—formally transfer the loyalty of the cultors from Sophos Mirabilis to Mr. Stanton." Miss Jesczenka paused. "He hasn't explained this to you?"

"There hasn't been time," Emily said.

Miss Jesczenka took a deep breath. Then she let it out. "My, it is warm in here, isn't it?" She stood, going to the windows to open them. A welcome breeze of cooling evening air stirred the silk curtains.

"Credomancers draw their power from how strongly people believe in them—you know that, of course." Miss Jesczenka settled herself back in her chair. "But there's a structure to that belief that allows power to be focused and distilled. That structure is called a credomantic pyramid. Most institutions of power, whether they're political, military, or commercial, are credomantic pyramids. The broad base consists of the cultors—that's Latin for 'worshipper' or 'follower.' At the Institute, those are the students. Fortissimus himself has hundreds of very powerful cultors—the employees of his Agency. Now, above the cultors are the praedicters—middle managers, if you will. As the holder of a Jefferson Chair, Mr. Stanton was a sub-praedictator, because he had no cultors of his own. Above the praedictators are the magisters—the professors, here at the Institute. Finally, at the very top, there is the Sophos, in whom all power is concentrated, collected, and focused."

Emily pondered this. "So you're a magister?"

"I am now the only female professor at the Institute since the departure of that dilettante Mrs. Quincy." Miss Jesczenka frowned at the old woman's memory. "And she was only given the position in San Francisco because her dead husband endowed the extension office. But I am a faithful practitioner. I have given my life to the study of credomancy, and I will be proud to serve as one of Mr. Stanton's magisters."

"Then you have cultors?"

"Over two hundred of them. I have four instructors under me and each instructor has about fifty students under his direct tutelage."

"So it really is a big leap for Mr. Stanton to go to being Sophos all at once, isn't it?" Emily remembered Stanton's words at the blockhouse.

"An unprecedented leap," Miss Jesczenka said, but then said nothing more. Emily bit her lip. The shortness of the woman's replies indicated that Emily was asking questions Miss Jesczenka didn't particularly want to answer, but those were usually the questions that most needed to be asked. She pressed on.

"Mr. Stanton took the power of the Institute with sangrimancy," Emily said softly. "I'm sure some people believe that he shouldn't have the position at all."

"I am sure many people believe that," Miss Jesczenka said.

Emily remembered Stanton bent over Mirabilis' blood-soaked corpse, his fingers tracing arcane patterns in the gory pool of red, muttering guttural words of power. Emily had seen magic, grown up with magic, known magic all her life . . . but she'd never seen power like that. The memory of it sent spiders up her spine.

"Well, he didn't steal Mirabilis' power, no matter what anybody says," Emily snapped, feeling a strange sudden need to defend Stanton. "It was the only thing he *could* do."

"I'm sure Mr. Stanton did what he thought was best," Miss Jesczenka said mildly. Then she gestured toward the rolling cart. "Shall we have dessert?"

Emily sat brooding while Miss Jesczenka served her a plate of something frothy with a decorative sprig of mint arranged elegantly on the top.

"Speaking of Mr. Stanton," Miss Jesczenka said in a sprightly tone, "I met Rose Hibble earlier today. She said she'd given you a card for Mr. Stanton. She was quite worried about whether she'd gotten the inscription right. Did you give it to him?"

"Oh heck, I forgot," Emily said.

"You must encourage her, you know. She has the potential to be an incredible asset to Mr. Stanton. She is a true zealot, veritably aflame with faith. Best of all, she has the energy and drive to foster admiration in the people around her. She can develop cultors for Mr. Stanton right and left. Really, as Mr.

Stanton's wife, you will be expected to fill that role eventually. But in the meantime, you can help by treating her well and encouraging her, even if Mr. Stanton hasn't the time."

Emily chewed over this. Could she ever be like Rose, hanging on Stanton's every word and action, either real or imagined? She doubted it. Just the thought of it gave her a mild headache and made her feel tired.

Emily looked down at her untouched dessert, and decided to leave it in its pristine state. It was so pretty, it seemed a shame to spoil it. She placed her napkin gently beside her plate, as Miss Jesczenka had taught her. The woman nodded approvingly.

"Very nice," she said. "You didn't knock anything over. I believe you're learning, Miss Edwards."

Emily blushed, thinking of the piles of soaked damask she'd been responsible for sending to the Institute's laundries over the past month. She stood.

"Shall we retire to the Library?" Emily said with extravagant formality.

"That would be delightful," said Miss Jesczenka.

The Institute's Library featured a huge central room, a Palladian space ringed with stained-glass windows depicting arcane scenes. From high skylights above, sunset brilliance slanted through the dust of ancient texts.

The shield-shaped chandeliers that hung from the carved ceiling had not been lit yet, but the shelves along the walls, and on the mezzanine above, were lined with glowing gas fixtures under green glass shades. The whole room had a strange twilight aura—the odd feeling of summer when the hour grows late, but light remains.

In the very center of the room, inlaid in brass on the floor, was a compass with the Institute's motto: *Ex fide fortis.* From faith, strength. The compass' arrows pointed to an archway leading to a different wing in each of the cardinal directions.

Even though the day's classes had long since concluded, the library was full of students. Several quiet young men looked up as the women passed, then just as quietly returned to their studies.

Their steps echoed dully against the stacks of leather-bound books. Finally they came to a door over which was written, in letters of gold, "Social Practices and Customs." The room was lined with dark wood shelving, close packed with books and smelling of parchment and vellum and ink. Miss Jesczenka went straight to the circulation desk, where a young man sat in close concentration before a pot of ink that was levitating in the air directly before his eyes.

"Excuse me," Miss Jesczenka said softly, but not softly enough; the young man startled and flinched. The pot of ink began to fall—but before it could hit the desk, Miss Jesczenka darted out a hand to catch it without spilling a drop.

"Thanks awfully," he said. "I ruined a whole ledger of entries that way, just last week—" As he reached up to take the pot of ink from her, he realized for the first time just who was standing before him. He blanched. "Oh! Professor! I didn't know . . . forgive me . . ." He hurried to stand, brushing his hands on his trousers and smoothing back his hair.

"I need the Boston Social Register," Miss Jesczenka said.

"Certainly," the young man said crisply. "Allow me to fetch it for you."

The young man was gone and back in moments, bearing a thick volume.

"It's an updating copy, just refreshed this month, so it should be current." He laid it on a nearby table for their use.

"Updating copy?" Emily asked, as she came to peer over Miss Jesczenka's shoulder at the book, on which the title *Boston Social Register* was stamped in gilt letters.

"It automatically updates itself with current information every quarter." Miss Jesczenka opened the book, and pointed out the date: June 1876.

"But if my mother were in it, she wouldn't be in it now," Emily said. "She died when I was five . . . in 1856, I guess that would make it."

"By 1856, she wouldn't have been Miss Kendall anymore," Miss Jesczenka pointed out. "So let's start with 1850, a year before you were born. She should still have been Miss Kendall then."

Miss Jesczenka gestured to the clerk. He came over with great dispatch, a look of helpful eagerness on his face.

"We need this returned to 1850," she said, handing him the book.

"Certainly, Professor Jesczenka. Of course you're welcome to use the Chronos Cabinet yourself, if you've got several years you need to return to."

They followed the young man to the desk, behind which was a large ebonized cabinet, decorated with scrolling floral patterns. On its lid was a series of wheels, white dials enameled with black numbers. The young man turned the wheels with his thumb. Then he opened the cabinet and laid the book inside.

"I'll be just here if you need me," he said, taking his seat and resuming his attempts at ink-pot levitation.

"What is this thing?" Emily asked as Miss Jesczenka closed the lid of the cabinet and latched it shut. She pulled down a large handle on the cabinet's side. There was a small whirring sound, like the sound of something being sucked up through a pneumatic tube.

"The space within the cabinet reorients itself briefly to the year you direct it to," Miss Jesczenka said, waiting a moment before she raised the handle and lifted the lid. "Anything inside it returns to that year as well." She lifted the volume out of the cabinet, laid it on the counter before her, and opened the cover. Emily read the date on the frontispiece.

June 1850.

"Would that work with anything?" Emily breathed, astonished. "If you put a cat in there and turned the dial back a year or two, would it come out a kitten?"

The young man sniffed disapprovingly from his chair. "Don't think there aren't cutups around here who haven't tried it."

"It's not advisable," Miss Jesczenka said. "Living creatures are not meant to travel in time."

"Can it be turned forward?" Emily persisted. "Could we find out who is going to be in the Boston Social Register in 1900?"

The young man stifled a chuckle. Miss Jesczenka gave him a frosty glance.

"No, Miss Edwards, because 1900 hasn't happened yet." She said this so kindly that Emily was willing to overlook the slight smile that curved her lips. "Now, Kendall . . ."

She leafed through the pages until she found the K's, then let her slim finger travel down the columns. It stopped at a point on the middle of page 132.

"Kendall," she read. "Rev. and Mrs. James (Emily Grace Nesbitt)." And, below that, connected by a line, read "Kendall, Miss Catherine Olivia."

Emily felt her heart flutter, leaned forward for a better look. There it was, in black and white. Catherine Olivia Kendall. And other names, too, the names of Catherine Kendall's parents . . . Emily's grandparents. And beside the line that connected them, an address.

Emily's mouth felt dry again, and she longed for another drink of the ice water that Miss Jesczenka had given her when she'd stepped out of the Haälbeck door.

"Pemberton Square," Miss Jesczenka mused. "I believe that was a good address in those days."

So it was entirely possible that her mother was respectable, Emily thought. On one hand, it was nice to think that she might be able to lay claim to an actual heritage even more respectable than the cattle-baron history the Institute wanted to manufacture for her. But on the other hand, it raised so many more questions than it answered. How did a respectable girl from Boston end up frozen to death in Lost Pine? Why would a respectable girl from Boston be looking for the Sini Mira?

"Now, we need to find exactly when she ceased to be a Kendall and took on her husband's name," Miss Jesczenka's voice broke through Emily's thoughts. "The register is updated every quarter, in January, April, July, and November. We'll just have to go one by one until Miss Kendall vanishes and Mrs. Whoever-She-Is shows up on the marriages page."

They didn't have far to look. They advanced the book through the remaining issue of 1850—November—and Miss Kendall remained firmly entrenched below her parents. But when the register was advanced to January 1851, her name was missing from below James and Emily Kendall's.

"I believe we've got her!" said Miss Jesczenka, turning quickly to the page titled "Marriages of 1851." Miss Jesczenka ran her finger carefully down the page, and Emily looked intently over her shoulder, but Catherine Kendall's name did not appear on the marriages page. Miss Jesczenka said nothing, but advanced the register to the next issue—April 1851. Still no Miss Kendall, and no wedding. Miss Jesczenka tried a third and last time, advancing the register to the July 1851 issue, before she finally closed the book.

"Thank you, we're finished with it now." Miss Jesczenka returned the book to the young clerk. "You've been a great help."

"My pleasure, Professor," he said, the ink pot hovering satisfactorily before his eyes.

Miss Jesczenka seemed sober as they walked back; Emily couldn't help but notice the furrow in her brow.

"Well, we found something, at least," Emily ventured. Inwardly, she was bubbling with excitement, but there was something in Miss Jesczenka's face that worried her.

"We found more than you may like," Miss Jesczenka said quietly. She looked around them to make sure that no one was close enough to hear her next words. "Miss Edwards, there's only one reason a woman's name would be expunged from the Social Register like that. She got into a . . . difficulty."

Emily stood stock-still, looked at her. "A difficulty?"

"The date of her expungement coincides with the time she would have been carrying you. Don't you understand what that means?"

Emily shook her head. Miss Jesczenka sighed.

"Your father, whoever he was, was not married to your mother."

Emily was silent for a long moment. The excitement in her chest took on a slightly queasy cast.

"So I've gone from orphan to bastard in one fell swoop?"

"I am afraid so," Miss Jesczenka said. "No one needs to know, of course—"

"Of course not," Emily muttered. No problem at all. The Institute would pay people to believe she was some mysterious cattle baron's daughter, and the fact that she'd sprung from the wrong side of the sheets would be covered up just as completely as the fact that she'd grown up in a timber camp in California. The shortcomings of her unseemly history would be eradicated with the Institute's money and power—because she was going to be the wife of the Sophos, and the wife of the Sophos had to be beyond reproach.

"Miss Jesczenka," Emily asked as they reached the threshold of the Library's main door, "what does fait accompli mean, exactly?"

"Something already done," Miss Jesczenka said. "Something that cannot be helped."

And at that moment, Emily felt very fait accompli indeed.

It didn't take long—from the Library doors to the high vaulted Main Hall—for Emily's despondency to mellow and her excitement to rekindle. Well, she was a bastard. So what? She was no worse off than she'd been before. If Stanton was willing to marry someone with no parents, he should be willing to marry someone with just one. And she was more excited at having discovered a mother—a real mother whose existence could be empirically verified—than at losing some small measure of legitimacy. She had a mother, and her name was Catherine Kendall, and the Sini Mira were looking for her. And Emily was going to find out why.

"What is the time?" Emily asked as they headed back toward her rooms.

Miss Jesczenka consulted the gold watch that hung at her waist. "Nearly nine-thirty. Why?"

"I'll see myself up," Emily said. "I'm going to drop in on Emeritus Zeno."

Miss Jesczenka quirked an eyebrow, indicating that Emily's whimsical fancy to "drop in" on the father of modern credomancy was unprecedented, but she said nothing.

Emily said her good-nights to Miss Jesczenka at the Veneficus Flame. The flame burned in the uplifted hand of a wise-looking goddess whose statue occupied an honored place in the very heart of the Institute. As had become her habit, Emily looked up at the flame that the goddess held aloft, pleased to see how high and strong it was burning. To her, the strength of the Veneficus Flame was the material representation of the benefits she'd bought at the price of her hand. The knife flashing down, the dull thud, the sudden blinding pain . . . the memories made her wince. If only she could trade *those* memories for the ones in the Lethe Draught.

She shivered and laid her living hand on the goddess' ankle, closing her eyes to steady herself. She could feel the power surging beneath the smooth cool surface, the strength of the Mantic Anastomosis rushing beneath her fingers. And then, suddenly:

Treachery.

Emily's heart jerked, and she pulled her hand from the statue as if she'd been burned. A message from Ososolyeh, as clear as if the word had been whispered in her ear. She looked around the darkened hall, but there was no one there. Her heart beat in her throat as she hurried away from the statue. Wasn't that just her luck lately—to look for comfort and find only something more alarming.

She turned down the hall to Zeno's office, pausing when she heard the sound of men talking around the corner. It was probably just a few students, or a cluster of instructors. None of them had ever paid a moment's attention to Emily. She was willing to wager nine-tenths of them didn't have the slightest clue who she was or why she was hanging around the Institute. She kept on walking.

But as she turned the corner, it wasn't an instructor or a student that she ran into.

It was Rex Fortissimus.

Fortissimus wasn't a large man—he was a little over medium height and somewhat paunchy of build—but he carried himself like a colossus. He had neatly groomed steel-gray hair, a luxurious silver mustache, and the sharpest, whitest teeth Emily had ever seen. He wore a ring on every finger—two on some. His watch chain glittered with jeweled fobs and ornaments, and the enormous blazing diamond set in his gold stickpin made Emily frown at her own ring. The thought of the Institute buying her engagement ring was bad enough, but the thought of Fortissimus procuring it from his own jeweler—some snooty joint, no doubt—was simply unbearable.

Fortissimus was wearing evening clothes and an overcoat and had his gloves in his hat. Even though he was dressed to go out he stood entirely immobile, critically examining a large swag of gold bunting. He was surrounded by a group of tired-looking laborers.

"I'm so sorry," Emily said quickly when Fortissimus finally noticed her. What was it about Fortissimus that always made her apologize?

"Miss Edwards," he said, flashing his white teeth at her scornfully. "Good evening."

Suddenly Emily regretted very much not having changed into a dinner gown; she felt Fortissimus' eyes over every inch of her limp and rumpled afternoon dress. She crossed her hands in front of her and attempted to look composed.

"Where is Miss Jesczenka?" Fortissimus' eyes continued to scan Emily's body, as if she might have secreted Miss Jesczenka somewhere on her person. "Is it not her duty to accompany you?"

Keep me from causing trouble, you mean, Emily thought. "Oh, I just . . . I was just stretching my legs."

"It would be better if you *took your exercise* away from the master's wing," Fortissimus said, obviously unwilling to let a reference to Emily's legs proceed from his lips. "Emeritus Zeno must not be disturbed."

"Of course," Emily said. "I didn't know you had business with him tonight."

"I do not," Fortissimus said curtly. "But I fear that the arrangements for the Investment tomorrow haven't been seen to with the care I'd hoped." He directed the last words like spitballs at the hangdog laborers standing before him. "But correcting such incompetence will have to wait until morning, as I have an engagement this evening." The way he said "an engagement" made it sound as if he was having the

Empress Eugenie over to buff his nails. This infuriated Emily, and she lifted her chin impetuously.

"Yes, if by 'an engagement' you mean beer at Delmonico's," she said, striving to match his supercilious tone. "Mr. Stanton told me."

"Most gentlemen would hesitate to impart such knowledge to a lady," Fortissimus said. "Perhaps next time Mr. Stanton volunteers such vulgar information about his schedule, you could remind him that you are his fiancée, not some common female who is expected to take such things as a matter of course."

Emily bit back a harsh retort. She remembered what Miss Jesczenka had said about Fortissimus being a powerful enemy—but she could not imagine anything she could possibly do that would be likely to gain his alliance. Anything, that was, short of magically transforming herself into one of the simpering daughters of the New York aristocracy that everyone thought Stanton should be marrying.

So inwardly she seethed, but outwardly she made no show of it as she allowed Fortissimus to take her arm and lead her back to the domed entry hall where the Veneficus Flame burned.

"Now, if you can find Miss Jesczenka, I'm sure she will be happy to accompany you on a walk through the gardens," said Fortissimus as he pointed Emily up the stairs that led to the private rooms. "Though the hour does grow late, and the gardens are better appreciated by the light of day—"

"Mr. Fortissimus!" It was Miss Jesczenka's voice. She was coming down the stairs, and her face was painted with worry and concern. "Miss Edwards! What are you doing still up? How fortunate that you happened to run into Mr. Fortissimus. You've told him, then?"

Emily blinked, not quite sure what she was supposed to say.

"No," she said finally.

"It's good of you to be accommodating, Miss Edwards, but we really must consult Mr. Fortissimus on this matter."

"Matter? What is the matter?" Fortissimus looked at Miss Jesczenka, and Emily noticed that his eyes when he looked at her were softer, less disapproving. This was probably because Miss Jesczenka was standing in a particular way—a way Emily had never seen her stand before. She looked vulnerable and soft and innocent and lost. She had removed her tortoise-shell glasses, let them swing from a gold chatelaine around her waist; her velvet-brown eyes gleamed moist and plead-ing. Fortissimus, for all his stature as a credomancer, did not seem to have a defense against this particularly feminine wile.

"I'm terribly sorry to trouble you about something so in-significant, Mr. Fortissimus," she said, and she sounded as if she truly regretted wasting a moment of his time, "but it's about the dressmaker you engaged for the final fitting of Miss Edwards' gown for tomorrow. The wretch was supposed to arrive today, but she never did and . . . oh!" Miss Jesczenka laid a hand against her cheek and let out a little sigh of frus-tration, as if the retelling of the incident were upsetting her beyond the capacity for speech. Fortissimus clucked his tongue sympathetically, his whole posture becoming strong and paternal.

"I'm sure it was simply an oversight," he said, taking her slender hands in his large ones and giving them a consoling pat. He glanced back disdainfully at the laborers, who were busily rehanging the bunting. "So many details have been overlooked, it's quite vexing. I'll send a boy tonight to make sure the fitters are here first thing in the morning."

"Oh, thank you so much, Mr. Fortissimus," Miss Jesczenka gushed, her voice dropping to a lower register. "You manage such difficult situations so . . . masterfully." Then Miss Jesczenka turned and fixed Emily with a calm brown gaze, and when she spoke her voice was as severe and disapproving as Fortissimus' had been.

"Really, you should retire, Miss Edwards. It simply won't do to have you running around the Institute like this. I'll see you up."

Fortissimus grunted in satisfied agreement. Emily saw a look pass between them—a look of complicit sympathy for Emily's impossibility.

"Certainly," Emily said through gritted teeth.

After many more effusive thank-yous to Fortissimus, Emily and Miss Jesczenka retreated up the stairs. But as they reached the landing, as Emily was about to continue up the next flight, Miss Jesczenka laid a hand on Emily's arm. She paused, listening silently as Fortissimus' footsteps retreated down the corridor.

"Now you can go back to Emeritus Zeno's office if you like," Miss Jesczenka said.

"I could have given him the slip just as easily," Emily said, "without you having to make a fool of yourself."

"With how full of secrets you looked, he wouldn't have been satisfied if he'd seen you to the door of your bedroom himself." Miss Jesczenka sighed. "I don't know what you're seeing the Emeritus about, and it's probably better that I don't. But you'd better go ahead, if you're going."

Emily turned to go, then hesitated, brow wrinkling. She turned back to Miss Jesczenka.

"Why on earth should anyone prefer us to behave so stupidly?" she said. But Miss Jesczenka's eyes revealed no answer to this question.

"Go on, now," was all she said.

Emily crept back downstairs on swift silent feet, past the Veneficus Flame, not pausing to risk another message from Ososolyeh. She reached the door of the Sophos' office, laid a quiet hand on its gold-plated doorknob. She turned it quietly, opened the door, and crept into the large book-lined antechamber. There were voices coming from within the office, from behind the tall heavy wooden doors with their magical sigils emblazoned in gold and mother-of-pearl. Could Fortissimus have snuck back when she wasn't looking? It couldn't be, she thought. No one was that sneaky.

"Emeritus Zeno," she called softly, before opening the door. "Emeritus Zeno, forgive me for bothering you—"

As Emily walked into the office, she saw two men: Benedictus Zeno, small and friendly and benign, with a face that looked as if it did not know how to express meanness or malice. And another man, sitting casually in one of the carved-wood chairs that was drawn up before the vast desk.

A man with ice-blue eyes and hair as white as paper, with a

brown cigarette between his fingers from which silver smoke curled.

Emily knew him in an instant, but when he saw her, he lifted his chin and lamplight illuminated his face wholly, and any doubt she might have harbored was dispelled.

He was called Perun. He was the leader of the Sini Mira.

Emily blinked, looked from the face of the Russian to Zeno's face and back again.

Treachery.

Without speaking a word, Emily slammed the door behind herself and ran back the way she had come.

CHAPTER SEVEN

The Bad Investment

Emily's first impulse was to leave the Institute that very night. But as she sat trembling on the soft bed in her silent room, she realized that such a move would be too impulsive, and that it would be far better to take herself in hand, review the situation coolly and calmly, and *then* leave the Institute.

Her fear, as it often did, took the form of anger—anger at Stanton mostly, for having told her she'd be safe in the Institute. He was always telling her she'd be safe in the Institute, and he was always wrong about it! Here was the Sini Mira, lounging in Zeno's office, in the very heart of the Institute, trading pleasantries with the man who was supposed to be protecting her.

Relax, she commanded herself, breathing deeply. *Review the situation coolly and calmly.* But her attempts to mathematically outline the problems arrayed against her, and solve for whatever value would show her the way out of this mess, led her to one irreducible conclusion. Catherine Kendall was very important to someone, for some reason, and that reason was very likely contained in the little blue bottle of memories in her pocket.

Emily pulled out the bottle and looked at it, holding it up against the low flickering glow of the gas jet. There seemed to be two distinct layers to the contents within. She took off the cap and sniffed it. It smelled of clove oil and iron filings. She wondered what it tasted like, and nearly touched a drop to her tongue before shaking her head and wedging the cap firmly back on. Tomorrow was Stanton's Investment. Certainly

Zeno would let the Sini Mira do nothing to disturb that. Assuming, of course, that Zeno had any kind of power over the Sini Mira at all.

There was a knock at the heavy mahogany door, which Emily had taken great care to lock. Emily drew her nightrobe more tightly around herself, her heart thudding against her ribs.

"Miss Edwards?" Zeno's soft voice came through the door. "Miss Edwards, it is important that I speak with you."

Emily was distinctly aware that she did not have to open the door. Indeed, every particular of Miss Jesczenka's training over the past few weeks advised against it. She was clad only in a nightgown—never mind that the nightgown had more fabric in it than any dress she'd ever owned in Lost Pine—and a lady did not hold conversations in her nightgown. But that didn't stop Emily from stalking over to the door and crouching by the keyhole.

"It's not a proper hour for calling, Emeritus Zeno," she hissed through the small opening. "You and whoever's with you can just go away."

A soft chuckle filtered through the wood.

"Miss Edwards," the voice was so reasonable and soothing, a grandfatherly voice that made Emily suddenly long for her pap. "There has been a misunderstanding, and I feel it must be rectified immediately. Please let me come in. I'm alone, I promise."

Emily weighed her options. Turn Zeno away and spend a sleepless night wondering about his motives, or open the door and hear what he had to say. She knelt with her forehead against the cool doorknob for almost a minute, trying to decide what to do. She remembered the barked insistence in her ear: *treachery.* But who was the traitor? Zeno? The pale Russian? And who, precisely, was being betrayed?

"Miss Edwards, I swear to you that no harm shall befall you." Zeno's voice made the wood of the door vibrate slightly. "Please let me speak to you."

Her fingers played over the heavy lock. He only wanted to talk to her, after all. Finally, she opened the door with a jerk.

While Zeno was revered as the father of modern credomancy, he was a particularly unimposing figure, so unlike the swaggering, braggartly credomancers Emily had become accustomed to. He was small and unassuming, his bearing vaguely apologetic. He looked at her with large calm eyes.

"I am sorry to have to come to you like this," he said. "I know that it's awkward, but I would like the chance to explain what you saw."

Emily retreated from the door to one of the large chairs by the window. Zeno followed silently, taking a chair across from her and regarding her through steepled fingertips. He did not speak for a while, but when he did, his voice was clear and resonant.

"In the position of Sophos, one must deal with a variety of individuals," he began. "Those individuals may not always be friendly, but they must be dealt with nonetheless."

"The Sini Mira are Eradicationists," Emily said curtly. "They want to poison magic!"

"They seek to implement a formula that may have some baneful properties, yes," Zeno said. "You remember Komé referred to it at the Grand Symposium."

The poison, Komé had said. *The poison hidden by the God of Oaths. It did not die with him. Ososolyeh desires it.*

"The poison hidden by the God of Oaths." Emily repeated the words as they had sounded in her mind. Zeno nodded.

"In the Russian cosmology, Volos is the God of Oaths. The poison she was speaking of is called Volos' Anodyne. The Sini Mira wish to know where it has been hidden. The man you saw—Perun, the leader of the Sini Mira—came to me to find out."

"Why would he think you would know?" Emily snapped. "And even if you did, why would he think you'd tell him?"

"He did not wish to ask me, he wished to ask *her.*" Zeno reached inside his coat and produced the golden rooting ball in which the acorn that contained Komé's spirit floated gently. It glittered as he turned it over carefully in his hand.

Emily fixed him with a hard stare. "What did you tell him?"

"I told him it would be impossible for him to speak with

Komé," Zeno said. "You must understand, I seek to protect her, and you, and the whole Institute. It is a dangerous time now. It is always dangerous when great power is transferred. It is the only reason I agreed to meet with him. If I had turned him away, the Sini Mira might have felt it necessary to cause some disturbance at Mr. Stanton's Investment tomorrow."

"Then you didn't tell him anything?"

"I told him nothing he did not already know," Zeno said.

"They went to talk to my pap," Emily said. She hadn't meant to say it, but the words seemed to tumble out of her mouth all on their own. "The Sini Mira. They sent men to Pap's place, and asked him questions about my mother—" She halted abruptly, pressing her lips together tightly. She hadn't meant to tell him about that. But everything about him seemed so certain, so comforting . . .

"Did he tell them anything?" There was an intensity to Zeno's voice that made Emily tremble. She felt suddenly as if there was nothing she could do to keep from telling him about the little blue bottle in her pocket. But something still made her feel she shouldn't. She struggled against the impulse to speak. These were her memories. She would not let the Institute have them. She swallowed hard, looked away from him.

"No," she said finally. "He didn't have anything to say."

Zeno was silent for a long time, and the force of his benevolence seemed to hum in the air between them.

"If you know anything, Miss Edwards, it could be very important."

"Why?" Emily said.

"Obviously they believe your mother had some connection with the poison. It is the only reason they would be looking for her now. What connection that might be, I cannot say." He paused. "If the Sini Mira finds the poison, they will implement it. It will have immediate and terrible repercussions for magic. If you know something about your mother that might lead to us finding the poison before they do . . ." He let the words hang. He stared at her. His eyes were terrifying.

"He told me my mother's name," she said abruptly. Miss Jesczenka knew about that anyway, Emily reasoned, and she would certainly tell Zeno if he asked. "Catherine Kendall. She was from Boston."

"That is something," Zeno said.

"And . . ." the words were on Emily's lips, to tell Zeno about the bottle of memories. The words were already forming in her mouth, all on their own. She had to tell him; it could have huge ramifications for magic if she didn't. For Stanton. *Fatally unpleasant,* he'd said . . .

The memories in the bottle could be the turning point between the Sini Mira finding the poison and implementing it and the credomancers finding it and stopping them. But she bit down on the words, chewed them, swallowed them. Not now. She was not ready, and an impulse of wariness still buzzed at the back of her mind.

Treachery.

What if Zeno were lying about everything? She'd trusted Mirabilis—rather against her better judgment, she reflected— and for all his assurances that she would come to no harm, she'd still lost her hand. She looked at the ivory prosthetic. It glowed softly in the room's low yellow light, and the hand that was gone seemed to ache faintly. No. She would not tell Zeno anything. Not now, not until Stanton's Investment was over, until he was Sophos. She trusted Stanton. Right now, she wasn't sure if she trusted anyone else.

"Is there anything more you have to tell me, Miss Edwards?" Zeno prompted gently.

"The Sini Mira," Emily murmured, seizing desperately on something she could tell him that didn't reveal the existence of the bottle of memories. "They sent a man to follow me in California."

"Did you speak to him?"

"He said his name was Dmitri. He rescued me from an Aberrancy." Emily described the events. She hadn't even told Stanton about her encounter with the Aberrancies, but each word she spoke to Zeno seemed to demand another, and sentences strung on sentences until she'd told him everything.

"It sounds like your visit home was quite eventful!" Zeno smiled. "And it is comforting to know that the Sini Mira find you more useful alive than dead."

"What do you mean?"

"The man could have killed you easily if the Sini Mira meant you harm," Zeno pointed out. "Instead he saved you, and let you go on your way without impediment. Actions do speak loudly, Miss Edwards."

That was true, Emily thought. The Sini Mira didn't seem to mean her harm—at least not yet. But who knew how their feelings might change if they knew about the blue bottle? This resolved her even more strongly not to speak of it again.

"You are safe here, Miss Edwards," Zeno said in a rich soothing tone. It made Emily feel sleepy. "The Sini Mira have gone. They will not be allowed to return. I'm sorry you were upset."

"It's all right," Emily found herself saying.

"I can see that you're tired," Zeno said. "And I apologize for having kept you up so late. Tomorrow will be a busy day. I trust you will get some rest."

And indeed, not five minutes after Zeno was gone, as if his last few words had been a command rather than a heartfelt hope, Emily had crawled into bed and fallen into a deep and dream-filled sleep.

The next morning, Emily woke from muddled dreams well before dawn, her head aching slightly. She splashed her face with cold water from the basin. The events of the previous night were vague, as if remembered through a fever.

Craving fresh air to clear her head, she opened the windows wide and climbed onto the windowseat, drawing her knees up to her chest. The predawn air was cool on her face and her bare feet. She closed her eyes, inhaling the fragrance of dew and darkness. So this was it. The big day, after which everything would be different. Leaning her head back against the cool marble, she looked out over the smooth lawn of the Institute, curving downward toward the crystal-paned conservatory. The only light came from the Institute itself, from the gas fixtures that blazed at each exterior door.

In the light from one of these fixtures stood two people.

Emily's first instinct was to duck back inside, so whoever it was wouldn't see the fiancée of the future Sophos sitting in the window in her nightgown. But it soon became clear that the two individuals—one male, one female—had eyes only for each other.

The young man was familiar only in that Emily had seen hundreds of his type during her time at the Institute. Dark-suited, the fresh-faced youth was such a standard-issue Institute student he could have been used for an advertisement. The woman held him in her arms, their heads drawn together in intimate converse. As if hearing a sound, the woman startled, cast a guilty glance from right to left. When the light caught her beautiful face, Emily almost gasped. Miss Jesczenka! Quickly, flushed with embarrassment at having intruded on such a private moment, Emily slid down from the windowseat. Well, *that* put paid to the idea that no one at the Institute saw Miss Jesczenka's loveliness. And a boy half her age! Well, good for Miss Jesczenka.

When Miss Jesczenka arrived just after breakfast to help her get ready for the Investment, Emily certainly didn't mention what she'd seen. She did, however, ask how anyone could possibly spend a whole day getting ready for an event that didn't begin until midnight. In response, Miss Jesczenka proceeded to fill every hour with a procession of experts. Emily was bathed, massaged, oiled, perfumed, and manicured. Her short hair was creatively arranged in something called "Roman curls," each curl brilliantined smooth and secured with a little diamond-tipped pin.

When the fitters arrived from Worth, it was clear that Rex Fortissimus had given them an earful. They profusely apologized for any perceived misunderstanding; it was their understanding that they were supposed to come that afternoon, not the previous. Miss Jesczenka had nothing but sympathetic comfort for the poor young women, impeccable in white aprons over black dresses.

"Oh please, don't apologize," Miss Jesczenka purred, giving the lead fitter a glance that was both sympathetic and conspiratorial. "Mr. Fortissimus does get things so muddled."

Emily stood like a mannequin in a lace-trimmed chemise and petticoats while the women bustled about her, drawing tight the corset lacings until her waist had been compressed to the nineteen inches that the Gods of Fashion had handed down as the standard of female beauty.

"You'll need to let that rest for a while," the lead fitter said, as she went to busy herself with the gown. "We'll have to tighten it again before we put the dress on."

"Tighten it again?" Emily moaned, looking at Miss Jesczenka. The woman was sitting in a corner, sipping tea and watching the proceedings.

"The laces and fabric will stretch," she said. "You wouldn't want to ruin the fit of the dress with a slack corset."

"I still don't know why I couldn't have worn one of those nice flowing dresses that so many ladies are wearing now."

"Yes, I can see that you'd be much more comfortable as an aesthete." Miss Jesczenka dipped a cookie into her tea. "But this is not England, and you're not going to be romping through fields of poppies."

Emily grunted discontentedly. "I shall surely faint."

"That will be very becoming and maidenly," Miss Jesczenka said. "And you can be assured that I shall be nearby all night with smelling salts to revive you. But do take care to fall in an attractive arrangement, won't you? It wouldn't be very nice to sprawl yourself out in front of all the Institute's distinguished guests."

Emily glared at her, but Miss Jesczenka just smiled and dipped another corner of her cookie into the tea.

After a half hour of letting the corset relax itself as it would—a half hour after which Emily found she could breathe a little easier—the fitters attacked her again, drawing the laces tighter and tying them off with seemingly sadistic satisfaction.

"Nineteen inches on the nose!" said the lead fitter, using a tape to measure Emily's waist. Emily tried to take some comfort in the fitter's pride, but there wasn't much to be found. Her blood pounded in her ears, and every time she moved, little black sparkles danced behind her eyes. She wondered how one went about falling in an attractive arrangement.

Miss Jesczenka consulted her watch.

"I'm going to see to my own dress. Will you have her ready for me in about an hour?"

The fitters nodded efficiently as Miss Jesczenka left, then proceeded to bring out the gown.

It was the first time Emily had seen it completed, and looking over the extravagant draperies of white satin spilling luxuriantly from the fitters' clean white-gloved hands, she just knew she was going to spill something on it. A linen cloth was placed over her head to protect her Roman curls as the heavy, rustling satin was slid down over her. The girls moved about her in a dainty dance, fastening the tiny satin-covered buttons up her back, using miniature silver scissors to trim away errant threads. It took about three-quarters of an hour, but finally they were finished. They stepped back and let Emily examine herself in the mirror. The gown had a broad row of ruching from hem to breast, dainty kick pleats of white satin, and ruffled sleeves that looked like old tea roses turned upside down. The effect was simple, but the draperies that seemed so carelessly elegant were really quite complex; the girls had spent a good quarter-hour fussing with them to get them to pouf and hang just so.

As she stood before the mirror, the fitters proceeded to warn her very sternly about the grave sartorial dangers associated with sitting, eating, drinking, treading on her hem, or letting anyone *else* tread on her hem. Once they'd exhausted their litany of potential disasters—and most of her remaining patience—they left, and Emily was alone for the first time all day.

Since sitting was out of the question, Emily stood in the middle of the room, feeling rather foolish. A soft baaing sound came from within her reticule. She pulled out the slate quickly.

A HORSE IS TIED TO A 10-FOOT ROPE, Stanton's writing read. THERE IS A BALE OF HAY 25 FEET AWAY. WITHOUT BREAKING ITS ROPE, THE HORSE CAN EAT THE HAY. HOW?

Emily went to lean against the high dresser to write her answer, the sound of slate against slate squeaking through the quiet room.

MAGIC ROPE. Emily tapped the period at the end of the sentence.

I SHOULD KNOW BETTER THAN TO ASK YOU RIDDLES.

DON'T YOU HAVE ANYTHING BETTER TO DO? Emily wrote.

I'M SUPPOSED TO BE MEDITATING DEEPLY ON THE NATURE OF SOBRIETY AND SELF-DISCIPLINE, Stanton replied. BUT THIS IS MORE FUN.

WELL, JUST WATCH OUT FOR FORTISSIMUS. HE'LL RAP YOUR FINGERS WITH A CANE IF HE CATCHES YOU PLAYING HOOKY.

NOBODY WILL BE RAPPING MY FINGERS TONIGHT, DARLING. NOT IN *THIS* HAT.

Emily grinned, pressing her lips to the slate. Forget all the words; the kiss was what she really wanted to send. She was wondering how she might phrase her desire in a manner more evocative than a long string of X's and O's when she heard the sound of Miss Jesczenka's gentle knock. Quickly, Emily erased Stanton's words—and the faint smudges left by her lips—and tucked the slate into the dresser's top drawer.

Miss Jesczenka had changed into a restrained gown of rich copper brown, embroidered with geometric figures in bronze thread. She pressed steepled fingers to her lips as Emily obliged her with a spin.

"Perfect," she nodded approvingly. "A vision from head to toe."

"Well, that's my head and toes sorted," Emily said, nodding toward her right arm. "But what about this?"

From shoulder to elbow, Emily's arm was smooth and rosy; below the elbow, however, began the sturdy leather fastenings that held her prosthetic hand in place. Displayed against a background of gleaming white satin, the ugly rigging looked like a set of sock garters laid in a fancy presentation box.

"Easily fixed," Miss Jesczenka said, producing a pair of evening gloves with the skill of a prestidigitator. They reached well above her elbows, hiding the prosthetic from direct view, though the buckles did bulge through the tight satin. Once she had fastened the tiny pearl buttons at the wrists, Miss Jesczenka carefully replaced the glimmering diamond ring on Emily's finger.

"That certainly is stunning," she said, tilting Emily's hand up to the light.

"I'll do my best not to hit anyone with it," Emily said.

"Now, one last touch." Miss Jesczenka reached into her pocket and pulled out a cylindrical silver powder box. Withdrawing a soft pink puff, she dusted Emily's face with a cosmetic that smelled of talc and lavender. Emily fought the urge to sneeze. Tucking the box back into her pocket, Miss Jesczenka stepped back to scrutinize the effect.

"Oh, yes." The woman smiled with the pride of an artist regarding a masterwork. "Just the thing for that shine. I believe you're ready, Miss Edwards."

The clock on the mantel struck nine. As if to confirm the clock's opinion of the time, Miss Jesczenka consulted the small gold watch she wore at her waist. "And without a minute to spare. The photographer will be waiting."

Emily gathered her skirts, kicking her train behind herself in a rather donkeyish way that made Miss Jesczenka's smile dim.

"Photographer?" Emily followed as the woman led her briskly down the hall. "I'm going to be photographed?"

"You must have an official portrait made. The Institute will have no end of uses for it. And it's a good idea to have it done while you're looking your best, don't you think?"

"But I thought I was being kept under wraps," Emily puffed as she hurried to keep up. "I was told it was part of Mr. Fortissimus' plans."

"I could not comment on Mr. Fortissimus' plans or lack thereof," Miss Jesczenka said archly. "But I can say with absolute assurance that after tonight, whatever wraps you have been kept under will be off. There will be no end to the newspapers, journals, and ladies' monthly digests that will be clamoring for information about you."

Emily's heart thudded dully behind its casing of silk and steel.

"Who, me? I can't be in papers. I don't have anything to say!"

"Having something to say is not a requirement for being in the papers, especially not for a lady," Miss Jesczenka said. "As a matter of fact, they prefer it if you don't. You need only be a pretty face in a pretty dress. The Institute will handle the rest."

Just as it has handled everything else, Emily thought as

they turned into a room that was usually used for classes. It was brightly lit; all the curtains had been drawn back, and the last brilliance of sunset streamed in through the tall panes of glass. A small studio area had been set up in one bright corner; velvet draperies hung behind a strangely shaped chair with one fat velvet-upholstered arm. The photographer and his assistants bustled around a large box camera, fussing with broad, flat glass plates.

The photographer posed Emily carefully, her head turned to one side and her ringed hand resting lightly on her opposite shoulder. Her gloved prosthetic was carefully left out of the shot.

"Smile pretty," the man said as he ducked under a heavy black hood at the back of the camera. "And for God's sake, don't move."

Emily realized, with a sudden flash of foreboding, that the direction was likely to summarize her entire mode of existence for quite some time to come.

At ten o'clock, after the photographs had been taken, Miss Jesczenka said that it was time to go down.

While the Investment ceremony was to be held in the Institute's Great Trine Room, the reception that preceded it was to occur in the great hall—a soaring space with the magnificent dimensions of a cathedral. At one end, a wide marble staircase swept down from the broad mezzanine that ringed the hall. At the room's far end stood two enormous black doors—the highly polished ebony guardians of the Great Trine Room.

The room was garlanded with swags of crimson and gold, and it was filled with a multitude of people—Emily knew the Institute had almost four thousand students, and that another thousand notables had been invited beyond that number. The air buzzed with conversation and energy—a brilliant contrast to the Grand Symposium, the last function Emily had attended here. Then there had only been a handful of participants, and the mood had been dark and ominous. But tonight the air itself seemed to sparkle, as if a million tiny fireflies had been released in the room. She tried to brush one away, but it vanished as soon as she looked at it. The excitement and energy of it all buoyed Emily up, made her feel cheerful and strangely eager, as if it had suddenly become intensely clear that unimaginable wonders awaited her.

"It would be best if Mr. Stanton could take you down," Miss Jesczenka murmured into Emily's ear, "but we can go down together if—"

"There will be no need for that." From behind them came Zeno's grandfatherly tone. The little man offered Emily his arm. He was dressed in ornate robes of black silk brocade, embroidered in gold with figures that much resembled the figures seen on the doors of the Great Trine Room. He wore a small cap on his head, black velvet that sparkled with jewels and intricately wrought gold charms. "Miss Edwards, may I have the honor?"

Emily gave him her arm, and together they descended the wide marble staircase. The rich perfume of hundreds of flowers rose to meet them, the scent wafting up from the deep-red blooms on the orchid vines that twined up the walls, from blush-pink summer peonies and plump cream-colored roses massed in large silver vases.

A few people near the bottom of the staircase looked up as Emily and Zeno descended. Some put their heads together to comment; here and there were grins. Emily put on her most tranquil smile and tried to look like a cattle baron's daughter.

"You look lovely, Miss Edwards," Zeno said as they arrived on the floor and began making their way through the murmuring onlookers. "I hope the events of last evening did not disturb your rest?"

"Not in the least," Emily said, acutely aware of a fresh desire to tell Zeno everything about the bottle of memories. But she kept her mouth shut and said nothing more as Zeno ushered her to the center of the great hall.

"Mr. Fortissimus did an exceptional job of arranging the event, don't you think?" Zeno finally said, after some moments of silence had passed between them. She followed Zeno's gaze to where Fortissimus stood in the center of a large group of people, holding court. He gestured around himself now and again, obviously detailing specifics of the lavish decor. "You might wish to congratulate him on his accompishment."

"That would be diplomatic of me, wouldn't it?" Emily said. Zeno grinned up at her.

"You have made great strides, Miss Edwards," he said. "I will be honored to stand next to you tonight in the Great Trine Room."

Emily brought her brows together. "Stand next to me?"

"Didn't they tell you?"

No one ever tells me anything was Emily's first choice of response, but she remembered what Miss Jesczenka had said about swimming with the current, and so restrained herself to inquiring politely: "Tell me what?"

"You will be participating in the Investment," Zeno said. "Tonight will be your first public appearance as Mr. Stanton's fiancée. You will not be called upon to do anything, don't worry. Just stand with us as Mr. Stanton is Invested. Ah, Mr. Stanton. There you are!"

Emily looked up quickly as a flash of red caught her eye. A pair of gentlemen in dark evening dress parted to reveal Stanton, clad in robes of crimson brocade that were like Zeno's, but infinitely richer, embroidered in some strange kind of floss that seemed to glow from within. He wore a high arched hat that, combined with his tallness, made him tower above everyone else in the room.

"Emily," Stanton said as she was transferred from Zeno's arm to his. His voice was formal, but he gave her arm a secret press of greeting. "Allow me to present you to Mr. Asphodel and Mr. Jenks, two prominent supporters of the Institute . . ."

And thus began a whirl of introductions and presentations, throughout which Emily smiled and murmured her pleasure. She met Schermerhorns and Schuylers, Schlesingers and Sinclairs. The names mushed together upon themselves like lumps in a bowl of exceptionally sibilant porridge; Emily was astonished that Stanton could keep them all straight. She concentrated intently as Stanton peppered her with name after name. She was acutely aware of the necessity to master the trick of remembering them, and fast. She started repeating people's names back to them once they'd been presented to her, as she'd noticed Stanton doing; she felt somewhat dimwitted doing so, but it did help her keep the names in her head for at least as long as she was talking to them. The presentations went on for hours, it seemed, with Stanton steering her from one clot of evening-dressed gentlemen to another.

They seemed to be walking toward another group of fat businessmen; the men lifted hands and smiled in Stanton's direction, but then Stanton muttered something under his breath in Latin and the men's faces went all confused. As Emily and Stanton walked right past them, she heard them commenting among themselves, "But I just saw him coming this way . . ."

Emily looked up at Stanton, and realized that his entire form had gone a bit spectral. She looked down at herself quickly and noticed that hers had, as well. Under their cloak of invisibility, or semivisibility, or whatever sorcellement Stanton had worked, they walked briskly toward a secluded alcove. Ducking inside, Stanton jerked the velvet curtain closed. Emily blinked, as if waking from a particularly odd dream.

"Impossible!" he blurted through clenched teeth, as his form solidified. "If I have to shake another sweaty, greasy hand—"

"What did you just do?" she asked, looking down at herself. She had regained her substantiality also. He grinned, laying a finger to the side of his nose.

"Zeno's been teaching me some wonderful tricks," Stanton said. "That one's quite useful, don't you agree?" Before Emily could agree, he had reached up and was scratching his scalp vigorously. "I only wish I'd thought of it sooner. This thing is murdering me!"

"It's very imposing," she said, gazing upward. The thick encrustation of gold embroidery had to add ten pounds to its weight.

"I have all those sixteenth-century engravers to thank for it," Stanton said, replacing the hat on his head and adjusting it so that it would balance properly. "Elongated headgear has always symbolized heightened spirituality and power, as if one could reach out to God with one's hat. Think of bishops, archdeacons—"

"I'd rather not, thank you, especially not if you're going to name them," Emily said. "And to answer the question I'm sure you'd ask if you weren't too busy thinking about hats, I am bearing up quite nobly. Though I wish those waiters would make their way closer to me once in a while."

"That makes two of us," Stanton said. He reached out from behind the curtain. She heard him issue a curt "excuse me" and when he ducked back, he held a whole silver platter of canapés. "I'm famished."

Emily watched him demolish the decorative arrangement of lump crab and caviar on crackers. Stanton offered her a morsel, but she shook her head. Food was the last thing she wanted; she was more interested in the thin crystal flutes of champagne the waiters were offering. He cleaned off the plate quickly, even swallowing the decorative sprigs of parsley. Finally he set the platter on the ground and licked his fingers.

"I know this is awful. I'm sorry."

"It's not awful at all!" Emily said with an enthusiasm she didn't feel. "It's wonderful. Spectacular."

"The Institute hasn't had an Investment since Mirabilis assumed power thirty years ago," Stanton said. "Fortissimus has outdone himself."

"Zeno said I'm supposed to congratulate him," Emily said.

"Oh, I'll just bet he did," Stanton snorted. "But maybe it wouldn't be a bad idea. He's not entirely on my side yet, I'm afraid. That became quite apparent to me last night."

"Oh yes." Emily arched an eyebrow at him. "The 'beefsteak.' Were there many pretty girls there? How were their legs?"

Stanton blinked, then smiled broadly. "Why, Emily Edwards. You're *jealous*! That's adorable. Don't worry, dearest, I didn't have time to notice any pretty girls or their legs. I was too busy trying to fend off Fortissimus' party bulldogs. They're all hoping the Institute will contribute toward Tilden's campaign, even though Fortissimus knows damn well we can't afford to take sides. I spent the whole evening avoiding the outstretched hands." He paused, reflecting. "At least the steaks were good. Grilled them on shovels. I wouldn't mind one right now."

Emily reached up to touch his flushed face. Through the soft satin of her glove, Emily could feel how hot his skin was. Stanton caught her hand, pressed it to his lips.

"So you were able to speak to Zeno?" he said, bringing up his other hand to clasp hers. "What did he say?"

Emily looked away, at the velvet curtain that separated them from the clamoring crowd beyond.

"Yes, I saw him," she said softly.

"Did you speak with Komé? Did she tell you anything?"

Emily blinked. No, she hadn't! She'd forgotten, until that very moment, that she'd been meaning to. Last night, Zeno had gotten answers to all his questions, and Emily had gotten answers to none.

She let out a breath, shook her head. *Credomancers.*

"I didn't get to speak to Komé. And I *didn't* tell him about the Lethe Draught," she added with pert emphasis.

"Why not?"

She bit her lip. She didn't want to go into it all at the moment, not with thousands of people milling about just outside the curtain. "I didn't want to ruin things before your Investment," she said. "There will be time enough later."

"But surely it's important. He might have been able to advise you—"

"Surely he would have had a very decided opinion on the matter," Emily interjected, a little sharply. "What if he'd wanted me to drink it right then? I didn't want to be pressured to take a step that maybe I'm not ready to take. All right?"

She was aware that there was too much vehemence in her voice. She softened her tone. "You won't tell him about it, will you?" she added. "Let's just take things slowly."

"Of course," Stanton said. "Emeritus Zeno does have a way of convincing one to do things one would rather not." He reached up and ruefully touched his hat. Emily stifled a laugh behind a gloved palm. Stanton looked at her, his eyes searching her face.

"Do you know, I haven't had a moment to really look at you all evening."

Emily stepped back as far as the confines of the alcove would allow and stretched her arms. He appraised her critically, rubbing his chin.

"You have the most wonderful throat," he said, as if reaching a conclusion. "I am completely convinced that it's the smoothest, creamiest, most delicious-looking throat I've ever seen in my entire life."

"My *throat*?" Emily lifted her chin indignantly, no doubt showing her laudable throat to its best advantage. "I go through agonies of waist compression, and train dragging, and bustle balancing, and you compliment my *throat*? The one feature of my person that hasn't been extensively fiddled around with?"

"I am very glad to hear that no one else has been fiddling around with your throat," Stanton said, bending down carefully to place a series of warm kisses from her chin to her shoulder.

Emily shuddered pleasantly at the touch of his lips. She might have chaffed him a bit more, but it was difficult to speak with someone kissing—no, nibbling now, nibbling maddeningly at—her throat. Stanton's ridiculous hat bumped her cheek, and she lifted a hand to keep it from falling. He wrapped one arm around her waist, and with the other he threw the offending haberdashery to the floor.

"Damnable thing," he growled, giving the hat a kick. He looked into her face. His eyes sparkled brilliant green, but it was worry in them now, worry and dismay. He drew a deep breath then shook his head.

"I don't think I can do this, Emily," he said suddenly.

Emily's brow knit. Her heart gave an unpleasant thud.

"What, the wedding?"

"No! I mean all of this." He looked around. "The Institute."

"You mustn't doubt yourself," she said, weakly repeating what she'd heard a million times from Miss Jesczenka.

"There's a difference between doubting oneself, and telling oneself the truth," Stanton murmured curtly. "Let's run away. Elope. Live in Europe and read books and drink good coffee. We can even live in *California,* for all I care."

"The Institute needs you."

"I don't want anyone to need me," Stanton muttered sullenly. "Except you."

She took him into her arms again, the fingers of her good hand toying with the hair on the back of his head. They held each other, cheek to cheek, for a long time.

This was everything he'd ever worked for, everything he'd ever wanted. She didn't want to be the one that spoiled it for him. She certainly didn't want him to look back on his short life and feel remorse for what could have been, if it hadn't been for her. She determined to redouble her efforts. She'd remember names, she'd squeeze into nineteen-inch corsets, she'd suffer through tea parties . . . She'd swim with the current.

"Tonight," she whispered. "We only have to get through tonight."

At that moment, the velvet curtain was jerked aside. Before them stood Rex Fortissimus, disapproval etched across his features. Emily and Stanton startled away from each other like guilty children caught fooling around in the haystack.

"Mr. Stanton," he said, "you are required." He nodded toward Emily coolly, his recognition of her dismissive in the extreme. "Miss Edwards."

"Mr. Fortissimus," she nodded back, with coolness that matched his. She was alarmed at how quickly her resolve to help Stanton achieve the heights of credomantic success melted away in the face of the man's sneering contempt. "It has been suggested that I congratulate you on the wonderful job you've done. While I am sure that some small and unenlightened minds might dismiss the decorations as vulgar and extreme, I will say that you have clearly done an excellent job spending the Institute's money—"

Stanton quickly caught Emily's hand and tucked her arm through his. He steered her out of the alcove, past Fortissimus' outraged glare, and back to the thronging masses before she could say another word.

"And you're giving *me* lectures?" he whispered in her ear

as they dove back into the teeming crowd. She felt, rather than saw, his smile become brilliantly broad. "Come along, my dear," he boomed, in a voice that seemed to be an echo of Professor Mirabilis'. "Let's mingle."

They mingled. The evening wore on, and Emily's silk-slippered feet began to ache, and her ankle (which Miss Jesczenka had directed the masseuse to pay special attention to) began to throb again. She became more aggressive in her efforts to corral the bustling waiters and relieve them of their delicate flutes of champagne, and her efforts paid off. After downing a half dozen glittering glasses, she found that the salmagundi of names was growing pleasantly ridiculous. She collected them like one might save oddly shaped buttons. Her current favorite was Ambassador Haemeneckxs. Emily had to struggle not to shorthand him in her mind as Ol' Ham 'n Eggs—his air of patrician distance made her feel quite sure that he wouldn't be amused if she called him that to his face. There was also a Sir Eustace Blackbottom-Hound, a Mr. Radley "Call me Bob" Gildermeester, a Mr. Stone Mason, a Dr. Wiley Camelback and—most astonishingly—a gentleman with shining black-lacquered hair named Mr. Propinquity Flounder Spintop. Upon being introduced to that elderly gentleman, Emily cast a skeptical glance up at Stanton, biting back the words "you're kidding" just in time.

"Mr. Spintop is in oil," Stanton added soberly. But his eyes glittered, daring her to make the subsequent joke that he knew she was itching to make. A small grin played at the corner of his mouth.

Their shared amusement came to an abrupt end, however, with the arrival of the Blotgates. There was nothing funny about the name, and there was nothing funny about the couple. In fact, Emily thought that after meeting them, it was entirely possible she might never find anything amusing ever again.

Emily saw the pair of them before Stanton did; indeed, her gaze was drawn to the man and woman inexorably, as it might be to a horrible accident. They had an air of destruction about them. The man was compactly built, muscular, with close-cropped gray hair. A thick, keloided scar ran down the side of his face, across his throat, and down into his collar; it looked as if someone had tried to take his head off diagonally.

He wore the full dress uniform of an Army officer, stiff with gold braid and resplendent with medals and decorations. The woman on his arm was stunning—certainly in her fifties, but with a kind of luscious ripeness that would make any younger woman seem half formed by comparison.

When Stanton saw the direction Emily was looking, he pulled up short, his body tensing. It was as if he longed to turn abruptly and move the other direction, or go invisible again, but there was no time. The collision was imminent and unavoidable.

"Stanton," the man called, inclining his head. His voice was low and cracking, like someone who'd just recently left off screaming. "I wondered when we'd get around to seeing you."

"General Blotgate," Stanton said, his eyes traveling quickly from the man to the woman. "Mrs. Blotgate."

"Dreadnought! How long has it been?" the woman purred, extending a slim gloved hand. The way she said Stanton's given name was a miracle. Coming from her magnificently formed lips, it sounded noble and melodious and absolutely correct. Emily could never get Stanton's name to sound like that, and at the moment, the failure seemed egregious indeed.

Stanton nodded stiffly over Mrs. Blotgate's glove, the sketchiest demonstration of respect he could offer without actually letting her hand hang in the air.

"Ten years," he said. There was an odd paradox in his voice; the implication that it had not been long enough, yet he still cared enough to count. Stanton looked down at Emily, and in the instant their eyes met, she saw warning there. "Allow me to present my fiancée, Miss Emily Edwards."

"Oh yes. The cattle baron's daughter." Mrs. Blotgate turned heavy-lidded eyes onto Emily's face, let them roam over her Roman curls and extravagant white satin dress. Mrs. Blotgate herself was dressed in a simple, elegant gown of light blue silk, and looked as chic as an edged weapon. Emily felt suddenly sparkly and fussy and squat.

"Emily, this is General Oppenheimer Blotgate, and his wife, Alcmene." Stanton paused. "General Blotgate is the director of the Maelstrom Academy at Camp Erebus, which I briefly attended."

"Briefly?" General Blotgate snorted, his scar flaring red from temple to windpipe. "Three years in a young man's life can hardly be called brief. And you certainly left your mark, being the only burned cadet we ever had. They still tell stories in the beast barracks about those stunts you used to pull." He paused, looking at Emily. "Has your fiancé here ever shown you what he can do with Black Exunge?"

"Chrysohaeme and Black Exunge are two states of the same substance," Stanton murmured to Emily. "Just as I was able to work with the chrysohaeme in Charleston, I can handle Black Exunge. Its transformative properties do not affect me." To Emily's gape of astonishment he added, "It's not an ability I find worthy of note."

"Your fiancé was the terror of the mess hall chicken coop." Blotgate grinned wolfishly. "He'd steal some Black Exunge from one of the student laboratories, Aberrate a biddy, and when it was nice and big, he'd roast it alive. Just took a finger snap, you know. The biddies didn't much like it, but he always did have an appetite." He looked at Stanton for a moment. "Ah, old times. I can see why you want to distance yourself from them now. You've got a good thing here. It would be a pity to ruin it."

Stanton smiled humorlessly, his green eyes glinting hard. "I'm surprised to see you here, General. I wasn't aware you'd been invited."

"Shall I produce the pasteboard?" the General said, fumbling pointedly in his pocket. "I know it's here somewhere . . . quite an overwrought thing, all those damned scrolls and gold leafing and such—"

"I'll take your word for it," Stanton said.

"How very *white* of you, Dreadnought." Mrs. Blotgate managed to make the words sound fluty and sneering all at once. "One could always count on you to do the right thing. Usually at the wrong moment, of course."

Emily's eyes traveled between Mrs. Blotgate's face and

Stanton's. To her dismay, she saw something pass between them—something she didn't understand and didn't want to. Mrs. Blotgate noticed Emily's confusion and savored it, her jaw relaxing like a python preparing to swallow a struggling creature whole.

"I see you are bewildered, Miss Edwards," she said. "You see, I knew Dreadnought when he was a real Warlock. Before he sacrificed his true potential to become"—she waved a dismissive hand—"a priest."

"Better a priest than a murderer." Stanton said the words with malicious cheer. His voice was so hard it gleamed.

"You don't belong with these crepe-paper prestidigitators, Dreadnought," Mrs. Blotgate said, looking around at the garish spectacle that surrounded them. "It's like the third act of a vaudeville show. It's revolting."

"Those who kill to obtain power are revolting," Stanton said. Emily had never seen him so tense. His body seemed ready to spring at the woman.

"Everyone must get power from somewhere," Mrs. Blotgate returned, obviously relishing the challenge. "Sangrimancers are at least honest about how we take it. We seize it from the weak and use it in support of the strong. Those who die in our service die nobly, sacrificed for greater goals they could never themselves achieve." She paused, piercing him with gunmetal-gray eyes that seemed to be all pupil. "But you *credomancers* . . . you sneak your power. You steal it from people's minds and their hearts. You manipulate them and make them believe whatever provides you with the most tangible benefit. We may violate them physically, but you violate them spiritually. Which is better, Dreadnought? Which is more pure?"

Stanton said nothing, just stared at her, his eyes igneous with hate. She stared back, smiling, like a snake warmed by the sun of his despising.

General Blotgate let out a strained bark of a laugh.

"Old Home Week." He gave his wife a look of mild exasperation but made no effort to break her gaze, locked with Stanton's. "These two were always like bulldogs in a crate."

"Oh, quite the opposite, Oppenheimer," Mrs. Blotgate said. "Dreadnought and I were great friends at the Academy. It is amusing to remember how desperately attached he was to me, but I'm sure that was just the madness of youth." She paused, her lips curling with pleasure. "Don't you agree, Dreadnought?" She paused again, exhaling malice. "Tell me, do you still have the scar?"

"Enough," Stanton growled. "You've done what you came to do."

And then the intensity that surrounded Mrs. Blotgate abruptly faded. Like a cat that had tired of playing with a struggling mouse, she lowered her head to murmur to the General, "Yes, perhaps we should be moving along. We'll want to find good places for the Investment ceremony before they're all taken."

"Interested to see how it all works," the General concurred. "I'm quite looking forward to the fireworks."

"Oh, and a word of warning." Mrs. Blotgate leaned in close to Emily, her breath hot and strangely spiced. "Lay off the champagne, my dear. Your cheeks are getting quite red."

Then, with a bright little laugh, she allowed her husband to lead her away into the swirling crowd. Stanton stood, watching them go, his face pale with fury.

"Scar?" Emily hissed.

"A six-inch gash above my third rib," Stanton said. "She tried to kill me. It's how sangrimancers amuse themselves."

"Who invited *sangrimancers*?"

"Obviously someone who wanted to make sure that my past is never forgotten."

Emily bit her lip. She furiously desired to ask him what Mrs. Blotgate had meant by *desperately attached*. And how exactly that tied in with a six-inch scar and an amusing murder attempt. Now wasn't the time, but she couldn't help herself.

"She was . . . a friend?" Emily spoke the word with all the distaste usually reserved for words describing rotten things.

"I had no friends at the Academy," Stanton bit back. Then, pulling his gaze away from the retreating Blotgates, he looked down at her. He put a warm hand over hers, pressed it reassuringly. "Never mind. Asinine insinuations. A petty attempt at a squink."

"Then there was nothing between you?" Emily said.

"I just told you," Stanton said. "She tried to kill me."

"Yes, and what if she tries it again?"

"You think she could hide a knife under that dress?"

"You know what I mean. What if they use magic to disrupt the Investment?"

"No hostile magic can be worked in the Great Trine Room, especially not tonight," Stanton said. "The wardings are very thorough, and there is no chance that the two of them could do the slightest thing with all the magisters assembled. There's nothing to worry about."

There was a warmth to his smile, a calmness to his voice, that filled Emily with a great feeling of peace. She let out a long breath and pressed closer to him.

At that moment, there was a blast of trumpets and the people around them lifted their heads, looking toward the Great Trine Room. Stanton straightened and took a deep breath.

"Nothing at all," she heard him say very softly, almost to himself.

They made their way to the Great Trine Room, through throngs of guests who parted to watch them pass. Emily walked next to Stanton, her chin held high, not looking at the people who surrounded them, at the students who offered deep bows of respect, at the scions of society who lifted their glasses and laughed as if it were all a great show.

"The Investment itself won't take long," Stanton murmured as they walked. "A few ritual words, an anointment by Zeno, and then the swearing of allegiance by the magisters. It'll be over before you know it."

"Mr. Stanton! Oh, Mr. Stanton, over here!" The words were cried out from among the crowd. Emily looked and saw Rose and her coterie of followers from the Dreadnought Stanton Admiration League. An ornate banner that bore the word "Congratulations" was draped before them, and they threw roses and lilies in Stanton's path. Stanton raised a hand in Rose's direction; the girl seemed on the verge of swooning at this show of recognition.

Together they passed through the enormous black doors and entered the Great Trine Room. The room was much larger than Emily remembered it, but the last time she had been here, she'd hardly been interested in the surroundings. Together, they walked over the place where Mirabilis had been murdered, his chest slashed open, his heart ripped from its moorings. Emily shuddered at the memory.

The brilliance of the room seemed designed to dispel such dark associations. Every gas jet was lit, and this, combined with the heat from the thousands of white taper candles that burned along all the walls, made the room stifling. Emily dabbed at trickles of brilliantine-tinged sweat running down her forehead.

As its name implied, the room was a great triangle, with walls of gold-veined marble and carvings of highly polished ebony. The pyramidal ceiling soared high above, coming to a sharp point directly above a wide raised dais that was festooned with more red and gold bunting. Stanton led Emily to stand at the end of a row of people whom she recognized as the Institute's senior professors, the magisters. Miss Jesczenka stood among them, hands clasped before herself and her back straight. She gave Emily a small nod, but said nothing.

In the very center of the dais stood Zeno, in his voluminous robes of black brocade. Stanton came to stand beside him, towering over the little man. Zeno clasped Stanton's hand with a great smile before stepping forward to address the crowd. The simple act of drawing his breath to speak caused the entire room to fall abruptly silent; it was a wondrous effect.

"Gentlemen and ladies," he began, and it was astonishing that such a towering, majestic voice could come from such a small figure. "Tonight we are gathered for the formal Investment of Dreadnought Stanton as the Sophos of this great and august institute of learning, which shall henceforward be known as the Stanton Institute. I am firm in my assurance that under its new leadership and with the benefit of a new name of such unparalleled distinction, the Institute will only grow in dignity and magnificence . . ."

Was it Emily's imagination, or was Zeno beginning to glow? She peered closer, watching as golden brightness grew around him. At first, she assumed that it was some credomantic tactic, a spotlight of brightness to focus all eyes on the Emeritus. As such, it was unnecessary. All eyes were focused completely on the little man. In the front row, Emily noticed General and Mrs. Blotgate watching intently.

But the glow was growing brighter with each word Zeno spoke. He seemed unaware of it, pressing on with his speech. "Many of you may know the history of this Institute, founded almost a hundred years ago under my own leadership. At that time, the art of credomancy was yet unrefined, its powers the province of priests and holy men. But over the past century, the powers of this noble tradition have been examined, refined, explored, reaching the zenith of might at which you see them today."

Zeno was glowing like a torch now, and Emily was aware of the magisters behind her, muttering among themselves. Emily saw Miss Jesczenka look up, toward the very pinnacle of the room's pyramidal ceiling. Emily followed the woman's eyes, and saw a glowing pinpoint of brightness there, shining down like a beacon.

"I can promise you, with unreserved assurance, that in the entirety of that long and august history, there has never been a man more admirably suited to serve as the Institute's Heart than the man who stands before you today . . ."

Stanton was now looking concerned; he, too, was looking upward toward the source of the brilliant beam of light that surrounded Zeno. He looked back at the magisters; Miss Jesczenka gestured toward Zeno urgently. Emily saw, with horror, that Zeno was now not just glowing; he had begun to elongate. He was growing taller and taller, stretching upward like a growing tree. Alarmed, Stanton leapt forward, reaching for the old man. From the assembled crowd came murmurs of concern, then shouts of apprehension.

Suddenly, Zeno himself seemed to realize what was happening. He stopped speaking and looked around himself desperately. Then, in an instant, he became terrible. His whole form expanded, his eyes glowed, and he gave a thundering roar of power, issuing commands in Latin that made the floor of the Institute shake. Power streamed from his hands, clutching desperately at the floor of the dais, trying to hold himself down; his whole being glowed with the effort. He struggled, shaking the floors and walls of the Institute with magnified intensity, and for a moment he was able to forestall his upward movement, able to struggle against the strange force that was drawing him in. But then he began to move again, pulled like taffy, the thundering roar of his voice growing smaller and smaller.

Zeno was sucked upward, his feet remaining on the ground as his body became thin as a thread. His head and shoulders soared toward the ceiling, toward the pinprick of light at the pyramid's apex, his futile words of power vanishing into a long babbling stream of nonsense as he was drawn into the light, his hands reaching downward, trying to grab for Stanton's. And then his feet flew up from the floor, and there was the sound of a loud crack, and he disappeared with a brilliant flash that left black sparkles dancing behind Emily's eyes.

And everything fell utterly silent.

Emily's head spun. It was hot, and she couldn't breathe, and around her all was a sudden welter of chaos, magisters rushing forward from behind her and students swarming up onto the dais, and then she was falling, forgetting entirely to arrange herself attractively as she hit the ground and everything went dark.

CHAPTER EIGHT

Chaos and Disorder

Emily woke from a dead faint to the acrid odor of camphor and rosewater being waved under her nose. Jerking away from the smell, she found herself looking up into Miss Jesczenka's concerned face. But the concern on the woman's face was not for Emily; rather, she was watching the men who stood clustered around Stanton, the magisters and Fortissimus. Stanton had removed his despised hat and was running his fingers through his hair with a rough gesture of annoyance. Everyone was talking loudly, fast, and all at once.

Emily sat up. They were no longer in the Great Trine Room. They were in the Sophos' office, and a group of students and instructors hovered by the doors to the antechamber, looking worried and pale.

"Enough, Fortissimus!" Stanton barked, in response to something that Emily had not heard. "The situation will not be improved by indulging our fears."

"I am certainly not *afraid,* Mr. Stanton!" Fortissimus stood before Stanton with his fists clenched, seeming to tower over him even though Stanton was much taller. "But if I were, it would be because I have no confidence that you understand the gravity of what happened tonight. Can you even conceive what kind of a blow this is? An attack on the Institute at the very moment when all its power was amassed for a transfer?"

"Of course I understand," Stanton said. "And to respond to this attack, we must first determine who launched it. We still do not know who kidnapped Emeritus Zeno."

"I think we have a very good idea," one of the magisters

said quietly. "The transportational device used for the kidnapping was a Nikifuryevich Ladder, I'm sure of it. I've sent some of my cultors up to retrieve it, but it will do no good. From what we know of the device, it opens a transdimensional portal for a brief instant, then destroys itself to thwart any attempts to follow those who pass through it." He paused. "It's a Sini Mira device, Mr. Stanton. An Eradicationist technology."

"It certainly wasn't a magical attack," another one of the magisters said. "We were fully warded against hostile magic, and there was no taste of power in the room other than Zeno's own. It could only be one of the Sini Mira's blasted machines."

"But how could it have gotten into the Institute?"

"And what on earth could the Sini Mira want with Zeno?"

The questions flew fast and thick, and Emily sat up as if to catch them in flight. She knew exactly how the Sini Mira had gotten into the Institute—Zeno had let them in himself! And she knew what the Sini Mira wanted with Zeno—they wanted the rooting ball in which Komé's acorn resided. She opened her mouth to speak, but Miss Jesczenka restrained her with a gentle hand.

"Whatever you know, it might be in Mr. Stanton's interest if you tell him privately," she murmured.

Emily sat back, lips pressed tightly together.

"These are matters which require further investigation," Stanton answered all the flying questions at once.

Fortissimus stomped an angry foot, which drew the attention of all the men in the room. "Further investigation?" he roared. "We know it was the Sini Mira! There's no one else it could have been! All this is just wasting time—time we should be using to preserve the power of the Institute! We have to get to all the papers, come up with an explanation that . . ."

"As I recall, Mr. Fortissimus, you are not a fellow of the Institute," Stanton said, leveling a dark, steady gaze on him. "And these matters do not directly concern you."

"The Institute is the living, beating heart of credomantic power," Fortissimus spat. "As I am a faithful credomancer, matters pertaining to it do concern me, *very* directly. If you think I'm going to stand around while everything I've built is eroded by incompetent leadership . . . well, then, you're a bigger fool than I ever imagined."

Stanton said nothing. The magisters around him muttered among themselves, shocked. But Fortissimus pressed on:

"You cannot deny, Mr. Stanton, that this has happened at the worst possible time. You haven't been formally Invested. You're no more Sophos than I am."

Stanton drew himself up. Now he towered over Fortissimus, his face terrible.

"I was selected for the position of Sophos by Emeritus Benedictus Zeno, the father of modern credomancy." He spoke very softly, but his voice rang and resonated through the office, resounding off the walls. The magisters stopped their muttering, but Fortissimus just smirked derisively.

"You were the only one Zeno *could* choose," he said. "And every man in this room knows why. You stole the power of this Institute. You stole it with blood magic, worked with Mirabilis' blood as he lay murdered."

"Someone made very certain that fact was remembered tonight, didn't they?" Stanton said. "Was it you who invited the Blotgates, Fortissimus?"

Fortissimus lifted an eyebrow.

"No one is blaming your old friends for what happened tonight, Stanton."

"They are not my friends!" Stanton bellowed, making a sharp movement with his fist that caused Fortissimus to pull back quickly. "I know who my friends are, Fortissimus. And I know who they are not."

Fortissimus did a strange thing then. He relaxed and smiled, the very act making him seem infinitely reasonable and Stanton seem hotheaded and rash.

"Mr. Stanton," he began calmly, raising his hands in a placating gesture. "Please. Let's not make this more difficult than it needs to be. Let's review this calmly. It is true that Emeritus Zeno selected you, but mere selection is not enough. The power must be formally transferred. You have not been Invested with the power of the Institute. You can try to run it on your own merits, slender as they may be . . . or you can do what's best for everyone and hand over the reins to someone who is better suited."

There was the sound of indrawn breath, and a long silence.

"Someone better suited, Fortissimus?" Stanton said, his voice low.

"I'm more powerful than you. I have an established base of cultors. I have a history of authority. You have none of these."

"What I have is the power of the Institute."

"Not formally, you don't."

"And I'm sure that serves your ends admirably!"

Miss Jesczenka's soft, reasonable voice cut through the rising anger between Fortissimus and Stanton. "Perhaps it would be useful to consider how the Sini Mira technology was smuggled into the Institute in the first place." Miss Jesczenka rose from Emily's side and went to look at Fortissimus with a slightly puzzled look on her face. "Your men, Mr. Fortissimus, have been all over the Institute for the past two weeks. A very convenient arrangement for someone hoping to secretly install a device like the Nikifuryevich Ladder."

Fortissimus goggled at her, his mouth moving in silent outrage. "Surely . . . *surely* you're not suggesting I had something to do with Zeno's disappearance?"

"There is an old saying about a shoe, and wearing it if it fits," Miss Jesczenka concluded calmly.

Fortissimus reeled back, looking around at the faces of the magisters. "And make my Agency the laughingstock of the magical community? We were hired to arrange this Investment, and Emeritus Zeno's disappearance has turned it into a debacle of the first water! Do you think, Miss Jesczenka, that that will be good for my business? For my *image*? With the election only a few months away? What kind of idiot do you think I am?"

"I have no idea what kind of idiot you are," Miss Jesczenka said. "That's why I'm asking."

Fortissimus thrust his red face close to hers.

"Is that the best theory you can come up with?" he snarled through clenched teeth. "Undercut the power of the Institute until it was next to worthless, then undercut my own power to take it? Only the vaporous brain of a *female* could conceive such nitwitted lunacy. The minds of men are more rigorous, Miss Jesczenka. But then, I suppose expecting logic from a dried-up old maid is like expecting a pig to know how to play billiards."

"Get out, Fortissimus," Stanton growled. "Your services are no longer required."

Fortissimus whirled on his heel and grabbed his hat from a table.

"This is not finished, Stanton," he said, looking at the magisters, fixing each one with a piercing gaze. "Any of you with a thimbleful of intelligence knows where to find me."

Then, pushing past the students who were massed around the entrance, he went out into the hall and slammed the door behind him. Silence reigned in the room for a long moment, a silence broken only by a low chuckle from Miss Jesczenka.

"How hard it is to find good help these days!" she smirked at the men surrounding her. Some smiled back, but most remained strained and grim. "Gentlemen, it is clear that we have much work to do tonight. Perhaps Mr. Stanton can make his good-nights to Miss Edwards so we can proceed." Miss Jesczenka nodded to Stanton, who nodded back before coming to crouch by Emily's side.

"How quickly can you be packed?" he murmured in her ear.

"Packed?"

"Yes. I want you to leave as soon as possible. Take Miss Jesczenka with you. The two of you can go to . . . Boston. You said you had a name there. This is a excellent time for you to do some research."

"Research?" Sudden anger made Emily stumble over the word. "You want me to go to Boston to do *research*? Emeritus Zeno and Komé have just been kidnapped!"

"Exactly so," Stanton snapped. "And the last thing I need is—" He stopped abruptly, closed his eyes, drew a deep breath. He composed his face carefully before speaking again. "I'm sure you want to help. But there's a lot I have to do in a very short period of time, and I will be able to do it better if I'm not worried about you."

Emily said nothing for a moment, her eyes searching his face. Then she sighed heavily. *Swim with the current,* she told herself. *Swim with the goddamn current.*

"Fine. I'll go to Boston. But listen to me." She dropped her voice low. "It *was* the Sini Mira. Their leader, the one named Perun . . . do you remember him? The man with the white hair, from Chicago? He came to the Institute last night, and Zeno met with him. He was asking about the rooting ball. He wanted to get information from Komé, find out what she knew about the poison . . . Volos' Anodyne, he called it. Zeno said he wouldn't allow Perun to speak with her. That must be why the Sini Mira kidnapped him."

"Have you told anyone else this?"

"No," Emily said. "What did Fortissimus mean, they know where to find him? They can't believe a word he said, can they?"

"If they do, I will change their minds." Stanton pressed a swift kiss on her forehead. "Don't worry. This kind of thing is always a danger with transitions of power. It's certainly going to be harder with Zeno gone, but Fortissimus will back down. He knows that it's not in his best interest to start an all-out credomantic war. Not now. You'll come back in a day or two, and all this will have blown over. I promise."

"Mr. Stanton," one of the magisters said. "Mr. Stanton, please, time is of the essence!"

Stanton stood, helping Emily to her feet.

"Go now," he whispered in her ear. "Miss Jesczenka will follow along later."

And Emily went, the white satin of her train rustling past disconsolate students and the torn, trampled remnants of gold bunting.

Well, I'm certainly not going down without a fight, Emily thought as she ripped the diamond-tipped pins from her hair and slammed them down onto her dresser.

She'd leave the credomancers to play their games of power and hierarchy, but she was as much a practitioner as they. And she had something that none of them had. She shared, however unreliably, the same connection with Ososolyeh that Komé had. And if she could contact Komé through that connection . . .

She owed it to the old Holy Woman to try to help her. The woman had sacrificed her life to speak for the earth, had left behind a daughter and a tribe and a family. Komé didn't deserve to end up in the hands of Eradicationists who would do heavens knew what to pry information from her weakened, constrained spirit.

Pulling off the fancy white dress, Emily let it fall to the floor in a frothy heap. She kicked off the now-tattered silk shoes and slid off the embroidered silk stockings. Then she sat on the edge of the bed, tucking her leg up behind her, absently massaging her sore ankle.

To contact Komé, she would have to be close to the earth. The closer she was to the soil, the stronger her connection to the consciousness of Ososolyeh. And her rooms on the Institute's fourth floor certainly didn't fit that bill. Springing up, she threw on her old gray dress and a dark cloak. Hurrying out of her rooms, she moved quickly through the Institute's dim, forlorn halls. She was sure that everyone was too busy to pay any attention to her, but she was also painfully aware that the whole air of the Institute was changing even as she moved through it. The walls seemed damp with gathering dread. All in all, the thought of getting outside onto the grounds seemed very attractive.

And indeed, once she was out in the warm, fragrant night air, she found herself breathing easier. She paused on the gravel path, considering her options. There were private copses where she could attempt a séance unseen. But then she thought of a much better place.

She turned her footsteps toward the conservatory—the great white building of glass and steel in which Zeno bred and grew his beloved orchids. Pap always said that the objects that were especially beloved by a person had a connection to them. These orchids were sure to have some connection to Emeritus Zeno, and that would be useful.

When she reached the conservatory, she pushed open the

door and entered cautiously, listening for any sound of occupancy. As she'd expected, the large glass building was deserted. The smell of sand and crushed coconut shell and cork surrounded her as she wound her way along the narrow paths, past white-painted wood containers. The air smelled thick and loamy and earthy and damp; the plants had been freshly watered just after sunset, and some of the night-blooming varieties had just opened, releasing sweet, strange perfume.

Emily found her way to a special growing bed in the very center of the conservatory. In this bed grew Zeno's favorite orchid, his pride—the Dragon's Eye orchid, a hugely tall vining plant that massed over a fifty-foot pillar of cork. Its blooms of chartreuse green and chocolate brown had a strange smell—a mix of sugary sweetness and animal rot. Zeno had once told her that the roots of this orchid extended far down into the native soil, hundreds of feet down, to the place where loam met bedrock. It was an excellent place to attempt to commune with Ososolyeh.

Emily looked around furtively. Then, swiftly, she stripped bare, keeping her dark cloak within easy grabbing distance. It was doubtful anyone would come wandering out to the conservatory at this time of night, but it certainly wouldn't help Stanton's chances of solidifying his control of the Institute if his fiancée were discovered rolling around in the dirt naked. She found a comfortable place on the ground and arranged herself cross-legged.

She had sought messages from Ososolyeh before, but never in such a formal way. There had never been any need. But now, with things tumbling all around them so abruptly, and with answers so desperately required, she had to make Ososolyeh speak to her, make the great consciousness acknowledge her and help her.

But how, exactly? She tapped a thoughtful finger against her chin.

During the Grand Symposium, a séance had been performed to bring forth Ososolyeh's consciousness through Emily's mind. She remembered exactly how it was done, and it seemed her best chance.

She drew a protective circle around herself in the dirt, then closed her eyes, wishing she'd brought some candles with her, or at least some lavender and sage. She let the smell and feeling of the earth saturate her. She relaxed into the center of herself, finding the place where her spirit lived, small and round and bright, and she sent it outward through her skin, out onto the warm air of the night, down into the moist soil beneath her. She murmured rhymes to herself—cadent rhymes that stirred power around her, drawing the earth to her, drawing her to the earth and to the ancient consciousness that suffused it. Around her the orchids nodded and swayed.

Ososolyeh. She murmured the Indian name for the living spirit of the earth, again and again, letting the word become a drumbeat in her mind. *Ososolyeh.*

Distantly, she was aware of something touching her— something slithering up her leg and along her bare side. Her impulse was to pull away, but the power of the magic that was gathering around her was too great. From the corner of her eye she saw what it was: a tendril of the Dragon's Eye orchid. It was sliding up her leg, around her bare waist, gripping her.

She felt her mind floating away from her, away from the immediacy of time and reality, to the deep eternal place where Ososolyeh slept and stirred and dreamed. Her mind stretched, thinned, frayed at the edges. She felt herself soaring backward from the comforting reality she'd always known; she saw how little her life was, how it was just a small chamber in a vast chambered sphere—a sphere that was always turning. She felt her being growing larger and her self growing smaller. She saw everything—the Institute, Stanton, her life, everything that was important to her—become laughably insignificant. She felt herself growing.

Emily struggled against panic, focusing on the drumbeat in her mind. But she was being stretched so broadly, so thinly, that she felt herself tearing in a hundred tiny places. She fought to keep her edges together. She had to be able to find her way back. She could be lost here forever, so easily.

She focused on Komé, remembering the old Holy Woman's friendly brown face and faded black tattoos, remembering her coarse salt-and-pepper hair and her smell of smoke and moss.

Komé, she called, against a shuddering eternity of wind and emptiness. *Komé, where are you?*

But no answer came, only the tiny echo of her own insignificance. She felt time jumbling in boulders around her—huge eras like pebbles, eons like cliff-faces. Here she was less than nothing, a moment's flitting thought, an article of a sentence elided quickly then forgotten. She was nothing, Komé was nothing, they were drops in an ocean immeasurably vast. Despair coursed through her. It was like one grain of sand trying to find another. It was impossible.

Emily struggled to disengage, to find her way out. And then, panic seized her utterly. The vast sphere had turned; she could not remember the way back to where she had been. She was lost. Around her there was only eternity and indifference. Her heart shrieked in fear. She would be lost here forever.

Be still.

Images of rocks, quiet things, old things that understood silence.

Do not fear.

Images of water lapping at the shore, calm and implacable.

Watch.

And then, he was there.

A brown-skinned man, tall and well formed, with eyes black as dead embers. He was arrayed in magnificent ceremonial garb, with a beaded headdress from which long spikes of iridescent blue feathers swayed in a glimmering halo. His face was smudged with glossy red and black paint. He wore huge hoops of gold and jade in his ears. He was naked, save for a heavy loincloth beaded with jade and shells. His feet were drenched in blood to the knees. On his breast, a brilliant mark glowed with divine radiance; it was the shape of a hand, fingers outstretched.

He was not alone.

Beside him stood a being, female in form, but nothing like human. She was not made of flesh. She was made of something cold and hard and glossy, something brittle and cutting—it was glass. She was made of black glass. Her tenebrous edges were sharp as razors; frosty light streamed through her. Her face was hidden by a mask—a twisted sneer, two massive ivory fangs curling out from it.

Together, they stood atop a stair-stepped pyramid of skulls. Blood dripped down the sides of an altar, heavy-rimed with frost. Bodies were piled all around it, hundreds of thousands of them.

The woman—the thing—stroked her hands over the man's bare flesh. Her caresses left welting trails of blood, more brilliant than any shade of red Emily had ever seen.

Xiuhunel, the black glass woman whispered, her voice rich with vast longing. *Beloved.*

The seams of blood on the man's body welled, and his flesh fell away from his body in strips. But beneath the first skin was another skin—a far different one. It was the skin of a young blond man with blue eyes. Only the mark of the hand remained, shimmering and burning. And then the black glass woman flayed the flesh from that man's body, and then he was another man, and another, and another . . .

Soon, we will be reunited.

When the twelfth man fell to pieces, all that was left of him was something gelatinous, something red-brown and glistening, like a lump of meat. Orange light pierced it, knifing outward with supernatural brilliance. Light so bright it hurt even to imagine it.

Do you see, beloved?

Spread out before the pyramid, as far as the eye could see, stretched a frozen ocean of blackness—stinking oily blackness that bubbled and churned. Voider than void, colder than cold, deader than dead.

It is your world.
It is the world we will make for you.

Emily woke shivering and choking, her overstretched mind collapsing back in on itself like a punctured balloon. Her heart was racing. She could barely breathe.

Her face and mouth were smothered with leaves. Tendrils of the orchid were moving over her arms and ankles and cheeks—the only exposed parts of her body. The rest of her was buried in the soil of the garden, black loamy grit and stubby white roots holding her firm. Leaves and vines were crackling up around her, tying her down, binding her fast. Struggling in panic, she broke free, tearing juicy, verdant greenery from her body. She pushed leaves and roots from around her mouth and nose; sitting up, she tore plants up with her.

Flashing memories of the black glass woman tore through the thin parts of her mind, as if the thing were right there in the conservatory with her. Climbing to her feet, Emily threw the cloak around herself, but found that it offered no warmth. Even in the hot summer night she was freezing, as if she'd just climbed out of her own grave.

CHAPTER NINE

Mrs. Blotgate

The next morning, Miss Jesczenka came to Emily's room early, looking fresh and composed despite the fact that she must have been up all night in close deliberations with Stanton and the other magisters. She stepped over the frothy white remnants of Emily's hastily discarded dress, then opened the curtains to let light into the room.

"See now, the sun did not fail to rise," she said cheerfully. "After all, the troubles of a bunch of credomancers don't matter one whit to it. Time to get up. We have a train to catch."

"Then we *are* going to Boston?" Emily said. "Aren't you needed here?"

"Mr. Stanton asked that I accompany you, and I am glad to obey the will of my Sophos." Miss Jesczenka retrieved a stray hairpin that dangled from Emily's ruined curls. She stared at Emily long enough to make Emily look down at herself. She was filthy, streaked with dirt and mud from the night before.

"I'm afraid there's no time for a bath, but there's hot water in the basin," was all Miss Jesczenka said, as she turned and discreetly cracked open a window to air out the smell of loam and leaf mold.

Moving to the basin, Emily was surprised to discover that her twisted ankle didn't hurt at all anymore. She balanced on it experimentally as she wiped streaks of dirt from her arm. It was as if the injury had never happened. Ososolyeh had healed her once before, the time she'd been shot in Dutch Flat. It was nice to have something working in her favor.

"How about you do something about the hand next time?"

she muttered to Ososolyeh as she squeezed dirty water out of the cloth.

She thought about the images Ososolyeh had showed her. Last night they'd seemed so terrifying, but in the clear light of morning, they were just puzzling. A knife-edged woman made of black glass? Twelve men flayed into strips, leaving a lump of meat that glowed orange? What a useless jumble of nonsense. It certainly didn't help with the puzzle of what had happened to Zeno and Komé. She hoped Stanton and his credomancers were having better luck.

"How did everything go last night?" Emily asked as she began to get dressed. Miss Jesczenka bustled about the room, picking up the discarded white satin gown and laying it carefully over a chair.

"As well as could be expected," Miss Jesczenka said. "The other magisters are worried, of course, but Mr. Stanton is approaching the situation with a level head. He shared the information you provided him. We will be contacting the Sini Mira immediately to open negotiations for Emeritus Zeno's return."

"And Fortissimus?" Emily fairly spat the name.

"He will try to stir up trouble however he can," Miss Jesczenka said. "But leave Fortissimus to Mr. Stanton. It's his first challenge, and I have no doubt he'll be equal to it."

Her words made Emily feel a little better. But what did not make her feel better was the fact that Miss Jesczenka had pulled out a huge leather steamer trunk and was packing all of Emily's belongings into it.

"But we're only going to be in Boston for a day or two, right?" Emily asked, as Miss Jesczenka knelt over the trunk, folding chemises.

"Better safe than sorry," Miss Jesczenka said. "Who knows what you might discover in Boston? If we do find your grandparents, they might wish you to stay longer. You wouldn't want to have to send back for your things, would you?"

Emily said nothing, but went to her dresser to retrieve the slate Stanton had given her. She wished suddenly that she hadn't rubbed out the last words he'd written on it. It would

have been comforting just to see them. She tucked it carefully
into the trunk, beneath some folded petticoats.

"Tell me honestly," Emily said. "Will I be coming back to
the Institute?"

Miss Jesczenka rolled back on her heels and looked at
Emily in astonishment. "Why, Miss Edwards, what a question! You make it sound like we're on the run. How grim.
We're just taking a brief trip to Boston. There is nothing at all
to be concerned about."

Not for the first time, Emily noticed the way credomancers
had of giving an answer that was not an answer at all.

The Grand Central Depot at Forty-second and Fourth was
a tangle of tracks and steam and people. As the city boomed,
the station had to keep expanding to accommodate it, and
thus it existed in a state of constant enlargement and revision,
like a schoolboy's novel written in pencil. And like a schoolboy's novel, it boasted a variety of odd quirks. Trains could
exit only in reverse. At Fifty-seventh Street, the tracks went
under a tunnel and didn't emerge until Ninety-sixth Street.
And at the moment, a current project of construction made
the ticket windows inaccessible except through a narrow
causeway along which a long single-file line stretched.

"Why don't you wait with the baggage?" Miss Jesczenka
suggested. "I'll get the tickets and meet you back here."

"Why aren't we taking a Haälbeck door?" As Emily was
feeling cross, she said this more snappishly than she had intended. She gestured with her eyes to a line of commercial
Haälbeck doors, where businessmen were lined up with bags
and briefcases. Traveling by Haälbeck was not cheap, but
since the doors were operated by the Institute, Emily supposed that they might at least get a discount. "There *are* Haälbeck doors that terminate in Boston, right?"

Miss Jesczenka opened her mouth, then closed it. She
shook her head, obviously deciding not to favor Emily with
an explanation.

"I'll get the tickets, Miss Edwards," she repeated, then
melted into the crowd.

Emily sat down on the edge of her trunk, fanning herself. Even though it was early, it was already stifling. Paperboys were crying their wares, their voices echoing against the white-tiled walls of the station. One of them thrust a paper under Emily's nose.

"Paper, miss?"

Emily could see only part of the headline—the words "Dreadnought Stanton" and "Unprecedented Debacle." She dug into her purse for a dime and handed it to the boy. It was one of the seedier metropolitan tabloids, replete with red ink and tawdry engravings. As Emily read through the article, dismay as heavy as a lead shawl slumped her shoulders. She was no expert in credomancy, but even she knew that bad press was damaging. And this was *disastrous*. It was written in a bombastic style, a sharp, clever satire of the pulp novels in which Dreadnought Stanton had been celebrated as a mythic hero. Suspiciously well done—too good for the paper it appeared in, certainly—it bore the stamp of a professional hand. Fortissimus? Had he left the Institute, gone straight back to his Agency, and had someone write it up? Or worse, had he had it written beforehand?

Emily thought about what Miss Jesczenka had said about Fortissimus having the perfect opportunity to plant a Sini Mira technology during his arrangements for the Investment. But why would he do such a thing? It seemed clear that the Sini Mira had kidnapped Zeno to get at Komé and what she knew about the poison. But if that was the case, why would Fortissimus help them? Why would anyone who made a career of magic want to help the Sini Mira eradicate it?

Emily folded the newspaper—offending headline inward—and mulled it all over as she watched the throng of travelers pass by. What Fortissimus had said the night before made sense. If he'd wanted to get his hands on the Institute, there were surely better ways than tearing it apart.

A woman in a black silk dress glided by, and Emily shuddered as she remembered the woman from last night's séance, the woman made of black glass with knives for fingers. The more she thought about it, the more the strange vision disquieted her. What could it mean? Ososolyeh had meant to show her something, but what? She suddenly felt very annoyed with the ancient consciousness of the earth for being so all-fired obtuse. One would think that an ancient consciousness might be a bit more obliging, but apparently not. Apparently it had its own concerns, which had nothing to do with Komé and the Sini Mira.

Poor Komé. For Zeno, strangely enough, Emily felt only a kind of vague dismay. She remembered the snow-white man sitting in his office, calmly smoking a cigarette. Zeno had played with fire, and got his fingers burned. But Komé hadn't asked for such troubles. Once again, she'd been drawn into someone else's machinations.

What would the Russians do to Komé? What kind of horrible methods could they employ to extract the information from her if she would not give it to them willingly? And what was to say that the old Holy Woman would *not* give it to them willingly? Komé had told her to go with the Sini Mira in Chicago. If they'd found some way to make her trust them then, what was to say that they could not do it again?

Too many questions. Emily's head swam with them. She hardly noticed the woman standing before her until it was too late.

"Miss Edwards, isn't it?" The voice had a smirk in it.

Of all the people she'd met last night, Alcmene Blotgate was the only one branded upon her memory. To her disappointment, Emily found that the woman was even more beautiful by the light of day. Exquisitely dressed in a rustling dress of iridescent taffeta that shifted colors from blackish purple to saffron, she looked like an elegant bruise. Her husband was nowhere to be seen.

Emily stood, straightened. She tried to look dignified and imposing, but the look of disdain on the woman's face made her feel certain that she wasn't succeeding.

"Mrs. Blotgate," Emily said, not extending a hand.

"Leaving New York? I can see why you'd want to, after that bizarre event last night." Mrs. Blotgate's eyes touched on the newspaper Emily held under her arm; Emily squeezed her arm down over it tightly.

"It has nothing to do with that at all," Emily said quickly. "I'm going to . . . see some family. You're leaving New York, too, I hope?" She did not mean to add the last two words—at least not out loud.

Mrs. Blotgate did not answer, but just stared at her for a long time with those vast-pupiled gunmetal eyes. Emily felt quite nervous under the scrutiny. She felt like running away, but she stood her ground and stared back as best as she could, answering the challenge in the woman's eyes with a challenge of her own. Finally, Mrs. Blotgate rippled a laugh.

"How charming. You're a Witch, aren't you?"

"I have been trained as an animancer." Emily tried to make it sound impressive. Mrs. Blotgate lifted a derisive eyebrow; it was clear that she thought even less of animancers than she did of credomancers.

"Dirt magic," Mrs. Blotgate said. She lifted a slender hand and brushed a speck of dried mud off of Emily's face. "You really must be more careful to wash."

Emily pulled away from the touch, anger thrilling through her. The woman licked her tongue over her lower lip, letting her hand drop back to her side.

"It was so lovely to see Dreadnought last night," she said, each word carefully enunciated. "It has been such a long time. But he's just as dull and humorless as I remember him."

"In the days when you were *desperately attached,* you mean?" Emily said.

"Oh, that was all very long ago," Mrs. Blotgate shrugged. "And humorless boys never hold my interest. It was merely a fleeting—if exceptionally *pleasurable*—liaison of youth."

"It didn't sound very . . . pleasurable," Emily stumbled over the word. "You tried to kill him."

Mrs. Blotgate frowned. "The coward deserved it. Running away to become a credomancer instead of claiming the power that should have been his. Death would have been a mercy for him." A pause. "But that mercy will be granted him soon enough, won't it?"

Emily opened her mouth to say something, but Mrs. Blotgate drove on.

"I'm absolutely fascinated by the fact that you haven't seen the scar. Is it possible that you haven't touched each other? If he hasn't even told you the secrets of his skin—"

"He's told me everything."

"You believe that?"

"Yes," Emily said.

The sincerity in Emily's voice made Mrs. Blotgate smile again—a soft queer smile that reminded Emily of the underside of a rotten mushroom.

"Then perhaps you will make a good credomancer's wife after all," she said. "As credulous and self-immolating as Dreadnought could desire." She paused. "On the other hand, you must have something rattling around in that pretty skull to entrap him as cleverly as you did. You're a pretty little puzzle, Miss Edwards. How I would love to take you apart."

Emily imagined herself a block of ice, and her breath fairly congealed white as she spoke. "I didn't entrap anyone. And you could not take me apart if you tried."

Mrs. Blotgate's eyes glinted like hard gemstones and she flexed her long fingers.

"Why, I can take you apart just as we stand here. I know every low grimy inch of you. I know you're no cattle baron's daughter—you're just a climbing little tramp, a skycladdische dirt Witch who fuels Dreadnought's fantasies of having *integrity*."

Heat rose up Emily's throat, but she said nothing. Mrs. Blotgate continued, her voice calm.

"Of course, fantasies should be paid for by the hour, not married, so Dreadnought tried to call things off gently, in a civilized fashion. But you chased after him until there was nothing he could do but propose."

"I didn't . . ." Emily began, her voice shaking despite her best efforts to steady it. Then she drew a deep breath. "You are a horrible person. I wish to have nothing more to do with you."

"Don't try to play that prim little card with me," Mrs. Blotgate snarled. "You never had it in your hand to begin with. I'm only applauding you for a trick well turned."

"There's no trick here."

"Of course there's a trick. There's always a trick. From what I hear, you have the habit of throwing love spells at any man who looks at you sideways. Why shouldn't you use a little magical encouragement on our dear Dreadnought? Catch yourself a senator's son to lift you up out of the mud and dress you in diamonds?" She eyed Emily's ringed hand meaningfully.

"That's a lie," Emily spat, quickly hiding the hand behind her back. "I would never—"

Mrs. Blotgate, who had opened her silk reticule to dig for something within, cut Emily's words short with a crisply proffered card.

"Well, delightful as this has been, I do have a train to catch." She slid the card down the front of Emily's dress. "Call on me when you're back in town." She leaned close, put her mouth by Emily's ear. "I can tell you everything he likes."

At this, Emily brought her hand out of hiding and was lifting it to slap the woman across the face. But then, Miss Jesczenka returned with tickets.

"The train is on platform twenty-two, Miss Edwards . . ."

Emily let her hand fall quickly. She stepped back, flushed with rage.

Miss Jesczenka stopped when she saw Mrs. Blotgate. She stared at the woman for a long time. Her eyes narrowed. A quizzical look stole over her face, replaced quickly by cool reserve.

"I'm sorry, we haven't been introduced." Miss Jesczenka stretched a hand. "I am Miss Edwards' companion, Miss—"

"Yes, I know who you are." Mrs. Blotgate looked at the proffered hand as if it were covered in excrement. "Tiza Jesczenka. An immigrant from Prague. A rabbi's daughter." She turned to Emily as if Miss Jesczenka weren't there. "This is your companion? A dowdy old Jewess?" She shook her head ruefully. "I suppose this shows what the Institute really thinks of you."

Miss Jesczenka looked at the woman for a moment. There was a sense of her marshaling some terrible force within herself. She lifted a hand, murmured something softly under her breath, and then said, in a very loud voice: *"Duze!"*

And then, just like that, Miss Jesczenka was gone, replaced by someone else entirely. Someone like Miss
Jesczenka, but as utterly unlike her as Emily could imagine.
Her neatly tailored clothes sagged into ratty unfashionability,
her neat hair wisped carelessly, her eyes brightened with
strange madness, and her cheeks reddened as if she were
drunk.

"Oh, Duze, it's you! How long it has been!"

Mrs. Blotgate looked around herself in alarm.

"What the hell are you talking about?" she snarled.

But Miss Jesczenka did not answer her. Instead she broke
into a maudlin flood of loud Polish. She rushed forward, gathered Mrs. Blotgate into her arms and sobbed theatrically.
"Duze! My dear! Don't you remember me? The *Bierstube* in
Praha, the Golden Tiger, *U Zlateho tygra* . . . do you not recall? The boys, they used to call us their little flowers!"

"Don't touch me," Mrs. Blotgate said, her face a mask of
horror as she pushed Miss Jesczenka away. Her eyes darted
around herself at the passing pedestrians; embarrassment
flushed her cheeks. But Miss Jesczenka wouldn't be denied;
she hung on Mrs. Blotgate's hand, pawing at it.

"Duze! Duze, don't play so. It's me, your dear little Alme.
Such times we had!"

Men were watching now, pausing in their hurried transits
to take in the spectacle of the two women wrestling with each
other. Mrs. Blotgate saw them watching, and her eyes traveled down to what they were looking at. Her face went from
red to purple. Gone was the elegant taffeta gown, gone was
the sneering polished veneer. Suddenly she looked a hundred
years older. Her face was haglike, her cheeks sunken from
missing teeth. Drab clothes hung from her in rags. She
smelled like beer spilled in a bucket of cigar ash.

"Stop it!" Mrs. Blotgate screeched, pushing Miss
Jesczenka back. "Get back from me, you lousy Jew, or you'll
wish you were never born!"

Still Miss Jesczenka held her tight. She put her face close
to Mrs. Blotgate's and Emily heard her whisper fiercely:

"Don't struggle, Duze! Don't you remember all the fun we
had?"

With a shriek of hatred, Mrs. Blotgate shoved Miss Jesczenka back, knocking her to the ground. Miss Jesczenka just rolled on the floor as if it were a great joke and laughed up at her—the laugh of a drunken whore.

"Oh, Duze, you naughty thing, don't be standoffish!"

But the words were shouted at Mrs. Blotgate's back as the woman staggered away from them, pulling her cloak around her. As she got farther away, Emily could see her true form returning to her, her armor of silk and velvet, but that did not stop the gapers from staring after her, elbowing one another and laughing.

Heart pounding, Emily hurriedly helped Miss Jesczenka to her feet. The woman seemed completely unflustered. She stood calmly, smoothed back her hair, straightened her hat. She glared at the staring men with an old maid's steely frigidity. Emily watched the looks on their faces mutate from amusement to puzzlement, as if they weren't quite sure of what they were watching, or why. Soon, the audience for the little drama had dispersed and Emily and Miss Jesczenka were left utterly alone.

Emily was flabbergasted. The sudden silence was deafening.

"What did you just *do*?" she managed.

"Miss Edwards, you must learn more about squinking," Miss Jesczenka said, taking Emily's arm with the utmost decorum. "The key is to find your opponent's greatest fear and attack it. The greatest fear of a woman—particularly an evil woman—is that she be made trivial and insignificant." Miss Jesczenka looked in the direction Mrs. Blotgate had gone. "A woman's power is tenuous enough as it is. Having that power mocked is the most terrifying thing that woman who lives in the service of evil could face."

"But what about you? You're a woman, and you had to humiliate yourself . . ."

"Humiliate myself?" Miss Jesczenka clucked as they turned toward the archway that read *Tracks 21–30*. "It's hardly humiliating if no one remembers. Anyone who saw that has already forgotten that the woman pawing Alcmene Blotgate was me; they will remember an inebriated harlot who has already ceased to exist. If they even thought to wonder what became of her, they would wonder only that she vanished so quickly and completely."

Emily said nothing for a moment. Then she gave Miss Jesczenka a sidelong glance.

"Could you teach me to do that?" she asked. She found suddenly that she very much wished that she could have been the one to send the odious Mrs. Blotgate scurrying in such a satisfying, ugly way.

"I very much doubt it," Miss Jesczenka said. "You haven't a dissembling bone in your body. Unfortunately. Hurry now, or we'll miss our train."

On the train, they found their seats in a ladies' car that bustled with late-morning activity. Emily watched New York recede into the distance as the train gathered speed, its wheels humming and clattering on the steel tracks. It wasn't until they were well out of the city that Emily thought to reach down the front of her dress and pull out Mrs. Blotgate's card. Without a word, Miss Jesczenka reached over and took the card from Emily's hand. She tucked it away in her own bag.

"A very unpleasant couple, the Blotgates," Miss Jesczenka said, as if the card had never existed. "They are mainstays of conservative Washington society. General Blotgate is the highest ranked practitioner in the military. He is first in line for the position of Secretary of War if Hayes gets the presidency."

Hand on her chin, Emily stared out the window.

"Mrs. Blotgate comes from a very old and very feared family in the South, known for producing generations of sangrimancers." Miss Jesczenka tilted her head. "The fact that she takes a new lover every year from among her husband's cadets is widely known, but never mentioned for fear of reprisal."

Emily pressed her lips together, stared out of the window harder.

"What was she bothering you about?"

"Nothing," Emily said, hoping that the shortness of her reply would indicate her desire to stop talking about Alcmene

Blotgate. The encounter with the woman had left her feeling greasy and unclean. Emily tried to sort out the confusing welter of feelings knotted beneath her breastbone. The images that kept flashing through her mind were those of the flayed man from last night's séance, the man with the halo of feathers and the hand-shaped birthmark. The man with seams of blood on his skin.

Miss Jesczenka's hand touched her knee, drawing her out of the morbid recollection.

"You mustn't worry about it." Emily looked up at her abruptly, into Miss Jesczenka's mild eyes. "There's an old saying: *He that can't endure the bad will not live to see the good.*"

"That's hardly comforting," Emily said. Unbidden images of blade-edged fingers leaving blood trails on smooth brown skin flashed behind her eyes. "Especially when it's all so bad."

"Oh, it's never as bad as you think it is," Miss Jesczenka said.

The Institute is in a shambles, Komé has been kidnapped, the Sini Mira is on my trail, and the man I love is probably hiding something from me. Emily allowed herself a small, grim smile. Exactly how could it be worse?

As if intuiting the drift of Emily's thoughts, Miss Jesczenka shrugged.

"Schisms of the type currently afflicting the Institute have always been part of credomancy," she commented. "Sometimes they can even be beneficial, like dividing a plant. The separated halves may thrive better for the separation. The magisters who remain loyal to Mr. Stanton will be stronger and more focused for their loyalty. Those who defect to Fortissimus' camp will always have the taint of treachery on their conscience. A credomancer with a guilty conscience is always at a disadvantage."

Emily reddened, thinking of Mrs. Blotgate, and hoped that Stanton's conscience was clear.

They rode the New York Central out of the city, winding along the Hudson up toward Albany. At suppertime they transferred to the Boston & Albany Railroad, which cut across the belly of New York State and into Massachussets. They arrived in Boston well before nightfall, and checked into the American Hotel—a foursquare brick pile that commanded a view of the smooth green commons.

The rooms were comfortable and well appointed, but even in a room with a hundred feather beds, Emily would not have slept that night. Opening her trunk, she pulled out the slate Stanton had given her, regarding its smooth surface. She chewed on the end of the pencil, thinking of all the things she could possibly write. *I miss you. I need you with me. I don't want to be in Boston. I saw Alcmene Blotgate at the train station.* None of the statements were brave or helpful, none could be adequately discussed via a slate with lambs on it, and at least one seemed dangerous to mention even at all. With a heavy sigh, she slid the pencil back into its slot.

In the morning, Emily dressed carefully in a solemn mauve twill, placed her mother's amethyst earrings in her ears, and tucked her mother's hair sticks into a reticule of knitted black silk. Certainly the Kendalls would want some proof of her claims. Then she went downstairs to meet Miss Jesczenka for breakfast.

"I'm going alone," Emily said abruptly, over her eggs. Miss Jesczenka shook her head brusquely.

"Out of the question. It's far too dangerous."

"This is my family." Emily paused. "I won't have the Institute interfering with that, at least."

Miss Jesczenka slowly removed the tortoiseshell glasses from her face. She looked at Emily, her eyes soft and sad.

"Miss Edwards, you must trust that the Institute wants only what's best for you."

"I've heard that before," Emily said, meeting Miss Jesczenka's gaze with all the firmness at her command. "I'm going to meet my family alone. If you want to stop me, you'll have to tie me to a chair."

Miss Jesczenka sighed heavily. "All right, then. I'll wait for you here. As long as you take a cab directly there and ask it to stand for your return, I can't imagine anyone will bother you.

But you must promise me you will be careful. I won't have you coming back to me covered in insect parts."

Emily smiled slightly, but said nothing.

"Your grandparents' neighborhood is no longer as desirable as it used to be," Miss Jesczenka warned. "All the best families have moved to the Back Bay, and Beacon Hill has gone over to tenancy. So come back quickly. If your grandparents wish to get reacquainted, ask them to come and call on you here, where I can protect you. All right?"

"I'll be fine," Emily promised, but was sharply aware of having learned that it was a promise she should not make.

After breakfast, the concierge called Emily a cab, and Miss Jesczenka hovered protectively by the hotel's front door as she climbed into it. Emily gave the driver the address they had found in the Boston Social Register, and he touched his cap smartly.

The cab took her to Pemberton Square. Tall redbrick houses rose high up on each side of the broad cobbled street. The street itself was bisected by fenced garden plots that probably used to contain neat flower beds, but now contained small kitchen gardens. Here and there, laundry was hung out over the black-enameled fencing that held the sidewalk at arm's length from the homes. Children played on stoops. On one set of stairs sat a man in his shirtsleeves, apparently indifferent to the overcast sky, reading a paper. It seemed friendly and cozy to Emily.

The cab stopped before a large home. It was very evenly balanced in construction, with four windows on each side of the house and a large red-painted front door right in the middle. There was a fan window above the door, and stone urns that held nothing more than dirt and the twiggy remnants of dead geraniums.

Emily climbed the steps. The front door had a small iron-barred grille in its center that could be slid open from behind to judge prospective callers. On a scuffed and tarnished brass plate beside the door was engraved *The Reverend James Kendall,* with a simple cross shown beneath it. This was the right place.

Taking a deep breath, Emily rapped her knuckles against the wood. The sound hung in the air.

There was no answer for some time, though Emily could hear shufflings behind the door. The little sliding door behind the iron grille was jerked open, and two eyes peered out at her. They peered for quite a long time, Emily thought. Then, finally, the door cracked open slowly.

An elderly maid in limp black and white leaned against the edge of the door, her heavy face pale and slack. She stared at Emily, dumbfounded. The careful words Emily had prepared to introduce herself evaporated at the sight of the woman's obvious shock; Emily half wondered if she'd have to catch her from a dead faint. But after a moment the old woman managed to force two whispered words past her leathery lips.

"Miss Catherine."

CHAPTER TEN

Creature of Filth

"No," Emily said, staring at the stricken old woman. "My name is Emily. Emily Edwards. I'm here to see . . . Mrs. Kendall." Remembering, she felt for a card, one of the new ones she'd had made, engraved in simple black letters.

The maid blinked. Emily tried to hand her the card, but the old woman would not take it.

"I've come from New York," Emily fumbled for something to say. "From California, actually—"

"Wait," the maid blurted and disappeared from the door, closing it loudly. Emily stood on the doorstep, her face flushed. The woman had recognized her—or rather, had recognized her mother in her. Emily's heart pounded like a drum, blood rushing madly between her ears.

There was more shuffling behind the door, and more sounds. Emily heard a muffled: "Don't be silly, Liddy!" and small crisp steps coming toward the door. Then the door was jerked open to reveal another old woman, different from the maid in every respect. She was neat and small and pretty, with smooth white hair. Emily was sure she would look nicer without the expression of anger and suspicion that disfigured her face. Her mouth was set in a way that said she was about to tell Emily to shove off, but then her eyes caught Emily's. The blood drained from her face, but she did not falter. If anything, she stood up even straighter.

"You do look like her," she said softly. "Very much."

"My name is Emily Edwards," Emily said. "Or Kendall. I

don't really know. I've come . . . I've come to speak with you about Catherine Kendall. She was my mother."

The woman blinked, her face softening for a moment, then hardening again abruptly. "Was?" she said. "She is dead, then?"

Emily nodded.

The old woman blew out a breath, as though a long-held suspicion had finally been confirmed.

"Come in," she said.

Emily was shown into a large sitting room, and though she hardly considered herself au courant in matters of fashion, even she could tell that the decor was severely outdated. The furniture in the room was gothic and austere, all angles and corners. There was a notable absence of the kinds of ornamentation—needlepoint pillows and wax flowers, cut paper and painted china—that Emily had become accustomed to. One prominent piece of decoration, however, caught Emily's eye. On the wall, a simple red cross. Her heart thumped nervously, but she pushed the anxiety away. Lots of people had crosses in their homes, she thought. And red was a very popular color.

The old woman perched on the edge of a horsehair settle.

"My name is Emily, too," she said.

"I know this is very unexpected." Emily clutched her reticule tightly. The action made the diamond ring on her finger flash like a shooting star. The speck of brilliance was sufficient to draw Mrs. Kendall's attention to Emily's good hand, and from there to her prosthetic of ivory. The old woman looked away from the appendage quickly. Emily cursed herself for forgetting to wear gloves.

"And you believe Catherine was your mother?" The old woman's voice caught upon speaking her daughter's name. "In what manner do you intend to support this claim?" There was a high tense note in the woman's voice, both eager and forbidding, as if she wanted Emily to both prove and disprove her kinship.

"I have this." Emily pulled out the calling card with her mother's name on it. She showed the card to the old woman, who took it with trembling hands. "That's how I found you. It was in my mother's things."

"My daughter handed out hundreds of cards," Mrs. Kendall said, turning the card over with slender fingers. "That means nothing."

"There are also these." Emily reached into the reticule and withdrew the hair sticks, holding them out for Mrs. Kendall to examine. The woman shook her head curtly.

"I have never seen them before."

Emily fought discouragement. Was it possible this was all an elaborate mistake? It just couldn't be. She leaned forward, gesturing to her ears.

"And these," she said. "She was wearing them when she died."

This time, the old woman paused. She leaned forward, too, so that she could more closely scrutinize the eardrops. She lifted a trembling hand, touched one of the glimmering amethysts, then let her hand drop wearily. She said nothing, but stood, and went to the drawer of a tall sideboard. She pulled out a velvet box. Without a word, she handed the box to Emily.

Awkwardly, aware that Mrs. Kendall was watching her, Emily opened the box. Inside there was a velvet separator with a place for earrings and a necklace. The earrings were missing, but Emily knew exactly where they were—in her ears. The necklace was there, a perfect match.

"Tell me what happened to her," Mrs. Kendall said.

"I don't know all of it," Emily said, thinking guiltily of the bottle of memories and the knowledge that this woman would relish of her daughter. "She died in California, at a place called Lost Pine. I was with her. She was going to San Francisco—"

"San Francisco?" Mrs. Kendall snapped in disbelief. "Why on earth would she go there?"

"I don't know," Emily said. "That's why I've come to you—"

"What do you want here?" The words came from the doorway. Emily looked up and saw an old man with a sour face and acidic eyes. Tufts of white hair stood out over his ears. He wore a suit of black and a priest's collar. He bore an electricity of anger into the room with him, anger that focused on Emily.

"James!" Mrs. Kendall said, taking one unconscious step back from him.

"I asked what you want here, young woman." Mr. Kendall's words were for Emily alone, spat with barely restrained fury.

"I wanted to meet you," Emily whispered.

"Why?" he barked.

"Because Catherine Kendall was my mother."

"My daughter is dead," the old man said. "And any bastard she had died with her. Or should have."

"No," Emily said. "I didn't die. I was raised up in California. I have her earrings—"

"You could have gotten those anywhere."

"James, please," the old woman said. "Look at her. She looks just like Catherine."

"And a poisonous mushroom looks edible until you die from eating one." The old man looked sidelong at his wife. "The Russians have been back here, Mother. They steal my daughter, lead her to a strange death somewhere in the wilderness, and then they have the brass to come back!"

"James!" Mrs. Kendall said. "What did they want?"

"They were here less than a week ago, asking me questions about Catherine, and about *you.*" The last word was punched at Emily.

"The Russians?" Emily said softly, the words catching in her throat. "The Sini Mira?"

"Oh, you know about them, do you?" Mr. Kendall came closer to her, so close she could smell the mentholatum and talc on his clothes. "If you think that knowing will help your cause, young woman, you're wrong."

"Why didn't you tell me?" Mrs. Kendall said to him, her voice low and hot.

"I saw no need." The Reverend Kendall's eyes continued to burn into Emily. "I didn't want you to know. She was raised a *Witch,* Mother. And she intends to marry a *Warlock.*" The word "Warlock" was spoken with such disdain that

Rev. Kendall's mouth went through precisely four discrete contortions.

Mrs. Kendall lifted her hand to her mouth.

"No," she whispered against her fingers. "It can't be."

Emily's amorphous fears seemed to coagulate all at once as she saw the horror in the eyes of the woman who had just begun to soften toward her. Now there were two pairs of hostile eyes scrutinizing her. The red cross on the wall wasn't just an ornament. It *did* mean what she'd feared.

Emily remembered New Bethel, the knife-faced preacher and his parishioners, Stanton tied in preparation for being burned at the stake for the sin of being a Warlock . . . they had been adherents to an ultraconservative theology, Eradicationists who wanted to see all Witches and Warlocks wiped from the face of the earth . . .

"You're Scharfians," Emily whispered.

"I count the good brother as one of my closest friends," Rev. Kendall said. "My church was the first in Boston to loose itself from the shackles of sinful appeasement and reform under the Scharfian banner. The banner of decency and godliness." His voice seemed to gain intensity as he spoke. "You are a sinner, girl. You are a foul and accursed thing, an abomination before the Lord—"

"There's nothing wrong with being a Witch," Emily stammered, standing quickly. She suddenly felt as if she might need to flee at any moment. "And the fact that I'm a Witch doesn't have anything to do with what I came for—"

"You came here to make some claim to being a Kendall," the old man interrupted. "But even if my daughter did have the misfortune to give you life, you're no Kendall. The Kendalls have hated Witches for three hundred years. The hatred is in our very blood."

Emily said nothing, but felt her way backward, toward the archway that led to the hall that led to the front door.

"The Kendall family moved to Boston only recently," Rev. Kendall said, driving her before him as he advanced on her, step by step, fingers held like claws.

"James, no," Mrs. Kendall said, under her breath. He did not seem to hear her.

"We arrived in Boston a hundred years ago. Before that, we were residents of Salem." He paused. "We were Witch hunters. Celebrated Witch hunters. My great-grandfather personally executed two hundred Warlocks, and almost as many Witches. Burned most of them. Hung a few. Chopped the heads off the rest. Hell-shackled sinners, each and every one. Sinners just like you."

He had backed her all the way to the front door. The large brass doorknob pressed into the small of her back. He stopped right before her, his face a mask of abhorrence.

"Mark my words, creature of filth." Spittle flecked her cheek; she did not dare reach up and wipe it off. "If I have anything to do with it, you and everyone like you will be dead before the century is out."

"James, please," Mrs. Kendall was saying. She was coaxing him backward with pleading hands laid on his arm. It gave Emily just enough space to reach behind herself and open the front door.

"Leave my house." Kendall shook his wife's hand away as Emily hurried out the door and down the steps. The old man watched her go, his voice rising in fury to follow her.

"Leave, and return to the bed of Satan from which you came! Leave, that the earnest faithful may not be sickened with thee! Leave, foul and accursed thing . . ."

Emily stumbled along the sidewalk, epithets ringing in her ears, until finally she heard the door slam shut. Then she stopped, and stood still for a moment, fighting tears that prickled the corners of her eyes. She looked around, suddenly realizing that in her nervousness, she'd forgotten to tell the cab to wait. Cursing her own stupidity, she wrapped her arms around her trembling body. Surely she could find a cab if she walked. And she wanted to get away from the Kendall house, far away.

She turned her steps back in the direction that she remembered coming. It felt good to walk, to let her legs do the thinking for her. Her head certainly wasn't up to the task of sorting it all out . . . that her mother had been born into a family of Eradicationists, Witch hunters who had killed hundreds of

Witches and Warlocks . . . hung them, decapitated them, burned them alive . . . it was a point of family pride!

And again, the Sini Mira. They were all around her now. The bottle of memories—it had to be what they wanted. She felt for it in her pocket, but it was not there; she suffered a momentary panic before she remembered she'd left it in the hotel, carefully hidden at the bottom of her trunk. Relief flooded her, and then she was glad she didn't have it, that she wasn't walking around with it. It seemed so dangerous all of a sudden.

She looked for a cab, but there were none on this quiet residential street; only the soft reassuring sounds of ordinary people going about their lives. It made Emily feel a little better. She walked on, wrapping her shawl tightly around her shoulders. The sky had turned grayer, and the air had a chill in it. There were no Russians around her now. The Sini Mira were far away. She kept telling herself that. The Sini Mira were far away.

Or were they?

Almost experimentally, Emily stopped in her tracks and looked around herself. There was no one near, but that did not stop Emily saying in a loud voice, "Dmitri! Dmitri, if you're here, show yourself!"

The words rang around her. Silence was the only answer.

She sighed, feeling better and worse at the same time. There was no reason to believe the Russian was still following her. There was no reason not to believe, really, that he hadn't been left behind in California. But deep frustration and anguish made Emily raise her voice again.

"Dmitri, come out and face me! Tell me what you want with me . . . or my mother . . ."

Again, only silence answered, and after a while, Emily trudged on, her brow furrowed darkly.

By the time Emily got back to the hotel, the skies had opened and drenched her in a downpour. She paused at the front desk and asked for paper and pencil. She wrote a short note to Miss Jesczenka, assuring the woman that she had made it back safely.

After a moment's thought, she added a little postscript explaining that she wished to be alone with her thoughts for the evening, and that she would meet her for breakfast in the morning. She handed it to the clerk and asked that a bellman be dispatched to deliver it.

Then she climbed up the stairs wearily and let herself into her room. She sat down to dry herself before the little gas grate in the corner.

There was a knock on the door. She stood wearily, expecting that it was Miss Jesczenka, come to check on her despite her expressed desire to be left alone. It annoyed her, and she jerked open the door, intending to address the woman coolly. When she saw who stood in the doorway, however, the words froze in her throat.

It was a woman in a heavy black cloak that was dripping with rain. She put back her hood, revealing shining white hair. It was Mrs. Kendall.

"I had to find you before you went," she said. "I thought you might be at the American. It's where all the Witches and Warlocks stay . . ."

Emily stood frozen in surprise for a few moments before she was able to speak. When she did, words tumbled over words quickly, and she opened the door wide.

"Come in," Emily said. "Please, come in."

Mrs. Kendall came into the room, and Emily showed her to two small chairs arranged before the mean little grate. The old woman sat slowly, her back straight, as if anticipating the need to bolt.

"I came as soon as James went to the church for Wednesday evening service," Mrs. Kendall said. "I usually go with him, of course, but I told him I didn't feel well. After what happened today, he thought I should rest—" She stopped abruptly, collecting herself. "James would be furious if he knew I'd come."

"So I gathered," Emily said.

"But I couldn't . . ." Mrs. Kendall let out a breath. "You should know what happened. Where you came from. She would have wanted that."

"Then you believe me?" Emily said. "You believe . . . about my mother?"

"I believe you," Mrs. Kendall said, fixing Emily with a clear blue gaze. "But if you think that will entitle you to anything, you're wrong. James will never accept you."

"I don't want anything from you or him," Emily said. "I just want to know."

"Then I will tell you," Mrs. Kendall said. She shrugged the wet black cloak from her shoulders. She drew a deep breath. "Your father was a refugee from Russia—Saint Petersburg. His name was Vladimir Lyakhov, and he was a member of a group called the Sini Mira." She looked up at Emily. "You seem to know the Sini Mira."

Emily said nothing. Her mind went back to Chicago, to the words Perun had whispered in her ear . . . *a daughter would more properly be called Lyakhova* . . . So it *was* her name after all.

"The Sini Mira and the Scharfian Brotherhood have worked together for many years. Their beliefs have always been compatible with our own."

A chill climbed Emily's spine. Stanton had said that the Sini Mira and the Scharfians shared the same views, but he'd never gone so far as to say they actually worked together. But it made terrible sense. They were both Eradicationists, except that the Scharfians wanted to eradicate magic by killing those who practiced it and the Sini Mira wanted to eradicate magic by making it unpracticable.

"It was before the war," Mrs. Kendall continued. "The war engineered by Warlocks, as an excuse to massacre young Christian men, both Northern and Southern—" She checked herself, then continued. "Many, like the Scharfian Brotherhood and the Sini Mira, put their finest men into the service of one noble cause—eradicating the use of magic. Of course, your Warlocks wanted nothing more than to find these men and destroy them, so everyone shared in their protection. We opened our house in service of the greater good. We sheltered your father."

"He was in danger?"

Mrs. Kendall nodded. "He had a mentor in Russia, a scientist. The man had been working on important research before he died, and your father was his assistant."

Emily felt her body go cold. "Important research?"

"Important enough that the Warlocks who murdered him felt it necessary to burn down his laboratory with him in it." Mrs. Kendall's tone was harsh. "I don't know any more about it than that. But yes, your father was in danger. Great danger. He sought safety on our shores, and we took pride in opening our home to a hero of the cause." Mrs. Kendall paused, looking into the glow of the gas grate before adding bitterly, "Little did we know that he would take our daughter in the bargain."

"My mother," Emily said.

"She was only nineteen. You do look very much like her, except you've got your father's eyes. They make you look like you're always keeping a secret, poorly." Mrs. Kendall drew a breath and continued. "We had high hopes that she would make a good marriage. In fact, she was engaged to marry a very nice young man, the son of one of my husband's most prominent parishioners. It would have been an excellent match."

"What happened?" Emily asked.

Mrs. Kendall's blue eyes glided up to meet Emily's.

"The Kendall Curse," she said, simply. "It destroyed any chance she had of a normal life. After the Curse descended upon her, I often thought that it would have been better if she'd never been born."

There was a long silence. Emily stared at the old woman; the old woman stared inward, delicately examining memories like fragile antique lace stored in a dusty trunk.

"You heard James refer to our Witch-hunting ancestors," Mrs. Kendall said softly. "Witches do not like to be hunted. Their wrath can be bitter, and it can extend beyond the grave, even for many centuries. Our family incurred the wrath of Aebedel Cowdray."

The name made a chill chase up Emily's spine. It sounded familiar in a terrible, unsettling way, like remembering a long-unpaid bill.

"Who was Aebedel Cowdray?" Emily asked.

"A very powerful Warlock in Salem, Massachusetts, in the 1690s. Civil Magistrate Anson Kendall—your great-great-great-great-grandfather—had him pressed between two stones. He vowed revenge. He cursed the Kendalls with his dying breath, and the curse was as powerful as his spite and hatred." She trailed a hand along the fabric of her skirt. "The curse allows his unsettled spirit to claim the body of its victim during the full moon. A half dozen Kendalls over the past two hundred years have lost their lives to it, usually after decades of great suffering." She looked at Emily. "It is good for you that you are well past your eighteenth birthday. The curse always manifests itself then."

"But my mother—"

"Every full moon, the spirit of Aebedel Cowdray would possess her, make her foulmouthed and cruel. We would lock her in her room to keep her from wreaking havoc, but Cowdray could always find ways to make her do evil. We tried to keep instruments of violence away from her at such times but—" Mrs. Kendall shuddered. "She killed her own cat . . . or rather, Cowdray killed it. A little yellow tabby she loved so much. Her fiancé gave it to her on her eighteenth birthday. She killed it with a heavy leather-bound Bible that we'd left for her to take comfort in. Crushed its skull and broke its back. Once Cowdray left her, she was disconsolate over its death. She was a good girl, a gentle child. She would never have hurt anything of her own volition."

Sudden understanding broke over Emily. Pap had said her mother was evil. But what if it hadn't been her mother Pap had met? What if it had been Aebedel Cowdray in her mother's body? The idea gave her hope, as though the image she'd always had of her mother could be reclaimed.

"The Russian—your father—did not approve of how we addressed her condition," Mrs. Kendall said. "It is true, James wrestled mightily with her to exorcise the demon, but what other choice did he have? *Rebuke them sharply, that they may be sound in the faith.* But the Russian believed that gentler ways would work better."

"One day, we found them both gone. We did not know where they went. Catherine sent one letter, posted from a hotel, saying that she was not coming back. James wanted nothing to do with her after that. And he wanted nothing more to do with the Sini Mira. He didn't speak with them again until just recently, when they came here asking questions."

"What did they want to know?"

"James wouldn't tell me. He said only that they were looking for Catherine, and that he'd told them good riddance to bad rubbish."

Sudden anger surged through Emily. "She was his daughter!" Emily bit the words. "How could he say something like that? How could he be so cruel?"

"James is a man of principles," Mrs. Kendall said. "And it has been such a long time. But I never stopped wondering what happened to her. I always hoped she would come back. I hoped she was still alive. But I think I knew long ago that I would never see her again—" Mrs. Kendall's voice broke. She raised a handkerchief to her mouth. She squeezed her eyes shut. Emily reached out a tentative hand to her, but Mrs. Kendall drew away.

"Please, don't." Mrs. Kendall said. "I have come out of respect for my daughter. I know she would have wanted me to come. But for you, Miss Edwards—and for the sinner's path you have chosen—I have only pity and contempt."

Emily pulled back as if struck.

"I'm sorry," Emily said softly.

Mrs. Kendall stood. "James will be home soon."

Emily said nothing, but rose along with her.

"There is one last thing," Mrs. Kendall said, reaching into her bag and pulling out a small box. She handed it to Emily. "She would have wanted you to have this. I have no use for it anymore."

It was the velvet box containing the necklace that matched the amethyst earrings. Emily smoothed her fingers over the silken nap.

"You do look so like her," Mrs. Kendall said, staring for a long time at Emily's face. "I will pray for your soul, Miss Edwards. Whatever of it is left."

Then she turned and went quickly to the door, and was gone.

Emily was left standing in the middle of the room, bewildered and silent. She lifted the lid of the velvet box, gazed at the necklace again. She touched it with the tip of her thumb. But it was not thoughts of her mother that occupied her at the moment. It was thoughts of her father.

Emily was not used to thinking about her father. In all honesty, what had happened to her father never concerned Emily much. Because she'd had a father. She'd had Pap.

But now, however, she'd learned more about her father than she'd ever even thought to wonder. His name was Vladimir Lyakhov. He was a member of the Sini Mira. He had been working on important research . . .

Emily shook her head. The Sini Mira weren't looking for her mother at all.

She released a breath she didn't know she was holding. They were looking for Vladimir Lyakhov. What did the Sini Mira want with him now, over two decades later? She'd come to Boston for answers, and now she just had ten times as many questions.

Well, you know where the answers are.

Emily's eyes found her trunk, in which the blue bottle of memories lay hidden between neatly folded stacks of undergarments. She realized now why she had told Miss Jesczenka not to bother her that evening. She realized now that she'd already decided what she had to do.

She had promised Stanton she would wait for him—but with all the uncertainty at the Institute, who knew how long it would be before he could help her?

She remembered Pap's words:

These Russians . . . these Sini Mira . . . if they're after you . . . You may have to know, Em. If you don't know, then you might not know how to stay away from them . . .

She was sick and tired of not knowing. She was sick and tired of question piling upon question on question. She wanted her memories back. She wanted answers.

Hurrying over to the trunk, she pushed clothing aside and retrieved the bottle. She uncapped it, tilted it between her lips, all in one movement, as if the haste of the gesture were required to maintain her resolve. The liquid spilled down her throat, bitter and stale tasting. Remembering Pap's admonition not to drink it all at once, she restoppered the bottle when it was half emptied, placing it carefully on the table beside the bed as the spell made its way down her throat, setting fire to her belly and chest. The smell of hay and sunlight and roses and warm, warm summer engulfed her, time dissolved, and then . . .

CHAPTER ELEVEN

Light and Sweet

. . . Emily was five.

Emily was five, and she lived on a farm with chickens and cows and goats, and her father always smiled. Her *papasha* was made of smiles, and chasing, and tickling. Her life was lived in light that seemed golden and diffuse, as if she were moving through an ocean of sunlight. It was autumn, she had just had her birthday, and the leaves of the trees were becoming gold and red.

"Well, *moya devuchka,* have you come to watch me again?" her father said, as he saw her peeping from behind the fence. He was working with his machines again. Father loved his big machines, his great thumping machines that stomped on the ground like feet. He swept her up in his arms, his thick brown beard tickling her face. She giggled.

"But what do they do?" Emily asked again. She'd asked before, and he'd answered before, but she liked to hear him tell it.

"They stomp and they stomp on the earth, like the feet of giants," her father said, making his face look terrible, like the face of a giant. "They stomp on the earth, and they make noise. And the earth hears that noise, and it listens, and it understands. And the earth talks back, sometimes."

"You talk to the earth?" Emily asked, wrinkling her nose with disbelief. "And it talks to you?"

"I do."

"What do you talk about?"

"About what the earth likes, and what she doesn't like. What she wants."

"What does she want?"

"She wants people not to hurt her," her father said. His face became mischievous. "She wants little girls like you not to use your da's shovel to dig holes."

"I only dug one hole, and Vas was the one who started it, anyway!" Emily was outraged. Vasily, the big black dog with such soft sweet eyes, was always digging. That's what dogs did, and Emily didn't see why little girls shouldn't be allowed to as well.

Her father tickled her and put her down, and she ran away, laughing, her feet flying beneath her.

"Emily, sweetling, come here now and let me braid your hair."

It was her mother, soft and young and gentle. Her face was kind and tired. Emily had a strange feeling that she'd seen that face in a mirror looking back at her. But Emily didn't look like that when she looked in mirrors. Emily was five, and she was small and brown and she had already lost two teeth.

Mama was sitting in her rocking chair, and she had an ivory brush in her hand.

"I hate having my hair braided," Emily spat. "I don't want to."

"Come, you can't run around with your hair flying around your face," her mother chided. "And your hair is so pretty! Like mine, look. Look, we have the same hair. And I always wear my hair in braids to keep it nice."

Grudgingly, Emily came to sit in her mother's lap and submitted to the torture of having her hair brushed. Her mother's hands, though, were gentle and the brush moving over her scalp made her feel sleepy. It made her think things she didn't want to think about. She clenched a handful of her mother's skirt in her fist, feeling the softness of it.

"Mama," she asked, "when is it the full moon again?"

Emily felt her mother's body tense.

"Why do you ask that, sweetling?"

"I don't—" Emily paused and reconsidered. "Vas doesn't like it when the full moon comes." The big dog, who was laying on the floor at their feet, raised his head when he heard Emily speak his name. He stood up and put his nose under Emily's hand. She petted him. "Vas doesn't like it when you have to stay in your room."

"I'm sorry that Vasilly doesn't like it when I stay in my room," Emily's mother said, the brush still moving gently in her hand. "But Mama has to stay in her room when she's feeling ill."

"People yell a lot when they're sick," Emily said matter-of-factly, but it was really a test, to see what her mother would say. But her mother said nothing, just sectioned Emily's hair into two parts and began braiding, pulling the long hanks of hair together tightly as she worked down.

"He only stays five days," Emily stated the fact with precision and finality. "Five times that the sun goes up and down. And then he's gone."

Mama's hands stopped braiding. They lay heavy against Emily's head. Emily felt them trembling slightly.

"That's right," Mama said. "Five days. Five days he's here, and then he's gone. You're a very smart girl, Emily."

"So when is it, Mama?" Emily asked, after a long time of her mother not saying anything, a long time of Mama's hands still against the back of her head. "When is he coming back?"

"Very soon, sweetling," her mother said, and there was a terrible apologetic sadness in her voice that Emily hated. "Very soon."

And then, Emily was in her father's lap, and he was holding her tight, rocking her. One ear he pressed against his shoulder, the other ear he kept covered with his big hand so she could not hear the screaming.

"Let . . . me . . . out!"

The voice coming from the other room was her mother's voice, but not her mother's voice. There was nowhere they could go in the house where they could not hear the screaming, and now it was winter, and too cold to go outside, where there was snow swirling. There was a big fire in the fireplace. It glowed orange and red, and sometimes the logs in it fell apart into shimmering, shattered embers. Emily could see the snow through the frosted windows, little bits of white reflected in the candlelight.

"I know you're out there, you and that brat of yours! You think you can lock me away forever? One day you will be careless. I will find a way out. Oh, and when I do . . . when I do! That will be such joy, Lyakhov. I can hardly wait."

Her father began humming—a low soft tune that resonated from his deep chest and filled Emily's ear. She concentrated hard on listening to it, trying to block out the terrible words that rang through the house from behind the locked door upstairs, the sounds of things being turned over, things breaking and shattering.

"I'll kill her in front of you first, that mewling brat, that squealing little get of a Kendall. And I won't let you die, I won't *allow* you to die, until she's cold on the ground in front of you in a pool of her own blood . . ."

And Emily closed her eyes, and listened to the humming as hard as she could, until her father stood up abruptly, still holding her in his arms. His face was dark and horribly sad and he did not smile.

"Emily, *devuchka,* come with me."

He quickly bundled her in her coat and shoes, put a scarf around her neck and a hat on her head, and they walked out of the house, into the swirling snowy darkness until they came to the barn, where he set her on a bale of hay. Even though Emily was very cold, and the barn was very dark, she was glad to be away from the screaming.

Shivering, she watched him light a lamp. It gave a thin yellow flame. He came close to her, setting the lamp beside her.

"I want to show you something," he said, his breath frosting white. He spoke to her in Russian, the language he always used when it was something important. Some secret the two of them shared, something secret that Mama should not know, for Mama did not know Russian. He pulled something from inside his coat, something that gleamed in the low light. He showed it to her. It was two sticks made of silver—the kind of sticks her mother wore in her hair. But she had never seen Mama wearing them before. They were so pretty. Emily reached out to touch them with her finger.

"It is very important that you keep this secret."

Emily listened very hard, looking into her father's face, and then at the hair sticks.

"These are very special things. There is writing on them. It is called Faery Writing. The writing says something very important. There are people, friends of mine, who will need to read this writing."

Emily looked at him, confused. She didn't understand, so she listened harder.

"We may have to leave soon, Emilichka." He used her baby name. It made her feel very small and very grown up at precisely the same time. "We may have to leave and go see my friends. Maybe it will happen that you find them and I don't. If you do, you have to tell them that there is a secret written on these hair sticks. A dangerous secret."

"Will Mama go with us?" Emily asked. She was still confused. He was talking about going somewhere but he hadn't said where, and he was talking about friends, but he hadn't said who. How was she to know who his friends were? What if they were going someplace she didn't like? She shivered more, her small bones rattling, and it was only partly the cold that made her do so.

"My friends are Russians, just like me. You will know them because they are called the Sini Mira."

"Sons of the Earth," Emily said, in English.

Her father nodded, smiling at her. His smile was like a new-kindled fire; it warmed her all through her body. But it vanished so quickly, it was almost as if it had never been there.

"That's right," he said. "It is very important that they get these, Emilichka." He touched her cheek, let his warm hand linger on her face. "And there's another important thing for you to remember. You must never tell Mama. You must never tell her about the Faery Writing. Promise me, Emilichka. Promise me that you will never say a word to her."

"I promise," Emily said, the cold around her seeping into her body like darkness, swallowing her up, swallowing her whole . . .

CHAPTER TWELVE

Return to the Institute

"Miss Edwards! Miss Edwards!"

Emily stirred slowly, her entire body heavy as a sodden quilt. She felt too long and stretched out. There was an arm before her eyes; it was long and slim, like her mother's arm, but then she wiggled her fingers and the fingers of the arm wiggled, and she knew it was her arm. Her own arm, no longer short and chubby but long and slim, and there was her other arm . . . it was strange, dead, made of some kind of white stone, and those were her feet in the boots so far away.

"Da?" she said tentatively, and her own voice vibrated in her chest strangely, low and resonant. "Da, where's Mama? Is she better yet? When will she come out?"

"Miss Edwards?" Miss Jesczenka said again, and her voice was full of real concern. "Miss Edwards, are you all right? Why are you speaking *Russian*?"

Emily sat up, looking around at the unfamiliar room, bright morning sunlight streaming through the tall windows. She wrapped her arms around herself, terrified.

"Da!" she screamed, looking around wildly. She did not know where she was. This was not the farm, this was nowhere she knew. Had they already gone? Had they gone to find Father's friends?

"Emily," Miss Jesczenka said, wrapping her arms around Emily's shoulders and holding her close. Despite her soothing presence, there was a firm, clear note to her voice. "Emily Edwards, listen to me. What has happened? What is wrong?"

Emily Edwards.

She was Emily Edwards, Pap's girl.

She looked around herself again, strange tendrils reconnecting in her mind, stretching toward one another like the fingers of lovers through the bars of a jail cell . . .

She was in a hotel.

She was twenty-five years old.

She let her eyes travel over the flowered carpet and up to the table beside the bed, where she saw a blue bottle, capped with iron. She reached up and grabbed it. It was half full, its contents murky and swirling. She turned to look at the woman who was kneeling by her. Miss Jesczenka, that was her name. Miss Jesczenka from the Institute.

"I'm all right," Emily said, in English. Her voice sounded strange and unfamiliar to her. She was in a hotel in Boston. She'd come to Boston to meet her grandmother, Mrs. Kendall. Emily was a Witch, and her grandmother hated Witches. "I'm all right."

"What happened to you?" Miss Jesczenka said, looking at the bottle in her hand. "What's that?"

"Nothing." Emily tucked the bottle into her pocket. "I . . . fell asleep."

"On the floor?"

Emily did not answer.

"I must have been dreaming," she said, pulling away from Miss Jesczenka and climbing to her feet. She felt so tall, a monstrous version of herself. There should be a fire, and snow outside the window. It should be cold. There should be screaming, but she was glad that there wasn't.

She felt for the hair sticks her father had given her, but she did not have them.

"My hair sticks," Emily said, looking around herself feverishly. "Where are they?"

"They're packed with your things," Miss Jesczenka said, looking up at her. "They're safe. Don't worry."

Emily brushed a hand across her eyes.

"Faery Writing," she said, under her breath, hardly realizing she spoke the words aloud. "Very important. Remember, Emilichka."

"Faery Writing?" Miss Jesczenka said. "Miss Edwards, what are you talking about?"

Emily stopped, blinking. The warmth of the room surrounded her, and she looked down at Miss Jesczenka. The woman's face was full of worry. She was not screaming. She was not the one who had been screaming. The one who had been screaming was dead. Emily swallowed hard, looked around the room some more, slowly reorienting herself. She was twenty-five years old. Her mother and father were dead, long dead, and she had drunk her memories of them.

"What is Faery Writing?" Emily said.

"It's an old-fashioned kind of magical code," Miss Jesczenka said, her tone vaguely puzzled. "No one uses it anymore. It was used quite a bit during the war, but since then, it's been superceded by better types of encryption. I believe there are still a few Faery Readers around Chatham Square, back in New York, but—"

"I want to go back to the Institute," Emily said firmly, staring into Miss Jesczenka's soft brown eyes. "I have to see Mr. Stanton."

"That's not a good idea right now," Miss Jesczenka said.

"I don't care," Emily said. "I have to see him."

Miss Jesczenka stared at her for a long time.

"All right," she said finally.

They took the afternoon train from Boston—one that would not arrive in New York until late that night. Miss Jesczenka had suggested that they wait until the next morning to depart so they could arrive at a decent hour, but Emily insisted on leaving immediately. She wanted to get away from Boston, away from the choking congestion of Witch hunters and the Sini Mira that she imagined all around her. Ever since she'd sampled the Lethe Draught, she'd felt paranoid and twitchy, as if every shadow contained something horrible within it. She remembered the revolvers she'd once carried, the comforting heavy weight of them in her pockets. She wished she had them now.

Explosions of memory kept detonating within her. A whiff

of stewed cabbage made Emily remember a time her father had cooked dinner, and she'd refused to eat because she didn't like cabbage. She'd never liked cabbage. Now she had a hundred new memories of hating its sulfury smell and nauseatingly slippery texture. It was so disorienting that Emily often found herself falling silent in the middle of a conversation, freshly experiencing pieces of her past.

If Miss Jesczenka noticed this change in Emily, she didn't comment upon it. But she did press Emily for details of her meeting with her grandparents as they clattered over the iron tracks toward New York.

"They are Scharfians," Emily said. "The Reverend Kendall is a great friend of Brother Scharfe."

Miss Jesczenka looked horrified. "Did he put you out of the house?"

Emily nodded.

"I'm sorry," Miss Jesczenka said, laying a hand over Emily's. "Truly I am."

Not as sorry as Emily felt. But the disastrous encounter with the Kendalls and their prejudices was, oddly enough, the furthest thing from Emily's mind at the moment. She was still trying to sort out the gout of memories she'd recovered the night before.

She understood now why Pap had said her mother was evil. Remembering her mother's voice, her soft gentle voice in the service of Cowdray's filthy words, made Emily feel helpless and small. How desperately she'd wanted her mother to get well. How deep the sorrow in her small, remembered heart. How she wished she could speak to her mother one more time, just for a moment, and tell her that she understood now, even if she couldn't understand then.

Emily sighed, pushing back her thoughts of her mother. They were too raw, too painful to examine for very long. She thought instead about the hair sticks and about what her father had said; that they contained an important secret, which must have been why Mrs. Kendall hadn't recognized them among her daughter's other things. They'd never belonged to Catherine Kendall at all. And the secret that her father said was written on them probably had something to do with the important work he'd been doing with his mentor in Russia. Work important enough that Warlock murderers would chase him halfway across the world to destroy it.

Emily and Miss Jesczenka arrived at the Grand Central Depot just before midnight and took a carriage uptown to the Institute. The building blazed with gaslights; it seemed that even in the darkest night, they kept all the lamps lit. The light revealed dozens of men clustered around the outer walls of the Institute, men in dark overcoats with notebooks in their hands. They stood chatting companionably, smoking cigarettes, taking furtive swigs from hidden flasks.

"Reporters," Miss Jesczenka said. There was an equal measure of delight and dread in the word. "I hardly know whether to hope they are graduates of the Institute, or to hope they are not."

The carriage pulled up at the gate that guarded the drive to the Institute, and a young gatekeeper approached. His face was held hard, in a manner that suggested he'd had to send a dozen people packing already that night. But when Miss Jesczenka leaned forward from the shadows of the carriage to speak to him, his manner became one of attentive respect.

"Who is your Sophos?" Miss Jesczenka demanded of him.

"Mr. Dreadnought Stanton," the young man said after pausing a moment and looking at Miss Jesczenka's face for reassurance. She smiled at him as if he'd done something extremely clever.

"Make sure you tell it to that pack of hoodlums out there whenever they ask." Miss Jesczenka tilted her head toward the shadowy milling reporters. "You know how easily they get their facts mixed up."

"Yes, ma'am!" the young man agreed as he hastened to swing open the gate for their carriage. It didn't open easily; it seemed to not be sitting quite right on its hinges. He had to put his shoulder into it to get it to move, but finally he managed. As they rode up the driveway, Emily saw the look of concern on her companion's face.

"He wasn't sure how he should answer," Miss Jesczenka

noted. "And that gate has never given anyone a whit of trouble before. I am afraid Mr. Stanton has not made the progress I had hoped."

"It's only been a day!" Emily said. Miss Jesczenka raised an eyebrow.

"An empire cannot be *built* in a day," she said. "But it can topple in one. Mr. Stanton must work quickly if he is to succeed. I only hope . . ." She trailed off, then gave Emily a bright smile. "Never mind. I'm sure everything will be fine."

Inside the Institute, the air was dead-still and strangely foreboding. Even though it was past midnight, there was an air of desolation and abandonment that went beyond the late hour. The glittering luster of the interior seemed to have been rubbed off by grimy, unseen hands. The polished marble walls looked flat and dull, like old sugar crusted on a plate. The red orchids, once so fat and fragrant, were withered and shrunken. Festive swags still hung, dispirited and dispiriting, drooping down in places. Miss Jesczenka planted her hands on her hips, regarding the scene with distaste.

"As many credomancers and would-be credomancers as there are in this place, and none of them think to clear away the remnants of failure and defeat?" She reached up and began pulling down bunting and wadding it up, looking for an ash can to stuff it in. The next words she spoke were under her breath, as if meant for herself alone: "Or is it that more people find it convenient to remember than to forget?"

She jerked down another swag of bunting. But this time, instead of paper and fabric fluttering gently to the floor, a huge chunk of decorative molding came crashing down. Emily leapt backward with a small cry as the hall exploded with plaster dust. She looked up with astonishment at the lathwork peeping from behind the gaping hole in the ceiling. Miss Jesczenka waved her hand before her face to clear the air.

"What is happening?" Emily blurted.

"The integrity of the Institute is a direct reflection of the strength of its leadership," Miss Jesczenka quoted in a weary textbook voice. "The Institute is falling to pieces. Literally."

"Miss Jesczenka!" The voice came from the end of the hall. Rose stood before the doorway to the office of the Sophos. Standing with Rose, peering down the hall through the settling dust, were three girls of similar attentiveness and intensity. Standing somewhat apart from this group of women was a well-fed man in a very nice suit. He looked annoyed.

"Rose?" Emily looked at Miss Jesczenka with puzzlement, as they moved toward the door of the office. "And her Admiration League friends? What are they doing here?"

"Emeritus Zeno's secretary resigned his position with the Institute on the night of Zeno's kidnapping," Miss Jesczenka said. "He was made an attractive offer by Mr. Fortissimus' Agency. It was necessary to find someone to serve as Mr. Stanton's secretary until a suitable replacement can be hired. Miss Hibble came to mind."

Emily lifted an eyebrow.

"I am satisfied that Miss Hibble's qualifications are adequate for the position. She does have an advanced secretarial degree from a . . . college," Miss Jesczenka said, obviously considering, then discarding, the adjective "well-respected." Then she bent closer, putting her lips next to Emily's ear. "Most importantly, she can be trusted. At this moment, that is an extremely rare commodity."

When Emily and Miss Jesczenka reached the door of the office, Rose stopped issuing orders to her female charges and clasped Emily's hand.

"Miss Emily! Oh, how good that you've made it back!" Rose's face was flushed and her eyes sparkled. It was clear that she was thriving within her new position. "Mr. Stanton has been simply tormented by your absence. I can't believe you went gallivanting off in his hour of need."

The three girls behind Rose nodded solemnly, regarding Emily with an odd mix of resentment and awe. Emily opened her mouth to say something, but Miss Jesczenka cut in quickly, gesturing around at the bunting and decorations.

"Miss Hibble, will you see that all this rubbish is pulled down . . . carefully . . . and that mess down there is cleaned up.

Immediately, please." Rose nodded efficiently, lifting a finger at one of the girls who stood behind her. The girl sprang to action, lifting a notebook and jotting down another item on a list that stretched down very far on the page.

"Mr. Stanton will be so glad you're back," Rose said to Miss Jesczenka under her breath. She gestured with her eyes to the well-fed man in the very nice suit who hung back from the group. He was tapping his foot and frowning, and kept consulting a pocket watch at increasingly frequent intervals. "There's trouble. *New* trouble, I mean."

"I'll speak with him," Miss Jesczenka said.

"Is Mr. Stanton in his office?" Emily asked, her hand going for the doorknob. Rose nodded seriously, subtly interposing herself between Emily and the object of her reach.

"But Miss Emily, he's ever so busy! He's in a meeting and mustn't be disturbed." Then, reverently, she opened the door herself and gestured Emily into the office's book-lined vestibule. She gestured to an uncomfortable wooden chair. "If you have a seat, I'll show you in when he's finished."

There was a steely quality in Rose's hushed voice that surprised Emily. She sat down. Rose beamed, nodding approval, then went to introduce Miss Jesczenka to the well-dressed man. Emily did not catch his name, but she could hear a quality of heavy formality in his voice. Rose and Miss Jesczenka and the man spoke for a moment, then moved away from the door of the office, and then Emily could hear no more.

Emily sat alone, in the silence. From somewhere behind the walls of books came a creaking sound. It was like being on a rigged sailboat. She fancied she could see the walls bowing inward, books tilting floorward. Gripping the arm of the chair tightly with her good hand, she heard a loud crack and watched as a half dozen particularly thick volumes tumbled from a high shelf down to the floor. She jumped to her feet, hurrying toward the door of Stanton's inner sanctum. She'd be damned if she was going to be smothered in an avalanche of books.

Quickly she opened the two large ebony doors that led to the inner office of the Sophos, and went in.

The last time she'd entered the office, she'd seen Zeno standing behind the desk, and Perun, the leader of the Sini Mira, sitting before it. This time, the scene was similar; a man stood behind the desk, and one in front of it. Only the characters in the tableau had shifted.

Stanton was standing behind the desk. His face was pale and drawn—with anger or exhaustion, she wasn't sure which. It made her catch her breath; she had never seen him look so discomposed.

Before the desk stood one of Rose's Admiration Leaguers, the sallow young man with anarchist eyes and an overbite. Emily remembered him; he'd been with Rose in the entry hall when Emily had been waiting for the carriage to take her to Central Park. Now he was staring at Stanton with adoring fervor, his hat held tightly between his fingers. He was speaking as Emily entered the room.

". . . we don't have to stop at taking these off the street, sir! We could teach the vendors who sell them a lesson. Make them think twice about—"

Emily caught a glimpse of something bright red on Stanton's desk. When he looked up and saw her, he grabbed it and shoved it into a drawer with annoyed haste. The young man whirled, his hand going to something at his waist. Something dark. A gun, Emily realized.

"Emily," Stanton said, with surprising calm. He gave the young man a look that made him duck his head and step back respectfully.

"I have to speak with you." Emily looked between him and the young man. "It's important."

"I believe we're finished," Stanton said.

"But what is my direction, sir?" The young man leaned forward, his knuckles resting on the desk. His eyes seemed to burn. "May I do as I see fit?"

Stanton looked at the young man for a moment. His jaw tensed, and rippled. Finally he said, "No, Gormley. It's out of the question."

"But, Mr. Stanton—"

"I don't want to hear about it again!" Stanton blazed, his

voice resonating off the walls. There was a pause. A strange mean smile crept over Gormley's face.

"Of course not, sir. I understand. You won't hear about it again." The young man gave Stanton a little bow. As he passed Emily on his way out, he touched the brim of his hat.

When he was gone, Emily crossed the room with short quick steps and threw herself into Stanton's arms, burying her face in his chest. She felt Stanton's shoulders relax as he drew her in closer, his lips finding the top of her head. Neither said anything. For that silent moment it was enough to share warmth, to appreciate the fact that both of their hearts still beat strongly.

"What's happened?" Stanton said finally. "What's wrong?"

Emily looked around the room, aware of a budding suspiciousness that was alien to her trusting nature. She did not trust this office, did not trust this place. Everything around her seemed suddenly menacing, malignant.

"Are we safe here?" she asked. The question made Stanton tense and look around the office.

"Safe from prying ears, you mean?" Stanton asked. "That is one thing I can vouch for." He paused. "For the time being." He paused again. "If nothing else."

Emily did not like the descending string of clauses, but she pressed forward urgently. "It's about my trip to Boston. My family—"

At that moment, the door to the office opened and Rose's blond head poked through the door. When she saw Emily, her face became reproachful.

"Oh, *there* you are, Miss Emily! You were supposed to wait outside." She looked at Stanton nervously, as if terrified she'd made a horrible gaffe. "I'm so sorry, Mr. Stanton, I told her you were busy—"

"Not now, Rose," Stanton said curtly.

"It can't wait, I'm afraid." The words were brisk; Miss Jesczenka stepped past Rose into the office. She closed the door behind herself softly. The older woman had a very worried look on her face.

"It's about the Institute's public Haälbeck doors." Miss

Jesczenka's tone made it clear that whatever business the well-dressed man had brought was urgent, pressing, and unpleasant.

Stanton let out a breath, unfolded Emily from his arms. He sank wearily into his leather desk chair.

"What about the Institute's public Haälbeck doors?" Stanton said, pressing his fingers to the bridge of his nose.

"They've been malfunctioning. Misdirecting travelers. There is a lawyer outside, representing a half dozen highly placed business interests who are claiming a loss of income resulting from the Institute's negligence. He intends to file suit in the New York County Courthouse first thing in the morning, unless the Institute wishes to discuss a settlement. He's waiting in the vestibule."

Stanton pounded a fist on the heavy polished wood of the desk.

"Settlement?" he roared. He threw himself back into his chair, raked his fingers through his hair. "You must be joking."

Miss Jesczenka gave him a look that indicated that she wasn't. Stanton exhaled exasperation through clenched teeth.

"Fine. I'll speak with him. Meanwhile, is anyone looking into this matter of the malfunctioning doors? Anyone?" Stanton looked from Miss Jesczenka to Emily; the look on his face was a bit too demanding for Emily's taste.

"Well, don't look at me," she snapped.

"Rose!" Stanton bellowed. The door from the vestibule opened quickly; the blond girl had obviously been leaning on the doorknob.

"Mr. Stanton?" Rose breathed.

"I want Professor Eames and Professor Leigh to look into this matter of the Haälbeck doors—"

Stanton paused at a small shake of the head from Miss Jesczenka.

"Not Eames," Miss Jesczenka murmured. Stanton's eyes held a moment's silent conference with hers. He sighed.

"Fine. Not Eames. McAllister, then. I want to see them first thing in the morning."

"First thing in the morning," Rose repeated to herself as

she wrote down the instructions in her notebook. Emily almost expected the girl to salute.

Then, like the blast of a cannon, there was a loud crash from the antechamber, accompanied by the sound of a suddenly muffled masculine shout. At the same moment, Stanton doubled over, grunting with pain and nearly falling off the chair.

"Mr. Stanton!" Rose hurried to his side. She was kneeling beside him and patting his cheek before Emily even knew what had happened. Miss Jesczenka jerked open the office door; stray pages fluttered into the room from the vestibule. She hurried out of the office, and Emily could hear her speaking with someone. There was a moan, and then a sharp cry of agony. Emily remembered suddenly that the lawyer had been waiting for Stanton in the vestibule. Miss Jesczenka reappeared at the door.

"The bookshelves collapsed," Miss Jesczenka said. "And it seems that our visitor now has a broken leg." She looked over at Stanton, who was climbing slowly to his feet. "Sophos, are you all right?"

"I'm fine," Stanton grumbled, pushing Rose away as she tried to help him stand. He brushed himself off, straightened his coat. His face, lined with pain, seemed immeasurably weary. "I didn't expect the office to start going so soon."

"Rose, please go and fetch a doctor," Miss Jesczenka said.

"I can help," Emily said quickly. She'd healed broken bones before; it had been one of the services she offered in Lost Pine. She looked at Stanton. "I still need to speak with you."

"As you like." Stanton was leaning heavily on the desk, his face pale. His voice sounded uncertain. Miss Jesczenka shook her head sharply.

"No, Miss Edwards. It's better that you go. It's late, and you can speak with Mr. Stanton in the morning."

For the first time in her acquaintance with Miss Jesczenka, Emily felt truly furious at the woman.

"No, I'm going to stay," she blazed. "I am going to stay, and I am going to help!"

"Miss Edwards!" Miss Jesczenka barked. Anger kindled in

her eyes, but was quickly hidden. The woman made an exasperated gesture. "All right, come on."

The vestibule was a wreck of papers, books, and bindings. The lawyer lay buried under a pile of leather-cased tomes, moaning. His left leg was twisted at an agonizing angle. Emily bent over him, her fingers finding the broken place through the fabric of his trousers. It wasn't good; the bone was shattered like a summer-dry stick.

"This place . . . this place is a shambles! It's unsafe! I'll have the buildings division here in the morning! Just see if I don't!" The lawyer's voice was high and hysterical; his eyes glinted miserably. He looked up at Miss Jesczenka, who was picking her way carefully through the wreckage. "If you think you had problems before, madam, you can't imagine the problems you have now—"

"Oh, hush," Miss Jesczenka snarled, laying a soft hand on his forehead. In an instant the man fell into unconsciousness, his head lolling back on his shoulders.

Emily looked up at her. "It's badly broken," she said.

Miss Jesczenka came to kneel next to her, sighing heavily. "Of course it is." Her voice was leaden with resignation as she looked sidelong at Emily. "You just can't take a hint, can you?"

"I want to help," Emily said fiercely. She could take a hint just fine. She knew what the woman was going to say. That she was a distraction, a nuisance. But if *Rose* could stand at Stanton's side, why couldn't she? There were things she could do, legs she could heal, bunting she could pull down . . .

"You *can't* help him now," Miss Jesczenka said softly. "Watching him suffer will make you suffer, and watching you suffer will make him suffer more."

Emily looked away, looked at her hand lying on the dark fabric of the lawyer's leg.

"You wanted to tell him something," Miss Jesczenka said. "Can it help him regain control of the Institute?"

Emily thought about it. Some new memories, the whiff of old secrets, and Witch-hating grandparents?

"No," Emily said.

"Then it can wait. You need to go away and stay away for a

while," Miss Jesczenka said. Her words were even and measured. "If you truly want to help, that's what you must do."

"And where am I supposed to go?" Emily tasted the bitterness of the words.

"There's only one safe place." Stanton's voice came from the doorway of the office. Emily looked up and saw him leaning against the doorjamb, surveying the wreckage with red-rimmed eyes. "Rose can take you."

CHAPTER THIRTEEN

Red Hand,
Gold-Colored Eye

It was almost 2 a.m. by the time the carriage conveying Emily and Rose arrived at the safe location of Stanton's promising. When Emily saw where she was being sent, she felt like climbing out of the carriage, turning tail, and taking her chances on a bench in Central Park.

"Oh, how *elegant*!" Rose breathed as the carriage came to a stop before the Stanton family brownstone on Thirty-fourth Street. "How *sophisticated*! Of course Mr. Stanton would have grown up in a place like this. Like a prince in a castle!"

Emily let out a long breath through clenched teeth. A prince with frogs for parents. That certainly was a new twist on the old stories.

At least the Senator actively ignored her. But Stanton's mother . . . Oh, she was going to just *love* having her son's malingering fiancée turn up on her doorstep, unannounced, at two in the morning. This was going to be a night to remember, though Emily doubted that she'd wish to.

Emily and Rose climbed the high narrow stairs to the heavy oak door. No light showed through the leaded glass window. Rose seized the handle of the bell and gave it three insistent pulls. There was a long wait, but finally the light of a lamp bobbed up the hallway and Broward came to the door, silver-templed and forbidding. His face was a mask of unpleasantness—unpleasantness that tempered itself only slightly when he saw that it was Emily who waited on the doorstep.

"Miss Edwards!" he said. He looked at Rose. "What can I do for you at this hour?"

"Mr. Stanton has sent a note," Rose said, briskly offering an envelope. Broward took it between two reluctant fingers, as if he were taking a soiled handkerchief. Then he opened the door and ushered them into the entryway, which was tall and decorated with classical urns.

"If you'll wait here, I'll go wake the Senator and Mrs. Stanton," he said.

Emily and Rose sat on a pair of chairs upholstered in slippery horsehair. Rose was beside herself at the honor of being admitted into the Stanton family home. She kept looking around herself like a child at an amusement park.

"How refined!" she chattered to herself. "Such excellent taste! Do you know the Stantons were one of the first families in New York? Mr. Stanton's grandfather was a general in the War of 1812, and Mr. Stanton's great-great-grandfather was the state's first attorney general." Rose paused, giggling as if catching herself being silly. "But of course you know that! You're going to marry him, after all."

Emily said nothing. She hadn't known any of it. It hadn't occurred to her to research Stanton's family tree, but she certainly wasn't going to admit that to Rose.

"Yes, the Stantons are very distinguished," was all she said.

After a long time, Broward came back down.

"Mrs. Stanton is in the library. Follow me, please."

Mrs. Stanton was sitting in a carved walnut chair, her back perfectly straight. She was immaculately turned out, having obviously taken the time to dress with great care. Or maybe she just never got undressed to begin with. Maybe she didn't sleep at all, just wrapped herself in brocade and hung upside down from a rafter.

As they entered the room, the old woman eyed Emily keenly, waiting until Emily and Rose had come to a complete stop in front of her chair before rising to greet them.

"Miss Edwards," she said coolly, leaning forward. She let her lips hang over Emily's cheek, not touching it in the slightest, and offered her an embrace that was remarkable only for how far she was able to remain from Emily and still have it seem an embrace. She hissed in Emily's ear: "You missed my lunch."

Emily bent her head. "I'm sorry," she said. She looked up at Mrs. Stanton. "I'm feeling much better now."

"Yes, it seems you recovered from the plague with astonishing alacrity." Mrs. Stanton pulled back, stared at Rose up and down, lip curling involuntarily. "I fear I have not been introduced to your . . . companion."

"Miss Rose Hibble, of Reno, Nevada." Rose smiled, extending a friendly hand. "It's an honor, Mrs. Stanton, to meet the woman who gave Mr. Dreadnought Stanton to the world."

Mrs. Stanton accepted Rose's hand limply. Emily saw her try to draw her hand away, but Rose continued pumping it enthusiastically.

"Your son is the greatest man of the nineteenth century," she said breathlessly. "How proud you must be!"

"Yes, quite proud," Mrs. Stanton said, finally reclaiming her hand with a little jerk. "Won't you both have a seat?"

"Such a grand room!" Rose said, looking around the library. "So many books! Did Mr. Stanton read them all?"

"I feel certain he read a great number of them," Mrs. Stanton said, then turned her gaze to Emily. Emily took a very mean comfort in the look, which indicated that whatever her own failings, she at least compared favorably to Rose.

There was a long silence as Mrs. Stanton withdrew her son's note from the pocket of her dress. She made a great show of unfolding it. She lifted a small pair of silver spectacles to her eyes and reread the letter slowly. There was a look of amazement on her face that seemed quite carefully cultivated. Finally, she folded the letter back into its envelope and regarded Emily with gimlet eyes.

"Miss Edwards, this letter from my son requests . . . well, perhaps *requests* is not the appropriate word . . . rather, *demands* that you shelter here for a few nights. Perhaps you can elaborate on the astonishingly scanty explanation he offered in support of this . . . scheme?"

"She's in danger, Mrs. Stanton!" Rose blurted. "Terrible danger, from all types of—"

"I believe I addressed Miss Edwards," Mrs. Stanton said to

Rose. Her eyes were as green as her son's, but colder than the deepest part of the coldest ocean. Even Rose—whose buoyancy was typically sufficient to lift her above even the most pointed dismissals—could not escape the crushing weight of the old woman's disdain. She curled back in her chair and turned red.

Mrs. Stanton turned her cool green eyes back to Emily. "Is this true, Miss Edwards? Are you in danger?"

"Yes," Emily said. "Mr. Stanton felt that I would be safest here. But I don't want to be any trouble. Maybe I should go to a hotel."

Say yes, Emily prayed, during the woman's long silence. *Please say yes.*

"No," Mrs. Stanton said finally. "Of course you must stay here. My son's note indicates that he will come for breakfast in the morning and explain everything." She paused. "What kind of danger are you in, precisely?"

Emily pressed her lips together and cursed Rose for her prattling nature.

"Things are unsettled at Mr. Stanton's Institute," Emily said carefully. Mrs. Stanton waited for more, but Emily did not offer it. Mrs. Stanton turned to Rose.

"Perhaps you can elaborate, Miss Hibble," Mrs. Stanton said. "You appear to be intimately acquainted with the circumstances."

Being invited to speak, especially after the sharp rebuke she'd received previously, worked like a tonic on Rose. Her cheeks flushed eagerly.

"They want to hurt her because she's Mr. Stanton's fiancée, of course! They will do anything to get to him."

"They?" Mrs. Stanton said.

"Rex Fortissimus and his thugs," Rose said, her voice dropping low. "He's a despicable cad. There's no depth to which he will not stoop. Of course it's all lies . . . that awful garish red color . . . you know, they say red is the most grabbing of the colors. That's why Fortissimus used it, of course—"

"Used what?" Emily broke in, looking between Rose and Mrs. Stanton. "What are you talking about?"

Clumsy guard stole into Rose's gaze.

"Oh, you haven't seen it?" When neither Emily nor Mrs. Stanton gave any sign of understanding what she was referring to, she looked uncomfortable and shifted in her chair. "Well, never mind then. It's nothing to worry about."

"Rose, if it's something about Mr. Stanton, you have to tell me." Emily said this too fiercely, forgetting Mrs. Stanton and the need for propriety. She did, to her credit, restrain herself from taking Rose by the shoulders and giving her a shake.

"It's nothing, honest." Rose hastened for safer subjects. "Poor Mr. Stanton! He's bearing up as well as he can, of course, but I must remind him to eat. He's a shadow, an absolute shadow—"

"Why on earth are you concerned with my son's appetite?" Mrs. Stanton asked, arching an eyebrow.

"I am helping him as his secretary," Rose said proudly. "He needs people around him he can trust. He can't trust any of those magisters of his, I can tell you that. They're a rebellious, treasonous lot. Half of them have thrown in with Fortissimus, but it's finding out which half that's presenting the problem . . ."

Emily listened with more interest, and even Mrs. Stanton seemed to have lowered her customary shield slightly. Rose, sensing her audience's focused attention, leaned forward and continued in a conspiratorial tone.

"What's worse, Fortissimus has been recruiting students away right and left, offering them apprenticeships at his Agency. And some of the professors have left, too. But of course, there are many who are loyal to Mr. Stanton. And Mr. Stanton is doing everything he can." She paused. "I swear, I don't know why he doesn't send Fortissimus packing like he did the Dark Sorcerer of Trieste!"

"I don't think he has enough power to do that yet," Emily said.

Rose looked at her with a mixture of sympathy and dismay. "Not enough power? What a thing to say! And to hear it from you, Miss Emily—well, never mind! We shall stick by Mr. Stanton until the very end. We shall not believe any of the lies Fortissimus puts out about him!"

"What lies?" Mrs. Stanton said.

Rose pressed her lips together again, adjusted the intricate flounces of her dress. It was clear that she knew something that no force on earth could induce her to reveal. The naked cherubs on the mantel chimed three times. Rose stood quickly.

"Oh, is that the time?" she said. "I must be getting back. And don't worry, I'm sure Mr. Stanton will make everything all right. You must believe in him."

Emily said nothing as she watched Rose go. There was a long silence in the room, unbroken until Mrs. Stanton finally spoke.

"I'll have Broward show you to the guest room, then," she said.

Emily wouldn't have rushed downstairs the next morning if she hadn't been expecting to see Stanton at the breakfast table. But the only Stantons she found seated around the table were the ones she didn't want to see—the impassive Senator and his sour wife, and Euphemia (munching on a triangle of dry toast) and Ophidia (sipping weak milk tea). Hortense appeared to be missing in action. Just her luck, Emily thought; Hortense was the only other member of the family who didn't seem to despise her.

"I've saved you the morning papers, Miss Edwards." Mrs. Stanton pushed them toward her. "You seem to follow the news so fanatically."

Emily glanced down at the headlines. She intended just to scan them for the sake of politeness, but she was shocked to see that the news of the disasters on the Pacific Coast had been supplemented by accounts of similar horrors in other parts of the country—Tennessee, Arkansas, Kentucky—and even other parts of the world.

"Warlock Experts Surmise Ongoing Problems Are Due to Expanding Earth, with Black Exunge Being Released at Rip Zones," read a headline in *The New York Times*.

As Emily read, she was aware of Mrs. Stanton's pointedly consulting a small gold watch on a chain. After an extended scrutiny of the timepiece, the old woman clucked disapprovingly and snapped it shut.

"One can only assume my son has decided not to join us for breakfast," Mrs. Stanton observed with astringent crispness. "How very like him."

Emily did not look up from her papers.

"He said he'd be here," she said softly. "And he will."

And indeed, at that moment, Broward leaned in beside her, her reticule in his hand. A soft noise came from within it.

"Excuse me, miss," he said. "But your bag has been bleating."

Emily withdrew the slate eagerly, holding it in her lap to evade scrutiny. Her excitement dimmed as she scanned the words Stanton had written: IMPOSSIBLE TO GET AWAY . . . CAN'T EXPLAIN . . . FORGIVE ME . . .

"I do hope that is some kind of magical gimcrack," Mrs. Stanton said, interrupting Emily's furtive examination of the slate. "We haven't room here in town for livestock."

Emily gave her a glimpse of the slate—long enough for the old woman to note the leaping lambs but not long enough to read the message written on it. She'd be damned if she'd give the old battle-ax the satisfaction.

"It's just a toy," she said. "It lets us send notes."

Mrs. Stanton knitted her brow, as if the idea of lambs—or perhaps toys—pained her. She inclined her head toward her husband.

"How utterly puerile," she murmured, her voice carrying like an opera singer's.

The Senator, obviously accustomed to ignoring his wife completely, did not comment. Emily lifted her chin.

"He'll be here tomorrow morning without fail," she said brightly. But no amount of brightness was sufficient to mask the dark worry she felt. He'd looked so completely lost in that crumbling office, surrounded by the hallmarks of failure. And there was nothing she could do about it except sit here in this house, surrounded by people who didn't want her, and pray that he would have the strength to prevail.

Using her napkin, she quickly wiped the slate clean, then laid it in her lap, where prying eyes couldn't read the words she wrote on it. ALL IS WELL. HAVE CHALLENGED YOUR MOTHER TO A GAME OF HORSESHOES. WILL INFORM OF RESULTS. Then, slowly and with care, she added the words I LOVE YOU. She stared at the slate with a low heart. The sentiment looked so small and uninspired when written.

She was surprised when the words vanished from the slate, as if erased by an unseen hand. The slate baaed softly as new words appeared on it.

I LOVE YOU, TOO, Stanton's handwriting read. BE CAREFUL. MOTHER CHEATS.

With a secret smile, Emily tucked the pencil away and returned the slate to her reticule. Now, speaking of horseshoes—what the hell *was* she supposed to do here all day?

As if reading the question in Emily's face, Mrs. Stanton lifted a teacup to her lips.

"Do you sew, Miss Edwards?"

Emily contemplated the question. Certainly she sewed. She used to sew patches in Pap's overalls. But she didn't figure that was the kind of sewing Mrs. Stanton was referring to. She lifted her right hand, the one of ivory, regretfully.

"I'm afraid not," Emily said.

"Oh," said Mrs. Stanton with a frown. Emily wasn't sure if the frown was because she didn't sew, or because she'd lost her hand, or because she was so badly bred as to admit both of these things. "But I suppose you read?"

Emily flushed hot under her collar; Mrs. Stanton had already asked her that question once, and knew the answer full well. But she nodded anyway.

"How extravagantly fortunate," Mrs. Stanton said. "Perhaps we could have some more Wordsworth after breakfast."

Emily cringed. She hardly knew the words were on her lips before she said, "I'm sorry, but I must . . . go out."

"Go out?"

"I have an appointment downtown," Emily lied. She wasn't sure where the lie came from, but it was a blunt and convulsive response to the thought of having to read Wordsworth to Mrs. Stanton all morning.

"Certainly someone should accompany you," Mrs. Stanton said, giving Euphemia a pointed look that Euphemia did her best to avoid by scrutinizing a crumb on her napkin. "Being that your life hangs in the balance under the Damoclean sword of some kind of unspecified danger."

Silently, Emily cursed Rose once again.

"Rose may have overstated the case a bit," Emily said. "I'm sure it's perfectly safe, and I'd hate to be any trouble—" Then she had a flash of inspiration. She lowered her voice. "It's a *banking matter.*"

Ever since she'd earned twenty thousand dollars from Professor Mirabilis, Emily had learned that money was a ready excuse for any occasion. Whenever she spoke of it, people shuffled their feet and looked away, as if she'd spoken about her drawers. She knew that banking matters were private, and that no one would interfere with her if she had to go out to attend to one.

"Farley can take you," the Senator said gruffly, not looking up from behind his paper. Farley, Emily assumed, was the name of some ancient Stanton family retainer, a grizzle-pated old man with his back bent from bowing and the custom of twisting his hat around in his hands.

After breakfast, Emily went upstairs. She hadn't really had a plan in mind when she'd made her excuse for an escape—her only thought had been to avoid Wordsworth and all those semicolons and larks. But now, as she thought about it, a plan formed in her mind. She needed to find out about those hair sticks. Miss Jesczenka said that there were Faery Readers near someplace called Chatham Square. So that's where she was going.

Tucking the hair sticks into her black silk reticule, she hurried downstairs to where Farley was waiting. Far from being a bent old graybeard, Farley was actually a nice-looking young man with bright red hair. He wore a ridiculous green livery that made him look like an overgrown leprechaun. He touched his cap and gave her a smile.

"Where to, miss?" he asked, as he handed her into the carriage.

Emily cast a glance back to the Stanton house, so solid and respectable. She gave him the address of the bank where she had her money on deposit. She didn't know New York well enough yet to know if the bank was anywhere near Chatham Square, but at least it would take her away from here.

They drove through the bright morning streets, beneath tall stone edifices and past old wooden buildings that hinted at the city's long history. Within a few minutes they arrived before the bank's sober facade of white marble. Farley unfolded the step and extended a hand to help her down. When she did not descend, he looked at her quizzically.

"Miss?"

"Mr. Farley, this is going to be a great shock to you, but I have no banking to do."

"No banking, miss?"

"No. I have another errand. One I would prefer the Stantons not know of." She knew that she was skating on thin ice. She remembered stories from *Ladies' Repository* in which women had been blackmailed by carriage drivers who'd been entrusted with secrets, but she didn't quite know what other choice she had. Give the man the slip and hire a different carriage? He'd gossip about that, too, if gossip he would. There seemed little alternative.

"You need to go somewhere else, miss?" His voice was low and conspiratorial, but with a friendly cast to it. "I can take you wherever you require."

"Well, that's the thing," Emily said. "I don't really know where I'm going." She leaned forward. "I need to find someone called a Faery Reader. I've been told that I might find one around Chatham Square."

Farley whistled. "That's the rough end of the Bowery. I'd catch hell for taking you there, excuse my saying so."

"And I'd catch hell for going," Emily said. "But neither one of us have to catch anything if we keep our mouths shut, right?"

"Right enough," he said. "And better someone you can trust taking you down there than one of these rummy b'hoys who'll leave you to get your throat cut."

"And I do need to go." She reached for his hand and pressed a gold piece into it. She felt that she'd gotten quite skilled in the niceties of bribery, and knew that gold usually smoothed over any objections most democratically. "Will you take me?"

"Sure thing, miss!" he said, looking at the gold piece with astonishment before climbing up into his seat and clucking to the horses.

The area surrounding Chatham Square was lively and rowdy, even at that early hour of the morning. Straggling merrymakers from the night before clustered before bars and saloons; newsboys with satchels full of papers darted past penny-cup-rattling veterans in tattered uniforms. Soot-bricked lodging houses shouldered up against museums featuring mermaids and sword swallowers. Advertisements for magical nostrums, boxing matches, politicians, and brands of tobacco had been pasted up on most available surfaces. Everything was designed to be seen by night; by the light of day the colors were brassy and overbright. Above the street, the black, greasy cast-iron framework of the elevated railroad hulked like an Aberrated centipede.

Farley pulled up to a stop at an intersection where a police officer stood directing traffic.

"Hey, Mack!" Farley called down.

"Aye?" The police officer strolled toward the carriage.

"You ever hear of such a thing as a Faery Reader?"

"Faery Reader?" The police officer tilted his hat back with his billy club and tried to peer into the darkened carriage. "Why, ain't noon of 'em left, save old Pearl." The officer gestured with his stick. "Block and a half oop on the right. Look fer the sign; red hand, gold-colored eye, ye'll not miss it."

The driver tipped his hat to the officer, and clucked to the horses.

Emily sank back in her seat as the carriage lurched forward. *Red hand, gold-colored eye.* Many Witches and War-locks in trade used the sign of the open hand with an eye winking from its palm to denote the services they provided; the individual businesses differentiated themselves by changing the color of the hand and the eye color of the orb in the palm. Just driving the block and a half, Emily saw a blue hand with a black eye (that was a curse worker), a black hand with a red heart (love spells, the fool), and, finally, a red hand with a gold-colored eye hanging outside a dilapidated shop. Surrounding the image was flowery script in faded gold letters:

Abner S. Pearl, Warlock De-Lux.
Palms Read, Fortunes Told, Faery Writing Decyphered.

Emily lighted from the carriage, pausing before the front of the shop. The sidewalk before the building was piled high with boxes and furnishings, around and on which a half dozen children of varying ages climbed and swung and played. A plump older woman in a neat white apron came out of the shop, bearing a box that she set with the others. She gave Emily a friendly smile.

"Abner Pearl?" Emily inquired, looking up at the sign.

"Just inside," the woman said with a pleasant Irish lilt. "Ye'll have to hurry, though. The movers will be here presently, and then he'll have no time for ye."

The door creaked as Emily entered, and somewhere above her was the tinkle of a bell. The shop was high ceilinged but dark nonetheless. It was dusty and smelled of old lacquer, and had a freshly emptied feeling; it was obvious from the bright shadows where pictures had once hung, and the walls where shelves had once rested, that the owners were just packing up shop.

From the back room came the sound of hammering.

"Hello?" Emily called. The hammering stopped and a late-middle-aged man emerged from the back. He wore a black eye patch. The frayed hems of his cuffs showed past his too-short jacket sleeves. He wiped his hands on a dirty-looking cloth as he regarded Emily with his one bright eye.

"Can I help ye, miss?"

"My name is Emily Edwards. I'm looking for a Faery Reader," Emily said.

The man threw the dirty towel over his shoulder, grinned at her.

"Abner S. Pearl. But if you're looking for a Faery Reader,

I'm afraid you're a few days late on that score," he said. "Shop's closed."

"Closed?"

"No custom from folks wanting Faery Reading anymore, and too much competition for all the other work. The swells with the money go to the fancy hand-and-eye shops on Broadway. And with times tight like they are, the poor folks in Chatham Square can't afford such extravagances." He paused, leaning forward onto the counter. "Family and I are movin' west, out to California."

"Why, I'm from California!" Emily said. "What part are you going to?"

"San Francisco," Pearl said. "You know it?"

"A little," Emily said. "I've been there once or twice. But aren't you worried about—"

"The earthquakes and Aberrancies?" Pearl waved a hand, made a scoffing sound. "And how do you think we got ourselves a place out there so cheap? I got my rifle and my silver bullets. If I have to dispatch a few of the slimy beasts for a chance at a better life, then that's just what I'll do. Mrs. Pearl!" Pearl raised his voice in a shout, and the plump woman ducked her head in the front door. "This lady here's from California. Knows it right well, she does!"

"You don't say." Mrs. Pearl stepped into the shop, hands on her hips. "Well, perhaps ye can answer me a few questions. I'm thinking of starting a dressmaking concern when we get there, but I haven't the first clue what ladies in that area might like." She looked Emily up and down, scrutinizing her costume. "Fashion minded, are they?"

"Some are, I'm sure—" Emily began, thinking that the Pearls would probably be better off opening an ammunition supply store, but Mrs. Pearl broke in, eagerly.

"Many dress shops? I've heard that it's all gold miners and horse thieves and crazy men, but then I said to Mr. Pearl, crazy men got to have wives like anyone else, ain't they?"

"I suppose," Emily said. She wasn't quite sure why Mrs. Pearl was staring at her with a such a puzzled expression, until the woman blurted:

"Why, it's a downright boggler! I could swear I've seen you

somewhere before, but I just can't place you. What did you say your name was? Emily Edwards?"

Emily nodded.

"That sounds awful familiar," Mrs. Pearl said, shaking her head. "Can't place it, though. You sure we haven't met?"

"I couldn't say," Emily said. "But I doubt it."

"Hmm." Mrs Pearl shrugged. "Well, perhaps it will come to me. Mr. Pearl, are you coming out? The movers will be here shortly."

"Coming, Mrs. Pearl, coming . . ." He looked at Emily. "Now, if there's nothing further—"

"But there is!" Emily said. "I came here for Faery Reading services. Is the shop really closed for good?"

"Closed for good," Pearl said with finality. "I've had it up to here with the headaches."

"Is there anyone else in the neighborhood I could go to?" Emily asked.

Pearl gave a great laugh. "Anyone else in the neighborhood? Sure, there's no one left in all New York does Faery Reading anymore. No call for it. I'm the last." Pearl fell silent for a moment. "Makes me feel right-out old, it does. Last of a generation."

"Enough of yer moonin', Mr. Pearl," Mrs. Pearl said. She tilted a confiding head toward Emily. "He does take on about things."

Two children thundered in the front door, whooping their way through the shop. They leveled fingers at each other and made shooting sounds.

"They're here! They're here! Movers are here! Off to California! Hooray!"

Mrs. Pearl laid a hand on her cheek and clucked.

"Oh dear, they're starting to run wild already. Boys, calm yerselves." Mrs. Pearl glanced out the front window. A large moving van was parked at the curb, horses stamping and shaking their harnesses. "Mr. Pearl, tell your sons to behave."

"*My* sons?" Pearl lifted his hands with good-natured incredulity. "Heavens, woman! *My* sons when they run about like wild creatures?" He gave Emily a kind smile. "I'm sorry, miss. I wish I could help you, really I do. But I'll have to bid ye good day now."

Emily caught his sleeve as he began walking past her.

"Mr. Pearl, please. I know you're busy, but—"

"Careful with the china now, that was me Gran's!" Mr. Pearl shouted past Emily, at the movers who were already beginning to load boxes under Mrs. Pearl's efficient direction.

"Mr. Pearl—"

"It's out of the question," Pearl said. "Me and me whole family, we're on the ten a.m. train tomorrow morning. And anyway, all my tools are packed up. Nothing to be done."

"I'll pay you well," Emily said, but Pearl just shrugged.

"Got all the money I need for the trip," he said. He was still watching the movers, wincing as he heard a box rattle when they lifted it. "Have a care, now!" He shouted past her again. "I'd better get out there, or they'll smash me things to bits—"

"Wait." Emily's voice was vibrant with urgency; it made Pearl stop and look at her. Quickly, Emily dug in her black silk reticule for the hair sticks. She showed them to him in the palm of her hand. They gleamed in the low, dusty light. "There's something written on them, I know there is. Something my father wrote. I never knew my father, and this is the only way I'll ever be able to find out anything about him. Please, Mr. Pearl. If you're really the only one who can read them . . . Please help me."

Pearl looked at the hair sticks, and then at Emily. For the first time, he seemed to see her. Gently, he took the hair sticks from her hand and examined them, holding them up to the light and peering at them closely.

"Well, if there's writing on these, there's not much," Pearl said, examining each long side of the square-sectioned, tapered sticks. He tapped his finger on the widest, thickest end of one of them. "And see all this engraving near the top. Ye can't write anything over engraving. But there's a smooth bit just below it, I suppose there could be something . . ." He paused, stroking his chin. Then he smiled at her again. "Well, I must say. I know about fathers, and I know about secrets. It's a shame when one gets tangled up with th' other . . ."

He shook his head sharply, then handed her back the hair

sticks decisively. "No. I'm sorry, but no. I've promised the kids that I'll take them out for ice cream. One last bit of fun before we leave New York forever. I can't disappoint 'em. I promised. I'm sorry, Miss Edwards. Good day to you."

Emily was turning to go, bitter disappointment burning under her breastbone, when Mrs. Pearl reappeared in the doorway. She was goggling at Emily.

"Emily Edwards!" she breathed, pressing her hands against her red cheeks. "Why, that's who you are! Miss Emily Edwards, in my shop! And me going to California in the morning, or I'd have the whole neighborhood in to see. Of course I know you; your picture is in the window right next door!"

Emily stared at the babbling woman.

"Excuse me?" she asked.

"Why, your picture's on sale at the photographer's shop right next door, up there with all the pictures of last season's debutantes! Mr. Pearl, this is Emily Edwards, the girl who's to marry Mr. Stanton of the credomancers' Institute! Surely you've heard of her?"

"Why, sure," Pearl said. "The papers say the Investment didn't go too well, though."

"Well, never mind that!" Mrs. Pearl waved a hand. "All any man needs is a good woman to straighten him out. Are you to be married soon? What will you wear? Do you have a dressmaker yet? Oh, what am I saying, I'm off to California in the morning . . . Mercy! To think that you're in my very shop!"

Emily was suddenly struck by an idea.

"I'll make you a deal," she said, looking at Mrs. Pearl. "If they know about me here, they'll surely know about me in San Francisco. If I buy one of those pictures you say they're selling next door and sign it . . . sign it 'To my most esteemed dressmaker in New York'"—Emily turned to Pearl—"will you read my hair sticks?"

"Why, that would be a boost for business," Mrs. Pearl said, looking at Mr. Pearl. "Having a famous customer would be as good as money in the bank!"

Emily looked at Mr. Pearl. "Furthermore, if anyone writes me for a reference I will write them back on Institute stationery, and assert that Mrs. Abner S. Pearl is the most talented dressmaker in New York, and that her moving to San Francisco is a loss from which I have yet to recover."

"Oh, Abner, please!" Mrs. Pearl said.

Pearl sighed. He reached up one finger to scratch the skin under his black eye patch. He thought for a long time.

"I promised the children," he said. "Ice cream, remember?"

"I'll take them," Mrs. Pearl countered swiftly. "Please, Abner. Please!"

"You know I can't say no when you call me Abner," Mr. Pearl said, reddening and smiling at the same time. He shrugged. "Well, then, get along, Mrs. Pearl, and tell the movers not to pack the green box. I guess I'll be needing it."

The green packing crate was retrieved from the sidewalk and carried into the big, empty backroom. Pearl picked up a hammer and started prying up the wooden lid. Iron and pine squeaked. When he'd gotten the lid off he set it to one side. He took off his jacket and rolled his sleeves, holding them up with black elastic garters. He reached into the box and pulled out a black velvet charm cap, decorated with cheap decorations of stamped and gilt pot metal. He adjusted this on his head. Then he reached into the box and pulled out newspaper-wrapped pieces of brass. These he assembled swiftly, slotting and tightening wing nuts. Assembled, the brass pieces made up a kind of stand, like the kind a jeweler might use. Two clamps stood ready to hold a piece for examination, and on the sides were two lamps with shades to focus their light down on the work. Pearl set this apparatus up on a swept-clean worktable, then returned to the green box. From it he pulled a large metal case, enameled with black and girdled with a pencil-thin gold pinstripe. It had a lock on the front. He unlocked it with a key that he wore around his throat. As he opened it, a faint glow escaped from beneath the lid.

All of this was done with an air of quiet solemnness that was abruptly shattered when two boys, both with black hair and blue eyes, thundered in and seized their father's elbow.

"Everything's loaded up, Dad!"

"The boxes have gone down to the station!"

"You promised to take us for ice cream!"

"Hold on!" Pearl bellowed at the boys. He held down the lid of the box, obviously nervous of spilling any of the contents. He gave the boys a fierce look. "You hooligans will upset the whole works! Off with ye. Go find yer mother—"

"Their mother's right here." Mrs. Pearl stood by the doorway, hands on her hips. "Boys, don't annoy your father. Go on upstairs and tell yer sisters to get cleaned up. I'm taking the lot of you over to the ice cream parlor." This news set the boys whooping up the stairs. Mrs. Pearl gave her husband a conspiratorial smile, and he smiled back gratefully. He gestured her over, gave her a fond peck on the lips.

"Wife, yer a marvel," he said.

"One good turn deserves another," she said, winking to Emily as she followed the boys upstairs.

Once silence had returned to the room, Pearl lifted the lid of the black enameled box. Inside were many small brushes and glass pots of powders in variously glowing colors. Oranges and pinks and blues, shimmering like gold at the bottom of a stream.

Pearl took one of the hair sticks and fastened it into a clamp on the brass apparatus. Then he lifted his hands to both of the lamps and muttered the words *lux ingens.*

Emily had to shade her eyes against the violent brightness that flared from the lamps. While most of the glare was directed downward, toward the scrutinized object, it still was bright enough to make her eyes water. The light was perfectly clear and white. The hair stick shimmered under the brilliant illumination, and Emily fancied she could already begin to see something more on it than the simple surface engraving.

Pearl lifted three of the pots of glowing powder from the black-enameled box. He unscrewed the top of two of the pots, then selected a pair of brushes—a large one and a smaller one. Then he pulled out a long, soft leather case. From this, he withdrew a long loupe, about nine inches long, wider at one end and narrowing to the size of a dime at the small end. Emily watched with fascination as he fastened the loupe over his head with a strange kind of head harness. He did not drop the loupe over his good eye, though; instead, he lifted his eye patch and gave Emily a wink. She stifled a gasp.

She had assumed that he wore an eyepatch because he'd lost an eye, but this was not the case at all. The eye beneath the patch was not destroyed. In fact, it was perfectly normal. But where his right eye was blue and correctly proportioned, his left eye was gold-colored, much larger, wider, and fringed with red lashes. It was an eye that did not belong in his face.

"Have to keep it covered up, or Mrs. Pearl gets after me." He brought the loupe up over this strange eye. "Gives her a turn. She never liked the idea of me having someone else's eye."

"Then it's not . . . yours?"

"Sure, it's mine! I paid enough for it. See, me own eyesight wasn't never that good, and you have to have good eyesight to be a Faery Reader. In one eye, at least." He fussed with the loupe until he'd gotten it just as he liked it. "So back in the Old Country, before I come over, I bought it off a young man with the consumption. He'd always had the best eyesight in the village."

"How interesting," Emily said, if by interesting one meant gruesome and queer.

"Well, his family had hit a rough patch, and he wanted to feel that he could be some use to 'em."

"Did he die?" Emily asked.

"Well, eventually, I suppose he did. But not from me buying his eye." Pearl lifted a hand. "That was strictly a money transaction, fair and square. I meant him no harm. We had an old Celt Witch do the honors for us. He woke up five pounds richer, and I woke up with one eye that could see for miles without strainin'. Didn't do much for my fine appearance, but somehow I managed to convince Mrs. Pearl to take me anyway."

Pearl took the larger brush and dipped it into one of the opened pots, which contained powder that glowed white. He carefully tapped the end of the brush over the pot and conveyed a minute amount of the white glowing dust to the hair stick in his hand.

"Ye don't want to be breathing too much of this powder,"

he commented quietly. "Faery Readers have gone mad from years and years of inhalin' this infernal stuff. Not as mad as the Faery Writers, of course, but that's why you never had one who was th' other."

"How do you mean?" Emily asked, watching as he gently brushed one side of the hair stick with the brush. His movements were clean and precise. "You mean that Faery Writing and Faery Reading aren't the same profession?"

"Completely different," Pearl said. "Faery Writing's about the most maddening magical occupation a man could undertake," Pearl said. "That's why no one does it anymore. There's better ways to hide secrets now. Cryptocrystalography, Otherwhere Encoding . . ." He paused, squinted closer at the hair stick. "Gar, look at that, will you! It's there all right. And bless me if it ain't in violet scale!" He turned to look at Emily, and it was as if his strange golden eye peered at her through the tiny end of his long loupe.

"Violet scale?" Emily prompted him.

"Why, I haven't seen violet scale since . . . well, ever! No one writes violet scale. No one in their right mind, that is."

"I don't understand."

"There are a variety of scales at which Faery Writing can be executed," Pearl said. "Red scale, that's the largest. Most Faery Writers, back in the day, they worked in the red scale. Most any Warlock with a pot of red reading could decipher it. The scales got smaller after that . . . orange scale, yellow scale, green scale, blue scale . . . You saw yellow scale sometimes, and blue scale almost never. But violet scale . . ." He shook his head. He opened a specially fitted compartment in the black enamel box and pulled out a very tiny vial of glowing purple powder. He paused, showing her the vial.

"In all my years, ever since I put this kit together, I've never had call to open this vial even once," he said. "And here it is, my last day in this city after ten years, and you come along. It's like fate, don't you think?"

"Oh, certainly," Emily said.

"The only folks who used violet scale much at all were the Russians. It was a particular favorite of Peter the Great's secret service. Maybe you got some old invasion plans for the coast of Malta scribbled on here."

Pearl lifted out the tiny vial of glowing purple powder and placed it carefully onto his workbench. He opened the vial and brushed it on the hair stick. Infinitely tiny writing appeared. Pearl peered at it for a long time.

"Oh, I'll have a headache for days from reading this," he said ruefully. "I've never seen tinier." He paused again, squinting harder. "Wait, I can just make out a name . . . Aleksei Morozovich. Just as I guessed. Russian!"

Aleksei Morozovich. She knew that name. Where had she heard it? She turned it over and over in her mind, trying to remember.

"Yes, I can decipher this," Pearl said after peering at the stick for a little longer. "It'll be tedious line-by-line business, and I'll have to stay up all night working on it, but I believe I can have it ready for you first thing in the morning, with a transcription written in my own fine hand. But I won't do it for a penny under two hundred." Pearl's tone was slightly apologetic, but firm. "That's the price of the headache I'll have once I'm done."

Emily licked her lips. Even though she was sure Pearl expected her to haggle, it sounded like a fair deal, and the thought of haggling over her dead father's memory was repugnant to her.

"All right," Emily said firmly, extending her good hand. They shook on it. "But I am sorry you'll have to stay up all night."

"Oh, I'll sleep on the train." Pearl waved a hand. "And I wouldn't have slept tonight anyway; all the beds have been packed up and we're camping out on blankets. The kids are all aflutter about it. Kids love adventures." He put a finger aside his nose. "Grown up folks, too, sometimes."

Emily smiled at him.

"Tomorrow morning, then?"

"Tomorrow morning," Pearl said, bending back over his work.

* * *

When she got outside, Farley was nowhere to be seen. Emily had been in the shop for quite a while, though, so it was to be expected that he'd found someplace to park the carriage and was waiting nearby. The traffic had picked up considerably as morning marched toward noon; the street hummed with flower sellers and fruit vendors and drayage wagons and light carts.

She went next door to the shop Mrs. Pearl had directed her to. And, indeed, there it was in the window—a large, full-length picture of her in the extravagant white ballgown she'd worn the night of the Investment, posed with her glittering ringed hand resting on her shoulder. It scarcely looked like her, the picture had been so carefully retouched and softened. She looked like an angel.

When she went into the shop, she was hardly surprised that the clerk did not recognize her. In the picture she was all white and glowing and sparkling and delicate. In real life, by contrast, she was grimy from spending two hours in Abner S. Pearl's back room and the feather on her hat was drooping limply from the already oppressive heat.

"Can I help you, miss?"

"I'm interested in obtaining a copy of the photo in the window . . . the photo of Miss Emily Edwards."

"Nice picture, isn't it?" he asked. "What size did you want? Cabinet or portrait?" He showed her both, and she selected the one that seemed small enough to pack but still large enough for Mrs. Pearl to show off in her store.

"So you sell these?" Emily asked. "But they have the name of another studio on them."

"Oh, we didn't take the picture," the man said. "We just sell copies. Pictures of well-known folks are sold all over town. I imagine you could find this photo in a hundred stores from the Battery up to Harlem. It's our most popular print."

"You have to be kidding me," Emily said.

"Well, especially after all the brouhaha that's been going on at the Institute. Everyone knows about Dreadnought Stanton, but no one knows about this mysterious beauty he's marrying. I hear she's some kind of cattle baron's daughter. Rich as Croesus, I'll wager. She's awful pretty, don't you think?"

Emily blushed, but didn't answer.

"That Dreadnought Stanton, I'm sure he's a fine man," the clerk continued. "Son of a Senator, he comes from good stock. But a man needs a good woman to stand behind him. To help him keep his feet on the ground." The clerk looked at the photo, and Emily saw something in his eyes—a mix of wistfulness and desire. It startled her. And it was so terribly odd, this man staring at her image so longingly while the real her was standing right in front of him, in flesh and blood, and he didn't even make the connection. The clerk was transfixed by the Emily Edwards in the photo, but he didn't give the real Emily Edwards a second glance.

After a long moment staring at the picture, the clerk looked up at her, gave her a cheerful smile.

"Let me wrap this up for you, then."

After Emily purchased the photo, she returned briefly to Pearl's shop to deliver it. Mrs. Pearl had gotten the children cleaned up for the promised trip to the ice cream parlor, and they waited in a neat—if somewhat disorderly—line as Emily used a steel-nibbed fountain pen to carefully write the promised accolades. Mrs. Pearl smiled at the inscription as she waited for the ink to dry.

"As good as money in the bank, an endorsement from the beauty queen of New York City!" the woman said gleefully. She looked at Emily. "Don't you worry about a thing, Miss Edwards. I'll keep my man working on those items for you all night, if required. And thank you . . . Thank you!"

Emily shook the woman's hand and left the shop quickly.

From the distance came a rumbling, creaking sound. Emily looked up at the elevated tracks above the street as a huge steam engine thundered overhead. Ashes and soot and sparks filtered down in a fine snowy drift as the train passed; passersby, apparently used to being showered with bits of debris, lifted newspapers or parcels over their heads. Emily darted forward, taking shelter behind a large wagon loaded with boxes of live chickens. The birds chuckled at the beauty queen of New York City as she brushed flakes of ash from her dress.

The sound of a whooping laugh from across the street made Emily look up from her dusting. Her eyes found a bookseller's shop across the street—a hole-in-the-wall with tomes piled high on rickety tables out front. On one of the tables was a great pile of red books, freshly printed. The color was quite eye-catching.

There were two men standing in front of the shop, laughing with a big man in sleeve garters who appeared to be the proprietor. They were holding up one of the red books, passing it between themselves, reading passages. The recitations, which Emily could not hear, sent the men into gales of impolite laughter that was accompanied with some pointed rib-elbowing. Emily's eye caught a flash of green; Farley in his leprechaun-hued livery was standing just behind the men. He appeared to be listening to them, but unlike the others, he was grim-faced and unsmiling. He snatched the red book from the hands of one of the men, and with a sour word, handed money to the proprietor.

The proprietor ripped a sheet of brown paper from a roll and began to wrap the book in brown paper and twine. Emily picked her way through traffic, crossing the street at a trot to avoid being flattened by a team of Clydesdales pulling a load of brewery barrels.

As she came closer to the bookshop, she noticed that a much larger group of men was walking briskly toward it as well. It was a gang of young men in brightly colored suits. They moved like schooling fish, swerving as the others swerved, kicking cans and conversing loudly among themselves. Emily had often seen groups of such youths in her clandestine travels through the streets of New York; she'd heard them called b'hoys, rowdies, or soaplocks. They had a rolling gait and surly manner, and Emily had always felt it wise to give them a wide berth. Achieving the safety of the sidewalk, Emily came to a dead stop as she watched the first of the young men—the loudest, the one who seemed to be their leader—come face to face with the bookshop's proprietor.

The young man planted his hands on his hips, looked over the display of red books with a frown, and began spitting curses in the proprietor's face—a string, indeed, of the filthiest expletives Emily had ever heard. Within an instant it became too much for the big man in the sleeve garters to bear. He lifted his hands in a pugilistic stance. The young man moved with the quickness of a striking snake. With one hand he grabbed the fabric of the bigger man's collar; with the other he delivered a vicious uppercut. In a heartbeat, the other b'hoys were throwing themselves on the older man, fists and feet flying. The big man, quickly overwhelmed, crossed his arms before his face and fell to the ground, yelling for help.

There were startled cries from all around. Farley, along with the two men who had been laughing and elbowing each other over the red book, hurried to pull the young men off. And in an instant, the beating became a full-fledged melee. Young men left off kicking the moaning proprietor and launched themselves at the would-be rescuers. Fists flew, women and children ran screaming, men tumbled to the pavement.

Emily watched, horrified, as two of the young men began to pay particular attention to poor Farley in his silly green livery. One of them cracked him hard across the mouth, sending him reeling; the other followed up with a hard sock to his midsection. Farley groaned, stumbled.

"Stop it!" Emily shrieked, running in Farley's direction. "You . . . thugs! You rotten dirty hooligans, *stop it*!"

The sight of a woman rushing them, screaming at the top of her lungs, made the two young men step back, grinning at each other meanly. Emily fell by Farley's side, putting her arm around his shoulders. She looked up at the pair of young men, who were now laughing at her. "Two on one? Shame on you!"

"Shut your rum-hole, lady, or I'll shut it for you," one of them offered, showing her a meaty fist.

"Rackers! Finnegan! Get over here and help me throw these down." The words came from the young leader who had started the brawl. He had beaten the proprietor into unconsciousness, and was now using his heavy boot to kick over the tables with the red books on them. With a joyful whoop, Rackers and Finnegan came like called dogs, gathering up handfuls of the red books and tearing them in half along the spine, sending ripped pages fluttering down the street in cheap, pulpy drifts.

"Miss Emily," Farley grunted, trying to rise, "we have to get out of here. The Stantons will have my hide."

Emily stood, helping him up. He remained half bent, his arms clutched around his belly. As he was rising, Emily saw the brown-paper-wrapped book on the sidewalk, and she snatched it, tucking it under her arm.

"Hey!" the young leader shouted at Emily, striding over toward her. Farley turned, tried to hurry her down the street, but the hooligan clapped a heavy hand on Farley's shoulder and made a grab for the book under Emily's arm. "You're not going anywhere with that. Give it to me!"

For the first time, Emily was able to get a close look at the young man, and to her astonishment, discovered that she recognized him. He had anarchist eyes and an overbite. It was the young man she'd seen in Stanton's office the day before. Gormley, that was what Stanton had called him. Emily stared at him as Farley put himself between Emily and Gormley's grabbing hand.

"Don't you dare touch her!" Farley spat at him, balling a fist. "You rummy bastards should know better than to touch a lady! Shove off or I swear to God I'll flatten you!"

Without a word, Gormley delivered two lightning-quick punches to Farley's face before the man in green even knew what hit him. Blood blossomed from Farley's nose, cascading down his chin; he reeled.

"Mr. Gormley, stop it!" Emily screamed.

At the sound of his name, Gormley disengaged, breathing hard. Rackers and Finnegan closed around him, a threatening phalanx. Gormley glared at Emily for a moment, trying to place her. Once he did, his face transformed from sneering menace to sullen complacency.

"Miss Edwards." Gormley dragged a dirty fist across his face, wiping some of Farley's blood from his cheek. He pointed at the brown-wrapped book under her arm. "That's one of the books, miss. Everything in there about Mr. Stanton . . . it's dirty lies!"

"Well, whatever they are, they're fluttering down every

street in the Bowery!" Emily pointed to the drifts of paper blowing down the street. "You've scattered them like dandelions! How many more people will get hold of those pages now, eh?"

Gormley clenched his teeth. His eyes burned into her like acid.

"I don't know anything about that," he snarled. "All I know is we're charged with getting rid of all of 'em. All of 'em."

"What do you mean, charged? Charged to destroy a business? Who charged you?"

"Why, you were in the office same as me when he said it," Gormley spoke through clenched teeth. "*He doesn't want to hear about it.* So he ain't gonna. He ain't gonna hear about businesses that sell lies and garbage. He ain't gonna hear about them getting just what this one got." He extended his hand, made a curt motion. "Now hand it over."

"No." She tucked her arm down tightly. Rackers barked a laugh, balled a fist, began to step toward her. Gormley restrained him with a raised hand. He looked at Emily.

"Give it to me," he repeated, softly and slowly. From the direction of the bookshop came laughing hoots and screams and the sounds of breaking glass. Emily realized that she was shaking, from the top of her head to the bottoms of her feet.

"No," Emily said, biting the word. "I won't."

Gormley took a step forward, grabbing Emily's shoulder, pulling her close. Farley grabbed for her, but Rackers and Finnegan swept forward as one, shoving him backward, following him as he stumbled back. Emily stood before Gormley, his head close to hers, his breath smelling of onions and whiskey. His fingers dug into the place where her neck met her shoulder, clasping hard, making her wince. His other hand was on the book, tugging at it, trying to pull it out of her grasp. She held tightly, wrapping her body around it.

"Listen, you stuck-up bitch," Gormley hissed. "I take my orders from Mr. Stanton, not from you. Just because you're his—"

The sound of a police whistle shrilled through the street.

"Run for it, Gorm!" Rackers was already sprinting away; Finnegan was not far behind. Spitting a curse in her face,

Gormley gave Emily a hard parting shake before taking one step back, then breaking into a run as well. He and the other young men faded into alley and saloon, swiftly and silently as dirty water running down a drain. Emily watched as the police arrived, three of them in dark-blue wool uniforms, running heavily down the sidewalk, whistles blasting.

"Miss Emily!" Farley was at her side. "Miss Emily, are you all right? Did he hurt you?"

"I'm fine, Mr. Farley," Emily said, her fingers playing along the edge of the brown-paper-wrapped book as she watched the police bend over the still-unconscious proprietor. The destruction wrought by the swarm of young men was awful. Tables and windows were smashed, and everywhere, the tattered remnants of red books fluttered in the wind.

Farley held one hand to his bloody nose as he took Emily's elbow, hurrying her up the street to where the carriage waited. As he opened the carriage door for her, he held out a bloodied hand.

"Miss . . . why don't you give me my book back?" he said.

Emily clutched the parcel tightly. "No."

"You really should," Farley said. Emily held it tighter. Farley sighed.

"I wasn't buying it for me, I just want you to know that. I wouldn't want you thinking I was a kind of person like that. I was . . . I was buying it for them. Because they'd want to know. The family has to know. That's all."

He closed the carriage door behind her, and she sunk back in her seat, letting out her breath. Her heart was still pounding like a freight train, and her hands were shaking. She felt up to her shoulder, where Gormley had grabbed her. The place still ached. The half-wrapped book lay in her lap, and a bit of bright red peeped from a torn corner.

All at once, fearing to hesitate, Emily tore the brown paper from the book.

It was cheaply printed on bad paper. The title, *The Blood-Soaked Crimes of Dreadnought Stanton,* was executed in stark gothic lettering.

The full-color engraving on the cover depicted Stanton, his

face twisted with evil intent. His hands and feet dripped with blood even more brilliantly red than the book's cover. In the picture, Stanton held aloft a squirming infant. At his feet writhed a half-clothed woman who looked disturbingly familiar. Black haired, black eyed . . . She was, Emily realized with a twist of disgust, the very image of Alcmene Blotgate. The woman's eyes glowed with lust—for Stanton or for the bleeding infant, it was not clear. It was hideous. It was also, Emily noticed, the very same color red as the thing Stanton had hidden in his desk when she'd been in his office last.

Back at the Stanton house, Emily spent the afternoon in her bedroom reading. It was not, as a typical afternoon spent reading, a pleasant occupation. It probably would have been more pleasant to read Wordsworth aloud, all things considered.

Though cheaply and hastily printed, the red book was completely successful in achieving its obvious intent—to make Dreadnought Stanton appear like the most depraved and disgusting individual ever to disgrace the earth's surface. Worse still, the message was driven home in such a fascinating and absorbing way, Emily could not tear her eyes away. On every page there was something more thrilling, shocking, or scandalous than the last. From a comparatively tame opening scene depicting the wanton defilement of a holy altar, it dragged the reader through a Grand Guignol of orgiastic blood-ceremonies, heartless ritual murder performed upon mercy-begging innocents, and gleefully creative and sadistic torture and mayhem—all peppered with prurient scenes of smut involving objects and animals better left uncoupled, even in the imagination. Emily shuddered. For God's sake, people didn't behave like that, even sangrimancers! How could anyone want to read about people behaving like that? Still, Emily turned the pages, even if it was just horror and dismay that kept her doing so.

Emily didn't mind much about some of the accusations. She was certain she didn't believe the part where Stanton breakfasted on a litter of newborn kittens. But some of them had the ring of horrible truth. There was the same story General Blotgate had told at the Investment—of Stanton's using Black Exunge on living creatures, then burning them alive for the amusement of the other cadets. According to the book, it wasn't just chickens. The descriptions made Emily shudder. And there was the depiction of Mrs. Blotgate (unconvincingly renamed in the book as Mrs. Blackheart) in Stanton's arms, the adulterous lovers swearing the eternal destruction of everything good and decent in the world . . .

For the fifteenth time that afternoon, Emily threw the book to the ground, temper flaring. Lies! Filthy, ugly lies designed to further weaken Stanton's position at the Institute. That's all it was. But if so, why had Stanton hidden it from her? The ways of credomancy generally bewildered her, but she knew from experience that trying to hide a secret only gave it more power. And what was he trying to hide, really? The lies . . . or the parcel of truth that lay behind them?

There was a knock at the door. Emily looked up guiltily, her heart jumping into her throat. She snatched the book up from the floor and managed to tuck it behind herself as Mrs. Stanton came into the room. The older woman paused, her hand on the doorknob, and looked toward Emily's arm, which Emily was holding awkwardly behind her back.

"I've been speaking with Farley," Mrs. Stanton said. "He was quite worried for his job. For good reason, as I have since discharged him."

Indignation flared up in Emily. "He was only doing as I asked him. It's not fair to—"

"My son sent you here to be safe, not to tramp around New York City getting yourself involved in street brawls." She gestured obliquely to Emily's hand, which was still behind her back. "Farley told me you'd managed to obtain one of those . . . things. I assume from your ridiculous posture that you've been reading it?"

Slowly, Emily pulled her hand out from behind her back and laid the garish red book on the side table. Mrs. Stanton advanced, took the book in between two fingers, lifted it disdainfully, and threw it into the fireplace. The cheap paper flared up quickly, issuing a great quantity of foul-smelling black smoke.

"It is an exceptionally transparent attack," Mrs. Stanton said, watching the flames and smoke rise together. She turned and looked at Emily. "I certainly hope you're not silly enough to have let it upset you."

"Why should it?" Emily said. "If it's all lies."

"If?" Mrs. Stanton's green eyes glittered. "Then you have doubts?"

Emily swallowed, but said nothing. Mrs. Stanton hmphed.

"Most of it, I'll own, seems rather unlike him. Blood strikes me as a highly unsanitary and disgusting beverage, and I can hardly picture him swilling jeweled goblets full of it. But the rest . . ." She paused. "Well, perhaps it is best that I refrain from sharing my opinion of my son's taste in intimate companions."

"You don't . . . you can't believe any of it?"

Mrs. Stanton lifted an eyebrow. "Dreadnought was a willful and perverse child. There is not a single earthly foolishness that I am unable to imagine him perpetrating. But whether he did any of those outlandish things or he didn't, it makes no difference. He is my son."

"Well, I'm sure he didn't do any of it!" Emily said. "But, for heaven's sake, if he did . . . you couldn't—"

"Of course I could," Mrs. Stanton said. She came to sit near Emily, in a chair that looked very uncomfortable. The way she sat in it, with her back straight as a poker, made it seem even more so. "And I would. What else would you have me do? Disown him? Denounce him? Ruin my world and my reputation in the service of some idealistic moral fantasy?"

"In the service of . . . decency." Emily could hardly choke out the words.

"Your frontier ethics are so rawboned, Miss Edwards, as rough-hewn and clumsy as the log cabin in which you must have been raised." Mrs. Stanton's face was like marble as she spoke; only her lips moved with ugly precision. "Decency is striving for perfection in a world in which every other hoglike creature satisfies himself with sloppiness and indulgence. Decency is not in failing to murder someone. It's in murdering the right person, and sparing your family the indignity of getting caught."

Emily stared at her. Mrs. Stanton blinked once, slowly.

"The Senator has gone through his share of difficult times over the past twenty years. There have been public scandals—allegations of bribery, graft, kickbacks. And there have been private disappointments. There will always be other women, Miss Edwards. To imagine otherwise is sheerest self-delusion."

She drew in a deep breath. "However, when my husband looks in the mirror, his reflection shows him an unblemished servant of the people, a faithful spouse, and a wise father. There is no doubt in his mind. He is a clear, unruffled pond. He is perfect in his belief in his own perfection. I have built this in him. I have killed all remorse, all conscience, all compromise within him. Because the strength of our perfection, the strength of our right to rule, is only as strong as our faith in it. Do you understand?"

Emily stared into the older woman's green eyes, lost in their ocean of implication.

"But what about the truth?" Emily whispered.

"The truth doesn't matter," Mrs. Stanton said.

A heavy silence filled the room. Emily moved to the other side of the room, wrapping her arms around herself. She felt dizzy and sick. Of course the truth mattered. It had to matter. What would life be if it didn't? Bitter self-delusion in the service of power? Despair flooded her. She pressed the back of her hand to her mouth, pressed it hard against her teeth to keep from screaming something foul.

"You have to rise above things like this, Miss Edwards," Mrs. Stanton said to Emily's back. "My son has explained many things about this 'credomancy' he practices. It is a fascinating art, though I can hardly understand why he had to spend a half-decade of intensive study on what seems to me little more than common sense. One of credomancy's foundational precepts has always struck me as extremely comforting: While false things can be made true with enough belief, true things can also be believed into becoming false."

Emily heard Mrs. Stanton rise. The woman went over to a carved walnut sideboard. She took a key from the small ring that hung at her waist and unlocked the cabinet. Inside, there was an arrangement of bottles and decanters. Mrs. Stanton selected an unopened bottle of brandy. She set it on a table, along with a cut-crystal tumbler.

"Personally, however, I prefer a more direct brand of comfort." Was that an attempt at kindness in her voice? If so, it was very difficult to distinguish from contempt. Emily watched as the old woman tore the seal off the bottle, poured herself a brimful glass. She brought the glass to her mouth, drained it slowly and fondly. When she was finished, she set the tumbler down softly, touched a fingertip to each corner of her mouth. She recapped the bottle and left it on the table.

"I'm sure you're very tired, Miss Edwards," Mrs. Stanton said. "You'll want to remain in your room this evening. I'll have something sent up. We all understand."

Emily turned violently, glaring at the bottle of brandy, at the old woman who hovered over it. She wanted to kick the table over. But at the moment, Emily did feel tired. Very tired. And the thought of locking herself in a room with a bottle of brandy didn't seem all that exceptionally bad.

Mrs. Stanton moved toward the door. Her hand was on the doorknob when she paused.

"It is a shame you must feel such heartache, Miss Edwards," Mrs. Stanton said, not turning. "It is as disappointing to me as it is to you. I did not raise my son to fall in love. I raised him to be like his father." She paused, and Emily heard her murmur as she closed the door behind her: "If only I knew where I went wrong."

Emily snatched the bottle of brandy and sat on the edge of the bed. She uncorked the bottle and tipped it down her thoat, forgoing the niceties of the cut-crystal tumbler. She assumed it was good brandy, but even so, it burned like hell going down. She wiped her mouth with the back of her hand.

So. The truth didn't matter. If there was truth in the red book, she was supposed to ignore it. Forget it. Polish Stanton into a gloss so fine that nothing real or honest could stick to him ever again.

She took another drink, the choking alcohol tickling her

nose. Warmth spread through her quickly, tingling and numbing. It would be easy. Drink a little more, go to sleep, smile pretty, and for God's sake don't move. Ignore the goblets of blood and sadistic ex-mistresses.

Swim with the current.

"To hell with that!" she growled to herself, dashing the bottle of brandy into the fire. It smashed with a satisfying sound, and blue flames leapt on the hearth. Swim with the current? Let Stanton stand by and get away with murder, if that's what he'd done . . . She swallowed hard. Three years at the Erebus Academy. How could she never have thought about what that really meant? Did she think that he'd spent those three years discussing theoretical abstractions? She trembled, wishing suddenly for another mouthful of brandy, wishing Mrs. Stanton hadn't taken the keys to the liquor cabinet with her.

Even if he hadn't gone to the diabolical lengths described in the book, he would have killed for blood. He would have tortured his victims to empower the blood. It was what sangrimancers did.

. . . it's in murdering the right people, and sparing your family the indignity of getting caught . . .

She put a hand over her mouth, trembling harder. These people really believed that! That life was worth nothing more than the power that could be bled from it.

And she'd told him it didn't matter. That it was all in the past.

She leapt to her feet, pacing the room up and down its length. She'd told him it didn't matter because she'd never really believed it of him. She'd never thought he could have done it. But he could have. She knew it now, with terrible certainty. He could have been that person. His mother's coldness, his father's reflective emptiness; the images drifted together, resolving into an image of Stanton, his face cold as marble, his soul uncluttered by doubt, driving needles into the flesh of a struggling victim . . .

Emily ground the heel of her hand into her eyes, trying to rub the image away.

And what if . . . what if he was *still* that person? The kind of person who would send thugs to smash bookstores, beat an innocent man to a bloody crumpled pulp . . .

She couldn't marry someone like that.

Using her mouth, she stripped the diamond ring from her finger, teeth raking her skin. She spat the thing into her hand, then slammed it down on a side table with a fierce cry. Then she stood looking down at it, watching it wink and glitter. As she watched it, her anger crumbled, tumbling into little shards of brandy-fueled misery. She thought of the afternoon up at the blockhouse, with Stanton's warm hand on her sore ankle. That was the man she wanted to marry.

Emily shook her head hard, as if the action would drive the thoughts away. She wasn't going to think about it anymore. There wasn't anything left to think about, really. Misery transmuted into bitterness. "Mrs. Blackheart" and the leather bindings imputed to her were not Emily's true rival. Her true rival was far more abstract and far more demanding. The Institute. The Institute would never relinquish him. It would always be the arms that held him fast, black glass hands tracing blood trails on his smooth flesh . . .

Emily shook her head. Stupid thoughts, all getting mixed up. She had to think of something else. She sat down and crossed her arms, squeezing her eyes shut tight, making herself small and hard.

Aleksei Morozovich. The name the Faery Reader had found on the hair sticks came back to her, and she pounced on it, eager for the distraction. Aleksei Morozovich. She had heard the name before. But where?

She tried to concentrate on the name, tried to remember where she'd heard it, but all she could see in her mind were young men in plaid suits, tearing up red books. Drifts of paper, white as ash, tumbling down the muddy streets of Chatham Square, balling in gutters . . .

Stop it! Emily used her good hand to give her own cheeks a smart slap. It didn't hurt as much as she'd expected it to. She slapped herself again, experimentally.

Aleksei Morozovich.

She remembered the sun shining down through the ivy-covered roof of the blockhouse, Stanton's warm hands. She was about to slap herself again for letting her mind wander, when she remembered Stanton's words, the words he'd spoken thoughtfully while his fingers played over her ankle, finding the sore places with perfect accuracy:

. . . They propose to implement a sort of toxin . . . a poison, deployed within the Mantic Anastomosis itself, that would make magic toxic to any practitioner channeling it. The idea was put forth by a scientist named Aleksei Morozovich . . .

Emily blinked.

Aleksei Morozovich. The scientist who'd been working on the poison.

Her father. A member of the Sini Mira. Mrs. Kendall had said he was working on an important project, one that had driven him from Russia. She had said that he'd had a mentor who'd been killed for his research. If his mentor was Morozovich . . .

She remembered being young and small and cold, her father standing before her with the gleaming sticks of engraved silver in his hands, the sticks she had thought were so pretty . . .

. . . There is a secret written on these hair sticks, Emilichka . . . A dangerous secret . . .

Emily could not move. Her head felt as if little explosions were going off in it. The poison. The secret of the poison that would make magic unworkable. Volos' Anodyne, that's what Zeno had called it. The poison hidden by the God of Oaths. That was what had to be written on her hair sticks, in hypertiny violet scale letters. That was what her father had been trying to protect.

She leaned forward, staring at the carpet beneath her feet. It couldn't be. But it had to. That's what the Sini Mira wanted from her. They wanted to reclaim Volos' Anodyne. And now she knew where it was. At least, she thought she did.

She had to suppress the urge to leap to her feet and rush down to the Bowery that very moment. The Faery Reader's report wouldn't be ready until morning. She couldn't make the man work any faster, but the trembling anxiousness inside her was killing her.

She rocked back and forth in her chair, staring at her trunk.

Inside, the blue bottle of memories lay half full. The rest of her past was in there. Her past, her father . . . and maybe the poison that everyone was looking for. Maybe there was an explanation in there, a confirmation, a confession. Maybe there was more he had to tell her.

Falling to her knees, she scrambled across the floor to her trunk, unbuckling it and throwing the heavy lid back with a thump. She dug through fabric until her ivory hand clinked against the glass. She lifted the bottle, looking at it.

Father, she whispered in Russian. *Let me see.*

She uncapped the Lethe Draught and drank it down to the last dregs. The bitterness of it filled her mouth, tasting of blood and mold and mushrooms . . .

CHAPTER FOURTEEN

Bitter and Dark

Her hair was on fire.

Her entire scalp burned and itched, and Emily kept throwing her head back and forth, trying to make it stop. Her father had plastered something on her hair, something thick and rust-brown that smelled like the strange powders he kept in his workshop. At first it had tingled, then it had itched, and now . . . now it burned. It burned like swarming stinging bees, like fire. They were in the barn, and Emily sat on a wooden chair, tilted back over a tub of foul-smelling water. Emily shrieked and squirmed in her chair, but her father held her shoulders hard against the wood. She kicked against him, screaming, crying.

"It burns, Da! Oh, Da . . . it burns!"

"Oh, Emilichka. Shush, *devuchka.* I'm so sorry."

Emily screamed angrily, tears of pain and rage streaming from her eyes. Her father reached up to brush them away.

"It must stay on for a few minutes yet," her father murmured, gentle but implacable. "Only a few minutes, Emilichka. Shush now, shush. And I will tell you a story. Do you want to hear a story?"

Emily gritted her teeth and stared at her father, hating him. She snuffled, and tears continued to streak down her cheeks. She began kicking her heel rhythmically against the leg of the chair, and the feeling of the back of her ankle connecting with the hard wood was comforting. It didn't hurt as much as the burning, but it hurt enough. *Thump, thump, thump.*

"I will tell you a story about a Witch," her father said, his

voice rich and slow. "You know Witches are distasteful creatures, ugly and hideous. But they can be very powerful."

Thump, thump, thump. Emily did not want to hear about
Witches. She wanted this horrible stuff off of her head. She
wanted to reach up and stomp out the fire with her hands. She
whimpered as her father held her hands down tight against
her sides.

"Now, listen. Listen. Once upon a time, long ago, the God
of Oaths was being chased by demons who wished to steal the
heart of his one true love. He kept her heart locked in a box
made of gold and silver, and he kept it with him always—"

"Didn't she need it?" Emily said. Her father smiled,
reached up to rub another tear that was trickling down the
side of her nose.

"He was keeping it safe for her," her father said. "He had
sworn to do this. It was his greatest oath, his greatest promise.
That he would keep it safe for her and that he would never let
it be broken. So he kept it locked in a box made of gold and
silver. But the demons wanted to steal it. They wanted to tear
it into a million pieces and make the God of Oaths break the
greatest oath he had ever made, so he would not be the God of
Oaths anymore. He would just be a man, pathetic and forsworn."

Thump, thump, thump. Emily didn't know what forsworn
meant, but she figured it meant something bad. Bad like the
full moon, bad like the five days, bad like the fire that was sizzling her skin . . .

"Da, how much longer?" she wailed. "Two minutes?"

"Two minutes, *kapusta*." Little cabbage.

Emily wrinkled her nose. "I hate cabbage," she snuffled.

"Listen. The God of Oaths. He was wandering in a wood,
and the demons were hard on his trail. They were closing in
around him, foul creatures with black teeth like razors and
claws like the sharpest knives. He came to a cabin in the
woods, a queer little cabin that sat right up on four chicken
legs."

Emily tried to imagine it. "Chicken legs?"

"In this cabin lived a Witch named Baba-Yaga. She was a
nasty, wrinkled old creature who always cooked cabbage, and

sometimes cooked little girls, too. But she was powerful, and the God of Oaths had no choice but to ask for her help. The demons were coming to tear the heart of his true love into a million pieces. Even gods need help sometimes."

"What did she do?"

"She let down her hair," Emily's father said simply. "Her long hair tumbled all around her body, and in it she hid the box made of gold and silver that contained the heart of the God of Oaths' one true love. When the demons came, they could not find it."

Emily wrinkled her nose at her father.

"How could she hide a whole box in her hair?" Emily demanded angrily. It was the stupidest story she'd ever heard. She wanted to hear how the God of Oaths had battled the demons, sent them running away, made them go and never bother him again. She would have liked that story. "You can't hide a whole box in your hair. Even Mama's hair, and her hair is so long!"

"Things can be hidden in strange places," her father said softly, as he lifted a jug of clean water. He laid her back over the tub, poured the water over her head. "There we are, *kapusta*. All done. It will feel better soon."

The cool water played over her scalp, washing away the fire, washing away the pain.

Wagons.

It was autumn, and the leaves were orange and yellow. It was cold, and they were riding in wagons with men Emily did not know, across mountains that glowed blue with snow.

Father was not there.

She wanted him. She wanted him so badly, to hold her in his warm arms and smile at her and talk to her in Russian. But she knew she could not ask for him. She knew that she could never ask for her father ever again.

Mama was there, swaying with the rocking of the wagon, her eyes dead and flat. She was so tired all the time, so tired and heavy and slow. She kept drinking something, something that made her eyes like plates. Emily sometimes snuck looks at the bottle her mother drank from. She would look at the bottle and try to sound out the word written on its brown paper label.

Morphia.

She could not imagine how it sounded. But whatever was in the little bottle made the five days better. It dulled the edge of the full moon like a knife rubbed against a rock. When they were with the men in the wagons, Emily could hide when the moon made the sky glow, when Mama started to yell and break things. Emily could hide, and the men would hide her, let her sleep curled under canvas blankets and feed sacks.

But after a while they did not ride with the men in the wagons anymore. They went their own way, and they came to a cold, wild place, and the round moon stared down at them, and Emily was all alone.

"What did he tell you?" Mama's eyes were like marbles, glassy and hard. She shook Emily, and Emily thought that she would rattle to pieces. She closed her eyes, letting herself be shaken, because there was nothing else she could do. "He wanted to destroy magic. He wanted to destroy us. He wanted to destroy me!"

Her mother threw her down, fell on her with fists. Emily whimpered, putting her arms up. "Tell me, you stupid little brat! Tell me or I'll kill you, I swear, I will kill you like—"

The fists stopped. Something came across Mama's face, something like tears and fury seen in a mirror. She staggered back, holding her own hands. Holding them down hard.

"Run, Emily!" her mother whispered. "Run and hide, Emily. Run and hide! Stay quiet! Stay quiet!"

Emily ran, her small legs shaking and weak. Her face ached where her mother's fists had hit her. She ran, not knowing where to go. She remembered Volos, the God of Oaths, running through the woods with demons chasing him. Demons with black teeth like razors and claws like the sharpest knives. She did not find a cabin with chicken legs. But she found a thicket of blackberry bushes that scratched her, tore at her skin and her dress, and she climbed deep within them, curling her arms around her knees, staying

quiet, hoping that trembling did not make a noise, hoping that
her wildly beating heart wasn't too loud.

Quiet. She had to be quiet.

Mama did not come looking for her for a while, but finally
her voice called on the beams of moonlight:

"Emily . . ."

Emily tightened her arms around herself, quaking. She
hid her eyes behind her knees, squeezing them tight. She
heard her mother shuffling through the underbrush, cracking
twigs, her footsteps heavy and slow.

"Emily . . ." Mama's voice, sweet and honeyed and poisonous. "Come out now, Emily."

Emily did not move. Five days. Five whole days, the sun
had to rise and set.

"Come out, you miserable little brat. Come out or I'll leave
you here. I'll leave you out here all alone. All alone with the
wild animals. They'll tear your guts out with their sharp teeth.
They'll eat your bones, and there'll be nothing left of you.
Come out, Emily. Come out and tell me. Tell me what you
know, and I won't hurt you. I promise you, sweetling, I won't
hurt you . . ."

But Emily knew that Mama would hurt her. She would hurt
her if she ever told what her father had told her. She would
kill her. She would kill her like . . .

Kill her like . . .

The light of the full moon streamed through the windows
of the kitchen.

Mama with the knife in her hand, gleaming. The big knife,
the butcher's knife she used to hack bones to make soup.

"Stop it, Catherine! Fight him. For God's sake, fight him—"

Father's arms around her, holding her close. Father watching Mama, watching the knife in her hand.

"I read your papers, Lyakhov." Mama's voice, flat and old.
Her eyes like scratched glass. "You think you can keep the
woman drugged up on morphia all the time? I control her
more than you know. What she knows, I know. I read your papers. I know what you're going to do. And I'm not going to let
you."

"I swear to you, I won't let her die." Father's voice, desperate. "I swear to you, Cowdray. You don't understand . . . there's another way!"

"Lies!"

Mama struck out with the knife; Father pulled back, wrapping himself tightly around Emily. Mama took another step forward, but Father reached for the large table—the table on which Emily had watched her mother's hands kneading bread. He pulled it to the floor with a crash, crouching behind it.

"Catherine." Father's voice was low, pleading. "Please. I beg you. Don't let him."

Mama stopped her approach. She put her hands up to her face, swaying slightly. She moaned—a tight miserable sound. Father threw Emily out of his arms, sending her tumbling toward the door. He jumped to his feet, jumped toward Mama, his hands coming up to grab her wrists. He wrestled her backward against the dry sink, using the weight of his body to hold her. She fought against him wildly, screaming, the knife still clenched in her hand.

"I won't let you, Lyakhov! I won't let you give them the poison. I won't let you kill me—" The knife flashed down, sinking into Father's shoulder. He grunted, staggered; the knife flashed down again, finding his throat. Blood gushed over Mama's hands, over her wrists, over the white apron that covered her dress.

The knife came down again and again. Father slumped forward, falling to the floor, his hands scrabbling for something. He made a terrible sound deep in his chest, and blood came out of his mouth, spilling across the floor, flooding the entire world . . .

CHAPTER FIFTEEN

The Black Carriage

Emily woke with screams ringing between her ears.

Dried tears cracked on the sides of her cheek . . . or was it blood? Was it blood, flooding over the floor, flooding the world . . .

Her head ached and her gut was cramped with pain. She tasted vomit in her mouth. Something smelled bad.

She was outside. She was in the street, outside under a gaslit sky, her cheek pressed against hard cold stone. Hadn't she been inside? In a building? A nice building, made of brown stone . . . or a kitchen. A kitchen, terrible with moonlight. Where had she been? Where was she now?

There had been rain. It was early, the sun hadn't risen yet. But the sky was lightening, a heavy dead gray. She was outside, in the street, and it was damp. The pavement glistened. She was laying on the pavement, staring down into the muddy street, at the place where the cobblestones met the sidewalk.

Trash was swirling in the water that was running toward the gutter. She smelled earth and leaves. She felt the presence of something in her mind, something old and vast. *Ososolyeh,* she thought it was called . . .

Words formed in the water, in the scumming foam that swirled on its surface:

Gold Eye.

Words formed in the detritus flowing toward the gutter grate. Words built on words, spelled out in orange peelings, tobacco flakes, snippets of dung-stained hay . . .

You must get to Gold Eye.

Mama's knife, coming down and down again, and her father screaming an ocean of blood . . .

"Oh, Da . . ." she moaned.

Emily curled in on herself, wrapping her arms around her knees. Words trickled from her mouth like blood, and her chest ached as if Mama's knife had stabbed into her, not into her father.

She felt people looking at her, stepping around her. She was laying in the street, and she didn't know how she'd gotten there.

You must get to Gold Eye.

The Faery Reader.

Emily sat up abruptly, remembering a smiling Irish accent and laughing children. She sat up, looked around herself. Her feet were cold; something had happened to her shoes. They were gone, and her socks, too. Her feet were scraped and bruised. Her ankles were muddy.

"Here, you, move it along!" The voice came from above her. A policeman stared down at her. He hit the side of a cast-iron fireplug with his billy club; the loudness of the sound made her jump and shake.

"I said, move it along! Sleep it off somewhere else."

Emily climbed to her aching feet. She wrapped her arms around herself, staggering away from the policeman, her bleary eyes searching for a street sign. She found one. Third and Catherine Street. She was in New York, she remembered. New York.

You must get to Gold Eye. The message echoed through her head, vibrating insistently, and she knew that it was the message that had driven her from the Stanton house. She remembered it now, how she had run through dark tangled streets, stone buildings rising above her like murderous mountains. Everything in her head was so tangled and mixed up. Her father was dead, slaughtered, butchered. Mama had killed him. Mama had driven a knife into his chest, again and again, blood spurting and soaking.

Mama, no . . . please . . .

The Faery Reader.

You must get to Gold Eye.

The Faery Reader had given her a card. She felt in her pocket for it, and found that it was still there, crisp and hard. She brought it up to her blurry eyes, trying to make them focus on the small type. She squinted up at the street sign again. She thought she knew how to get there. It was important that she get there. She had to get something back, something she had left with him . . .

She started in what she thought was the right direction, leaning with one shoulder against the buildings as she walked. She felt unmoored, like a balloon that wanted to float up from the ground. She stopped to vomit again, letting her stomach heave itself up out of her throat. She wiped her mouth with the back of her hand then kept moving.

When she got to the Faery Reader's shop, there were dozens of people clustered about outside of it, their faces grim and nervous, their conversations low and regretful. And there were police, many police in blue coats with shiny brass buttons. And there was a black cart with the words "County Morgue" written on the side.

No, Emily thought. *No, no.*

Emily pushed through the crowd, not caring who she shoved. Some people looked at her and cursed at her, told her to watch herself, but she hardly heard them. She pushed herself forward until she came almost to the door of the shop, where a policeman put his hands on her shoulders, held her back.

Emily stared at the shop. The windows that opened onto the street were covered on the inside with blood, thin and viscid, a streaky red film. There was a terrible smell coming from the open door—a rotten charnel house smell.

"What happened?" Emily asked. Her voice was thick and phlegmy. The policeman gave her a scornful, harrassed look.

"I don't speak Russian, sister," he said. He said it very loudly, as if volume would help her understand him. She shook her head, tried again. This time the words came out right, but understanding the question didn't make the policeman any friendlier.

"Ain't no business of yours," he growled, pushing her back. "Move along."

"He had something of mine!" Emily's voice was a yell now.

"Well he don't have it now. He don't have anything. He's dead. Murdered. The whole family. Guts splattered all over the shop."

Emily felt her face drain. The policeman eyed her suspiciously.

"You wouldn't know anything about it? Hey!"

Emily was already pushing her way back through the crowd. Abner S. Pearl and his family . . . Mrs. Pearl, and the children . . . she felt like vomiting again, but her stomach was an empty sack. Everyone was dying, everyone was being murdered. Blood was everywhere; it ran in the streets like water.

She sank to the curb, bare feet damp against the pavement. She curled over her knees, hiding her eyes behind them, squeezing her eyes shut tight. Stay quiet, stay quiet. She felt so small. She was just a little girl. Her father was supposed to be here to take care of her. He wasn't supposed to be gone. She wasn't supposed to be here.

Sobs racked her shoulders. She was lost. She didn't know what to do. She didn't know where she was, or how to get home. Everyone was dead.

"Help me, please." She muttered, her face pressed into the dirty fabric of her skirt. She put her arms up over her head, shutting out the sounds. "Someone please help me."

Shush, Emily Edwards, another part of her mind, an older part, chastised gently. *No one's going to help you. You have to figure this out for yourself. You're Pap's girl. You can do it.*

But the younger part of her, the part that was still five and forgotten, only cried harder. Father had told her to take care of the hair sticks. Father had told her to keep them safe. He'd told her never to tell anyone. But she'd lost them. And Father was dead. Mama had killed him with the knife.

Had she told?

Emily searched her memory desperately.

Had she told Mama about the hair sticks? Had she? Was that why Mama had killed him?

Emily looked down in the gutter, where the trickle of ugly water flowed over her bare feet. And there were words again, another message, spelled out in letters of filth and muck and blood, shining with urgency:

Run.

She stared at the message, hands over her ears. She stared at it, feeling its urgency. But all urgency in her was gone. She should run immediately, as fast as her feet would take her, but it all seemed so hard now, like her feet were cast iron.

Then, suddenly, she felt eyes upon her. Two sets of eyes, men in the crowd outside the Faery Reader's shop. A tallish man followed by a shorter one; they wore black suits and bowler hats. They were looking straight at her. One of them said something; she could see his mouth moving but she could not make out his words. Then they began moving toward her.

"Run, you idiot!" Emily growled at herself, and the words spoken aloud seemed to bring her back to herself a little. She stood quickly, looking around. The men were pushing through the crowd, bearing toward her. The street was thick with traffic; she darted between a swiftly moving carriage and a heavy cart laden with crates of cabbages, running fast as she could on her bare feet. She could lose them in the confusion of traffic. But as soon as she was across the street, she could see them hurrying in her direction. She ran faster, past pedestrians and tradesmen, vomit-stained skirts tangling around her bare ankles, tripping her. Then she caught a glimpse of another policeman, friendly looking, swinging his club, whistling.

"They're following me!" She fell on him heavily, grabbing his arm. "Please, I have to get back . . . I have to get back to . . ."

The policeman stared down at her, and she watched his friendliness become hard distaste. Glancing backward, she could see that the men were still approaching. They were not hurrying now, but they were walking normally, keeping their eyes on her.

"One too many, sister?" the policeman asked her.

"Those men!" Emily quavered, pointing at them. "They're following me. They're after me."

"After you?" The policeman frowned at her. "Pick the wrong pocket?"

"No, I didn't steal anything. They're following me." Emily tried to make her voice sound calm, but tears were still streaming from her eyes. "Help me, please!"

The taller of the two men approached the police officer. He was young, with a stock-straight bearing. He had a strange bruise on his forehead, right between his eyes, and his blood-red tie was pierced with a silver stickpin that was set with gleaming obsidian. Emily cowered away from him, clinging more tightly to the policeman's sleeve.

"Leave me alone!" she screamed.

"Officer, we're from the Pinkerton Agency," the young man said, quickly flashing a badge. His voice was thin and raspy, as if his vocal cords had been dipped in acid until nothing but a fine cobweb of them remained. "This woman left the care of her relatives last night, and we've been sent to retrieve her."

"I'll need some proof of that," the officer said. "What's her name?"

"Her name is Emily Edwards." The shorter man procured paperwork and handed it to the police officer. With a burst of energy, Emily tried to run, but the man with the obsidian stickpin caught her easily. His fingers dug painfully into the muscles of her upper arm.

"They're lying!" she screamed at the policeman, trying to pull away. The hand around her arm tightened, and she winced. "I don't know these men. They're going to hurt me. They're going to kill me. I know it, I know it—"

"Miss Edwards has been drinking," Stickpin said calmly, fingers tightening even more. Emily could feel his nails cutting through the fabric of her sleeve. "But from the smell of her, I guess I don't have to tell you that."

"It is imperative that she be returned to the care of her fiancé's family," the shorter man said. "I think you recognize the name, don't you?"

The officer looked over the papers. He tilted back his hat and scratched his head.

"Well, that's something else," he said, handing the papers back to the man. "I don't argue where senators are involved." His face became stern as he looked Emily up and down. He shook his head and tsked.

Emily screamed, kicked, tried to hang on to the policeman's blue-wool sleeve, but Stickpin jerked her away, dragging her down the sidewalk.

He raised a hand, whistled for a black-curtained carriage that was waiting a ways down the street. There were more men in black suits riding on the back of the carriage, their faces covered with scarves, glittering eyes visible beneath their round black hats. They were going to put her in that carriage. They were going to take her away. She threw her body from side to side desperately, screaming at the top of her lungs, but Stickpin wrapped his arm around her neck, his hand pressing hard over her mouth. She kept screaming in her throat and tried to bite his dry, raspy palm.

"Stop fighting, you little bitch," he hissed, and with his other hand, he pressed the sharp tip of a hidden knife up under Emily's arm—a place where it could slide easily through her ribs. But Emily did not stop fighting. Something told her it would be better to be stabbed than to be put in that black carriage. She kept scrabbling and kicking and trying to scream until they came to the open door of the carriage. Then Stickpin was pushing her in, lifting her and shoving her inside. He climbed in over her, boot heels grinding into her back and legs. Closing the door, Stickpin knocked hard on the roof. The carriage gave a lurch and rolled forward.

"So you want to scrap, do you?" he growled, his voice cracking. He reached down and grabbed a handful of her hair. He pulled her up easily, threw her back into the seat, and raised a clenched fist.

"That's enough, Lieutenant." The words came from the seat across from them. "Your enthusiasm in the Goddess' service is duly noted."

Emily's eyes went to the voice. There was another man inside the carriage. Indeed, it was hard to miss him, as he filled an entire half of it. He was massively fat, in an ill-fitting black suit with a high collar. He had tiny shoe-button eyes. His lips were red and cracked, and his pink tongue kept darting over them, moistening them. Emily subsided into trembling watchfulness, staring at him. She knew him.

"You remember me, Miss Edwards?" The man's features lightened with obvious enjoyment of her fear. "Indeed, we have met before. That night at the Institute, the night of Professor Mirabilis' gruesome demise."

"The High Priest," she said stupidly, her voice a thin quiver. "Heusler."

"The Faery Reader told us you were to come back in the morning. And here you are."

"You killed them all." Emily breathed hard. "Even the children—"

"How do you think we got Pearl to tell us everything he did?" Heusler smirked. "Howling little monsters, but he seemed attached to them—"

Emily screamed, throwing herself at him. Lieutenant Stickpin held her back, but Heusler drew in a breath of sheer delight at the attack, gasping as if she'd offered him a tender caress. He licked his lips as the lieutenant pulled her back, held her down, his heavy hot hand pressing against her breast.

"What do you want?" Emily snarled at Heusler, trying—and failing—to push the hand away. "I don't have anything. I don't know anything."

"The Black Glass Goddess has everything she wants now," Heusler said. "The hair sticks, inscribed with the formula for Volos' Anodyne, are on their way to her as we speak." He paused. "But there is one small matter that remains. One little thing that she desires. You. Dead. In the most lingering and agonizing way I can imagine." He leaned forward and spoke the next words as solemnly as if he were swearing an oath of true love. "And I have a very good imagination."

The fat man lifted a soft heavy hand. He pinched her chin and cheeks between thick fingers, his palm clammy with sweat. He turned her face from one side to the other, scrutinizing her.

"You have very nice eyes," he said finally. She tried to flinch away, but Stickpin held her fast as Heusler put his puffy, slick thumbs over her eyes. He pressed them against her lids harder and harder. "The eyes are always such a good place to start . . ."

But then, suddenly, he let his hands fall away. He settled himself back into his seat. His belly was rising and falling rapidly. He licked his red, rough lips.

"I'm going to take you to a place where I can really get to work," he said, wiping the sweat from his palms onto his trousers. "No point in ending things too soon."

Then there was a jolt. The horses at the front of the carriage must have spooked, for the vehicle stopped abruptly, tossing all the passengers forward.

"What the . . . ?" Heusler braced himself against the walls of the carriage, and Stickpin scrambled to push aside the black curtains at the windows. Outside, there was the sound of guns. Rifle shots. In the confusion, Emily reached for the door, wrenched it open. She threw herself out onto the cobblestones. Lieutenant Stickpin jumped down after her, swearing in a querulous rasp. She scrambled backward. Stickpin snarled as he lunged for her.

There were men near the front of the carriage, men holding the heads of the panicking horses, men with shotguns, yelling to each other in Russian.

"Wait!"

"There she is!"

"Hold the horses!"

Emily wrenched herself from Stickpin's grasp and ran. He started on her heels, but one of the Russians was on him, striking at him with the butt of a rifle. Emily saw him reach inside his collar and draw something from beneath it.

More rifle cracks. Emily ducked as a bullet whizzed past her ear, and dived for cover under a heavy drayage cart. She watched as the carriage outriders—the black-suited sangrimancers—jerked down the scarves masking their faces and raised their alembics high in glowing fists. The sound of spells chanted in a guttural, ugly language filled the air. Dark sinuous magic wreathed a large man in a loose embroidered tunic—one of the Russians—holding the plunging carriage horses. He screamed, crossing himself as he fell to his knees, his body cocooned in smoke and green flame.

She could see where the gunfire was coming from now—dozens of men in rough clothing were pouring from side streets, rifles raised. Screams echoed as pedestrians scattered in all directions.

She saw one of the sangrimancers fall, half his head vanishing in a spray of red. But the rest remained standing, shielded with spheres of terrible power. Emily saw Lieutenant Stickpin, alembic held high, muttering up a heavy black storm cloud around his hands. Little strikes of lightning sizzled within it. With a cry he released it upward into the air, and it spread over the whole block, a churning tempest. There was a crack of unearthly thunder and rain began to pour down—black rain that hissed and sizzled as it hit the pavement. The men with the rifles screamed when the rain struck their bare skin. Arms over their heads, those who could not find shelter fell shrieking and writhing beneath the downpour. Under the heavy cart, Emily jerked back with a cry of pain as a few drops of the black rain splashed onto her bare arm. It burned like molten lead.

Heusler dragged his ponderous bulk from the carriage, his massive form surrounded by a glowing sphere of protection. He looked bored and angry. Emily tried to scramble backward under the heavy cart to the sidewalk beyond, where she would be free to run, rain or no rain. But Heusler's eyes found her. He lifted a hand, and magic glowed.

"Stay where you are," he muttered.

Emily felt her muscles cramping painfully, her hands balling into fists, even the bottoms of her feet tensing and curling inward. She felt as if she were being crushed under a terrible weight. Then Heusler turned away from her, lifting his hands like a preacher giving an invocation. He spoke words that rang off the tall buildings around them. From the puddles that had formed from the burning black rain, a huge snakelike thing grew, raising an eyeless black head. The thing struck out at whatever Russians were still standing, heedless of their bullets. Opening a huge mouth, it swallowed one of them whole. The man shrieked, dissolving in a conflagration of red and gold.

Over the sounds of the shrieking was another sound— a sudden cry, high and furious. Heusler staggered forward as a man threw himself onto the High Priest's back. Even though he was wearing a heavy overcoat and gloves, she recognized him.

Dmitri.

Dmitri wrapped a hand around Heusler's forehead and pulled the fat man's head back. Then he brought his hand up, slashing abruptly. Emily did not see the knife in Dmitri's hand, but she did see the blood fountaining from Heusler's throat. Heusler fell, his hands reaching up with futile magic streaming from them. Dmitri rode Heusler's body to the ground, then leapt up, pulling his shotgun from a holster on his back. Emily felt the spell cramping her muscles slacken, fall away. The writhing snake collapsed inward on itself, becoming a spreading thick puddle of black. Smoke rose from it, acrid and foul.

New waves of men were storming into the fray now, and they were all wearing heavy overcoats and dark smoked goggles. They fell upon Heusler's men, grappling wildly. With Heusler bleeding on the ground, it seemed that more rifle shots were finding their mark; Emily saw another sangrimancer fall, a cavernous hole blown in his chest. Everything churned—swirling freshets of black rain and humming waves of glowing red magic hissing up like mist and vapor, the close sound of firearms and breaking glass, the screams of the wounded and dying. Dmitri looked up the street. Emily followed his gaze.

At the end of the street a man stood alone, carefully working some kind of device. He was ice-white, neatly tailored, calm.

Perun.

He stood within some kind of egg-shaped shield that glowed yellow and green; the black rain sizzled and smoked against it. Like the other Russians, he was wearing dark goggles. A cigarette dangled forgotten between his lips. He glanced up at Dmitri and gave a small nod. Dmitri quickly lifted a similar pair of goggles hanging around his neck and fixed them over his eyes.

Then, to her horror, Emily realized that Heusler was not dead. He was inching his bulk toward her, his fingers clutching at the black, slimy cobblestones. The wound on his throat closed even as she watched, creeping magic seaming the lips of the wound, stanching the gouting spurts of blood. The black knife was in his hand.

At that moment, Perun punched a button on the device in his hand, then tossed it away from himself. She watched it roll out onto the cobblestones with a small *tink tink tink*.

It was the last thing Emily saw.

The device exploded with a rumbling boom and a flash of light that made everything go stark white, like the light of a hundred midday suns.

She felt Heusler's hand on her arm, then on her throat. He pulled her out from under the cart and pulled himself up over her body, panting like a dog. She felt him raise his arm.

There was a lone rifle crack. Warm sharp chunks splattered across her face. Something dropped beside her head, shattering. Shards of it sliced into the flesh of her neck. Burning pain flamed through her.

Heusler's bulk fell over her, a smothering weight.

"Cursed Warlock," Emily heard Dmitri's voice say. "Let him heal himself of *that*." She heard him grunt as he rolled Heusler's body off of her. Then he was helping her sit up. She felt warmth spill down the side of her throat, down into the well of her collarbone. His hand brushed something from her face, sharp bits scratching her skin.

"You see, Miss Edwards?" he said. "I told you I had been sent to protect you."

CHAPTER SIXTEEN

Pelmeni with Smetana

The next hour was a blur of shadows and pain.

Emily could see nothing, but she could feel herself being quickly lifted into a large covered drayage wagon, carried away swiftly from the sounds of screaming and scattered rifle pops. There was the sound of horses' feet, and the smell of blood and black acid rain, and the feeling of men's bodies all around her—wounded men, groaning.

The cut place on her throat burned, and the whole side of her neck was tight and sticky with clotted blood. But that pain paled in comparison to the pain searing her eyes. They ached as if they'd been put out with red hot pokers, and her head was splitting. She tried to blink away the blindness, but there was nothing, not even the faintest shadow of motion.

Dmitri sat beside her. He had a cool damp cloth, and he laid it over her aching eyes. It smelled of chamomile and mint and other smells she could not identify—chemical smells.

"The compress will help the blindness pass," he said, his body rocking against hers as the wagon moved. "The Solar Flash is hard on the eyes, but will do no permanent damage if treated quickly."

And after a while, Emily's vision did begin to return. First she could distinguish vague forms around her, the men sitting hunched forward, nursing injuries. Then, everything became very red, and she began to see details. Loose tunics stained with blood. Thick fingers fumbling with heavy wooden crosses on beaded strings, heads bowed, lips moved in prayer. A bottle of vodka, a bulwark against pain, being passed from dirty hand to dirty hand. Emily reached for it as it passed, taking a long swallow. Shuddering, she looked out the flapping canvas at the back of the wagon, trying to see where they were going.

Dmitri lifted the compress to her face again.

"Keep it over your eyes," he said curtly, and the way he said it made Emily wonder if it was really because he was worried about her vision.

But silently, she did as she was told.

The wagon stopped after a little while, and Emily, the compress still over her eyes, was led into a place that smelled good. There was the sharp tangy smell of tea, the rich earthy odor of beets and potatoes, the savory whiff of chicken broth. When Emily removed the compress, she found that her vision was mostly restored, and that she was in a big kitchen. A squat woman in a colorful headscarf was stirring a pot of soup and muttering to herself in Russian. Dmitri, in the far corner, was rummaging in a box, pulling out pieces of clean white linen. Laying these over his arm, he took up a steaming bowl and a small vial of iodine and came to sit next to Emily.

"Let's have a look." He seized her chin, looking at the place on her throat where she'd been cut. "It's not deep, and those heathen blades of glass cut cleanly, at least."

He dipped one of the pieces of linen in the warm water, and began to wipe the blood from Emily's throat without particular gentleness.

"Where am I?" she asked.

"Safe," he said. "A restaurant, actually. The *pelmeni* with *smetana* are particularly good, if you are hungry."

Emily winced as the cloth touched the wound. She thought about all the death she'd seen that day. "I'm not," she said.

"Certainly a healthy young Witch isn't going to let the death of a few dozen strangers ruin her appetite?" Dmitri said. He did not sneer, or speak with anger, but the bitterness of the words made Emily press her lips together. Dmitri dipped the cloth into the bowl again. The water turned abruptly red. He wrung the cloth and began wiping her face, removing scratchy chunks of bone and, Emily knew now,

Heusler's brain. Over by the stove, the woman was cutting potatoes into the soup unconcernedly, as if brain-spattered girls came to sit in her kitchen every day.

A door opened, and the smell of a brown cigarette preceded the opener into the kitchen.

As she watched Perun enter, Emily tensed. Even though the Sini Mira had saved her life, and even though her father had been a member of that group, they continued to make it very clear how they felt about her and her kind, and she continued to distrust them.

Perun came to Dmitri's side and cast his husky-dog gaze down on Emily.

"Miss Edwards, it is good to see you again," he said. His accent was even thicker than Dmitri's. "You remember, we have met before?"

"Yes, we've met once or twice," Emily said, pushing away Dmitri's hands. "Once when you tried to kidnap me. The second time before you kidnapped Emeritus Zeno." She paused. "Where is he?"

Perun gestured obliquely with the cigarette, smoke making patterns in the air. "How are your eyes, Miss Edwards? No permanent damage, I hope?"

"My eyes ache," Emily said. The words sounded too angular, too foreign. This place, with its smells, reminded her of her father. "I will be fine," she added, letting the words form themselves in Russian. Perun looked startled.

"Miss Edwards!" he returned, in Russian. "I did not know."

I didn't either, until last night, Emily thought. But now the sonorous tones of Russian were familiar and homey.

"What have you done with Emeritus Zeno?" Emily asked the question again, though it tasted no better in Russian.

"We do not have him," Perun said. "The Institute is mistaken in thinking that we do."

"I think the Institute can be forgiven for that," Emily said, "since he was kidnapped using one of your machines. Something called a Nikifuryevich Ladder."

Perun shook his head ruefully.

"The Institute does not seem to understand that our technologies can be used against us, as any technology can." He fell silent for a moment as he watched Dmitri pick bits of bone from Emily's hair. Then Dmitri stood silently, moved back to the box from which he'd gotten the supplies, watching his own hands as he replaced them slowly, item by item. Emily lifted her head to look Perun full in the face. The man bore the scrutiny, taking a long drag off of his spicy-smelling cigarette.

"Then if you don't have Emeritus Zeno . . . who does?"

"The same people who just tried to kill you, most likely."

"The Temple of Itztlacoliuhqui," Emily said softly. She remembered the vision she'd had in the Institute's conservatory, the vision of a knife-edged goddess of black glass. Then it was she whom Ososolyeh had been warning Emily against.

"The High Priest said that she commanded that I be killed. But if she's got the hair sticks, why does she want me dead into the bargain?" Emily shook her head. "Just for fun?"

"Hair sticks?" Perun reached for a chair, pulled it close to where Emily was sitting. He sat down and leaned forward. "What are you talking about?"

Emily snapped her lips shut. What did he know? What should she tell him? Her mother had been taking the hair sticks to the Sini Mira . . . at least, that's the best sense Emily could make of her jumbled memories. But her mother had also killed her father, to destroy the secret of the poison . . . so why hadn't she destroyed the sticks while under Cowdray's terrible possession?

Unless she'd never known.

Unless, after all, Emily had never told.

"Miss Edwards?" Perun prompted, and Emily realized she'd been silent for a long time.

"You first." She brought her eyes up to meet his. "I want you to tell me what's going on. What connection you had with my father, Vladimir Lyakhov. I know he was a member of the Sini Mira. I know you've been looking for him. Tell me why."

Perun let out a long breath. He let the stub end of his cigarette drop to the floor, and quenched it with his foot.

"All right," he said. "I will tell you what I know. As you said, your father's name was Vladimir Lyakhov, but within the Sini Mira, he was known as Volos, after the God of Oaths.

It was a title within our organization, a nom de guerre. My own name, Perun, honors the Heavenly Smith."

Volos' Anodyne, Emily thought. That was what Zeno had called the poison.

"The title of Volos was inherited by your father," Perun continued, his voice breaking through the little firecrackers of connection that were popping in her brain. "From his mentor at the Imperial Academy of Sciences in Saint Petersburg. After he was murdered, your father assumed his work. Thus, your father became Volos."

"Aleksei Morozovich," Emily said. "That was his mentor, wasn't it? The scientist who created the poison called Volos' Anodyne."

Perun's eyes widened. He glanced over at Dmitri, who had taken a position by the door and was watching Emily with arms crossed.

"You know more than you are telling, Miss Edwards!" He reached into his pocket, extracted a silver cigarette case. He took out another one of his brown cigarettes, tapped it on the back of the case.

"Aleksei Morozovich was indeed the creator of Volos' Anodyne. It was his life's work."

"His life's work was to poison magic, to make it unpracticeable?" Emily stared hard at Perun. "Why? Why tamper with the natural way of things?"

Perun lit his cigarette, gave it a few deep puffs before speaking again.

"Until about a hundred years ago, the practice of magic was self-limiting. A Witch or Warlock could only channel the amount of power his or her body could stand. As you say, this is the natural way of things. But humans always seek power beyond what is given by nature. The lessons of science and engineering began to be applied to the practice of magic. Methods for extracting raw power were developed—and now have developed to the point where they can be implemented on a large scale, as with the Terramantic extraction factory you saw in Charleston. Raw magic can be sucked straight from the earth in vast quantities. Exponentially larger magical schemes could be brought to fruition—resulting in exponentially larger production of Black Exunge, over-whelming the Mantic Anastomosis' ability to process it. And so there are eruptions of Exunge, and Aberrancies, and all manner of foul imbalance."

Perun swallowed smoke, exhaled.

"But worse than that," Perun continued, "is that the collection of such huge amounts of raw power makes possible unholy magical practices on a scale hitherto unimaginable. The Black Glass Goddess, Itztlacoliuhqui, who once required the blood of thousands of human sacrifices simply to *manifest* in a human body, can now easily be provided with enough power to wreak whatever havoc on the world she desires—all thanks to the bastard union of magic and modern technology."

"And just what kind of havoc does she desire?" Emily asked.

"Temamauhti," Perun said. Emily remembered hearing Sophos Mirabilis speak the word once before, and his scoffing dismissal of it.

"The half-baked apocalypse?"

Perun grunted.

"It is now quite thoroughly baked, Miss Edwards. Do you remember all the power from the Terramantic extraction factory? Power that Captain Caul was amassing to oppose the so-called 'half-baked apocalypse'? After Caul's death, General Blotgate, the Army's highest-ranking magical practitioner, advocated for a military alliance with the Black Glass Goddess. Instead of using all that power to oppose her, the United States Army has delivered it into her hands. And soon the calendar will ripen, and soon she will begin the Remaking."

Emily's flesh went cold.

A stair-stepped pyramid made of skulls . . .

"The earthquakes along the Pacific Coast, the Aberrancies terrorizing cities and towns . . . they are just the first manifestation of the Goddess' efforts," Perun continued. "They will continue to spread."

Blood dripping down the sides of a frost-rimed altar . . . bodies piled all around it, hundreds of thousands of them . . .

"The Army can't have given her that much power," Emily whispered.

"The power they have provided her is merely a match set to kindling," Perun said. "We believe the Goddess has discovered some means by which she can filter Black Exunge. Release the power trapped within it, just as the Mantic Anastomosis does naturally, except much more quickly, and far more efficiently. And as she does this, channeling evermore enormous amounts of pure raw magic, the more Black Exunge the Mantic Anastomosis will produce, and the more Black Exunge she will have from which to draw power." He paused once more, letting his silence hang. "Until, of course, the entire earth has been transformed into an Aberrancy—a sphere of lifeless filth."

Emily remembered another vision Ososolyeh had shown her. *A lake drained, leaving nothing but foulness behind, poison pumped into the deepest places, clogging them with filth and venom . . .*

At the time, she had thought it referred to the Black Exunge the Terramantic extraction plant was pumping deep into the earth to extract refined pockets of chrysohaeme . . . but it had meant this, too.

"Morozovich did not live to see these days come to pass, but he foresaw their coming. That is why he developed the Anodyne. It is a toxin, yes. But the toxic effects are aggregative. A practitioner doing a small work—a healing for example—might feel no effects. A practitioner doing a larger work might feel slightly ill from the exposure to a larger amount of the toxin. A practitioner manifesting a spirit as powerful as Itztlacoliuhqui's, giving her the blood and body she needs to wreak havoc on the world, would die like a rat given cyanide."

"And someone like my fiancé?" Emily said. "Someone burned?"

"That is not our concern," Dmitri said from his corner of the room. "And given what we know about your fiancé—"

Perun lifted an abrupt hand, and Dmitri fell silent.

"Miss Edwards, your fiancé had had ample opportunity to remove that baneful blight," Perun said. "He chose not to, and now, with Zeno gone, it is too late."

Emily's eyes darted between the men.

"What are you talking about? There's no cure for his condition. He told me so himself."

Perun frowned at Emily for a moment, then grunted a mild concession.

"Then I am mistaken, and I apologize," he said. He paused before continuing. "There is no way to know what the poison will or won't do to your fiancé. But I can promise you, if we do not stop *temamauhti,* your fiancé, and you, and I, and your pap and the very earth itself will suffer and die in miserable agony under the cruel reign of the Black Glass Goddess."

There was a long, horrible silence as Perun finished speaking. The sound of clinking china made Perun look over at the head-scarved woman, who was spooning heaping portions of food into large white bowls.

"It smells of heaven in here, Irina Sidorovna," he called to the woman. He looked at Emily. "Are you hungry, Miss Edwards? The *pelmeni* with *smetana*—"

"I know. Delicious," Emily said. "But for some reason I'm not hungry."

Perun shrugged as the woman called Irina Sidorovna slid a plate in front of him. Fat steaming dumplings were topped with a mound of glossy sour cream and sprinkled with fronds of dill and black dots of caviar. A bottle of vodka from an icebox and a small glass completed the meal. Without a word, Emily took the bottle of vodka and poured herself a glass. She tossed it back. Perun looked at her, but didn't comment. He ground out his cigarette and picked up a fork.

"When news of Morozovich's work leaked out, the Temple marked him for death. He went into hiding, of course, but Warlocks from the Temple found him. They tortured him, forced him to surrender every scrap of paper in his possession and made him swear that he had given the information to no one else. Satisfied that they had wrung the truth from him, they dragged his bleeding body to his laboratory in Saint Petersburg and burned it down with him inside. They believed that by destroying him, they had destroyed the poison."

Emily shuddered, the vodka spreading warmth through her gut. She watched Perun stab one of the small dumplings and pop it into his mouth. "But if no other copy existed—" she began.

"Of course the notes still existed," Perun interrupted curtly, touching a napkin to his mouth. "Morozovich had entrusted copies to his assistant—your father—then wiped his own memory clean with a cheap elixir bought from one of the old *koldunyas* around Gostiny Dvor. When the Temple Warlocks found him, he knew no more about the poison than you or me. They confronted him with his own notes. He said he did not recognize them. The torturers thought he was withholding information and redoubled their efforts."

Dmitri made a strangled sound. Perun shook his head, and picked up another little dumpling. He chewed it thoughtfully before continuing.

"Your father fled to America. We kept him in a series of safe houses. The Kendalls—your mother's family—provided one of the safe houses. There, he worked to complete Morozovich's work on the Anodyne. It was quite unexpected that he would fall in love with their daughter." He paused, reaching over to reclaim the glass from Emily. Uncorking the bottle, he poured some for himself. "He left their house and took your mother with him. And after that, we lost track of him." He threw the vodka back with a jerk.

"So you did not know what happened to him either?"

Perun exhaled, shaking his head.

"Our last contact with him was in 1856."

When I was five, Emily thought. So he'd contacted the Sini Mira just before he died. She remembered him telling her that he was going to meet his friends. Before her mother—before *Aebedel Cowdray,* Emily corrected herself fiercely—had killed him.

"He had arranged to meet with us in San Francisco to deliver the formula," Perun continued, "but he never arrived there. And we never heard from him again."

Perun was silent for a moment, his eyes searching her face as if to read an answer there. Emily looked away. She was not ready to talk about that night, that horrible moonlit night full of knives and blood.

"We thought the poison was lost to us forever," Perun said finally, "until the Indian Witch spoke of it at the Grand Symposium."

"You were not at the Symposium," Emily said. "How did you hear of it?"

"Zeno told us," Perun said. "I've known him for a long time, Miss Edwards. In some ways, we were even allies."

"I don't believe you," Emily said, looking at Dmitri. "I know how you people feel about Witches and Warlocks."

"You know what you have been told," Perun said, "but that does not mean you know everything." Reaching inside his coat, he pulled out something round and golden. Emily gasped when she realized what it was. It was Komé's rooting ball.

Perun handed it to her, and Emily cradled it against her chest with her good hand.

"Zeno gave it to me the night before the Investment, the night you saw us together." Perun scraped the last of the sour cream from his plate, licked it from his fork. "He was worried that something might happen, and he asked me to keep it safe."

Emily closed her eyes, feeling for the old Indian Witch's consciousness within it. To her joy, Emily could feel the woman's presence. She was there, but despite Emily's efforts to rouse her, she would not speak. She just sort of . . . *hummed.*

Emily looked at Perun. "What have you done to her?"

Perun smiled softly.

"Miss Edwards, we have done nothing to her. You are a Witch who knows the earth; surely you recognize the metamorphosis of nature. It was the very reason she was put in the rooting ball. She is sprouting, growing, transforming from what she was into what she will become. You cannot expect her to feel particularly conversational."

Emily held the ball tightly. She knew Perun's words to be true as soon as he spoke them. The satisfied hum of roots growing outward—it was precisely what she'd heard. Frowning, she looked up at him.

"I still don't understand why Zeno would ally with you. Credomancers use magical power just like anyone else."

Pushing his plate away, Perun extracted a fresh cigarette and tucked it between his lips.

"Of all the magical traditions, credomancy requires the least free magic—only a fraction of what is required by sangrimancy. It is theorized that the practice of credomancy will be only slightly affected if the poison is implemented," Perun said. "Perhaps Emeritus Zeno thought that the poison might be a good way to advance the cause of credomancy over the long term."

"Quite convenient for the credomancers," Emily said, waving a hand in front of her face to dispel the sudden cloud of smoke. "So you're saying that Zeno *wanted* to see the poison implemented?" Emily said. "To set the practice of credomancy above all others?"

"He *was* once a priest, Miss Edwards." Perun smiled wryly. "Old habits die hard."

"Then Zeno had no more moral high ground than the sangrimancers he claimed to despise!"

"He wanted to see the damage to the great consciousness of the earth halted." Perun squinted as he lifted the cigarette to his lips. "That is not a matter of human morals, it is a matter of human survival."

"I can't believe it," Emily muttered to herself. But actually, speaking the words, she found that she could believe it. Remembering Zeno's eyes, the soft storm of schemes that had churned behind them . . . yes, she could believe it.

"Now, Miss Edwards, I have answered your questions. You must answer mine. Tell me of the hair sticks you mentioned."

Emily looked down at the floor, stroking the golden ball in her lap thoughtfully. The Black Glass Goddess had the hair sticks now, and whatever secrets were on them. What use was it to hide the information from these people, even if she did not fully trust them? Now that the barn door had been left open and the horses had vacated their stables, what harm could it do?

"My father gave me a pair of silver hair sticks," Emily said. "They had Faery Writing on them, and the name Aleksei Morozovich. I am almost certain that they had the formula for the poison on them."

Perun and Dmitri exchanged glances. Shadows of rage and pain passed over Dmitri's face.

"So they have been lost," he said, his voice a horrible strangle. "And those poor people murdered, and . . ." Dmitri rubbed a hand across his mouth, turned away.

Despite how unkindly he'd spoken to her, Emily felt sudden sympathy for him. She understood the awful burden of guilt he felt. She'd brought the sangrimancers to the doorstep of Abner Pearl and his family . . . and for what? For a secret that was lost before it was even discovered. It was a waste—a terrible, useless waste.

"And what are we to do now?" Dmitri crossed the room in three steps. Obviously needing some outlet, he snatched the empty plate in front of Perun and threw it across the room. Emily winced at the sound of it smashing. "There is not a single hope left for the world!"

"Calm yourself, Dmitri Alekseivitch," Perun frowned. "Hope is never entirely lost. Even in the coldest darkness of winter, hope remains."

Dmitri made a sound of disgust. "You have been listening too much to credomancers," he said darkly. "And Witches."

Ignoring the barb, Emily held Perun's eyes. "Without the hair sticks, how can we have any hope at all?"

Perun laid a kind hand on her shoulder. "Get some rest, Miss Edwards. Dmitri will take you to a place where you can sleep. I am going out for a while, but I will be back soon. And I will have a plan."

After Perun left, Emily did receive a plate of *pelmeni* with *smetana,* pushed upon her by the woman he had called Irina Sidorovna—and it took only one bite to confirm that they were indeed delicious—creamy and oniony and dripping with rich meaty juice. But one bite was all Emily could manage, with Dmitri scowling at her. In the brooding silence, Emily's mind filled with the screams of the dying, both remembered and imagined. She pushed the plate away and reached for the bottle of vodka, her hand trembling violently. Dmitri took it before she could, uncorked it, poured himself a glass. He looked at her hard. Then, sighing, he poured her a glass as well. They drank together in silence. They both knew things could have gone very differently than they had, and that each of them could have done something better.

After they had finished half the bottle, Dmitri took her upstairs, to the restaurant's top floor. The rooms were mostly used for storage, but one had been cleared for her use. It had a comfortable-looking bed spread with a colorful counterpane.

"There is water, so you can wash, and I will find you clean clothes and shoes," Dmitri said. Emily looked down at her own bare, scratched feet. "You'll be staying here for a while."

"How long?" Emily sat down heavily on the bed. Climbing the stairs had made her realize just how much vodka she'd drunk.

"Until Perun can formulate his *plan,*" Dmitri spoke the last word with faint contempt.

"I should go back to the Stantons'," Emily said. "Or at least send a message—"

"No," Dmitri said. "Temple Warlocks killed two dozen of my men today, rescuing you. I think that's enough."

Emily bared her teeth at him. "You think I wanted it? I didn't ask for any of this, Dmitri Alekseivitch." She wasn't sure why she had added his second name, but she remembered it was what Perun had called him. Dmitri winced when she spoke it.

"You were perhaps too young then to understand the meaning of a man's patronymic, or too drunk now to respect it," Dmitri said coldly, "but it is derived from the name of a man's father. My father's name was Aleksei."

Emily looked up, finding the man's brown eyes.

"Aleksei . . . Morozovich?"

"Reclaiming my father's work and seeing it implemented is of great personal importance to me." Dmitri spoke through clenched teeth. "As is killing every Warlock who has ever spent a single moment in the service of the Black Glass Goddess." He bowed contemptuously as he opened the door to leave. "Sleep well, Emilia Vladimirovna."

* * *

Emily did sleep, but not well, and when she woke again it was dark outside and her head throbbed horribly and her mouth tasted as if she'd been sucking on a rotten potato.

Well, here I am in the hands of the Sini Mira, she thought, arm over her eyes to block out even the faint light of the low-burning lamp. Once it had been her worst nightmare, but she had discovered that nightmares could be much, much worse.

Even though Perun had given her so many answers, they did not balance against all her questions. And while she was very glad to have Komé back—she glanced at the side table to make sure the golden ball was still there—the old Witch was too busy growing roots to give her any answers. But, Emily realized suddenly, she didn't need Komé's answers. She could speak to Ososolyeh just as well as Komé ever could. Without even knowing it was happening, Emily had been growing into something new—just as Komé now was. Perhaps that had been the intention all along.

Now that she had learned more from Perun, perhaps Ososolyeh could show her the rest. Climbing out of bed, she tried the door. It was unlocked, which was a pleasant surprise. She was rather glad for the fact that her feet were still bare; it allowed her to move silently down the dark hallway.

She crept down three flights of stairs. At the bottom, the door to the restaurant's kitchen was open, and light from it spilled into the hallway. Laid over the smell of food was the acrid stink of cigarette smoke. Quietly, she crept to the back door. It opened onto a tiny, trash-strewn yard, hemmed by tall brick buildings on all sides and piled high with empty wooden crates. There was a chopping block by the door, bright with blood; chicken heads were piled in a basket beside it.

Getting as far away from the smell of blood as she could, she went back to the corner of the yard where a few small trees and bushes straggled. Stripping quickly, she crept under a tall weedy bush, her fingers and toes feeling for the soft, moist earth beneath it. Within moments, as if the earth guessed her haste, she was sinking into the ground, soil sliding over her like a lover's hands. Instead of fighting against it as she had before, she relaxed in the embrace, the sweet smell of rot and clay and life filling her nostrils, soothing her aching body.

Basket of Secrets. Ososolyeh cooed a resonant greeting, its eternity of memories thrumming through her like a heartbeat.

Emily breathed back, letting her body dissipate, letting her body expand into the vastness of the void, into the glowing bones of the world.

Tell me, she prayed. *Tell me more.*

Smooth black walls, slippery and gelid.

A pyramid of yellowed skulls. The smell of smoke, bitter and acrid.

A Temple in which something ancient and malicious crouched, razor fingers gleaming, dripping with fresh-drawn blood.

Zeno was there.

Zeno was dying.

He was dying, and it was a bad death, sick with agonized regret.

If only things had gone as they should have . . . She could feel, rather than hear, Zeon's fading thoughts.

But everything went wrong . . . so wrong . . .

Life pumped from Zeno's gaping throat, spurt after weakening spurt. His naked body, withered and pale, showed the horrible marks of extended torture—flesh battered, bones crushed. But he had not broken—she could feel it. He had outlasted the ancient and malicious thing, and death was his reward. He had been discarded, thrown into a pit, his blood a treat intended for the unholy thing within—an enormous hunk of meat, quivering slimy and slick.

But I can give him one more chance.

One more chance.

Emily could sense him marshaling power, all the power that he had or ever had. Collecting it for one final effort.

May good triumph over evil! The silent command, willed rather than spoken, made the earth shake. He drove the decree deep into the flesh that slicked and roiled beneath him. The flesh shuddered and cringed. She could hear cells rupturing, veins and vessels shredding, delicate internal structures collapsing. Zeno poured his vast will into the command, until only one tiny golden drop of himself remained.

Then, with his body's very last bit of strength, Zeno reached out to grab something protruding from the crumbling earthen wall of the pit.

A root.

A fat, deep, ancient root.

Zeno clutched it.

He sent the last tiny drop of himself outward, sent it soaring along a network of roots, tiny and large . . .

Freedom.

Release.

Escape.

A stripped soul singing along, borne away by sap and nectar, up bright living channels, up, up to where the sun was, to where leaves spread and rustled . . .

I am going home. Zeno's words floated on a last breath, spoken in the language of wood and water and leaves . . .

"Miss Edwards!"

The voice came from far away. There was the feeling of hands, but not the gentle soft caress of the earth. These were rough, hurried hands, digging at her, pulling her up like a root vegetable. Emily stirred, aware that she was well buried. Hands helped her sit up, brushed smothering dirt from her face. Then the sound of Dmitri's voice, harsh.

"Miss Edwards, for God's sake!"

She felt herself gathering back into herself, the threads of her human consciousness retracting from where they'd spread out in a thin, vibrant array. Dmitri knelt over her. A lantern glowed on the ground nearby.

"What are you doing?" He grimaced, averting his eyes from her mud-streaked nakedness.

"Getting answers," she said softly. She felt as if she'd forgotten how to speak. She hardly knew if she was speaking in Russian or English anymore. Maybe she was speaking some new language, the language of wood and water and leaves.

But it seemed he could understand her. He snatched her dress from where she'd discarded it and thrust it toward her with his face turned away. She could feel his disgust like a physical thing. She pulled the dress over her head slowly, still trying to remember how to move.

When her body was covered, Emily wrapped arms around herself and sat staring at the ground. "I lost my father, too, Dmitri Alekseivitch. A Warlock killed him to destroy the poison. I was very young. I watched the knife go into his chest. Again and again." She looked up at Dmitri. "I didn't tell Perun that."

Dmitri looked down at her, his face harshly shadowed by the light of the lantern he held. After a long silence, he reached down to help her stand, and escorted her back to her room, locking the door behind her as he left.

CHAPTER SEVENTEEN

The Plan

Not surprisingly, the door was not unlocked again until the next morning, when Dmitri came to retrieve her.

"Perun's got his plan," Dmitri said. "And he's ready to present it."

This time he led her into the restaurant proper—a cheerful room crowded with dozens of heavy wooden tables covered with bright cloth and flowers arranged in colored bottles. Morning sunshine glowed through the closed wooden shutters. At one of the tables, Perun sat. Sitting next to him, straight and prim in a chestnut-colored dress, was Miss Jesczenka.

"Emily." Miss Jesczenka stood quickly. She came over to where Emily stood next to Dmitri and took Emily's hands in hers. The older woman's gaze flew over her from crown to toe, taking in her dirty and disheveled appearance. "Are you all right?"

Emily wasn't certain how to answer, so she said nothing.

Miss Jesczenka scrutinized Emily's face, looked at the bandage on her throat. She put a worried hand on Emily's forehead, as if suspecting a fever—as if her bearing witness to horrible death and tragedy were like a bout of influenza.

"Mr. Stanton," Emily asked. "Is he all right?"

"He doesn't know I'm here," Miss Jesczenka said. "You ran away from his mother's house, left your ring . . . and she said you saw the book." She paused, looking at Emily again, carefully. "As soon as I get back, I'll let him know that you're safe."

"I told you, we mean no harm to Miss Edwards," Perun said. One of his omnipresent cigarettes smoldered between his brown-stained fingers. "Shall we begin our discussion?"

Irina Sidorovna brought out a samovar of tea and a plate of cakes and a bowl of raspberry jam. She set these in the center of the table. Perun turned the small spigot on the samovar, poured tea into little cups, and pushed the saucers across the tablecloth toward the women. He stirred a large spoonful of raspberry jam into his own cup, his spoon making small tinkling sounds against the china. Emily tasted her tea; it was bitter and strong. She dipped a spoonful of jam into it, and the sweetness did indeed help.

"The Institute is grateful to you for helping Miss Edwards," Miss Jesczenka began, not even looking at her tea. "If the events truly happened as you have described them, then you have done us a great service."

Perun chuckled. "Why should I lie, Miss Jesczenka?"

"There are many scenarios I can imagine in which lying would suit your purposes," Miss Jesczenka said coolly. "But whether or not you are lying is immaterial. I am here to take Miss Edwards back to the Institute. Mr. Stanton very much desires her return."

"I'm sure he does," Perun said. "However, the Institute is not a safe place for her right now. Is it?"

Miss Jesczenka colored slightly. Perun sipped his tea, took a cake and examined it. He ate it in one bite.

"I have called you here to explain the situation, and to see if there is some possibility the Sini Mira and the Institute could do together what neither of us can do alone. It may surprise you to know that we had a very amenable understanding with Emeritus Zeno."

"So amenable that you kidnapped him at the precise moment that it would be most damaging to the Institute he founded," Miss Jesczenka sneered.

Perun brushed crumbs from his hands. "As I've told Miss Edwards, we did not kidnap Emeritus Zeno. Rather, I believe it was the Temple of Itztlacoliuhqui, the sangrimancers who tried to kill Miss Edwards yesterday. The sangrimancers who have taken her hair sticks, on which her father inscribed the secret of Volos' Anodyne."

Miss Jesczenka turned astonished eyes on Emily.

Emily answered her gaze. "My father was an assistant to a scientist in Saint Petersburg," she said. "A man named Aleksei Morozovich. My father brought Morozovich's research with him to America. My hair sticks—he gave them to me when I was very young. He told me they had Faery Writing on them. So I took them to a Faery Reader in Chatham Square—"

"That's why you were asking about Faery Reading," Miss Jesczenka breathed.

"I'm sure the formula for the poison was on the hair sticks," Emily said. "If I'd known, I never would have left them. When I came back the next morning . . ." Emily dipped her head, shame reddening her cheeks afresh. "Temple Warlocks had gotten there before me. And it *was* the Temple, Miss Jesczenka. The man who tried to kill me was named Heusler. I met him at the Symposium."

"Selig Heusler, High Priest of the Temple of Itztlacoliuhqui," Miss Jesczenka affirmed, letting out a dismayed breath. "Why haven't you told us any of this before, Miss Edwards?"

"I didn't know any of it before," Emily looked up, heat rising under her collar. "And even if I had, what chance did anyone give me? Everyone kept putting me off, sending me away . . . I was a nuisance, remember? A distraction. What should I have done?"

She scanned Miss Jesczenka's face, honestly seeking an answer. But Miss Jesczenka had none. She just touched Emily's hand gently before turning hard brown eyes back on Perun. "So, Miss Edwards had the secret of Volos' Anodyne in her possession, and now she does not. The Temple of Itztlacoliuhqui has stolen it, and has probably already destroyed it, if it is as much of a threat to them as you imply." She tilted her head. "What do you hope to gain by keeping her here? What is keeping you from turning her over to me right now?"

"To answer your last question first, I believe it is Miss Edwards' decision as to whether she wants to go with you.

Therefore, I am in no position to turn her over," Perun said. "To answer your first question, I believe the Temple will not be able to destroy the poison unless they have Miss Edwards, and thus it is of utmost importance that she be kept safe."

Emily blinked at him. "What are you talking about?"

"The way the secret was hidden," Perun replied. "Why would your father have encrypted it on something like hair sticks?"

"They are small, easily concealed." Miss Jesczenka was brusque. "No one would ever think to look on them. Also, they are a woman's item. No one thinks women capable of such subterfuge."

"Believe me, Miss Jesczenka, I know all about women and subterfuges." Perun stared hard at her as he spoke. "But what you say is true. Hair sticks are very small. So small, indeed, that violet scale had to be employed to fit all the information onto them. Lyakhov would have had to search far and wide to find a man who could encrypt them, even in 1856, when Faery Writers were far more common than they are now. Why go to such trouble? Why not use a larger object?"

"Why not, indeed, use the broad side of a barn?" Miss Jesczenka said. "I don't see the profit in this line of inquiry."

"Because you do not know your Russian mythology," Perun said. "You never learned the story of Baba-Yaga and the God of Oaths."

"I know that story," Emily said. "My father told it to me." She searched her memory. "My father said I was supposed to tell it to his friends when I found them. And only in Russian, never in English."

Perun nodded, as if his suspicions had been confirmed.

"Tell us now, Miss Edwards," he prompted gently.

"Baba-Yaga had a house with four chicken legs," Emily said, remembering the strange tale. "The God of Oaths had the heart of his true love locked away in a box of silver and gold, and demons wanted to take it from him. Demons with knives for fingers, and razor sharp teeth. So he hid the box in Baba-Yaga's hair." Emily reached up, fingered one coppery-brown curl. "He told me the story when he was washing my hair. He washed it with something that burned."

Perun looked at Miss Jesczenka.

"Lyakhov would never have been so careless as to hide the complete secret in one object only. He would have employed more complex means—a two-part code. One part on a pair of hair sticks. The other on the hair itself."

"Then you are implying that he was a monster," Miss Jesczenka said, her words clipped. "For only a monster would have hidden such a deadly secret in the hair of his own child. What about his wife? Wouldn't she be a more likely candidate?"

Perun opened his silver case, tapped a cigarette against it quickly.

"He would not have put the secret in Catherine Kendall's hair. She was cursed. Possessed by the vengeful spirit of a Warlock one of her ancestors pressed to death," Perun said. "She could not be trusted."

"And a five-year-old child could be?" Miss Jesczenka said.

"Miss Jesczenka, I am looking at this logically," Perun slammed down the cigarette case on the table. The samovar rattled.

"No. You are looking at it desperately, as a man who has lost his last hope." Miss Jesczenka glared at him. "You have lost the poison. You are scrounging for a shred of promise where none remains."

The two of them glared at each other for long moments. Perun was the first to break the gaze, lifting his hands.

"Fine. There is an easy test to see if I am right. Shall we conduct it? If I am wrong, I will allow Miss Edwards to go her own way. Whether that's with you, back to that crumbling Institute and Mr. Stanton, who is in no position to protect her from the blood sorcerers who want to kill her . . . well, that's her decision to make."

"What test?" Emily asked.

"I will require a small piece of your hair." Perun reached into his pocket and pulled out a pair of scissors.

"All ready, I see," Miss Jesczenka observed, her eyes narrowing.

"I anticipated that this would be necessary," Perun countered. He looked at Emily, his gaze softer. "May I?"

Emily leaned forward. Perun snipped a small curl from behind her ear. He lifted his teacup and set it aside, sprinkled the strands of hair into the saucer. He snapped his fingers meaningfully at Dmitri, who stepped out of the room and returned quickly with a rattling leather bag.

"If Lyakhov encrypted the information as I believe he did, he would have chemically treated Miss Edwards' hair in a special way. The chemical will have changed the structure of her hair's follicles, so that no matter how much hair she loses, the hair she regrows will contain the same properties."

"What properties?"

"You know that it is the shape of the hair follicles that results in the hair's curliness, do you not? The exact shape of the curl defines a precise sine curve. The measure of that curve is the value to which the information on the hair sticks is coded." Perun took the leather bag, opened it, fished inside for a small bottle. "This type of two-stage encryption has been used within the Sini Mira before, for highly sensitive information."

He pulled the cork stopper from the bottle. A sharp odor filled the room as he swirled the liquid between his fingers.

"The chemical used to etch the hair follicles changes the molecular structure of the hair in a unique way. This chemical will indicate the presence of that unique molecular structure. If I am correct, the hair in this dish will glow with a blue color."

He dripped the chemical into the saucer. Emily watched as the hair curled, damped, and glowed the blue of a summer sky. Nodding, Perun pushed the dish toward Miss Jesczenka and Emily so they could examine it more closely.

"Ingenious, isn't it?" He capped the bottle, placed it back into his leather bag.

"And just as likely to be an ingenious deception," Miss Jesczenka said. "You scientists have chemicals that will make anything do anything. I know the tricks of science, just as I know the tricks of magic."

"This is no trick," Perun said. "It is the one slim advantage that remains to us."

"So slim, indeed, as to be indiscernible. Pray elaborate."

"I believe the sangrimancers will examine the hair sticks, find that they are unable to fully decipher them, and refrain from their immediate destruction. Thus, there may be a chance to retrieve them."

"Well, *that's* an optimistic supposition!" Miss Jesczenka snorted. Emily had never heard the woman snort before. "What conceivable need would they have to decipher the formula? There's no reason not to simply destroy the hair sticks and be done with it."

"But unless they decipher the writing on them, the Temple cannot be sure that they have what they think they have," Perun noted. "They cannot be sure that it is the formula for Volos' Anodyne. And so . . . they need Miss Edwards to be sure."

"Then Miss Edwards is our slim advantage."

"They've already expressed a very pointed desire for her death, so it's possible that they've intuited the connection already." He paused. "It's clear that no matter what, she's in grave danger. They will not stop at clipping a curl of her hair. They will not rest until she is dead, her body burned, and her ashes scattered to the wind."

Miss Jesczenka shook her head, sighed heavily. But it was a sigh of resignation, not disagreement. She tilted her head at Perun once more. "What do you want, exactly?"

"I want the Institute's help," he said.

"Even if the Institute were willing to help the Sini Mira, it is in no position to do so," Miss Jesczenka said. "It is not strong enough."

"But you have a way to rectify that situation, don't you, Miss Jesczenka?" Perun's voice was suggestive.

"What is he talking about?" Emily said, but Miss Jesczenka did not even look at her.

"How did you know?" Miss Jesczenka asked softly.

"I know enough about credomancy to recognize the makings of a classic Talleyrand Maneuver. And I know about you and Fortissimus. The rest was easy to deduce."

Miss Jesczenka studied the table's colorful cloth as if there were something fascinating in the paisley pattern.

"We must have the Institute's help if we are to reclaim the hair sticks," Perun said. Then more gently, he added, "It would also be nice to rescue Emeritus Zeno, don't you think?"

"But Emeritus Zeno is dead," Emily said.

Perun turned a piercing gaze on her that made Emily squirm uncomfortably.

"What did you say?" he said, his voice terribly quiet.

Hadn't they discussed this? If so, when? She couldn't remember now. But why had she thought . . . Emily knit her brow.

"I'm sorry. But . . . I . . ." She looked at Miss Jesczenka for help, but the woman's eyes were full of anxious hurt, ice to Perun's fire. She looked away quickly. "I saw it. I saw him die. In the Temple . . . his throat was slashed. He was bleeding, so much blood . . . I saw it all in a vision. A Cassandra."

"You see visions?" Miss Jesczenka prompted softly.

Emily fell into silent recollection and did not speak for a long time. Then she shook herself.

"I get them from Ososolyeh, just as Komé did. Ososolyeh . . . shows me things." She looked toward Perun, but did not dare meet his gaze. "Things as you have described them. *Temamauhti,* a world transformed by Black Exunge, a Goddess with knives for fingers . . ." She looked back down at the table. "All of it."

"Such a connection with the Great Mother is rare indeed," Perun said, his voice distant. "That is a terrible shame about poor Benedictus. A very great shame." He passed a hand over his eyes, held it there for some moments. When he let it drop, however, there were no tears—only the shine of uncompromising determination.

"I will give you one day," he said to Miss Jesczenka. "Make the arrangements necessary to deliver the coup de grâce of the Talleyrand Maneuver."

"One *day*?" Miss Jesczenka almost shrieked. "Perun, you can't—"

"When the power of the Institute has been restored, you must swear you will ensure that it is used to thwart the Temple of Itztlacoliuhqui."

"If I agree, I will be swearing to help you find the poison that could undermine the practice of magic. My entire life's work—everything I've built for myself—may be for naught." Miss Jesczenka's brown eyes sparkled with fury. "If I don't, my entire life's work will *certainly* be for naught. Destroyed, along with the rest of the world, in a blood apocalypse of unimaginable proportions." Miss Jesczenka spoke through gritted teeth. "Damn you, Perun. What do you expect me to say to that?"

"Checkmate?" Perun suggested.

CHAPTER EIGHTEEN

The Talleyrand
Maneuver

"Dmitri and his men will be at your disposal," Perun said, after Miss Jesczenka's long silence seemed to satisfy him of her acceptance of his terms. "He will see that you are provided with everything you need."

Miss Jesczenka narrowed her eyes at him. "You understand that I must return to the Institute to perform my work. I know Miss Edwards will have to stay, but—"

"You will work from here." Perun seemed to recall that he hadn't had a cigarette in quite some time; with a trembling hand he reached for the case on the table and the cigarette he'd tapped against it sometime before. He struck a match and lit it, looking at Miss Jesczenka through the flame.

"Impossible." Her voice was clipped. "All my things . . . address books, press lists, contacts . . . Those are the tools of my trade. How can you expect me to operate without them?"

"You're a brilliant woman, and I'm sure your memory is excellent." Perun blew out the flame with a small puff. "I cannot allow you to leave. This location is secret, and must remain so."

"I was blindfolded when I came. I can be blindfolded again." She paused. "Are you saying I am a prisoner?"

"I am saying that you must do what you can from here. You will not be allowed to return to the Institute. Miss Edwards' safety and the safety of Volos' Anodyne are now one and the same. I will not allow either to be put in jeopardy."

"I must be able to contact the outside world," Miss Jesczenka said. "Even you can understand that!"

Perun nodded. "Writing supplies will be provided for you. Dmitri will arrange for messages to be carried."

Miss Jesczenka glanced at Emily, and Emily could see her internally debating whether to speak the words she spoke next.

"Mr. Stanton won't be able to hold up without my help," Miss Jesczenka said finally, quickly. "He's upset about Miss Edwards' disappearance. You must let her contact him, or it could destroy the last bit of power he has left before I'm able to execute the Talleyrand Maneuver."

"No," Dmitri said curtly. "The less he knows, the less likely he is to send a squadron of his thugs into the streets looking for her."

"To send men to *rescue* her," Miss Jesczenka corrected him sharply. "From her *kidnappers*."

"Miss Jesczenka, why must you continue to hold us up in such an ugly light?" Perun asked. "We saved Miss Edwards' life. We mean neither of you any harm. We cannot afford the smallest of false moves. You must understand this."

It was his last word on the subject. He swept from the room in a cloud of smoke, slamming the door behind himself.

"Follow me, Miss Jesczenka," Dmitri said. "I'll show you where you'll be working."

Upstairs, in another small crate-packed room with a tiny creaky table for a desk and a dusty kerosene lamp to shed light on it, Miss Jesczenka threw up her hands. She looked at a pile of paper and a pen that had been neatly arranged on the table. She picked up the pen, looked at it, and threw it down with restrained fury, as if it was the sole author of her annoyance.

"One day? Without any of my tools? I can't possibly pull it off!" She sank into the chair and pressed a hand to her cheek. Her brown eyes darted back and forth, unfocused. "But of course, he's right, it must be on Thursday. Otherwise we'd have no choice but to wait until Tuesday, and by then . . ."

"Pull what off?" Emily asked. "What is all this about? What's a Talleyrand Maneuver?"

Miss Jesczenka glanced over at Dmitri, who was standing

guard by the door, then gestured to Emily. Together, they moved to a far corner of the room, sat on a packing crate by a window that overlooked the narrow backyard below. She put her head close to Emily's.

"There is something I must tell you, Miss Edwards," Miss Jesczenka said in a low quick voice. "I'm afraid it will be rather shocking." She paused, drawing in a breath. When she spoke, the words were slow and carefully measured. "I am the one destroying the Institute."

Emily gaped at her.

"I am the one subverting Mr. Stanton's power. I have been playing both sides of the fence. But not to destroy him," she added quickly. "To help him. It's a very advanced credomantic technique called a Talleyrand Maneuver."

Emily held her mouth tight, stared at the woman. Fury kindled beneath her breastbone. "Did you put out that book?"

"No." Miss Jesczenka held up her hands, as if she were afraid Emily might jump her. "I swear to you, that was Fortissimus. I'm sure he had that vicious thing ready and waiting long before the Investment. My suspicion is that he invited General Blotgate and that odious wife of his with the specific intention of reinforcing the book's destructive power. But everything else, everything after that, was me. I sabotaged the public Haälbeck doors. I made the shelves collapse in Mr. Stanton's office, and I caused that annoying lawyer to break his leg. Furthermore, I have been in discussions with disloyal professors who believe me to be one of their own. In all ways, I have worked to undermine Mr. Stanton's authority."

Emily couldn't think of even one word to say. Miss Jesczenka saw the hurt and puzzlement in her face. She placed a hand over Emily's, but Emily snatched hers away.

"Please, hear me out," Miss Jesczenka said. "What I've done, I've done for Mr. Stanton's benefit."

"Really?" Emily said softly. "Or are you lying, too, just like everyone else? To serve your own ends?"

"I'm not lying," Miss Jesczenka said. "I really do want to help Mr. Stanton. A Talleyrand Maneuver, if executed properly, will leave him stronger than he was before, with the full power of the Institute returned to him and then some. Now please stop scowling at me and let me explain."

She took another deep breath.

"The Talleyrand Maneuver takes its name from a brilliant French politician who was born over a hundred years ago. His name was Charles-Maurice de Talleyrand-Périgord. He was thoroughly corrupt, he was a blatant opportunist, and he was a traitor to every master he ever served, from the Pope to Napoléon Bonaparte to King Louis Philippe."

"It sounds as though the two of you have quite a lot in common," Emily commented frostily.

"While I understand that was not intended as a compliment," Miss Jesczenka said, "I am honored to be compared to Monsieur Talleyrand. He was one of the greatest credomantic practitioners in recent history. I have made a special study of his life and methods."

"So Mr. Stanton is to be your Napoléon?" Emily said bitterly. "You're going to throw him to the dogs for history to chew over?"

"No, Miss Edwards. Mr. Stanton is not Napoléon. He's not even Louis XVIII—though Talleyrand's manipulation of that monarch's fortunes most closely parallels my actual intent. Really, Mr. Stanton isn't any of the temporal heads of state that Talleyrand used as pawns. Mr. Stanton is larger than that, metaphorically."

Emily waited for the other shoe to drop. When it did not drop immediately, she prompted: "Metaphorically?"

"Talleyrand was a traitor to every master save one," Miss Jesczenka said. "France."

"So Mr. Stanton is France. And while you are a traitor to Mr. Stanton, you are not a traitor to France."

"Precisely."

"Well, then," Emily said. "That clears everything up entirely!"

Miss Jesczenka frowned at her. "Sarcasm really does not become you, Miss Edwards. And there is a difference between not understanding and being willfully obtuse."

Emily let out a breath. After a moment, she gestured for

Miss Jesczenka to go on. Miss Jesczenka smoothed her skirt and rested one slender white hand over the other.

"Talleyrand once said, 'The art of statesmanship is to foresee the inevitable and to expedite its occurrence.' After Emeritus Zeno's disappearance, it was inevitable that Mr. Stanton would lose control of the Institute. It was inevitable that Fortissimus would attempt to take it from him. It was inevitable that Mr. Stanton would not have the strength to defend against him, even with all the ammunition the Institute has stockpiled against Fortissimus—"

"Ammunition?" Emily lifted an eyebrow.

"Damaging information, slanderous assertions with basis in fact, things of that nature. We collect it on everyone who might be a potential threat. It's standard procedure for any credomantic institution." Miss Jesczenka paused, glancing back at Dmitri, who was still sitting by the door. He did not seem to be listening, but Miss Jesczenka lowered her voice anyway. "Unfortunately, the information we've collected on Fortissimus is nowhere near damaging enough to destroy and discredit him, not with the level of power he currently enjoys. Unless"—Miss Jesczenka lifted a finger—"it is leveraged."

"And how does expediting Mr. Stanton's inevitable defeat make you better able to leverage this damaging information?"

"*On n'aime point le tyran, petit connard,*" Miss Jesczenka said.

"What's a *petit connard*?" Emily asked.

"Never mind," Miss Jesczenka said. "I was quoting something Talleyrand is famously attributed as having said to Napoléon once, over dinner. Napoléon responded by throwing a glass of wine in his face. Translated, the sentiment is simply this: 'No one likes a bully.' This statement was made at about the time Talleyrand had decided to sell out *le Petit Caporal* to Russia and Austria. Talleyrand was not out for glory, nor for gain, but rather for the good of France. Napoléon was destroying it with his savage dreams of conquest. Talleyrand knew that he had to be stopped."

"So . . . wait. That means Fortissimus is Napoléon?" Emily was beginning to wish she had a pencil and paper.

"You're taking this all far too literally," Miss Jesczenka said. "The point is, in the end, everyone wants to see a bully get his just deserts. A bully who pushes things too far—like Napoléon, or Fortissimus—is laying the groundwork for his own defeat."

A glimmer of understanding kindled in Emily. She inclined a thinking finger at Miss Jesczenka. "But you knew that Fortissimus wasn't stupid enough to push things far enough. Not on his own."

Miss Jesczenka smiled at her. "Very good, Miss Edwards," she said. "I had to add a little extra malice to the mix. I had to make Fortissimus look even more of a bully than he already is. By making it seem that Fortissimus is behind these relentless, merciless attacks, he comes to be seen as the kind of fellow who'll kick a man when he's down. He becomes every villain the Dreadnought Stanton of the pulp novels has ever battled against. And thus, when the information is brought to bear against him, it will be more damaging than it would be otherwise, because the prevailing attitude will be that he deserves what he gets. If all goes as it should, the attack should be sufficient to nullify him as a threat forever."

"All right, so you destroy Napoléon," Emily said. "But you tear France apart in the process. I don't see how this is a good thing."

"Ah, but France was not destroyed," Miss Jesczenka said. "Indeed, after the demon Napoléon was exorcized from the poor unwilling body of France, the Bourbons were restored, the country was allowed to retain its original borders, and Monsieur Talleyrand went on to some of the greatest political victories of his career. Napoléon bore the full brunt of disgrace. All the damage was reflected back onto him. Every imperial aspiration, every greedy barbarism, every expansionist impulse. They lashed back and crushed him." There was a particular relish in Miss Jesczenka's voice when speaking these last words that made Emily feel surprised at exactly how passionately the woman hated Napoléon. But of course, Napoléon wasn't Napoléon. He was Fortissimus.

"All right," Emily said, summarizing for herself. "Mr.

Stanton is France. Fortissimus is Napoléon. The more of a despot Napoléon is made to seem, the more brutal the retribution when he is finally discredited."

"Exactly," Miss Jesczenka said. "But there's one more character in this credomantic drama that I've left out. The victim. The martyr. Someone who has been specifically and terribly damaged by the actions of the cruel bully."

"Well, that would be Mr. Stanton, wouldn't it?"

"Certainly, he is the logical choice, but he cannot be cast in that role. He must be fit to rule once Napoléon is exiled to Elba, and he cannot do that if he is seen as pitiable or pathetic."

Emily looked at her warily. She was aware of an uncomfortable certainty growing in the pit of her stomach. "If not Mr. Stanton, then who?"

Miss Jesczenka said nothing, but looked at her for a long time.

"The innocent, blushing virgin with dreams of a happy future, crushed under the loathesome weight of indecent suggestion," Miss Jesczenka said at last.

Emily let out a long sigh. Miss Jesczenka nodded a confirmation.

"You're going to be the martyr, Miss Edwards. You're going to save the Institute."

"You've got to be kidding!"

"I've never been more serious."

"But you said it yourself, I don't have a dissembling bone in my body!"

"Good," Miss Jesczenka said curtly. "The more truthful you can be, the more powerful you will be. Remember that."

"But how can I do that?" Emily said. "I don't know what the truth is. I don't know what Mr. Stanton did, or didn't do . . . I don't know what's true at all, anymore!"

"I didn't say this was going to be easy," Miss Jesczenka said.

A long silence hung between them. They stared at each other, calm brown eyes looking into troubled violet ones.

"What if I can't pull it off?" Emily whispered. "What if the

Talleyrand Maneuver isn't successful? What if Mr. Stanton can't regain control of the Institute?"

Miss Jesczenka smiled at her. "Of course it will succeed, Miss Edwards—" but Emily cut her off with a curt gesture.

"Spare me the credomancy," Emily said. "What happens if the Talleyrand Maneuver doesn't work? Will it hurt him?"

"Mr. Stanton *is* the Institute. He is the physical body of the Institute as much as the white marble mansion. And you have seen what's been happening to the mansion." Miss Jesczenka's face became serious. "As the power of the Institute crumbles, so does he. As long as the power of the Institute is in decline, he will continue to decline with it. If the Institute is destroyed . . ."

Miss Jesczenka did not need to finish the sentence.

Stanton regaining control of the Institute was a matter of life and death—not just for the world, but for him as well. She had to save the Institute—save the very thing that would take him away from her. She had to help him become a man who could never really be hers, ever again.

She shook her head and smiled at the neat horror of it, but her smile was small and bitter.

"Checkmate," she whispered to herself.

Miss Jesczenka was right about one thing. A single day was not nearly enough to satisfactorily execute the coup de grâce of an intricate Talleyrand Maneuver. But it was all the time they had.

"The first thing is the press conference," Miss Jesczenka said. Sitting at the makeshift desk with paper, pen, and ink, she wrote furiously as she spoke. Emily stood at her shoulder, watching the woman's steel-nibbed pen move swiftly over the paper. Quite amazingly, Miss Jesczenka was writing a catering menu, an order for a dressmaker, and a list of names while she spoke. "We will hold it at the Fifth Avenue Hotel. It's the nicest in town, and I am good friends with the manager. He will see that we're given the Imperial Suite. It's got wonderful acoustics." Miss Jesczenka paused momentarily, signed her name with a flourish, then lifted the piece of paper and wafted it in the air to let the ink dry. She looked at Emily. "We will invite every newspaperman not in thrall to Fortissimus."

Copies of all the morning newspapers were spread out before Miss Jesczenka. Emily reached over and pulled out *The New York Times* and scanned the headlines.

"Javanese Regent Declares Mass Evacuation of Batavia," that morning's headline read. "Aberrancies Swarm the City. Stadhuis Reported Destroyed."

Emily sighed, pushing the paper back. *Temamauhti*'s inexorable march. But she had enough to worry about at the moment without adding Java to the list.

Miss Jesczenka turned a disdainful gaze on Dmitri, who was watching from his accustomed place by the door. "Dmitri!"

Dmitri lifted an eyebrow, but said nothing.

Miss Jesczenka glanced at the paper, deemed it dry enough to fold and tuck into an envelope. She wrote a name and address on it and handed the envelope to him.

"See that it's delivered immediately," she said tersely. "And hurry back. I'll have quite a lot more for you very soon."

"I shall give it to one of my men," Dmitri said pointedly, turning to step out of the room.

"Russians! There's no getting rid of them," Miss Jesczenka muttered under her breath. "For pity's sake, I might as well be back in Poland."

"So what's going to happen at this press conference?" Emily asked.

Miss Jesczenka slid a fresh sheet of paper before herself, then dipped her pen into ink again.

"You, Miss Edwards, are going to put on a show like no one's ever seen before."

"I gathered that much," Emily said, "but I don't understand why anyone's going to care. No one knows who I am. And if they do, their whole notion of me is built around a lie, that I'm some kind of cattle baron's daughter. You said that we had to be truthful!"

"It wasn't my idea to make you a cattle baron's daughter," Miss Jesczenka said, chewing the end of her pen thoughtfully. "And of course, Fortissimus engineered that ridiculous cover story with just this kind of situation in mind. He's always known just how powerful a weapon you could be, if someone took it in their mind to use you. So he made sure to hobble you well in advance."

Emily lifted her hands in astonishment. "How far ahead do you people think?"

Miss Jesczenka smiled.

"It's like chess, Miss Edwards. The current move is of no importance. It's how the current move relates to the moves yet to come. And to answer your question, just for my own personal amusement, I've strategized your future out as far as the birth of your fifth child. After that, I'll admit, it gets a bit hazy."

Emily blinked at her. "Five?"

"As for no one knowing who you really are, it doesn't matter all that much, really. Fortissimus hoped that in trying to live up to his cattle baron's daughter story, you'd make some kind of hideous blunder. Once the truth about your background was revealed, you'd end up looking like a lying little gold digger, and you'd be nullified as a threat forever. He hoped, in short, that you'd cut your own throat. The tactic might have worked, if you'd gone around in society a bit more. But as you've done such a very good job of avoiding society, you've evaded his trap." Miss Jesczenka gave Emily a little look that recalled her old exasperation about Mrs. Stanton's lunch. Emily suddenly felt very pleased—quite undeservedly—with her own cleverness.

"Even if the Institute had been completely open and above-board about your background," Miss Jesczenka continued, ignoring the self-satisfied look on Emily's face, "that would have presented its own set of challenges. Ultimately, the specifics of *who* you are matter less than the truth of *what* you are."

"And what am I?"

"You are a young woman. You are pretty, and when I'm done with you, you'll be prettier still. And, most important, you are in love. Those are the ultimate truths that we will use to our advantage."

Emily said nothing, but wrinkled her nose. Three such simple components. A young woman. Pretty. In love. Each individually might be said to have truth in it, she supposed. But there were so many caveats, so many shades of meaning and doubt and conflict in each one. Taken together, they added up to a truth so oversimplified and abstract as to be nearly meaningless. How could such a truth have any power in it at all?

"It's a matter of symbology, Miss Edwards," Miss Jesczenka said, as if she could read the doubt on the curve of Emily's brow. "You signify something that people treasure, an ideal that they cherish. That is what is important. That is why you will be able to play this role, and why you will succeed in it."

"But it's still not the *truth*," Emily muttered. But if Miss Jesczenka heard, she did not comment.

"The good news is, your path has already been well prepared. You remember the photos that were taken before the Investment? They've proven as popular as I'd hoped they would be," Miss Jesczenka said with some satisfaction. "You did not notice, but I placed a subtle glamour on you while I was helping you prepare. You have no idea how lovely you looked. I was quite proud of the effect."

"I've seen the pictures," Emily said. "I saw one in a shop window in the Bowery. They didn't look like me at all, but the counterman said that they were selling well."

"Excellent," Miss Jesczenka said, and whether she was pleased that the pictures didn't look like Emily or that they were selling well was hard to discern.

"You really did have this all planned out, didn't you?" Emily looked closely at the woman.

"Someone had to keep a level head on their shoulders," Miss Jesczenka said. "Zeno and Stanton were larking around like a couple of schoolboys, with all their credomancer's assurance and bravado. It is a great weakness of credomancers, Miss Edwards. They often believe their own press."

"You're a credomancer, too," Emily said.

"I'm also a woman. Failure, struggle, and doubt are my constant companions. They are not always pleasant, but they inoculate me against overconfidence. As such, I would not trade them for all the arrogant bravado in the world."

There was the sound of the key scraping in the lock, and the door opening. Emily pressed her lips together and Miss Jesczenka turned back to her writing desk, resuming her elegant scribbling.

Emily expected Dmitri to take his chair, but instead he came to stand behind Miss Jesczenka, arms crossed.

"Yes?" Miss Jesczenka said without turning.

"You're going to present Miss Edwards to reporters at a press conference at the Fifth Avenue Hotel?"

"What of it?" Miss Jesczenka snapped, pen hovering briefly over the paper.

"Every Temple Warlock in the service of the Black Glass Goddess wants her dead," Dmitri growled. "And you're going to parade her around in front of reporters in a public place?"

Miss Jesczenka turned, fixed Dmitri with a blazing glare. "Well, that must be your lookout, mustn't it? I can hardly arrange for Institute security if you aren't going to let me contact them."

Dmitri said nothing. His jaw flexed uneasily.

"If you will keep me informed as to the arrangements, I will see that there is sufficient security."

He caught Emily's gaze. And for the first time, instead of something disapproving, she thought she saw a warning.

Miss Jesczenka worked unflaggingly into the night. By the time the small clock on the table chimed 1 a.m., Emily sat drowsing in a chair, her body quiescent but her mind feverishly active. She was remembering everything Ososolyeh had shown her, rubbing vision against vision, trying to strike the meanest spark of understanding. The Temple, a cold terrifying place of bones and blood; the Black Glass Goddess, ancient and malicious; twelve men, cut to ribbons . . . *Why twelve?* she wondered. Twelve was such a strange number. Twelve astrological signs, twelve disciples, twelve dancing princesses—Emily abandoned the line of contemplation as it went from promising to preposterous.

I can give him one last chance.

Emily shivered, remembering the horrible hunk of slimy flesh on which Zeno had died. What had Zeno's dying thoughts meant? Him *who*? Perun? The sly white-haired Russian had said that he and Zeno had been friends, and Emily believed it; she had seen the real sadness in his eyes when she'd told him that Zeno was dead. But how could Zeno's wasting the last bit of his strength on destroying that . . . thing, whatever it was, help Perun?

"Miss Edwards needs to rest," Dmitri said, as if intuiting the frenzy of Emily's thoughts. "I will escort her to her room."

"Well, don't be long about it," Miss Jesczenka said, not looking up. "We're working through the night, and I need you."

With dull complaisance, Emily followed Dmitri. When they reached her room, he followed her in and closed the door behind himself.

"I want to speak with you," he said brusquely, answering the question in her eyes. "There may not be another chance."

Emily settled herself on the edge of the bed. Dmitri sat on a chair against the wall, his straight back pressed hard against the wood. He frowned for some moments before speaking, finally shaking his head in frustration.

"I am not a man of schemes, like Perun. Nor of language, like Zeno. But I am a man who listens. I am a man who hears." He looked at the floor, at his feet on it. "I am a man who believes in good, and in evil."

He drew a deep breath.

"I do not believe you are evil, Miss Edwards," he said, glancing up at her. "Perhaps I have been too unkind. But after my father was murdered, I hated everyone who practiced magic. Everyone." He sighed heavily. "It does not do to hate everyone. Only those who do wrong. Who do evil."

Dmitri looked up at her, his face tight as a fist. "This man . . . Dreadnought Stanton. You love him very much?"

Emily drew a deep breath, her whole body tensing. She nodded, once.

Dmitri shook his head bleakly, as if he had just watched her put her signature to a confession of treason. "You have no idea what he is."

"I know what he is," Emily said.

"He is no better than a Temple Warlock. No better than the men who killed my father."

"If you're going to outline my fiancé's errors to me, at least keep your facts straight," Emily hissed. "Yes, he studied sangrimancy at the Maelstrom Academy—but he never had anything to do with the Temple."

"The Temple draws Initiates from Erebus Academy cadets all the time," Dmitri countered harshly. "Did you know that? No, I am sure you didn't. Why should anyone tell you *that*?"

Emily bared her teeth.

"Why should you tell me?" she spat. "What do you want from me?"

"There's a woman at the Erebus Academy," Dmitri continued, as if she hadn't spoken. "She recruits young men to serve the Temple. She takes them as lovers if they please her. The General's own wife, Alcmene Blotgate."

Emily blew out a breath as if she'd been punched in the gut.

"What do you want?" she said.

"I want you to admit that he's lied to you. Every time you turn around, you're faced with another one of his lies. He wants you to love him for who he is not." Dmitri's voice filled her ears, hard and demanding. "I want you to understand that he doesn't care if you're hurt."

"That's not true." Tears were standing in Emily's eyes now. Seeing them glitter, Dmitri nodded with harsh satisfaction, as if they indicated awakening understanding.

"You will be hurt when he dies, will you not?" Dmitri said. "In ten years, five years? He will leave you a widow, your children orphans. He doesn't *care*. If he did, he would have taken the cure from Zeno when he had the chance."

Emily looked up, stricken.

"There is no cure."

"He could have been cured anytime." Dmitri spoke the words with relish. "Anytime before Zeno was kidnapped. That was what Perun was speaking of, only he was too gentle

to make you face the truth." Dmitri stood, stalking the length
of the room, fists balled. "Zeno spoke of it once. An old custom called Touching the Evil. It takes nothing more than a
coin, a touch-piece of silver. Your fiancé could have asked the
blessing of his Sophos, and his illness would have been
lifted." He snapped his fingers for emphasis. "Like *that*."

"I don't believe it," Emily whispered.

"Of course, the cure comes at a cost. All magical channels
in a man's body must be fused, closed permanently. It would
leave him unable to work magic. But I suppose that would be
too much to ask. I suppose you're not worth such a great sac-
rifice. And anyway, it's too late now. Zeno is dead, and your fiancé's fate is sealed. And he never told you."

Dmitri stood in silence for a long time, looking down at
her. Tears spilled down Emily's cheeks, and she wiped them
away angrily.

"Leave me alone," she said finally. "Just . . . go away."

Dmitri did not move for a long time. When he did, he came
to stand next to her. He put a hand on her shoulder, let it rest
there for a moment.

"I am sorry, Emilia Vladimirovna," he said softly. "I really
am very sorry."

Emily lifted her head. She didn't know if she intended to
strike him or scream at him. But she could do neither, for
Dmitri was already at the door, and in an instant he was gone.

CHAPTER NINETEEN

The Ruined Woman

The press conference was scheduled for 10 a.m. "After breakfast and before lunch," Miss Jesczenka explained, "when the reporters will be at their peak of attentiveness." But Emily and Miss Jesczenka began their preparations well before dawn. Dmitri and his men moved silently in the early-morning darkness, some leaving to take up secure positions around Twenty-third and Broadway where the Fifth Avenue Hotel stood, some preparing the nondescript carriage that would take them there, some loading and polishing what sounded like an arsenal of rifles. Dmitri himself carried a large trunk up to Miss Jesczenka's room and set it down with a heavy thunk. The woman stood, going to the trunk quickly and throwing it open to make sure that nothing had been left out. She pawed through mounds of silk and lace, seemingly satisfied.

"Thank you, Dmitri," she said. "You'll have to leave us alone now. We must get her dressed."

Instead of leaving, Dmitri went to Emily's side. Emily didn't look at him, but he would not be ignored. He seized Emily's hand, the one of ivory, and held it for a moment, looking at it meaningfully. Then he bent over it with the stiff courtliness of a soldier.

"Think about what I told you," he said. "There are always other choices, Emilia Vladimirovna."

He straightened and walked from the room, closing the door behind him. There was the familiar scrape of a key in the lock.

When Emily turned, she saw that Miss Jesczenka was staring at her. Emily flushed and gritted her teeth.

"All right," Miss Jesczenka said quickly, turning her eyes down to the trunk. "The press conference starts in less than two hours. I need you to listen closely while I brief you on one of the most important elements of this little drama we're going to be staging."

Emily was already removing her clothes in preparation for being put into what she expected would be another extremely formal gown, if the profusion of shimmering silk peeping from the top of the trunk was any indication.

"I'm listening," Emily said, pulling her dress off over her head.

Miss Jesczenka reached into the trunk and produced a portfolio. She opened it, and nodded with satisfaction at the contents. Inside were letters. She handed the letters to Emily. It was a fat bundle; surely Miss Jesczenka couldn't expect her to read them all right then? But she seemed to expect no such thing, and was ready instead with a precise summary.

"Remember I told you that the Institute had ammunition against Fortissimus? That's the ammunition."

Emily looked through the letters. They bore familiar addresses, in both the delivery and the return sections. The addresses were those of the Fortissimus Presentment Arranging Agency and Tammany Hall.

"Those letters provide irrefutable evidence that Fortissimus' Agency extravagantly padded city contracts under the administration of Boss Tweed," Miss Jesczenka said. "Shocking, of course, but hardly fatal given that just about everyone in New York was the recipient of Tweed's graft. Without the leverage we're going to bring to bear, such information would hardly dull Fortissimus' shine. But it's the *way* we're going to give it to the reporters. We're going to call upon a belief more ancient, more deeply held, and more fondly cherished, than even the American urge to root for the underdog."

Emily laid the letters aside on the desk as she came to stand before Miss Jesczenka. "And what ancient, deeply held, and fondly cherished belief would that be?" she asked. Zeno's powerful command, the one he had driven deep into the flesh of the thing in the pit, flashed through her mind. "Good shall triumph over evil?"

Miss Jesczenka looked at her like an elementary school student who'd just spouted the solution to a trigonometry problem.

"Why yes, that is a credomantic concept of exceptional power," she said wonderingly. "Have you been reading Mr. Stanton's textbooks?" She paused, then shook her head. "But no. That's not the one we're going to use. It is not specific enough for our purpose."

"What is then?" Emily said.

"'True love conquers all,'" Miss Jesczenka said, pulling a chemise down over Emily's head with a jerk.

"The human belief in true love is perhaps the most powerful belief known to credomancy, next to the rather more general one you just quoted," Miss Jesczenka said as she tied Emily's corset strings and then left them to stretch, as she'd done before. She slid her arms along Emily's firmly compressed sides, apparently satisfied that Emily's waist was small enough, even without the benefit of a measuring tape. "Everyone wants to see two people who are truly and deeply in love come together in a happy union, regardless of the fact that the lovers must pass through trials of fire. It's trials of fire that observers like the best, as a matter of fact. They serve as proof that the love is true, and powerful enough to survive whatever cruel fate throws in its path."

Emily thought about cruel fate, and everything it had thrown in the path of her and Stanton. She pressed her lips together. Unlike a heroine in a romance story, she'd had her doubts. She had them still. Would her love be true enough?

Emily smiled wanly to herself. That last sentence certainly sounded enough like something out of *Ladies' Repository* to fit the bill. But the smile did not last, as she followed the metaphor along its logical paths of association. Because in all those romantic stories, the hero never had murderous blood sorcery in his past. He would never leave the heroine to face brutal villains on her own because his work demanded him elsewhere. And heroes in stories were honest and forthright and decent.

Stanton was not honest. And he certainly wasn't forthright. Well then, she could only pin her hopes on the last one. She had to pray that he was decent. And not decent the way the Stanton family defined decency. She could only hope after everything he'd done, after everything he'd been, there was an irreducible part of him that was the man she had fallen in love with. The man she imagined she saw in his green eyes when he looked at her.

That was all there was left for her to believe. Would it be enough? It would have to be.

"Hold your arms up," Miss Jesczenka said.

Miss Jesczenka had arranged for an exquisite afternoon dress of a tender pinkish hue. It was light silk, and skimmed over Emily's form with a delicate elegance. It suggested gardens, laughing hope, and swings decorated with flowers.

"Just the color," Miss Jesczenka said with approval, smoothing the fabric down over Emily's body. "Like a virgin's blush." At the word "virgin," Miss Jesczenka's eyes darted, ever so briefly, to the door through which Dmitri had exited.

"Then it will suit me perfectly," Emily bit back, snatching the skirt away from the woman's fussing hands. Without a word, Miss Jesczenka rose and began doing the dozens of tiny mother-of-pearl buttons that ran up the back.

"Mr. Stanton loves you very much," she murmured as her nimble fingers made the buttons fast. "You know that, don't you?"

"I wish I could hear it from him," Emily said, dropping her head as Miss Jesczenka's fingers moved to her nape. When the woman had finished the buttons, she took Emily by the arms and turned her. She looked into Emily's eyes, her brown ones soft and imploring.

"You have to believe that he does." She gave Emily a little shake. "You have to believe it in every bone of your body. If you could see what I've seen, if you could see how worried he's been about you . . . you'd know. He's not here to tell you himself, but he would want me to tell you. He loves you, and he never wanted any of this to happen."

Emily looked into Miss Jesczenka's eyes.

"A horse is tied to a ten-foot rope, and there's hay twenty-five feet away," Emily murmured thoughtfully. She was remembering another day, another dress, another life.

"Miss Edwards?" Her companion's voice was puzzled.

"The simplest answer is that the horse can't eat the hay. It's impossible. Some things just aren't meant to be." She paused. "I don't think that's the answer he was looking for. It's not the answer I was looking for. But maybe it's the right one." She looked at Miss Jesczenka, her eyes focusing. "You want me to be the heroine in a love story. But there's one thing missing. A *hero*. You say he never wanted any of this to happen. But it did. And he couldn't stop it."

"No, he couldn't." Miss Jesczenka's voice was firm. "Credomancy may seek to exploit the human desire for a tidy narrative where an unblemished romantic hero vanquishes all obstacles, but such ideals have very little to do with reality. Reality requires pragmatism and compromise. Men fail. Women fail. There are no heroes, only human beings who somehow find the strength to behave heroically, no matter how many times they have been unable to do so in the past. If you understand that, Miss Edwards—if you truly and deeply understand that, then you will understand the most powerful thing anyone with a heart can understand."

"And what's that?" Emily said softly.

"That love is not enough. But it's a start."

She released Emily's arms slowly, stepped back to look at her.

"You look beautiful." She smiled. "You'll do just fine."

At 9:30 a.m. precisely, Dmitri knocked softly on the door and told them that the carriage was ready. He led them downstairs to where a large black landau waited, harnessed horses stamping impatiently. Two men sat atop the carriage, behind the driver, and two sat on the carriage's back railing. They all had rifles.

Emily settled into her seat, drawing a deep breath as Dmitri fastened the door behind them. She looked at the letters she held in her white gloved hand, then at Miss Jesczenka, who had settled across from her.

"Well, you've told me everything about true love," Emily said as the carriage lurched and got under way. "But you haven't told me what I'm supposed to do with these."

"You are going to show them around to the reporters. Let them paw over them with their greasy hands and read enough to know that they want to read more. Whet their appetites, give them confidence that the letters are genuine. But make sure you get them back, and I'll make sure that everyone gets copies afterward."

Emily nodded, but the woman continued to look at her.

"But the letters aren't the most important thing. The most important thing is for you to charm them, to make them believe that you love Mr. Stanton so much that you're willing to throw yourself on their mercy for his sake. They'll love having a pretty girl supplicating them, even if you'll have them entirely at your advantage, as you will by the time you're finished with them. A few discreet tears would be nice, but don't overdo it. No one likes a sniveler. If things get really bad, faint."

"You really think I can do this?" she asked, half to Miss Jesczenka and half to herself.

"You must," Miss Jesczenka snapped. "You must, so that Mr. Stanton can be redeemed, the Institute saved, and Rex Fortissimus destroyed. Destroyed completely and utterly." There was bitter delight in these last words, more bitter than Emily had ever heard from the woman, or from any woman, for that matter. She looked at Miss Jesczenka as the carriage rocked them softly from side to side.

"Perun said he knew something about you and Rex Fortissimus," Emily said.

"He is trying to destroy everything I've ever worked for." Miss Jesczenka spoke as if the words were rehearsed. "Of course I dislike him."

"No, you don't dislike him," Emily said. "You *hate* him."

Miss Jesczenka was silent for a long time, and Emily thought that the matter would end with her silence. The woman looked at the window, reaching up to brush aside the drawn curtains, then thinking better of it. She touched a finger to the corner of her eye. Finally, she spoke again.

"It is not a polite story for a virginal bride," she said. "But since I've already told you about true love, I suppose I can tell you." She closed her eyes and drew a deep breath.

"I was sixteen years old," Miss Jesczenka said. "I had just come across from Poland. I didn't know anything about New York. I barely spoke any English. And the Mirabilis Institute wasn't taking women at the time." She paused. "I went to Fortissimus' Agency, knowing only that it was a place of powerful magic. I was looking for work, any kind of work that would help me learn magic—learn to have the kind of power the men I'd grown up around had . . . the rabbis, the wise old men of the minyan. They told me I could never study the mysteries of the cabala, that it was forbidden to women. They told me I should calm myself and learn to be a good, observant wife. That was power enough, they said. I did not agree. So I came to America. Because in America, anyone can do anything they want."

She paused, chewing her lip—a strangely nervous gesture from the woman Emily was used to seeing so calm and composed.

"A slimy little weasel of a man hired me to do simple clerical work for Fortissimus' Agency. I was overjoyed. I believed I could work my way up, learning as I went. Looking back, the fact that I was hired at all should have been a warning. I wasn't anything like a promising prospect. Except in one very specific regard."

She paused.

"I learned later that the slimy weasel of a man who hired me took presumptuous girls like myself off the street all the time. Girls who thought they wanted to learn something about the man's world. It was a great joke between him and Fortissimus, teaching us."

"Teaching you?"

"We would be directed to work late. And Rex Fortissimus would be there, waiting, in the dark offices with the heavy doors."

Horror spread through Emily's body.

"He . . . took advantage of you?"

"The word is rape," Miss Jesczenka said. "And yes. That's what he did."

She was silent for a long moment, looking thoughtfully at the curtain that she seemed still to long to push back, to let the light in.

"It wasn't just that he took my body. He took my ambitions. He made me a ruined woman." She looked at Emily. "And I mean that in a very specific credomantic way, just as Fortissimus certainly meant it."

"I don't understand," Emily said.

"Almost as powerful as the belief that true love conquers all is the belief that a ruined woman will never recover from her ruining. Fortissimus' rape wasn't simply a physical attack, though that was low and ugly enough all by itself. His attack was infinitely worse, because it mocked my desire to wield the kind of credomantic power that he was master of. By making me into a ruined woman, he attacked me with the force of belief. He made me into something that he believed I could never recover from being." She paused, her voice going almost too soft for Emily to hear her next words: "And indeed, it has been very difficult."

"But you did it," Emily said.

Miss Jesczenka nodded, a small movement.

"At a cost. I must maintain the weeds of a spinster to avoid any hint of the past I have defeated. That is a very lonely road." She looked at Emily, smiled sadly. "Everyone likes to believe that true love might one day find them, and I'm no exception. But in my case, I can't let it. Not ever. I must be satisfied with lesser consolations."

Emily thought of the young man she'd seen with Miss Jesczenka the night before the Investment. She watched the light play over the woman's face. She wanted to reach out to her, but she felt that it was better not to.

"I left the Agency after that, of course. And of course, there was a child. The bitter fruits of ruination. I gave the baby to an orphanage. What else could I do?" She looked at Emily, as if wishing Emily had an answer she herself had never been able to find. When she saw no answer, she let her eyes fall back to her lap. "I do not know what became of him, and I will never know. I could not even give him a name, only a description in my own language. Utisz. *Anonymous.*"

"How did you do it?" Emily asked breathlessly, imagining Miss Jesczenka young and lost and alone. She herself had often felt young and lost and alone, but she couldn't imagine how much worse it must have been for the woman who sat before her.

"I was hired by a flower shop that needed a quick-foot for deliveries. The flower shop specialized in orchids. My deliveries often took me to the Mirabilis Institute, to the conservatory. It was there that I met Benedictus Zeno. We became friends and I liked him very much. He was good to me, and he even spoke to me in Polish sometimes. After a while, I told him everything that had happened. I wouldn't ever have told anyone, but I told him . . ."

A look of fresh puzzlement at the unexpectedness of her admission came over Miss Jesczenka's face. How well Emily knew that puzzlement.

"He helped me gain admission to the Institute. Mirabilis didn't want to have anything to do with me. He didn't think I was a good risk, as he put it. But Zeno was kind. He understood. And I did everything I could to make him proud."

"I'm sure he would be proud of you," Emily said. A sudden question struck her. She wondered if she should speak, but curiosity overcame tact.

"But Fortissimus has seen you a hundred times since. How come he's never recognized you?"

"Fortissimus sees positions, not people," Miss Jesczenka said bitterly. "He would not recognize his own mother if she were dressed in the clothes of a beggar. And as I've told you, credomancers often have the weakness of believing their own press. He believed that girls he made ruined women would stay ruined women." She paused, clenching her teeth. "More fool he."

Then she rearranged her face brightly, and the note in her voice when she spoke next was as cheerful as if she'd just been talking to Emily about the bright morning sunshine, and how vexing it was that the heavy dark curtains must be drawn to keep it out.

"Now you know my darkest secret," she said. "My sad tale of woe."

Emily looked across the carriage at her. "It seems that you've done very well for yourself."

Miss Jesczenka smiled at her. "Yes, I have, haven't I?" Her note of cheerfulness became terrible, almost mad in its intensity. "I've come far enough to pay back Ogilvy Creagh Flannigan for what he did to me. I intend to repay him pound for ounce the humiliation and misery he caused me. Revenge is indeed a delicious dish, Miss Edwards, served hot or cold. I hope you never have cause to develop a taste for it."

And hearing the bitter note of obsession in the woman's voice, Emily found that she sincerely hoped so as well.

The Fifth Avenue Hotel occupied an entire block between Twenty-third and Twenty-fourth streets. Six stories of white marble, it faced onto the sweet-smelling gardens of Madison Square. The carriage came to a stop and Dmitri's face appeared through a crack in the door.

"The men are in place. Come in quickly, Miss Edwards."

Emily was ushered hastily into the luxurious grandeur of the hotel, Dmitri at her elbow, his eyes darting back and forth as they walked. Emily found that his nervousness was infectious; she found her eyes sweeping the beautifully dressed crowd for black suits and obsidian stickpins.

She was escorted into a box called a Perpendicular Railway—a little car with a liveried attendant who touched his hat to her as he slid the ornate grate closed. Emily felt her stomach fall to her feet as the box swept her swiftly up to the Imperial Suite on the sixth floor.

As they came down the hall, Emily glimpsed a beautiful large ballroom, in which the acoustics did indeed seem to be wondrous. Emily could hear every note of the reporters gabbling within, their loud voices carrying into the hall. But they didn't go directly into the room where the reporters were. Instead they entered the suite through different doors, into a large withdrawing room with arched marble windows hung with gold brocade draperies. Miss Jesczenka threw her bag down and immediately began rummaging through it.

"We're going to have to be even more aggressive than we were at the Investment." From the bag she withdrew a silver case that Emily recognized as the same silver powder case she'd used at the Investment. She pulled out the same pink puff, dusted Emily's face with it as she had before, but she didn't just stop there; she proceeded to sprinkle Emily's whole body, stopping just short of dumping the silver box's contents over Emily's head. Emily brushed away glittering dust, coughed chokingly at the overwhelming stink of lavender. "The glamour I applied to you for the Investment was subtle—I didn't want random ambassadors to start dying of unrequited love for you. This time, however, the more heartbreakingly lovely you are, the better our purpose will be served."

"It's like a love spell?" Emily felt a faint echo of panic, remembering the love spell she'd put on Dag Hansen. The love spell that had cost her so much.

"Exactly so," Miss Jesczenka said briskly. "You're going to make those reporters fall head-over-heels in love with you. They're going to find you so appealing and attractive that not only will they believe everything you say, they'll be driven to hit the streets immediately in your defense."

"But that's not *honest*!" Emily said.

"Forget about being honest," Miss Jesczenka said. "Worry about being convincing. Now, let's get these in your ears." She took out a pair of delicate pearl earrings and hung them in Emily's ears. "These earrings will allow me to communicate with you. Listen for me, and for God's sake, do exactly as I say." Indeed, Emily did not see how she could fail to listen to Miss Jesczenka; once the earrings were in her ears, Miss Jesczenka's voice became twice as loud.

"Won't the reporters hear?" Emily winced, putting a hand to her ear.

"No, only you," Miss Jesczenka said. "And don't wince like that, it's not maidenly at all. Now, one last thing." Her hand dipped back into the bag and when she removed it, something blazed between her fingers. Emily stared dumb-founded at the diamond engagement ring she'd left back at Mrs. Stanton's.

"How did you get it back?" Emily said.

"Much as it pains me to compliment Dmitri, I will allow that he's got some highly skilled footpads in his employ," Miss Jesczenka said. "Give me your hand."

For some reason, Emily hesitated slightly. Miss Jesczenka's brow knit.

"Is something wrong?" she asked.

"No, nothing," Emily said, holding out her hand, hoping Miss Jesczenka didn't see how much it trembled beneath its sheath of white satin.

When everything was ready, Miss Jesczenka positioned herself before the doors to the drawing room. She took a deep breath, and once again, she seemed to be gathering strength, marshaling force from deep within herself. Then she threw up her head, straightened her back, flung open the doors, and strode into the ballroom.

The room was large and high ceilinged. Dozens of reporters lounged on carved chairs that had been brought in for them; some of them had tipped the chairs back, some sat straddled over them, casually slouched forward. Emily's eyes swept the room, noting the arrangements that had been made for them: platters of delicious-smelling food—already mostly devoured—carafes of ice water and juice and coffee, lots and lots of coffee. But what Emily noticed most, and what gave her the most comfort, were dozens of Russian men—Dmitri's men. Gone were the loose peasant shifts; now they were all carefully suited, and they stood ranged around the walls, their bodies hiding the silver-loaded rifles behind them. Dmitri himself was standing by the door, staring stock-straight, his face impassive and watchful.

As she came into the room, the gabbling voices stilled. Dozens of eyes followed her as she walked. The reporters sat up straighter; some of the straddlers even swung their legs back over their chairs and hastened to sit in a more dignified fashion. Notebooks came out, pencils were pulled from above ears.

Emily came to sit demurely on a red velvet sofa as Miss Jesczenka took her place at a highly polished lectern. She lifted her chin, gathered the reporters within the compass of her velvet-brown gaze.

"Thank you all for coming," Miss Jesczenka began. "I am Miss Tiza Jesczenka, and I have the great honor to hold a position as senior professor at the Stanton Institute of the Credomantic Arts, the foremost institution of credomantic education in the United States. I appear before you today as Miss Edwards' representative. As you all know, she is engaged to be married to Mr. Dreadnought Stanton, the Sophos of the Institute. She has asked you here personally because it is her deep and heartfelt desire to defend her true love against the scurrilous accusations and ignoble attacks leveled against him by those who wish to see him damaged by such falsehood."

Miss Jesczenka paused, looking out over the reporters. Their pencils hovered over their pads, but they did not write. They were too busy staring at Emily. Emily blushed. The glamour Miss Jesczenka had cast on her was certainly quite powerful. Lowering her eyelashes made the men breathe hard. Lifting a hand—which she did experimentally to touch a stray curl—made them watch as if they were imagining her using that hand to do something shocking.

We're off to a fine start, Miss Jesczenka's voice whispered in her ear, as the woman lifted a glass of water to her lips. She put the water down carefully, looked out over the reporters again.

"First, she prays that you all imagine the grief these accusations have caused her. The terrible, heartbreaking grief of an innocent, virginal bride-to-be, with all the fondly cherished hopes and dreams that a young girl nurtures in her chaste bedchamber. She has been very hurt by these accusations. Very *deeply* hurt." Emily saw the agony her supposed pain caused the reporters. They looked at one another, concerned. She lowered her eyelashes again, and felt certain that one man in the front row was about to break into tears.

"Is it not unfair, gentlemen—is it not ignoble and unkind— that this beautiful child, who dreams only of true love and its appropriate sanction, should have to suffer the existence of such base and disgusting and utterly unfounded lies about the man she loves? The powerful, honest man who rescued her from dangers more terrible than should ever be imagined, the bold lover who brought this innocent girl from an innocent land to New York, with all its bright promise . . . where, instead of finding the welcome and adoration of its inhabitants, she was instead wounded—nearly fatally, perhaps—by their depravity, and cruelty, and sniggering prurience?"

The reporters looked among themselves, ashamed. They had all written stories about Dreadnought Stanton, Emily guessed. And they were all imagining themselves with beautiful, innocent fiancées reading them. Heads hung, feet shifted guiltily.

"Shame on you!" Miss Jesczenka cried suddenly, her voice trembling. "Shame on you all!" But at that moment, Emily rose softly and laid a gentle hand on the woman's shoulder.

"No, Miss Jesczenka," Emily said, keeping her voice very soft, as she had been instructed.

Don't worry if they can't hear you . . . they'll just listen harder, Miss Jesczenka had said. It wasn't hard to keep her voice soft, with her heart thudding in her throat as it was. Emily stepped before the lectern, putting herself, her lovely dress the shade of a shell's lip, and her shimmering glamour on display before them. She crossed her hands before herself, lowered her head.

"Please, don't be so hard on these poor men." Emily put a lilt in her voice. "They were only doing their jobs. They didn't know. They didn't know that it was all lies . . . all lies . . ."

Emily let her lower lip tremble and lifted a handkerchief to her eyes to catch supposed tears. Several of the men moved forward, looking to be in the right position to catch her if she should faint.

"Gentlemen, I understand that each one of you has a very important job. Mr. Stanton often says that reporters are the most powerful men in New York, and for the first time, I truly understand that terrible power. I understand that you must write stories that are interesting and . . . *titillating* . . ." Emily took care to hit every "t" in the word with tantalizing precision. "But my fiancé—Dreadnought Stanton, the Sophos of the Stanton Institute of the Credomantic Arts, the foremost institution of credomantic education in the United States—is truly a great man. He is kind and noble, decent and strong. I know that he could never do anything ugly. He could never do anything base."

"But he practiced sangrimancy, didn't he, Miss Edwards?" Emily's eyes came up quickly to a man in the back who spoke the words loudly. He was a very large man in a shiny gray waistcoat. He looked calm and pleased with himself. He wasn't sitting, but was leaning against the back wall with his arms crossed. He didn't have a notebook or a pencil; he was just watching Emily with cool appraising eyes. He was smiling, but not necessarily in a mean way.

Horace Armatrout! How did he get in here? Miss Jesczenka's words hissed in Emily's ears.

"There will be time for questions later, Mr. Armatrout," Miss Jesczenka said crisply.

Don't worry, he's not one of Fortissimus' men, but he's honest. Too honest. He writes for The New York Times *and he's impossible to manipulate. The womanly wiles may work on the other simpletons, but not on him. Be careful.*

"It's all right, Miss Jesczenka," Emily murmured, lifting a hand. The gesture made a cluster of reporters in the middle of the room fan themselves. But Emily paid them no attention. She looked at Horace Armatrout.

"Mr. Stanton did study sangrimancy," Emily said. "But that was a mistake he made long ago. He has paid the price for it. He admits his error of judgment." Not seeing any give in Armatrout's cool eyes, Emily looked rather desperately around at the men she knew she had under her sway. "Haven't any of you gentlemen ever made a mistake?"

"Oh, of course, of course . . ." Emily heard the men mutter among themselves. By that point, however, Emily was aware that she could have told them that they had all attended the Fifth Council of Reims and had gotten good copy out of it, and they would have agreed with her. All of them. All of them except the coolly smiling Mr. Armatrout.

"Short of a hangman's noose, I wonder how exactly one goes about paying for the mistake of killing people and stealing their blood," Armatrout said. But it was not a question, so Emily said nothing, just kept her lips pressed together tightly. "And speaking of errors in judgment, what about this 'Mrs. Blackheart'?" Armatrout reached into his pocket, pulled out a red book, and held it before himself. "Just another one of his mistakes, Miss Edwards? To be honest, I find your apparent acceptance of your noble fiancé's indiscretions kind of . . . puzzling."

All right, Miss Jesczenka's voice was clipped. *I think it's time we considered the fainting option.* But Emily did not faint; she just lifted her chin and stared back at Horace Armatrout.

"I have met Mrs. Blotgate," Emily said. "She was a guest at the Investment, in the company of her husband." Emily had to clench her teeth to get the next words out, but she got them out all right, to her credit. "She seemed very nice. I don't believe any of the things I read in that book, not about her or about my fiancé."

"You *read* the book?" Armatrout sprung the trap, his voice rich with pretended astonishment. "You read *The Blood-Soaked Crimes of Dreadnought Stanton*? Hardly nice material for an innocent such as yourself."

God no, you haven't read it. Miss Jesczenka's voice in her ears was horrified. *You can't even conceive of the kind of depravity described in that book.*

"Oh, no . . . I couldn't read it," Emily stammered. "I couldn't even concieve of the kind of depravity described in that book."

"Then how do you know about 'Mrs. Blackheart'?" Armatrout asked her. Then he shrugged. "Oh well, I'm sure you've been well prepared. Well *briefed*." He encompassed Miss Jesczenka and Emily in one pointed glance.

"I . . . I have heard a little about it. But I felt quite ill when I saw it. I felt the evil in it. The horrible, horrible evil. I felt that it was an evil book, and it . . . it made me feel ill."

Stop babbling, Miss Jesczenka's voice was hard. *Let him have the point. You've already lost it.* Emily pressed her lips closed, clenching her teeth.

"As I said, Mr. Armatrout," Miss Jesczenka quickly interjected, "there will be a time for questions later. At the moment, Miss Edwards has something to deliver. Something that will reveal the true author of these attacks, and the malicious intention behind them."

Emily wasn't listening as the woman continued to speak. She was watching Armatrout. He had apparently satisfied himself as to the idiocy of the proceedings and was lounging at the back of the room, using a pocketknife to pick his fingernails.

"Miss Edwards?" Miss Jesczenka's voice prompted. But Emily was still watching Horace Armatrout.

Emily, the voice barked in her ear, making her startle. *Bring out the letters. They're ready for you. They'll do anything you say now.*

Emily's hands dipped swiftly into her bag for the letters. She half pulled them out; the reporters leaned forward eagerly, like dogs waiting to be thrown a treat.

And then, Emily's hand paused. She looked at Armatrout again. He was watching her without seeming to watch her. She did not pull the letters from her bag. Instead, she tucked them back down swiftly and strode across the room, her silk skirts rustling. Dozens of astonished eyes followed her.

What are you doing? Miss Jesczenka's voice had a note of panic that Emily had never heard in it before. *Show them the letters! Miss Edwards, please, you must! That's what all this was for! You'll never have a better chance . . .*

Emily reached up, removed one pearl earring from her ear, then the other. She stepped carefully through the neck-craning crowd of men. She came to stand before Mr. Armatrout. He looked down at her, his face slightly amused. He folded the pocketknife and tucked it into his pocket.

"Wonderful show," he said under his breath. "For someone who obviously doesn't have much practice, that is."

"Thank you," she said softly. Her hand dipped into the bag for the letters. She handed them to him. He looked down at them.

"I'm supposed to show these around to everyone," she said. "The Institute wants them widely disseminated. Once you read them, you'll see why. They prove that Rex Fortissimus—his real name is Ogilvy Creagh Flannigan, I believe—embezzled millions while in the service of Boss Tweed. His Presentment Agency padded city contracts. These letters are the proof."

Armatrout looked over the letters, his eyes appraising.

"Are they the real deal?"

Emily nodded. Armatrout snorted laughter.

"Well, you'd say that in any case."

Emily looked at him. "The letters are real, and so is everything else. Mostly." He looked at her, his face registering surprise at the modifier. She held his eyes calmly.

"I do love Mr. Stanton, very much," she said softly. "He's made terrible mistakes, yes. He's made bad choices, yes. If I could stop loving him, maybe I would. But I don't know how."

Emily sighed, closing her eyes and opening them again. When she spoke, she did not look at Armatrout. It was as if she spoke the words to herself.

"Why should he be saved? Because I love him? No, love doesn't make anything different. It doesn't pay any debts. Should he be saved because he's really tried to do his best? Because every choice he made seemed right at the time? That doesn't make any difference either. Really, I don't know why he should be saved. Maybe he shouldn't be."

She looked up, saw that Armatrout was staring at her. She gestured to the letters in his hands.

"That's why I'm giving these to you. Because the truth does matter. And I think you serve the truth, the best you can find it. So serve it. Do what is right. I'm sure you can see what it is more clearly than I can. I only know that I love him. I do love him, despite everything. And that makes me blind. I don't want my blindness to lead to more evil. True love shouldn't do that."

Armatrout turned the packet of letters over and over in his hands.

"I know you can see right through all the credomantic mumbo jumbo," she murmured. "You think that this was all a show, and it was. But I wanted you to know it was more than that, too."

Armatrout stared at her. For a moment, his smirk was gone, replaced with a look of wonderment.

"He's a very lucky man," Armatrout said finally.

"No, he isn't particularly," Emily said. "But I believe that he is decent. And that's all I get."

Armatrout tipped his hat to her. She turned away from him. As she did, newspapermen around her surged, knocking over chairs to get to him. They were snatching the letters out of his hands, passing them among themselves.

"Give, Armatrout!"

"You're not keeping all the good stuff for yourself!"

Emily glided away from the scuffle like a beautiful, calm boat, closing her eyes. She thought of another credomantic precept that she could probably find in one of Stanton's textbooks somewhere, if she ever had a chance to look.

The truth will set you free.

"Not exactly the way I planned it," Miss Jesczenka said as Emily returned to stand by the lectern.

Together, they watched the pack of reporters grabbing at Armatrout. The big man was holding the letters high, protests roaring from his lips, but a dozen greasy hands had already reached up to snatch at them, and all around the room, reporters bent over their hard-won prizes, eyes scanning them greedily.

"Gentlemen!" Miss Jesczenka called to them loudly, over the din. "Gentlemen, I will see that you all get copies of the letters! Gentlemen, there really is no call for such dramatics . . ."

But then the dramatics really began.

There was the sound of kicked wood, and the doors at the back of the room, which had been closed for the conference, slammed open, banging back against the walls. Men strode in, a dozen men in gray uniforms bearing patches with the Institute's crest. The Russians, already nervous from the reporters' feeding frenzy, bristled and reached behind themselves for their rifles.

Leading the gang in gray was a tall, spare man in a black suit. It took Emily a moment to understand what her eyes were seeing. When she did, abrupt joy flooded through her.

"Mr. Stanton!" she cried, running across the room to him. She threw herself into his arms, and he folded her in them tightly. He pressed his lips against the top of her head, his hot breath stirring her hair.

"Goddamn you," he whispered fiercely. "You're not leaving me, Emily. I won't let you."

Emily ignored the words, ignored everything. She held him tight, squeezing her eyes shut, wishing everything else in the world would vanish. They stayed that way for longer than they should have, because when she opened her eyes, she saw that the reporters hadn't vanished. Indeed, they'd all flipped their notebooks to new pages and were scribbling furiously. Reluctantly, she pulled away from Stanton, aware that just a bit more reticence might be in order. She noticed that Dmitri and his men had clustered close behind her, rifles drawn and leveled. They were grimly eyeing Stanton and the clot of Institute security that surrounded him. Emily had the sudden, terrible urge to laugh. A couple of true lovers with their security teams facing each other down.

Stanton, too, became more aware of the situation. Emily saw his face change as he looked around the group of reporters. His face became guarded and he frowned.

"Smile," Emily whispered to him. But Stanton did not smile. In fact, if anything his scowl deepened. The reporters began barking in unison.

"Mr. Stanton! May we have a comment?"

"Mr. Stanton, do you feel confident in your ability to put these base and unfounded accusations behind you?"

"Mr. Stanton, are you terribly concerned by the anguish your fiancée has suffered?"

"If my fiancée has suffered from anguish, it's because you and everyone like you has been bothering her with your ugliness and insinuation and disgusting filth!" he barked at the reporters, his green eyes shining with rage. "She shouldn't be here, subjected to this kind of . . . pawing! You howling pack of wolves!"

Pencils scratched rapidly over page-turning pads. The story was getting better and better.

"Sophos, what are you doing here?" Miss Jesczenka's quiet voice came at Emily's elbow. "You know you shouldn't be out of the Institute—"

"And you!" he barked, whirling on Miss Jesczenka. "What are you thinking, putting her through a press conference? Parading her before them? Are you insane?"

"Mr. Stanton." Dmitri's voice was a low throbbing insistence beneath Stanton's keening fury. Stanton looked up, suddenly noticing the dozens of rifles that were trained on him. "I think it's time you leave. Now."

Stanton looked at him. He clenched his teeth. "Who the hell are you?"

"I represent the Sini Mira," Dmitri said, his eyes coming up to Stanton's, meeting them with hard brown determination. "We are here to protect her."

"The Sini Mira? Protect Emily?" Stanton fairly spat the words. "Eradicationists who want to see magic and those who use it destroyed utterly?" He pulled Emily closer, his arm closing protectively around her.

Sudden inspiration lit Miss Jesczenka's eyes. Stepping back, she drew a deep breath.

"Yes, indeed!" Her voice resonated through the room as her eyes turned on the Sini Mira men with a look of desperate terror revealed. "Oh, indeed! These are the very men who tried to kill her! The men who tried to murder her in Chicago! Gentlemen, we were not at liberty to disclose this fact, but we were forced to come here today against our will! These brutes forced us to come!" She leveled a trembling finger at Dmitri and his confused-looking comrades. "These men wish to *murder* Miss Edwards!"

"But they let her have a press conference first?" Emily heard Armatrout mutter, but no one seemed to pay any attention to him. The reporters were agape at the rifles, at the Institute security men who were already pressing forward, hands raised. Miss Jesczenka's terror was filling the room like a palpable thing.

"Run, Sophos!" Miss Jesczenka said, her voice extravagantly pleading. "Take your true love and run!"

"Oh, for God's sake," Emily heard Stanton mutter as he wrapped his arms around her. Flames flared up around them, flames that burned with extreme brightness but gave off no heat. In a moment they were gone, and in another moment they were tumbling heavily together onto the floor of the Sophos' office in the Institute.

Inside the Institute, the air was still as a tomb. Emily sat up slowly, pressing a hand to her head. She felt slightly dizzy, as if she'd been drinking vodka again, but the feeling passed quickly.

The office was a shambles, Emily noticed first. Pieces of colored glass from the huge stained-glass window behind the desk littered the floor, showing glimpses of the blue sky beyond; curtains drooped from their rods, and everything was covered with a thin film of crumbled plaster dust. Emily looked down at Stanton, lying on the floor. His face was pale, skeletal, and bruised. She put an arm around his shoulders, helping him sit up.

He grinned wanly, his green eyes flat as marbles. "I can't imagine how I did that. The Institute hasn't an ounce of power left."

"That wasn't the power of the Institute." Emily smiled, stroking his cheek. "That was true love conquering all."

"Have you been reading my textbooks?" His eyes fluttered closed for a long moment before opening again and focusing slowly on her. She brushed a speck of plaster dust from his face.

"I was doing all right. The Sini Mira didn't mean me any harm. Miss Jesczenka was just making the story better for the reporters. Please tell me you didn't hurt yourself with that silly trick."

"There is nothing else I can do, Emily," he murmured. "I've lost the Institute."

"Don't say that." She looked around the office, the despair in his voice making her imagine the roof crumbling to pieces on top of them. "Not here."

"There's not much more damage that can be done," Stanton said, seeing the direction of her gaze. He was silent for a long time, and when he spoke again, his voice was soft. "I was so worried about you. Are you really all right?"

"I have nine lives, just like a cat," Emily said.

"And you're just as careless with them." Stanton was silent for a long time before he spoke again. "I know you saw the book."

She didn't want to ask him about the hideous red book. Right now he was broken and tired, and all she wanted to do was soothe him and stroke the hair back from his broad hot forehead. But he did not want to be spared this, she knew. And sparing him this would be just like his mother . . . gliding over unpleasant things, encouraging his emptiness. Making him as empty as the Senator. She wouldn't do that to him.

"You killed people," Emily said softly. "You killed people when you were at the Erebus Academy, and you took their blood."

"Yes." There was no apology, at least.

"Were they good people?"

"I don't know," Stanton said. "We were never encouraged to ask."

"How could you?" Emily said, her voice thin with pain. "How could you have done it?"

"I did it because they meant nothing to me. They were only objects to be used to achieve power."

"But you're not like that now," she said. "I know you're not."

"I try not to be," Stanton said. "I try very hard."

He sank his head against her breast, breathing softly. She stroked his head.

"When I thought you'd left me, part of me was glad," Stanton murmured, after her long silence made him realize she didn't intend to speak. "I was glad you'd come to your senses."

"Hush," she said.

"I told you I wasn't someone you should fall in love with. I told you I'd done terrible things. I'm sorry I didn't let you go back to Lost Pine, where you could be happy."

"I didn't want to go back to Lost Pine," Emily said. "And I'm happy with you."

"Don't lie," he said. "That's my job."

"I'm not lying," she said.

"How could you love me?" The question was desperate.

Emily searched for the right answer, but finally just shook her head. "I don't know," she said.

Stanton was silent for a long time.

"I've always grabbed for the things that I wanted," he said at last, his voice low and sleepy. "The Erebus Academy, the Institute . . . but nothing is ever what you want it to be. The harder you grab for it, the more deeply it cuts. And it mocks you for being foolish enough to reach for it at all. You come to fear touching anything at all, because you know that if you do, it will become terrible."

Emily said nothing.

"I didn't want to touch you. There is no cruelty in you. There's no deceit. I've never known anyone like you. How could I bring myself to ruin that? Why do you think I kept telling you to go marry the lumberman? He'd never have to lie to you. He'd never ask you to accept so much ugliness. You deserve someone like him."

"Hush," Emily said again.

"I wanted to believe that somehow you would be invulnerable to all this. That you'd be armored by that wondrous common sense of yours. But it was a foolish thing to believe. It will ruin you just as it's ruined me."

"You're not going to ruin me," Emily said. "Keep your chin

up, Dreadnought Stanton. It's always darkest before the dawn, right?"

"Now I *know* you've been reading my textbooks." He smiled, closing his eyes and holding tight to the arms she held him with. Within a few minutes, he was asleep, breathing deeply.

"Oh, my poor love," she said, pressing her lips to the top of his head. "My poor, martyred love."

CHAPTER TWENTY

Dawn and Darkness

The next morning she woke before he did, stirring from dreams of frenzied reporters and rifles. His warm body was stretched out beside her. When she opened her eyes, the first thing she noticed was that the dawn was very bright. She raised a hand to her eyes, wondering if the stained-glass window had given up entirely and the sun was beaming down on them through the empty frame. But then she realized that it wasn't the summer sun glowing so brightly. It was Stanton, sleeping peacefully as a cherub.

He glowed as if lit from within. She sat up abruptly, staring down at him with astonishment. The clothes that had hung off him limply the night before now fit with perfect detail. He looked as if he had just gotten back from a month at a celestial spa drinking tonics made of starlight. Emily looked around the office. The wreckage of the night had vanished completely. The stained-glass window was whole and unbroken, colors streaming through it like individual elements of an extravagant promise. Every bit of plaster was in its accustomed place, gilt glittered madly, and it even seemed that a phantom cleaning crew of renewed power had taken a duster to the shelves and a broom to the carpet.

Beside her, Stanton sat up with the swiftness of a man waking from a nightmare. He looked around, blinked three times, and then looked at Emily.

"Am I dead?" he asked.

"I don't think so," she said. "I don't think heaven is this garish."

Grinning, he took her face in his hands and kissed her— a bright celebratory kiss. After having been apart so long, Emily found herself moving in ways that ensured celebration would quickly give way to something far more intimate. Before it could, however, the office door flew open with a bang.

"Mr. Stanton!" Rose burst in, waving a sheaf of newspapers. Breathing hard, Emily hastily climbed off Stanton's lap, glaring at Rose. "Miss Emily, thank goodness you're safe! Mr. Stanton rescued you from the clutches of those evildoers! I knew he could do it! Hooray for Mr. Stanton!"

"Yes," Emily muttered, pulling up the neck of her dress. "Hooray for Mr. Stanton."

"Good morning, Rose." Stanton had stood, and was brushing dust from his coat, even though there was no dust to be brushed. Rose, staring at him, dropped the bundle of papers she was carrying. Then she reddened and hastened to pick them up.

"Oh, me and my butterfingers! We can't have a mess, not when everything looks so . . . so wonderful now!" Rose looked up, eyes beaming around the office. "It's even more beautiful in here than it ever was!"

Stanton reached down to help Emily to her feet, his thumb stroking her palm suggestively. The touch sent a shiver up her arm.

"Rose, run along and fetch us some coffee and a big breakfast. I'm famished. Are those the morning papers?"

Mute, Rose offered the papers to him with trembling hands, then hurried out. He took them to his desk and spread them out. Emily looked at them over his shoulder, bringing up her good hand to twine her fingers in his hair. How had she never noticed how soft it was?

"Dreadnought Stanton's Fiancée Refutes Scandalous Allegations," read the first headline. It was accompanied by an above-the-fold engraving of her, posed in a modest and demure posture she couldn't remember having assumed. "Dreadnought Stanton Rescues Fiancée from Foreign Attack at Fifth Avenue Hotel," read another. "Dreadnought Stanton Defies All Odds to Rescue His Love from Clutches of Bloodthirsty Slavs."

They all carried some variation on this theme; the headlines were all on the front pages, and they all carried pictures of engravings of Emily in idealized detail. Stanton's eyes quickly scanned each of them, but it was a paper at the bottom of the pile—a sober, serious paper with only a few very small illustrations—that he lingered over. It was *The New York Times*.

"Rex Fortissimus Implicated in Embezzling Scandal, Ignoble Plot to Discredit Dreadnought Stanton Revealed," its headline read. It was smaller than the others, but seemed to command respect. Stanton read the article, then stared at the author's name.

"Horace Armatrout." He looked up at Emily. "Horace Armatrout!"

"He's a very nice man," Emily said.

Stanton grinned at her. "You really are full of surprises," he said, and the praise made her glow in a way it never had before. But he had no time to offer more, no matter how dearly Emily suddenly desired it, for there was a sound at the door. A pair of magisters peered inside, looking around the office, their faces astonished. Stanton waved them in.

"Professor McAllister. Professor Dyer. It seems the worst has passed."

"Indeed, Mr. Stanton," the one named McAllister said, shaking his head as he took a seat. He looked at Stanton, respectfully inclined his head. "Sophos Stanton."

Stanton inclined a head back at him, the reciprocation just one shade more remote.

"Fortissimus is already here, hat in hand, to negotiate a settlement of hostilities." McAllister's voice bore a great deal of satisfaction. "I made him wait in one of the classrooms. He's fuming, but he's not going anywhere. He knows when he's licked."

"Delightful." Stanton smiled wolfishly. "Let him wait a little while longer. I'll talk to him after I've had my coffee."

At that precise moment, Rose bustled in, bearing a huge silver platter loaded with steaming coffee and frosted pastries of all sorts. He grabbed for a thick hunk of something moist and sugary, downing it in three swift bites before grabbing another. Emily took up the pot of coffee and poured him a cup, then a cup for herself. Then, remembering, she looked at the magisters. They lowered their eyes and lifted their hands in respectful negatives.

Stanton, however, did not look up at her as he opened the sugar dish and spooned half of its contents into his cup. The small space that remained he filled with thick cream. He fixed McAllister and Dyer with a firm green gaze.

"Make it known that I'll be happy to speak with anyone who defected from the Institute during the recent hostilities. I will hear everyone out, of course. But I will not promise that they'll be reinstated at anything like their former positions."

McAllister and Dyer nodded obediently, hurrying from the office to see that the wishes of the Sophos were executed swiftly and completely. When they were gone, Stanton leaned back in his chair, coffee in hand, grinning up at her. She smiled back, raising her coffee cup from its saucer in an ironic salute.

"Now, this is more like it," he said, bringing his cup to his lips.

"Mr. Stanton." The quiet moment was scattered to the winds as Rose hurried back in, a note between her fingers. "This just came for you."

Stanton put his coffee on the desk and picked up a sharp silver opener. He slid it along the top of the envelope, unfolded its contents.

"It's from the bloodthirsty Slavs," he said. "They want a meeting so they can return Miss Jesczenka." He looked up at Emily. "Should we invite them in for coffee?"

"They prefer tea," Emily said. She found Stanton's eyes, held them. "You understand they didn't really try to kill me, don't you? They were helping me."

Stanton looked at her, his eyes scrutinizing, but he said nothing. Instead he turned to Rose.

"Go and tell the Sini Mira to come in," he said. "And see if you can't find them some tea."

A moment later, Rose led in Perun and Dmitri, and a very pleased-looking Miss Jesczenka, who had the self-satisfied air of the cat who had swallowed the New York press. Emily went to her side, gave her arm a fond squeeze.

"Did you see the papers?" Miss Jesczenka whispered.

Emily nodded. *"Horace Armatrout,"* she said.

"Horace Armatrout," Miss Jesczenka echoed, letting out a sigh of satisfaction.

"Gentlemen, make yourselves comfortable," Stanton invited. Lowering himself into the very same chair he had sat in the night before the Investment, Perun pulled his cigarette case from inside his coat and hung a cigarette from his lips. Seeing the action, Stanton reached into a humidor on his desk, withdrawing a cigar. After fussing with it for a moment, he lit it with a finger-snapped tongue of flame. He did not, however, move to offer the flickering werelight to Perun. The white-blond man smiled slightly, reaching into his own pocket for a match.

"Thank you for bringing my magister back to me," Stanton said, eyes moving from Perun to Miss Jesczenka. "You are unharmed, I trust?"

"Entirely," Miss Jesczenka said.

"Excellent," Stanton said. There was a long silence. Stanton smoked his cigar contemplatively, watching Perun. Perun smoked his cigarette down between brown-stained fingers, watching Stanton. After five minutes of this, Emily stomped over to the window and cracked it open.

"Honestly," she muttered.

"I am rather busy," Stanton said finally. "Do we have further business?"

"We do," Perun said softly. "We most certainly do."

And then, in low even tones, Perun explained everything. About the hair sticks, about Aleksei Morozovich, about Volos' Anodyne. Stanton watched Perun give the recitation, his eyes hard and glinting.

"Miss Jesczenka's execution of the Talleyrand Maneuver restored the power of the Institute to you," Perun concluded. "We allowed her to do so in exchange for her solemn oath that the Institute—that *you,* Sophos Stanton—would help us."

"Miss Jesczenka is a valued member of my staff," Stanton

said, "but she does not have the power to make promises for the Institute. Or for me."

Dmitri snorted, a dark scornful sound. "I told you so, Perun," he said.

"I see you have been reading the papers." Perun gestured to the pile of newsprint on Stanton's desk. "Tell me . . . have you noticed that *temamauhti* has begun, or have you been too busy with your own clippings?"

Stanton looked at Perun, not moving. Perun reached forward, began pulling paper after paper off the pile on Stanton's desk.

"America's Pacific Coast . . ." He lifted a paper. "Arkansas and Tennessee and Kentucky . . ." He lifted another. "Japan and China and Java and the good Lord knows how many other unfortunate places by now." He threw the papers to the floor, his face seizing with fury. "And all of those are just from the Black Glass Goddess gathering the Exunge she needs. It is *beginning,* Mr. Stanton. And we have to stop it— one way or another."

Stanton watched him closely, but did not speak.

"If you do not believe me, ask your fiancée." Perun looked at Emily. "She has seen it all, through her unprecedented connection to the Mantic Anastomosis—the consciousness she calls Ososolyeh."

Stanton looked at her. "What is he talking about?"

"Ever since the Symposium—" Emily began, then stopped. "No, since before that, actually. I can't even remember when it started. It seems like forever. Ososolyeh speaks to me. It shows me things. Awful things."

"What does it show you?" Stanton asked softly.

"The Black Glass Goddess, her fingers sharp as knives," Emily whispered, eyes turning inward as remembered images danced before them. "I have seen her cutting twelve men to pieces, leaving nothing but a mound of flesh, like some kind of monstrous . . . organ."

Her eyes stared forward, fixed and unfocused.

"A priest in gold and feathers and jade. The world remade in blackness and frost." Emily's mouth was moving, but she didn't feel in conscious control of what was coming out of it.

Words poured forth like humming, like roots growing. "Blood running down the sides of stepped pyramids. The air ringing with the screams of the innocent. The end of the world."

She did not know how long she was lost in the terrible memories; she only knew that when she came back to herself, Stanton was standing before her, a warm hand laid on her cheek.

"We have to get the hair sticks back," Emily said softly. "We have to find a way."

"This isn't about the hair sticks anymore, Miss Edwards," Perun said. "I'm afraid it stopped being about the hair sticks when we lost them to the Temple."

Emily looked at the Russian, astonished.

"Even if I had the hair sticks in my hands right now," Perun continued, "there would be no time to implement the poison. Tomorrow is June 30. By the Aztec calendar, it is the first day of Cuetzpalin, the thirteen days the Goddess rules. It is the day of her greatest potency. It is when she will strike."

"Then why—"

"I had to give you hope," Perun said. "Without it, you and Miss Jesczenka could never have accomplished the near-impossible and returned the power of the Institute to Mr. Stanton."

"But if there's no time to implement the poison, what does it matter if the power of the Institute is restored?"

Perun chuckled grimly.

"Do you not remember, Miss Edwards? Even in the coldest darkness of winter, hope remains." Perun paused, looking at Stanton. "And indeed, there is one last hope. It is one that only Mr. Stanton can deploy. The *desperatus*."

Emily turned her gaze back to Stanton. "What is he talking about?"

But Stanton did not speak, only continued to look at her face, as if trying to commit it to memory.

"For a decade now," Perun answered for him, "the credomancers have sought to perfect their own answer to the threat of *temamauhti*. Working together in greatest secrecy, Mirabilis and Zeno crafted a magical weapon called a *des-*

peratus. It will block the larger apocalypse by unleashing a smaller one. Fire to fight fire, as it were." Speaking of fire apparently made Perun crave one of his never-ending string of cigarettes; he took out his cigarette case. "We all hoped that it would never have to be used, for if it is deployed, it will be only slightly less destructive than *temamauhti* itself. Now, however, it seems we have no other choice."

As Perun spoke, Emily watched Stanton's face. She watched the emotions passing over it; frustration, then fear, regret, then resignation.

"Mr. Stanton, the *desperatus* is yours to deploy. The power of the Institute has been returned to you so that you can do so." Perun paused. "The time has come, Sophos."

Stanton turned, leaned on the desk, faced Perun squarely.

"You know as well as I do that no one has ever been able to ascertain the precise location of the Temple." The words were clipped, and there was a determined note in his voice, the sound of a man suddenly and swiftly convinced. "We must get to the Temple to deploy the *desperatus.* How do you propose we find it?"

"You have Fortissimus, do you not?" Perun drew a cigarette from his case, tapped it. Stanton jerked his head in a nod.

"It seems clear that he planted the Nikifuryevich Ladder that was used to kidnap Zeno, and your magister agrees with me." Perun looked at Miss Jesczenka. "If he is in league with the Temple, as I believe he is, then he is our only hope for finding it."

"I have promised him pardon," Stanton said. But it was a comment, not a protest.

"A little thing, compared to the end of the world," Perun said. Stanton nodded, then straightened.

"Rose!" he bellowed.

Rose hurried into the office, blond hair wisping about her face.

"Have Fortissimus brought here immediately," he said.

If Fortissimus strode into the office of the Sophos looking very sure of himself, clearly expecting that he would meet with Stanton alone, he was quickly disabused of that notion. The robust, dismissive bonhomie with which he had been intending to greet Stanton—as one would congratulate a colleague who'd just won a round of golf—mutated to cold suspicion as his gaze traveled over the faces of those who waited for him. Dmitri and Perun, Emily and Miss Jesczenka, and, finally, Stanton. Emily felt certain the man would have turned and fled had not Rose closed the door quietly behind him.

"Good morning, Mr. Stanton," he said, licking his lips.

"Good morning, *Flannigan,*" Stanton said. Emily saw the man wince as Stanton used his real name. "Rose, take his hat and coat."

"No . . . I'd like to keep them . . ." Fortissimus began.

But Rose already had them and was leaving with them through the office door.

"Please sit down," Stanton said.

"I'd really rather—"

"I asked you to sit down," Stanton said without raising his voice. Fortissimus dropped into a sturdy chair like a stone from an uncurled fist. Sudden sour fear bloomed from Fortissimus' pores. It made Emily's heart thud like a baneful elixir. At her side, she could feel Miss Jesczenka's body tense with anticipation.

"Perhaps you should leave, Miss Edwards," Miss Jesczenka murmured to Emily, but the woman did not take her eyes off Fortissimus. There was dark desire in those eyes, hunger and anticipation, and a smile played at the corners of her lips. Emily looked quickly away, foreboding chilling her.

Stanton stood over Fortissimus, looking down at him for a long time, his hands clasped behind his back.

"You're afraid, Flannigan." Stanton's tone was merely observational, but it set Fortissimus to trembling. His eyes darted from face to face.

"I came here on good faith," he said. "This is an outrage!"

"You planted the Nikifuryevich Ladder," Stanton said. "Under the direction of the Temple of Itztlacoliuhqui."

Fortissimus' eyes snapped up.

"How dare you suggest such an . . . obscenity," he spat, rage overmastering terror. "How *dare* you! I have worked all my life to hone my skills, improve my practice, build my Agency to prominence . . . and you have the *audacity* to suggest that I would toss it aside so stupidly? To such little benefit? I am a *credomancer,* Stanton. If you're interested in finding a sangrimancer, go look in a goddamn mirror."

Stanton merely had to twitch a finger, and Fortissimus' mouth snapped shut with such abruptness that blood trickled from the side of his mouth. As if proving some kind of point, he leaned his head down to wipe the blood off on his shoulder. Stanton took a deep breath.

"Tell me how to find the Black Glass Goddess," he said.

"I don't know! I don't—"

"Tell me how to find the Black Glass Goddess," Stanton repeated. "Stop lying and tell me the truth."

"How would you know the difference?" Fortissimus snarled. He looked over at Emily, his eyes gleaming insinuation. "For example, how much of what I printed in that book was a lie? And how much of it was just . . . *enhanced actuality?*"

"Do not change the subject," Perun barked, smoke trickling from between his lips. "You invited the Blotgates to the Investment. General Blotgate advocated a military alliance with the Temple, and his wife is known to recruit for them. You planted the device for them, admit it!"

"I planted nothing!" Fortissimus screamed. "Yes, I invited the Blotgates. I invited them to remind people what he has done. What he *is!*" Fortissimus glared at Stanton, eyes dancing with hatred. "To pay him back for making an utter travesty of everything I have ever accomplished! I wanted to destroy him, not the Institute."

Stanton crouched down before Fortissimus, looking into the older man's face. When he spoke, his voice was strangely kind. "Tell me how to find the Black Glass Goddess. This is your third chance, and you know that's all you get. You know that there are harsher methods."

Fortissimus moved his tongue around his mouth. Leaning

forward, he spat blood into Stanton's face. Stanton stood, pulled a handkerchief from his pocket, and wiped the blood away.

"Miss Jesczenka," Stanton said, tucking the handkerchief back into his pocket. "Please fetch the needle."

Miss Jesczenka returned with a black leather case. She unzipped it carefully as she moved, and the small sound seemed to echo through the office. Fortissimus watched her movements; they were sinuous with malice. Miss Jesczenka removed a large crystal syringe and a small glowing bottle. She plunged the syringe through the bottle's rubber top and filled the crystal chamber with the glowing liquid.

Stanton and Perun watched her actions with a kind of terrible calmness. Only Dmitri's face was pale and slack with horror. He looked at Perun, shook his head, began to speak—but Perun stilled the words in his mouth with a curt gesture of his hand.

Miss Jesczenka knelt silently before Fortissimus and stretched his arm out. She unbuttoned his sleeve and rolled it back delicately. She touched the smooth flesh on the inside of his elbow, and then slid the needle into it. She depressed the plunger slowly.

Within a moment, Fortissimus' face contracted sourly, as if he'd just bitten into a lemon. Before she stood, however, Miss Jesczenka leaned forward and placed her mouth close to Fortissimus' ear. Fortissimus listened, then stared at Miss Jesczenka's face. He stared at it for a long time.

"You," he whispered. "I *ruined* you!"

Miss Jesczenka smiled at him gently. "And yet, at the end of the day, I am the one holding the needle, aren't I?" she said. She replaced the syringe in the case, and laid it carefully at Fortissimus' feet. Then she stood, brought her hand back, and slapped him across the face. The crack echoed through the office as Fortissimus' head snapped to the side.

Stanton leaned back against his desk, crossing his arms. "Let us begin."

"No!" The word burst from Dmitri. "Not this way! Perun, I beg you."

"Peace, Dmitri Alekseivitch—"

"This is what the Temple Warlocks did to my father!" Dmitri's eyes went from Perun's face to Stanton's. But Stanton did not look at Dmitri; his dark gaze was fixed on Fortissimus.

"Tell me," Stanton said.

Fortissimus tensed, hissing agony.

"The harder you resist, the worse the interrogation acid will burn in your blood." Stanton's voice was soft and calm. "You think the pain is unbearable now, but it will get worse. Submit, Flannigan. Tell me and the pain will stop."

"Dreadnought," Emily whispered. "No."

"Tell me how to find the Black Glass Goddess," Stanton repeated, his voice perfectly level, as if striving to make each word balance precisely with the next.

Fortissimus threw his head back and cackled—something halfway between a laugh and a shriek. Tears streamed down the sides of his face, mingling with the sweat that ran in rivulets down from his forehead.

"I don't know!" he screamed. "I swear it, I don't know anything!"

"Tell me how to find her!" Stanton said, his voice rising.

"Dreadnought, *no!*" Emily seized his shirt in her good hand, shook him, made him look at her. "I did not help you regain the power of the Institute so that you could do *this!*" Her eyes searched Stanton's face frantically. "I told him the *truth!* I told him you were *decent!* And I told myself . . ."

"Emily . . ." Stanton looked down at her.

"Don't make it a lie," Emily whispered, her voice tiny and desperate. "Oh please. Please don't make it a lie."

She saw the flicker of anguish behind his eyes. His face softened for a moment, but it hardened again almost as quickly, like wax cooling. He put a hand on each of her arms. "It's the end of the world, Emily."

No sooner were the words out of his mouth than a vision knifed through her like a cold glass blade slid between her ribs. The agony of it drove her almost to her knees.

The Black Glass Goddess, thrusting a knife of obsidian deep into Stanton's side . . .

"Xiuhunel!" she cried, tearing herself away from his grasp, throwing herself away from him, running out into the beautiful, strong, powerful hallways of the Institute.

She ran until she came to the Veneficus Flame, and when she reached it, she collapsed beneath it, pressing her hot cheek against the cool marble pedestal. She pressed a hand over her mouth, her stomach heaving.

There were swift footsteps, and a warm hand was laid on her shoulder. A figure crouched down beside her. Dmitri. His eyes were wide with betrayal and anguish.

"Goddamn him," he growled. "Goddamn them both."

She stood quickly, intending to run, but he caught her arm and jerked her close. It was as if he needed to be comforted as much as he desired to comfort. He wrapped his arms around her, pulled her to his chest.

"A torturer. A sangrimancer. I told you so!" Dmitri said again, clinging to her. "And Perun . . . How could he let it happen?"

Emily pressed her face into Dmitri's shoulder, stared at the weave of his jacket. She didn't want to think. She wanted to lose herself in the calm, orderly arrangements of threads. Hot tears stung her eyes, flowing into the fabric of Dmitri's jacket. Then she was sobbing without restraint, jerking and shuddering.

"I will take you away from here," Dmitri said firmly. He sounded as if it was the only thing he could do that would make the world right. "Away from all of them."

She looked up at him, shaking her head, and in that instant Dmitri's mouth came down over hers roughly. She pushed against his chest, but he clung to her, embracing her with the desperation of a man seeking to replace a shattered illusion with a new one.

It was the sound of a betrayed gasp that finally made him release her.

Rose stood staring at them, her mouth open. Her eyes were

wells of anguish. She brought up a hand, put it over her heart as if it hurt her terribly.

"Shame," Rose whispered. "Shame on you!"

Sobbing, she spun on her heel and ran toward the Sophos' office. Pushing herself away from Dmitri violently, Emily ran, too—in the opposite direction.

Emily went back to her room on the fourth floor, where she could almost make herself believe that the beautiful summer day she saw out of her window did not contain torture, pain, and betrayal. She felt numb and old, so very old. She felt as if her body were made of poured lead, her limbs stiff and slow, her core hot and vitreous. She found a chair to sit in. She stared out the window at the tops of the trees, waving mutely in the warm afternoon breeze.

Not honest. Not forthright. Not decent.

"Why didn't you tell me?" she implored Ososolyeh. "How could you let me fall in love with him?"

Stanton came to her an hour later, the doors of the room flying open without his having to touch them. They closed behind him silently. She struggled not to look up, to keep her eyes fixed on the tops of the stirring trees, but just as she had been unable to ignore Mirabilis in his own Institute, just as she had been unable to ignore Zeno, she could not ignore Stanton. The Institute was his now; it belonged to him and he belonged to it. She glared at him, despising the intrusion.

He stared down at her silently. She could see that despite his mastery of the Institute, he did not know what to say.

Good, she thought, bitterly. As long as she could unsettle him, discomfit him, she'd never be totally under his sway. It was a horrible way to think about a fiancé, but it was a perfectly logical way to think about an ex-fiancé. She thought about taking the diamond ring from her finger and throwing it at him, but the action was unnecessary; the diamond itself spoke more loudly than even the most desperate of gestures. It sat on her finger as dead and flat and lusterless as a piece of glass.

"Fortissimus wouldn't tell us," Stanton said, looking down at her. "Pushing him any further would have killed him."

"Well, why didn't you just kill him, then?" Emily spat. "That's what sangrimancers do, isn't it?"

There was a long silence. He stared down at her as if expecting her to speak, but she held her lips together tightly.

"Rose saw you," he broke the silence, finally. "She told me."

Emily stared into his eyes, putting all her strength into the gaze. She pressed her lips together until they ached, until she tasted blood behind her lips from where her teeth cut into them. Stanton wanted her to apologize, to beg for his forgiveness, to say that the Russian meant nothing to her. And he *didn't*. But no one would force her to say the words. Not ever. Not with all the glowing needles in the world.

"Do you love him?" Stanton's voice was acid.

"I don't think I love anyone," Emily said. They were the words she wanted to say, not the words Stanton wanted to hear, and she said them with great relish.

"Perhaps you are not capable of love," Stanton said. "Perhaps you are only capable of making men desire you. With underhanded powders and potions and—"

"Stop it."

"Perhaps it's all a matter of convenience with you," Stanton continued, his voice low and brutal. "Perhaps that's what men are to you. Convenient harbors for the dingy little boat of your life. Creatures you can manipulate into loving you—"

"I said stop it!" Emily screamed.

"No," he said. "I won't stop. Not in my own—" Even though he checked himself, Emily knew perfectly well what he'd been about to say.

". . . in your own Institute." She completed the sentence for him, fury whipping her. "The Institute that you stole with blood magic . . . that I lied to get back for you!"

"Lower your voice," Stanton said through gritted teeth. "I've had enough of your shrieking."

Emily stared at him, breathing hard, her heart thudding. She wanted to fly at him, tear him into bloody strips. But with great effort, she calmed herself. She took a deep breath. When she spoke again, her voice was low and resonant—so low as to be almost inaudible.

"It's all right," she said finally. "You won't have to listen to it much longer. I'm leaving."

"You can't leave," he said.

"Can," she spat. "Will."

He seized her as she tried to dart past him, wrapped her in strong arms that had the force of iron bands. She struggled against him, but he held her fast. Finally she subsided, breathing heavily, staring down at his chest. She held her body stiffly. Her hand was a fist.

"Let me go," she breathed, the words growling in her throat.

"No," he said. "I won't."

They stood like that, locked in anger and fear, for a long time. Finally, without slackening his grip, Stanton murmured something by her ear.

"It will be terrible, Emily. More terrible than Perun described. More terrible than any of your visions."

"How do you know?"

"I just know that it will be terrible," he said.

"No, you know more than that," she said. "For God's sake, stop lying!"

"It will be terrible!" he shouted, the force of the words shaking her, rattling her bones. She couldn't stand under the force of those words; only his arms, wrapped tightly around her, kept her from sinking to the floor.

"You've seen it all, too," Emily said, awareness dawning on her. "How?"

Stanton's eyes were closed, his face was painted with terrible remorse.

"Alcmene Blotgate," he said finally.

"Did you love her?" Emily searched for an explanation, any explanation.

"Sangrimancers don't fall in love." Stanton's eyes remained closed. "They use each other for mutual benefit."

"Then how—"

"She took me to the Temple to be initiated into the Goddess' service," Stanton said, the words tumbling out in a rush. "When I was a cadet. I failed the initiation. The Goddess released my neologism, showed me the world remade. Showed me *temamauhti*. I couldn't bear it. I ran away."

"You knew?"

"That's why Alcmene Blotgate tried to kill me—because I was a traitor. Because I was a failure and a coward. I don't know why she didn't finish the job. I was ready to finish it for her when Mirabilis found me. He made me see that there were better choices—"

"You *knew*?" Emily cried. "You knew it was coming? You knew ten years ago, and you did nothing? When men like Morozovich, or my father—my *father*!—were dying, trying to save the world? How could you? How *could* you?"

Stanton opened his mouth to speak, and it was clear the intended retort was scalding. But in the end, he didn't say anything. He just shook his head and released her from his arms, as if finally realizing that it was futile to hold on to her any longer.

"You're right," he said. "About everything. Hate me. It will make things easier for both of us."

Taking a step back, she slapped him across the face, hard.

"Go to hell, Dreadnought Stanton."

He nodded, rubbing his face tiredly.

"I will," he said. "It was only you who ever made me think I could go anyplace else."

And as he left the room, the doors slammed behind him with a force that made the whole Institute rumble.

After he left, Emily sank to the floor, as if he'd taken all her strength with him. That was that, then.

At length, Emily got up. She took off the peach-blush dress, let it fall to the floor, laboriously removed her corset and chemise and everything soft and lacy, and stood savoring her nakedness for a long time.

Then she put on old things. She would have put on the clothes she'd brought from Lost Pine, if there'd been anything left of them. But there wasn't. So she put on the simplest gray dress she could find, dragging it down over her head and buttoning it slowly, her ivory hand tinking against the buttons.

Then she sat down wearily on the window seat to wait for the end of the world.

She watched the leaves of the trees swaying in the early evening wind. This time, she saw them moving a special way, a way she knew. This time, she already knew there would be a message for her in them. But she didn't want to see it. She tried to look away. She was tired of messages, tired of the responsibility they brought. But, still, she looked.

Zeno is in the Dragon's Eye.

Emily contemplated this with black amusement.

Ososolyeh, beloved earth-mother, Emily said to it, trying to send her reply down through the treacherous stone floors of the Institute. *I've had just about enough of you.*

She knew what the Dragon's Eye was, of course. It was the brown and green orchid, Zeno's favorite plant in the Institute's conservatory. In her vision, Zeno's last words had been soft and simple, spoken in the language of wind and water and wood: *I am coming home.*

Komé had transferred her spirit into an acorn; Zeno had sent the last drop of himself singing along a root. But that place, the place he'd died . . . it had seemed so immeasurably far away. How could he have made it all the way back here, to New York, to the Dragon's Eye orchid he loved?

Sighing, rising wearily, she thought about not going. She thought about ignoring the message, but she knew she could not. She went to open the door and found, completely unsurprisingly, that it was locked.

CHAPTER TWENTY-ONE

The Dragon's Eye

Emily pounded on the door, assuming it would do no good, but finding the act of pounding very satisfying indeed. After a moment, however, the handle turned. Emily stepped back as the door opened, praying that it wasn't Stanton. But it wasn't. Outside of the door stood Rose, flanked by two guards in Institute gray.

"Let me out of here!" Emily said.

"You've had your chance," Rose snarled at her. "He's got important business to attend to. He'll send for you when he's ready." She put a distasteful emphasis on the word "you," as if even the idea of Emily tasted bad.

"You can't keep me a prisoner here," Emily said. "You want me to go, I want to go. Now get out of my way."

"You *deserve* to be a prisoner!" Rose's mouth was tight with anger. "He should throw you into a pit and forget he ever met you. You're mean and deceitful and cruel, and I know for a *fact* that you never gave him my card!"

"Rose," Emily groaned. "Please."

"It was a very special token," Rose said. "Intended to convey my deepest admiration and respect. And yes, if you must know, I signed it 'with love' . . . something you'd know nothing about!"

"Rose, honestly, you can have him." Emily bit the words. "Take him with my blessing. Just let me the hell out of this room."

With a strangled cry, Rose slammed the door hard, and

once again came the sound of a key scraping a lock—a sound Emily knew so well by now.

She whirled savagely. With a high-pitched scream, she picked up a delicate chair and hurled it at the door, just to hear it smash.

Then she stormed over to the window, threw the casements open, and climbed up to kneel on the padded window seat. She looked down. It was a long sheer drop to the ground. She suddenly felt terribly certain that it had been planned this way from the beginning, and that giving her this room had been a very conscious choice.

Emily leaned a hot forehead against the stone frame of the window and watched the leaves of the ivy fluttering in the gathering evening breeze. They shone in the setting sun. There was the touch of a gentle hand on her shoulder. She startled, then looked back slowly.

But it was not a hand. It was a tendril of the thick English ivy that blanketed the Institute's exterior wall. Emily pulled back in surprise as the tendril slithered down across her chest and down around her waist. She tried to pull it off of her, but it grasped her tightly, pulling her out of the window. She screamed in surprise and protest, her voice hoarse from all the screaming she'd done previously, but more thick vines came up, pulling themselves away from the wall, their suckers making popping sounds as they released from the stone. Emily felt vines snaking around her ankles, around her knees, around her waist . . . she was being pulled out of the window, toward the sheer drop.

But more tendrils of ivy wrapped themselves around her, and she realized that she was being borne out of the window on gentle verdant hands. They conveyed her slowly down the wall, toward the ground below. Leaves and rough stalks tickled her skin as they passed her down, higher vines releasing as lower vines tightened. And then she was on the ground, the good soft ground through which she could feel Ososolyeh thrumming up. She was on the verge of sinking to her hands and knees in sheer gratitude for the closeness, but she saw students inside a classroom rush to a window; some pointed and called. She started running. If the lowest of the Institute's

cultors knew that she'd escaped, Stanton would know soon.
And he would come for her. She fled to the conservatory.

Inside the hothouse it was as warm as she remembered it.
She recalled how Emeritus Zeno had led them along these
crushed walnut paths, showing off his orchids like favorite
grandchildren. The orchid he had been most proud of was the
huge Dragon's Eye orchid, with its stinking flowers of chocolate brown and chartreuse. Its roots reached far down, to
where soil met bedrock and water.

Kneeling quickly, she placed her hands on the orchid's
thick, woody vine, closing her eyes.

Ah, something greeted her. *Emily, isn't it?*

Emily relaxed, letting her body slump against the vine, letting her consciousness reach into it.

"Emeritus Zeno," she breathed.

Is that my name? Oh well. If you say so.

"I saw you die."

Emily felt Zeno's consciousness spreading through the orchid, suffusing it, becoming thinner and less human with
each tendril he curled into. She had to hurry.

I made it home. Zeno's spirit breathed satisfaction and relief. *I went through a root, then another root, and another. I
lost my way a few times. Several times. But I went through another and another and another and another . . .*

"You have to tell me how to find the Temple," Emily asked,
trying to hold on to him, trying to pull his mind back together. "The Temple where you died. We have to get there,
stop *temamauhti . . .*"

Who are you, again?

Her fear stoked a sudden rage. He hadn't come all this way
just to melt into an orchid. He was Benedictus Zeno, father of
modern credomancy, a roil of calculation. He just had to remember. She had to make him remember. Taking a deep
growling breath, she gathered the power of Ososolyeh within
herself. Closing her eyes, she reached her spirit into the orchid and shook the old man, seizing every diffuse piece of
him. It was like rattling a box of marbles.

Damn it, she snarled silently. *You came back for a reason.*

Her sudden anger shuddered through the whole earth. *You must tell me.*

Zeno's mind, suddenly clear, said, *My goddess. Mat' syra zemliya . . .*

Tell me, Emily thundered again.

I thought he was just a failed Initiate. Something we could use. We even had a plan to get him into the Temple. After the Symposium, he was to find the High Priest, crawl before him, beg to be taken back in exchange for something of great value . . .

Emily tightened her grasp on Zeno's spirit; the effort of clarity seemed to make him weaker by the second.

But then, in her lair of despair and pain . . . such a cold, cold place . . . she showed me the horrible truth. The horrible truth of what he was . . . what he is. And then I knew. I knew how to get the desperatus *into the Temple.*

How? Emily shrieked the words in her mind. *How can we find it?*

He doesn't have to find the Temple, my Goddess, Zeno said. *The Temple will find him.*

And then, Zeno did not speak anymore, just spread out thinner and thinner, his spirit becoming flowers, becoming small chambered fruits, becoming tendrils. His mind filled with nothing but thoughts of blooms, luscious and meaty.

Emily removed her hands from the orchid's vine and fell backward. She smelled earth all around her. She felt Ososolyeh moving in her mind. She did not even need to tumble toward it, or allow her mind to expand—the consciousness was just there. It was part of her, like breathing in and out. She stopped looking for answers. She stopped asking questions. She just lay there, breathing in and out, as the vision unfolded in her mind:

The mound of flesh, slick and quivering, in a pool of Exunge. It began to glow, orange light knifing outward . . . and for the first time, Emily understood what it was doing. Why it glowed.

It was transforming the slick tarry Exunge around itself into a luminous golden substance.

Chrysohaeme.

We believe the Goddess has discovered some means by which she can filter Black Exunge, Perun had said . . .

Emily didn't open her eyes. Just kept breathing, in and out. That was how the Goddess purified Black Exunge. That was how she intended to marshal the vast amounts of power she needed. That unnatural mound of flesh was the engine that would power the remaking . . .

Emily felt someone bending over her, but it took her a moment to remember that she had human eyes, and that she should open them and look through them.

The someone bending over her was a young man. He looked like a standard-issue Institute student, black-suited and fresh-faced, but he had a strange bruise on the center of his forehead. He wore a blood-red tie affixed with an obsidian stickpin. In his hand, he clutched a sangrimancer's alembic.

"Miss Jesczenka's lover," she whispered, not sure if he was a vision or if he was real. He was the boy she'd seen Miss Jesczenka with the night of the Investment. And she had seen him somewhere else, too. "Lieutenant Stickpin."

"Lover?" He snorted, his voice cracking. He looked past Emily, down one of the gravel paths. "Did you hear that, Mother?" he called, his tone bitter and mocking. "I can't imagine where she got such a disgusting idea." Following his gaze, Emily saw that the words were directed to a motionless female form. A woman's body was laid across the path, the front of her dress bright with blood. It was Miss Jesczenka. "Of course, I use the term 'mother' in the loosest possible sense," he continued conversationally. "More important, she's my key to the Institute. Not an easy one to use—she's awfully damn canny—but she got me in to plant the Nikifuryevich Ladder. And she got me to *you.*" He paused, and at that moment she saw the knife of black glass in his hand, glittering in the gathering darkness of night. "You'd think a Witch, of all people, would know better than to abandon her own blood, leave it to wander the world anonymous and unattended."

"Anonymous." Emily remembered Miss Jesczenka's words. *"Utisz."*

"Better than Stickpin, anyway," the lieutenant sneered, bringing up the knife. Emily raised a hand to defend herself, but he knocked it aside easily, pinned it to her side.

"I hear your fiancé's looking to find my divine mistress," he said, as she struggled beneath him. "As it happens, she's looking for him, too. Let's give him a trail to follow, shall we?"

Then, with one brutal swipe, he slashed the knife across Emily's throat. Pain burned through her, and warm wetness gushed down from her throat to her chest. Her hand flew up to the wound, fumbled along the edges of sliced flesh, her fingers drowning in hot stickiness. She felt the vein throbbing beneath her clutching fingers, pumping her life out in gouting bursts with every beat of her hammering heart.

Utisz placed his hand over hers, let her spurting blood coat it. The bruise on his forehead glowed. He threw back his head, closed his eyes, bared his teeth, and screamed one word—a word that spun the world in a hurricane around them, dissolving reality into fragments that lashed Emily's skin like pellets of ice in a winter snowstorm.

"Itztlacoliuhqui!" he roared. The sound throbbed in her ears like the beating of her own slowing heart, and they were gone.

CHAPTER TWENTY-TWO

A June Apocalypse

"Wake up, Miss Edwards. Don't you know what day it is?"

Emily opened her eyes, saw Alcmene Blotgate kneeling over her, looking down at her with those terrible gunmetal eyes of hers that were all pupil. Behind her stood Lieutenant Utisz, the front of his dark suit drenched with fresh blood. *Her* blood, Emily realized. He had a blade of black glass in his hands, and he was playing with it, feathering his thumb along its edge.

"Finally," he said, watching Emily stir. "Now we can get on with this."

They were in a small frigid room with black walls that leapt with strange shadows. There was the sound of water, like a creek somewhere deep below their feet, and there were smells—the smell of rusty water, the bitter cutting smell of wormwood and sage. Emily was naked and shivering, laid out on the cold stone floor. Her whole body was wet, and her skin tingled as if she'd just been washed with a rough sponge. There was a silver bucket next to her that contained the rusty-smelling water. Mrs. Blotgate was touching places on her naked body with some kind of oil—that was the bitter cutting smell. Emily remembered the places as those Caul had once touched, when detailing the locations he intended to drive needles into her to bleed her dry . . .

Her throat.

Emily reached up immediately and felt at her throat for the gaping wound. Her fingers found a knotted cord, just loose enough to allow her to breathe. Beneath it, she felt the slight rise of a fresh-seamed scar.

"Oh, we've taken enough of your dirty blood for the moment," Mrs. Blotgate said, rocking back on her heels. Naked from the waist up, she wore an intricately embroidered skirt of red silk and an ostentatious necklace of feathers and gold and jade. "Much as I'd like to, I can't let you die just yet. He'll have a much harder time following your blood if you're dead."

"Mr. Stanton?" Emily said, knowing the answer already.

Mrs. Blotgate purred a confirmation. "Dreadnought."

Emily rolled up to her feet. With an angry cry, she kicked over the bucket of rusty-smelling water; it rattled and spun across the stone floor.

"Kick all you like, there isn't any way out," Mrs. Blotgate said. "This is the Temple of Itztlacoliuhqui, the Goddess of Obsidian Knives."

At the far side of the room were two tall doors made of hundreds of human bones arranged in decorative patterns. The doors were lit by torches that made the skulls seem as if they were moving. Emily did not go over to these doors, she could feel something terrible behind them, something that waited. She went the other direction instead, where the walls were tenebrous and indistinct, and she could feel even colder air rushing up from dark caverns too dark to see into.

"I wouldn't go over *there*," Lieutenant Utisz called, his voice ragged as sandpaper. "Bad things over there."

Shivering, feeling the eyes of bad things on her back, Emily returned to the light. She rubbed the puckered stump of her wrist with her good hand. They'd even taken her prosthetic.

Mrs. Blotgate, still kneeling in the center of the room, watched Emily pace.

"Miss Edwards, do you know just exactly how hard it is to bring a man back from the dead?"

Emily did not favor her with a reply.

"You wouldn't think it," Mrs. Blotgate continued, "but reclaiming one pitiful human life from the oceans of eternity is a task to challenge even a goddess."

"Maybe that's a hint," Emily snapped. "That there are some things even a goddess shouldn't mess around with."

Mrs. Blotgate went on, as if Emily hadn't spoken.

"Every human man has thirteen unique aspects, each aspect finding its natural seat in one individual organ. When he dies, those aspects are scattered, seeking rebirth. A man is never reborn whole, Miss Edwards. He is reborn in pieces. Finding these pieces of Xiuhunel has been the Temple's primary employment for almost four hundred years. But now, we have all of him." She touched a golden cage that hung from the necklace around her throat. It contained a dried heart, Emily noticed with disgust. Other golden cages were spaced along the necklace, each one containing a different piece of desiccated flesh.

"I guess one of the aspects is two-timing you," Emily noted. "You've only got twelve there."

"Aren't you a clever little saucebox?" Mrs. Blotgate hissed, annoyance finally getting the better of her. "For someone who's already dead."

"I'm not dead yet, you vile bitch," Emily snarled. "And I'm clever enough to know that destroying the world, just to bring back one man, is proof that your Goddess is as dumb as a sackful of hammers."

Mrs. Blotgate cringed, as if anticipating vengeance to rain down upon them all. When it did not, she leveled an acid gaze on Emily. "Clearly, Miss Edwards, you've got a lot to learn about love."

"Not from you," Emily said.

At that moment, the earth rumbled around them, like a great black beast growling low in its chest. The bones of the door rattled, the floor beneath them seemed to ripple. Mrs. Blotgate closed her eyes, releasing a long sigh.

"The Black Glass Goddess summons me," she said, rising swiftly. "I am to have the honor of being her last vessel."

Utisz made a noise of desperate protest, and was at her side in two long strides.

"You?" he murmured, grabbing her slender hands. "No . . . not you! Please! Her vessels always die, burned up by the force of the Goddess' spirit . . ."

She trailed a hand along his cheek, silencing him.

"In the world remade, there will be power enough to preserve this body, to preserve all who are faithful to her." She smiled. "You will join me there soon, dear boy. Do not fear, you will be remembered in her service."

Utisz turned her palm, pressed his lips against it fervently.

"Mrs. Blotgate," he said in a choked voice. He might have said something more, had the woman not pressed her mouth against his in a deep, attenuated kiss.

At that moment the doors of bone opened, swinging wide on hinges that creaked with a low groaning. Without looking at him again, she passed beyond them into the darkness.

Utisz watched her go, his eyes heavy with longing.

"Let me guess," Emily said. "You were a cadet at the Erebus Academy. I hear she takes a new one every year."

Utisz turned slowly. He smiled at Emily, a tight, strange smile. Then, with a furious motion of his clenched fist, he made the knotted cord around her throat slide tight. Emily coughed, sputtering as she fell to her knees. He came to stand over her, watching as she squirmed helplessly at his feet.

"You are nobody, and soon you will be nothing," he rasped. She could barely hear his voice over the blood rushing in her ears. He moved his fist another fraction, making the cord around her throat tighten again. Darkness sparkled behind Emily's eyeballs, darkness and pain, and it felt as if the cord around her throat would slice her head from her body.

"The Black Glass Goddess may be my divine mistress," he said, "but Alcmene Blotgate is the only woman I have ever loved. The only woman who has ever loved me."

Initiate, a voice commanded, a voice old and ancient. It reverberated in thought and in fact, like a million screams screamed all at once.

With a flick of his wrist, Utisz slackened the hold, but did not release it.

Bring her.

The Calendar Chamber seemed to have no walls, it extended so far around and above them. All around, brazen tripods belched thick dizzy smoke into the air. But the floor had captured Emily's attention first. It was a vast circular pattern carved into the slick black stone, and in the channels of the pattern ran Black Exunge, bubbling and stinking. She walked over the channels carefully, acutely aware that her feet were bare and even the tiniest touch of Black Exunge could fatally transform her.

We have been told you understand true love.

The Goddess' words, resonating in her mind, drew Emily's eyes toward the center of the room, where a slender shaft of sunlight illuminated a deep, bowl-shaped pit. At the edge of the pit knelt a woman in a skirt of embroidered red silk.

Emily recognized her immediately. It was Alcmene Blotgate's body, of course . . . but that was not whom Emily recognized. This thing kneeling at the edge of the pit was not Alcmene Blotgate. It was not even human. Power and sorrow rose from it, smoldering from sinuously carved shoulders. It was the Goddess of Obsidian Knives.

Emily squinted through the drifting smoke, looking into the pit. There, protruding from the pit's earthen sides was the thick gnarled root through which Zeno's spirit had escaped. And there was the mound of flesh that she recognized from her Cassandras. The thing Zeno had been thrown onto to die. The thing that could transmute Black Exunge into chrysohaeme—the engine of apocalypse. A pile of slick, healthy flesh in her vision, now it was gray and sickly, like a pile of badly cured leather.

It was not always as you see it now, the Goddess said. *Before we grew it, and loved it, and nurtured it, it was very small. A mere cluster of cells on the tip of a sharp knife, slid between the ribs of a traitor.*

. . . A black blade, sliding between Stanton's ribs, Emily remembered.

A little piece of his liver. The organ that gives a burned Warlock his most unique abilities. The ability to channel chrysohaeme—and the ability to transmute Exunge. We did not need his service. We did not need his soul. We needed only this.

"Then *that's* the thirteenth organ," Emily said. "The thirteenth piece of Xiuhunel."

It is the most important piece. The one we will use to reunite all the others.

"You're not going to reunite anything," Emily said with relish. "Zeno has broken it. He's broken your engine of apocalypse and there's nothing you can do about it."

The Goddess rose in a dark blur, teeth flashing white behind the sneering mask with its huge curving fangs of yellow ivory. She was huge, her edges shimmering and indistinct.

Credomancers, she growled, the low resonance of her voice making the pile of leathery flesh behind her shudder. *Always trying to believe inconvenient things into being untrue.*

"I'm not a credomancer," Emily said, her voice trembling despite her best efforts to control it. "I know what the truth is."

Indeed. Emily felt the Goddess trying to push into her mind, to explore her soft places. *You are the vessel of Ososolyeh. You see the truth through her eyes.*

"I see that your Liver is dying," Emily said. "That is all the truth I need."

But it is not all the truth there is. It is gravely injured, but it can be healed. It can be healed by the blood of the man from whom it was taken. The blood of my beloved consort's last rebirth. The blood of the Thirteenth Incarnation.

At that moment, a voice rang through the great Calendar Chamber.

"Itztlacoliuhqui, Misery of Humankind, Goddess of Black Glass. Let me enter!" Stanton's voice echoed through the Calendar Chamber, resonating off the cold vitreous walls. "I have come to destroy you."

CHAPTER TWENTY-THREE

The Thirteenth
Incarnation

Stanton materialized before the teocalli, seeming to form from the resonant syllables of the words he had spoken. His form glittered, half opaque; he was nothing more than an illusion, Emily realized. To truly enter this place, he would have to obtain her express permission . . .

Destroy us? The Goddess trilled amusement as she regarded Stanton's spectral form. *On our own hallowed ground? You have grown more powerful since last we saw you, but no less foolish.*

"Let me enter," Stanton repeated.

"Don't do it, it's a trap!" Emily screamed. "The Liver . . . it's yours! Zeno almost killed it, but now they need your blood . . ."

A flick of Utisz' wrist, and the knotted cord around her throat tightened like a hangman's noose. She staggered forward, choking. Seizing her, Utisz twisted her arm behind her back and forced her to the ground, slamming her head hard against the cold slick stone. He placed a knee on her neck, pinning her immobile.

Stanton did not look at Emily. His ghostly eyes remained fixed on the Goddess' impassive mask.

"Let me enter," he said a third time.

Enter then, she commanded diffidently, and Stanton's ghostlike image became heavy and solid, magic flying away from him like smoke from a blown candle.

"Fool," Emily rasped, her face still pressed against the cold stone. Utisz had released the ligature around her throat to allow her to continue breathing, but his knee pressed heavily on the back of her neck. "Oh, Mr. Stanton, you damn fool."

Kneel, the Goddess commanded.

Stanton dropped to his knees heavily, as if his long legs had been kicked out from under him.

Bow, she commanded.

Stanton lowered himself in a deep, slow bow. He let his forehead rest against the stone at her feet for a long time. She did not command him to rise, but after a while he did, kneeling stiffly, staring straight ahead, his jaw clenched.

"Why did you come?" Emily moaned, despair washing over her.

"Because I love you," he said very softly. "And because I have to save the world."

"You could have saved the world if you'd stayed away!"

Nothing could have saved your world, the Goddess said. *This is destiny. This is fate.* She paused, gently running her fingers through Stanton's hair. *This is true love conquering all.*

Then, in a movement of dark smoke and obsidian sheen too quick for the eye to comprehend, the Goddess flayed the shirt from Stanton's body. Strips of cloth fluttered to the ground around him; he was not even scratched. Emily sucked in air involuntarily. On Stanton's slender white chest, over the place where his heart was, blazed a garish red birthmark. A birthmark in the shape of a woman's outstretched hand.

The mark of our claim. Did you never see it? The Goddess traced a glass-knife finger over the birthmark. *How did this truth escape you? The truth that he could never be yours? He was always ours. From the time he was born and from all the times he died before.*

"I am not yours!" Stanton's face twisted with angry confusion. "I am not Xiuhunel, or even a piece of him! I'm nobody . . . I ran from you!"

"Would she have let you come back if you were nobody?" Emily said softly, the words catching in pain as Utisz twisted her arm harder.

"Let her up, you sadistic bastard," Stanton hissed.

Utisz made no move to comply. Instead, he twisted Emily's arm further—slowly.

"Stop it!" Stanton shouted. "Please!"

Emily clenched her jaw to refuse Utisz the satisfaction of her pain, but it was no use. First she whimpered, then she begged. Then she screamed.

Stop.

The word resounded through the Temple, ringing off the walls of black glass, making the ground shake and the braziers clatter. But this time, it was not the Goddess who spoke. It was Stanton.

Breathing hard, Utisz released Emily's arm, staggering to his feet. Emily pushed herself to kneel, arm limp and throbbing. She looked for Stanton . . . but when her eyes found him, she could not believe what she saw.

He was standing waist-deep in the Calendar's widest channel of Black Exunge. Tendrils of the black tarry substance slithered up his body like baby adders, plunging into his flesh—but he did not expand as he should have, as an Aberrancy would have. Instead, the Exunge spread itself out over his skin in a black shining film.

"My body is in contact with all the Black Exunge you have collected," Stanton said. He was trembling as if bearing a great weight. "Every drop of it."

Is this how you hope to destroy us? The Goddess was circling him, head tilted with fascination. *We know that your body can filter Exunge, it is the gift of the burned—but even with a hundred years and a hundred lifetimes you could not hope to work a magic large enough.*

"I don't need to work a large magic," Stanton whispered, ligatures of Black Exunge strangling the sound in his throat. "Sometimes smaller weapons serve better."

Then Emily saw him move the hand that hung at his side. He pressed his thumb and forefinger together.

She had seen him do it a hundred times. Snap his fingers. Summon flame.

"No!" Emily screamed. She threw herself across the few feet of distance that separated them.

"After I left the Academy, I told Zeno I would give my own life to destroy her." Stanton's eyes, glossy black, shone with oily tears as he looked down at her. "But you, too, Emily? Why does it have to be you, too?"

Stop, Thirteenth! It was clear that the Goddess suddenly understood what Stanton intended. *Relinquish this foolishness, and we will spare her life. She will live forever in the world remade. We swear it to you.*

"I'm sorry, Emily," he whispered. "I can't save you and the world, too. I have to choose the world."

It was a horrible choice. But it was the choice of a decent man. He *was* decent, she realized. With that truth to bolster her, Emily felt others flooding in behind it. It was why he hadn't taken the cure . . . why Zeno had wanted him to leave her . . . why they had exiled him to Lost Pine, treated with hatred and scorn and contempt . . . because he was something bad to be used against something worse. *He* was the *desperatus.* He was their weapon.

I can give him one last chance . . .

Zeno had cursed the Liver because it was the only way Stanton would be allowed back into the Temple. Zeno knew the Goddess would need Stanton's blood to cure the Liver they had taken from him, and that would give him one last chance to deploy the *desperatus.* Stanton would snap his fingers, cleanse the Temple in flame—the Temple, and all the other places around the earth where the Goddess had collected Exunge in preparation for *temamauhti:* San Francisco, Arkansas, Tennessee, and Kentucky. Japan and China and Java and all the other places Emily had read about in the newspapers . . . exploding in a vast unimaginable conflagration . . .

A smaller apocalypse to forestall a larger one.

Fire to fight fire.

Now she understood. Now Ososolyeh understood.

"No," Emily said. "This is not the right way."

Grabbing his hand, Emily threaded her living fingers through Stanton's Exunge-slimed ones. He gave an agonized cry, tried to pull his hand away, but she held on to it tightly. She felt the funguslike tendrils of Exunge burrowing into her skin. Ososolyeh turned them back.

"It's all right, love," Emily whispered to him. "Trust us."

There was a ferocious rumble that made the ground shake. It was the scream of the Goddess of Black Glass. She flew at Stanton, a blur of black and smoke.

Razor-edged fingers slashed his flesh in a hundred different directions. Blood blossomed all over his body. Stanton sagged, gory streams bright against the slimy black that covered him.

Utisz had Emily by the throat again, was yanking her backward. She tried to hold on to Stanton, but his fingers slackened in her grasp.

The Goddess gathered Stanton's bleeding form in her arms. She picked him up as easily as if he were a hollow shell of paper. Turning, she carried him toward the sickened Liver, one white foot sliding before the other, her steps making the ground shake.

CHAPTER TWENTY-FOUR

The Goddess' Triumph

Utisz laid his blade of black glass along Emily's throat, cold and sharp.

"Do you wish the honor of watching him die?" he croaked furiously. "Or shall I kill you now and spare you the misery?"

Emily spun beneath his grasp, knowing that the glass blade would cut her. She let it. She sank her teeth into his bare arm. He bellowed with surprise and pain as blood gushed warm between her lips. Words were forming in her mind—bitter, furious, guttural words.

She spat blood between her hand and the stump of her amputated arm, rubbing them together, the words forming on her lips at the same moment they were forming in her mind. She let them stream out in a foul ancient whisper.

"No!" Utisz wrapped an arm around her throat, reaching for his alembic with his other hand. Emily clutched at the arm around her throat, repeating the sangrimantic incantations as Ososolyeh spoke them to her, clutching Utisz' arm between her good hand and her severed stump. Fierce red magic surrounded her and burned through him.

Behind her, she felt Utisz' body began to jerk and spasm. There was the sound of something sizzling, like a steak on a hot griddle. She felt magic flowing through her body and smashing into his, charring muscle and bone. Utisz made a horrible sound like a rusting gate being torn from its hinges. His arm fell away. The black glass knife at her throat fell to the floor. Turning, she saw that he was dead—body charred

beyond recognition, his arms extended as if he were still trying to restrain her. Emily reached down for the black glass
knife. She knew she would need it.

Nothing knotted or tied.

Be skyclad.

Emily brought the knife to her throat and cut the cord that
bound her. Then she let cord and knife drop together to the
floor, similarly useless.

The Goddess had carried Stanton's bleeding body to the
very center of the Liver, and was laying him carefully atop
the quivering mound of gray flesh. She removed the necklace
from around her neck and placed it around his. Each of the
twelve golden cages began to glow. She laid one hand on his
chest, tenderly. Then, with one blade-edged finger of black
glass, she slashed his throat.

Emily screamed. Stanton's blood fountained. It bathed the
gray flesh beneath him, rejuvenating it, and within moments
the organ looked as healthy as it had before, slick and strong.

The Goddess lifted her hands and the Liver began to glow,
pierced with shafts of orange brilliance, and all the Black Exunge in all the channels of the great Calendar Chamber began
to glow with midday brightness.

Be reborn! She screamed, her voice high and wild as waves
of brilliant golden power rose around her. Tendrils of glowing
chrysohaeme slid up to encase the Liver in a fine mesh,
wreathing Stanton's body in a delicate, shimmering web.

And Stanton's body began to change.

The Black Exunge that had coated his flesh burned away
like a paper shell, revealing smooth dark-tanned skin,
adorned with black tattoos and paint of many colors. Ornaments of jade and feathers and gold swirled around him in a
glittering cloud, and the red handprint glowed on his chest.
Only his eyes remained black—black as wells of tar, black as
the darkness of the world he would rule.

Xiuhunel! The Goddess breathed, her voice rich with the
joy of reunion. She reached for him, sharp-edged arms outstretched. *Our true love.*

Emily squeezed her eyes shut, took a deep breath, and gave

a command with Ososolyeh's voice. Her voice. The voice of a Goddess.

The earth rumbled in immediate answer. Roots shot out from all directions, through the walls, up from the floor, down from the ceiling. Thick, hairy, tough roots, intertwined with hunks of masonry and obsidian. They seized the Black Glass Goddess, tangling her in their grip.

Xiuhunel! The Goddess screamed as the roots pulled her up, high up above the pit, suspending her in the light that shone down from the ceiling like an insect under a magnifying glass. *Rise! Rise and defend us!*

Emily ran for him, jumping from churned stone to overturned obsidian boulder as if she were wending her way along a steep, melt-rushing creek. The Liver was glowing with blinding brilliance now. Squeezing her eyes shut against it, she began to climb. She had to feel her way up the side of the disgusting slimy flesh against the tornado of power that tried to push her back. Blood and slime covered her as she inched her way up, the earth tumbling all around her, helping her gain purchase. And as she climbed, she summoned Ososolyeh's power, pulling it from stone and earth and root, driving it deep into the unholy flesh just as Zeno had.

"May good triumph over evil," said Emily.

Below her, the Liver squealed and cringed. The brightness of it subsided, and then she saw him, stretched out motionless, throat gaping like a silent scream. In the fading brightness, he didn't look like Xiuhunel anymore. The feathers and jade and gold were gone. His skin was corpse white, and his face was painted only with blood. He looked like the man she had fallen in love with. He looked dead.

Emily gathered his body in her arms, finding that it was as easy as if he were a hollow paper shell. She carried him to a place where good dark earth, untainted by Exunge, had tumbled up from the cracked floor. She laid his body down gently, directing Ososolyeh to slide its loving fingers over him, burying him deep within the rich black loam. Before the earth covered him completely, she put her hands around his throat, smearing her hands with his gritty blood. She would need it.

He is ours! The Goddess writhed in her prison of grasping roots, her blood-soaked feet kicking in the harsh light. *Our true love! We swore an oath on the blood of those who murdered him . . . we pursued him life after life . . . for love of him, we would remake the world!*

"And for love of him, I will save it," Emily said. She felt Stanton's life, his blood, singing along her fingers. She kissed each one of her fingertips, whispered good-bye.

Then Emily lifted her bloody arms. She let herself fall. She cast herself heedlessly into Ososolyeh's eternity, its mystery, its complete understanding. She knew that she was pouring herself into an ocean without shores, without bottom, without bounds. She knew that she would never find her way back. She knew that she would die.

And she began speaking in all languages at once—in Latin, in the foul guttural language of blood, in the words of earth and water and stone.

We are more ancient than you. Emily's voice was like the crash of planets. The ceiling began to disintegrate. Huge chunks of obsidian crashed to the floor. *This is our world, and it has been since before men existed to conjure you from their nightmares.*

No! The Black Glass Goddess screamed.

With all the powers we possess, Emily continued, her voice rising as huge boulders crashed around her and power rose to wreathe her, *with the faith that good will triumph over evil, and the blood of the man who was yours for twelve lifetimes but is yours no longer, and all the power of the ancient consciousness of the earth who despises you, false Goddess, ruined woman, misery of humankind . . .*

"*No!*" Alcmene screamed.

We command that you die.

Now.

Emily tightened her fist, feeling Stanton's blood singing triumphantly within the embrace. And the roots around the Goddess tensed like a thousand edged wires. Brilliance surrounded her as she screamed, the roots flaying her into bloody strips.

* * *

Pieces of flesh fell to the ground like filthy soaked bandages, making wet slapping sounds on the glassy boulders of obsidian. Then Emily, too, was falling, collapsing to the sundered ground beneath her feet. The roof had collapsed, and bright sunlight streamed down through the wide, ragged-edged hole. Emily could smell good growing things, the smell of water and leaves pouring down, displacing the stench of rot and blood and incense. In the silence, she could hear exotic birds calling to one another.

Full of life, she thought. *All around.*

An eternity later, she felt arms around her once again, pulling her up, brushing dirt from her face tenderly.

"Emily." Stanton looked down at her, his eyes searching her face. He was covered in dirt and blood. His throat was seamed with a thin white scar. "It's me."

"Xiuhunel?"

"No," Stanton said again. "It's me, Emily."

She smiled at him.

"Dreadnought," she breathed, her voice a stream of joy.

He clasped her tightly, his arms strong and hot. But even they were not enough. Her eyelids fluttered. Again, she felt herself falling. Ososolyeh was all around her now, around her and in her and of her, and it sang of memories she could only now understand, only now comprehend. The memories were pulling her back, and she was spreading out to greet them.

"No, don't go," a voice far, far away was pleading. "Please don't go. I'll get you out of here. I'll get you home . . ."

I am home, Emily thought, Ososolyeh swallowing her up with all the blackness of the places in between the stars.

CHAPTER TWENTY-FIVE

Lyakhov's Anodyne

"Wake up, Miss Edwards. Don't you know what day it is?"

Emily stirred groggily. Stanton was sitting by her bed, smiling down at her, holding her hand. As her eyes focused on his face, and she blinked at him, his smile became much wider.

"What day is it?" she asked, her voice a sleep-choked rasp.

"It's the happiest day of my life," Stanton said, thumb stroking her palm. "How are you feeling?"

"I don't know," she said. "Am I alive?"

"It would seem so," he said. The feeling of his hand holding hers was wonderful. The skin of her hand was exquisitely sensitive, as if she'd never felt anything with it before. With her fingers, she could see Stanton—see him clearer than with her eyes. He was well. He was whole and strong, and the power of the Institute—the power of faith—sang in his blood. The joy she felt pulsing through her fingers, from his hand holding it, made her blush furiously.

Then she noticed something.

She noticed that he was holding her right hand. The hand that should have been ivory. But it was not ivory anymore.

"What the hell is this?" she demanded, snatching her hand out of his and looking at the smooth new flesh with astonishment. She wiggled her fingers. She looked up at Stanton. "If you tell me this was all a dream, I swear I'll kill you."

Stanton laughed.

"I don't know how it happened either. I can only imagine it was Ososolyeh's doing. It has an astonishing capacity for healing." His hand went to his throat, to the faint white scar seamed there. His voice became softer. "I wasn't entirely sure you were coming back. You've been unconscious for days. The only hope I had was that little hand. It started growing back as soon as we got to the Institute. I watched it every day, and I thought that if it could come back, you could come back, too." He puckered his brow, remembering. "It was quite a strange process, actually. At one point it looked just like a peeled turnip. Disgusting."

"Well, I think it's quite pretty now," Emily said, turning it to and fro. "I can't tell you how glad I am to have it back."

"I'd say you'd earned it," Stanton said. Emily lifted an eyebrow at him.

"Earned it?" she said. "Hell yes, I earned it! And you lying there dead during the best part. We beat her. We beat her with every kind of magic all at once. Animancy and credomancy and . . ." She paused.

"Sangrimancy?" Stanton looked at her.

"I don't know sangrimancy," Emily said. "But Ososolyeh knows everything. We muddled through."

Stanton smiled. "You always do, Miss Edwards."

"And why do you keep calling me that?" Emily said. "Don't tell me you've forgotten my name already?"

"I'll never forget your name," Stanton said. "But I wasn't sure you wanted me to call you that anymore. I wasn't sure if we were still engaged."

"After everything we've been through? After true love conquered all?" Emily shook her head. "Being dead has done nothing to alleviate your obtuseness, Mr. Stanton."

"Being dead allowed me to learn the heart's deepest secret," he said. "That sometimes love—even true love—isn't enough."

"But it's a start," Emily said. And then she reached up and pulled him down to her, and began kissing him, and they might both have learned a great deal more had not a voice from the door startled them apart.

"Mr. Stanton!" Rose peeked in, and her cheeks flushed with excitement. She looked at Emily, and the meanness and spite had gone from them, replaced with her customary brown-eyed eagerness.

"Oh, Miss Emily. Miss Emily's awake! Dreadnought Stanton saves the day again! Oh, how wonderful!"

"What is it, Rose?" Stanton said with mild annoyance, quickly buttoning his shirt.

"Well, I'm so sorry to bother you, but the Sini Mira men have been here for hours waiting for you, and you really must speak to them . . ."

Stanton twisted in his chair and looked at the girl with astonishment.

"Rose, my fiancée has just stirred from what I feared was her deathbed. She's just saved the world from the depravities of a Black Glass Goddess who wanted to transform it into a nightmare of filth and despair. And you want me to come talk to the Sini Mira?"

"Well, I know, it's very inconvenient, but—"

"Go on." Emily laid a hand on the jacket of his coat, gave him a little push. He turned his green eyes down to her.

"No," he said.

"Yes," she said. "You've got an Institute to run." She wiggled her new fingers with glee. "I can't believe they're back! I'll never take them for granted again. I'll sign up for piano lessons immediately!"

He bent down and kissed her new fingers softly, his love thrilling through their sensitive tips.

"I'll be back soon," he promised.

He didn't come back at all that afternoon, which didn't surprise Emily in the least. But she had another visitor to keep her company, who came in carrying a great bouquet of fragrant peonies and began to arrange these in a crystal vase by Emily's bed without speaking a word.

"Miss Jesczenka," Emily said. She looked at the wide white bandaging around the woman's throat. She only half remembered the night in the conservatory, when Utisz had kidnapped her; she had seen Miss Jesczenka's body lying motionless on the gravel pathway, the front of her dress soaked with blood. "Are you all right?"

"The Institute is running wonderfully," Miss Jesczenka said. "Enrollments are up, and Mystic Truth sales have never been higher. Fortissimus is a broken man. He has retired from professional life and will be recuperating indefinitely in an asylum in the Adirondacks. We have completed negotiations for the purchase of the Fortissimus Agency. It will be re-named the Stanton Agency, and we will use it to branch out into the field of presentment arranging. It should be quite a profitable sideline, if what I've seen in Fortissimus' account-ing books is any indication." She paused, arranging another bloom. "Mr. Stanton has asked me to run the Agency for him."

Emily was silent for a while, looking at the woman. "That's not what I meant," she said.

Miss Jesczenka's elegant hands stilled. She drew a deep breath. "Sophos Stanton has graciously forgiven my trans-gressions, involuntary as they were." She was silent for a long time before adding, "And for some reason, my son did not cut my throat deeply enough to kill me. He spared my life."

Emily said nothing as she watched the woman position a stalk in elegant counterpoint to its mates. She gave the flow-ers a freshening fluff and adjusted the vase slightly. Then she sat down by Emily's bed, her brown eyes lowered.

"He began by sending me letters. He said that someone at the orphanage had told him about me. He said that he wanted to meet me, to learn about me. And then he just . . . showed up, the night before the Investment. He was falling-down drunk, loud, angry. He said he would wake the whole Institute and tell them what kind of a whore I was. I had to quiet him down. I brought him into my rooms. I allowed him into the Institute. All I could think of was my reputation, my position, all that I had made for myself. I was so ashamed. I was so ashamed of *him*."

She paused, eyes turned inward with thought.

"Shame is such a powerful emotion," she mused. "Almost as powerful as love. How clever of him to have used both against me."

"I saw you with him," Emily said softly. "The morning before the Investment. I thought . . . I thought he was a student. And I thought he was your lover."

Miss Jesczenka looked up at her in shock. Then her face softened into a small smile.

"I have always maintained a great deal of magic around myself to keep men from thinking of me in that way," she said. "It is nice that there's one person in the world who sees through it."

Then Miss Jesczenka lowered her head. "They used my child, Emily. They used my *shame*. What kind of monster does that make me? Why didn't I use the power of my faith to make a better life for him, instead of for myself?"

Once again, Miss Jesczenka's eyes searched Emily's face for an answer that wasn't there. With a shaking finger, Miss Jesczenka dashed a tear from the corner of her eye.

Emily laid her hand across Miss Jesczenka's. Through the exquisitely sensitive flesh of her new fingers, she could feel the weight of the woman's terrible guilt. But more than feel these things, the hand Ososolyeh had given her could soothe them. It could not take them away, but it could blunt them, make them like a storm seen from a distant ridgeline. When Miss Jesczenka opened her eyes, they were clear and calm, and when she spoke again, it was as if she hadn't spoken at all before then.

"By the way, Miss Edwards," she said. "I have something for you. A letter from your friend Miss Pendennis."

Emily's eyes widened in surprise as Miss Jesczenka withdrew a fat envelope from her pocket. As she handed it to Emily, Emily noted the abundance of exotic stamps decorating its face.

"My goodness, she sent this from Portugal," Emily said. She looked up at Miss Jesczenka. "She's on a lecture tour, you see. Do you mind?"

Miss Jesczenka inclined her head obligingly.

Emily slid a finger behind the flap and opened the envelope, drawing out its contents. Inside the envelope was a fat folded letter, as well as another envelope. Emily looked at the second envelope; it seemed to contain some kind of congratulatory card. She laid it on the bedside table as she unfolded

Penelope's letter. It started off with fond regards and her hope that Stanton's Investment went off without a hitch. Emily chuckled. She continued to scan the letter, which detailed Penelope's adventures at lecture stops from Senegal to Sumatra to . . .

San Francisco?

Stopped in San Francisco for a few days on the way back from Alaska, and took the opportunity to hop up to Lost Pine. Called on your pap. He's in fine fettle, got that lovely old woman to look out for him, and all those cats! Oh, and I met that lumberman of yours. What a topping fellow. He's everything that will ever make this country great. I told him I'd like to study him some more, if he'd let me. He said that any friend of yours was a friend of his.

Emily let out a breath and smiled.

I've sent along a card he wanted me to give you, and a couple of wedding presents, too. I've sent all the paperwork along to the Institute. I'm sure they can see that the shipment arrives safely . . .

It went on from there, but Emily didn't read more. She reached quickly for the second envelope and opened it.

It was a prettily printed card of congratulations with hearts and flowers on the front.

Best wishes from the Hansen Timber Company, someone with fine penmanship had written inside. Beneath the fine writing was Dag's friendly, blocky scribble: *Good luck to you both.*

She brushed her new fingers over the writing, feeling it sing up to her. He would have a daughter, Emily suddenly knew, and she would be very pretty. Emily knew that she would meet her someday, and would like her very much.

Emily pulled her hand away from the card, waved it as if burned.

"My goodness!" she said, blowing on her fingers. "This is quite a hand!"

Miss Jesczenka inclined her head. "You've bonded completely with the great consciousness of the earth—body, blood, and soul. I suppose that makes you kind of a goddess."

"Oh, hogwash," Emily snorted. "I'm just Emily Edwards

from Lost Pine, California. And what's this Penelope writes about wedding presents?" she asked, snatching up the letter again to reread it more closely. Miss Jesczenka smiled, touched a finger to her nose.

"I've seen to it all," she said.

After Miss Jesczenka left, Emily decided she'd had just about all she could stand of her near-deathbed, so she got up and tested her legs. They seemed to work just fine. Pulling on a dress, she buttoned it up with delightful alacrity, new fingers flying. She regarded her face in the mirror. Her own pert reflection stared back at her, same as it ever was.

Goddess, she thought, wrinkling her nose at herself. *Hogwash.*

She went to the door and tested it. It was unlocked. How nice to be in a world with unlocked doors again.

She walked through the halls, noting with satisfaction the air of hope and excitement that filled the mansion's white marble walls. Students chatted in eager clusters, stopping to watch as she passed. She waved cheerfully to them, but did not stop. She was going outside, to a place where things grew. She was going to the conservatory.

She walked along the gravel paths under the great arching roof of glass, brushing a trickle of sweat from her brow. Always so humid in here. She remembered roots and calling birds and sunlight streaming down through a broken and sundered aperture.

She came to a stop before the Dragon's Eye orchid and placed her hands on the thick woody vine. She closed her eyes.

The memory of Zeno greeted her. *Oh, hello there. It's you. What was your name again?*

Ososolyeh, Emily said.

Emily spent the rest of the afternoon sitting cross-legged before the Dragon's Eye orchid, searching for the bits of Zeno's memories that had been scattered like dandelion fluff all across the country. It was a pleasant pastime. She wandered through root and leaf and branch, from one shining ocean to the other, looking for pieces of his mind. It was a fresh pleasure every time she found another bit—a memory in the root of an elm in Chicago, a fleeting thought in the petal of a fireweed in New Jersey. She brought these memories to him like pinecones in her hands, proudly.

In the jungles above the ruins of the Temple, held in the broad heart of the tree Zeno had escaped into—the first one that had been his savior—they found the memory of a boy with white-blond hair. He was working in a field of wheat, calling to Zeno bad-temperedly to come and help. Zeno respired pleasantly through his leaves.

Ah, Nikolai, he said. *There you are! How I've missed you.*

Emily smiled, remembering with Zeno for a moment before giving the memory back to him.

A warm hand touched her shoulder. She flinched slightly, the pleasant memory of the wheatfield and the white-blond boy scattering with the jump of her heart. She remembered Utisz' hand, remembered a slashing black knife.

"It's all right," Stanton murmured gently. "It's only me."

Emily opened her eyes, smiled up at him. She looked past Stanton and saw that Perun was standing behind him, hat in hand, white-blond hair shining in the sunlight.

"We've come to ask for your direction, *mat' syra zemliya,*" Perun said, head low. "Goddess of the Earth."

Emily sat in the dirt with the Dragon's Eye orchid rising at her back, and Perun and Stanton sat before her, their legs crossed, hands resting on their knees.

"Dmitri Alekseivitch," she called. "I know you're back there."

Dmitri, who'd been hiding unsuccessfully behind a large stand of palms, came out. He would not look at her, but he came to sit behind Stanton and Perun, at a respectful distance.

"Emilia Vladimirovna," he said, with great formality.

"You were speaking with Emeritus Zeno." Perun's eyes traveled to the Dragon's Eye orchid, and there was sadness in them. "How is he?"

"Your brother is dead, Nikolai Illarionovich Zeno," Emily said, looking back at him. "Other than that, he'll be fine."

Perun smiled to himself, shaking his head as he looked down at his lap. Stanton twisted himself to look at Perun.

"Emeritus Zeno was your brother?" His eyes were astonished. "But he was over a hundred and seventy years old. He kept himself alive with magic. How could you . . ."

Perun lifted his cigarette.

"I keep myself alive with science," he said. "A preservative drug I inhale almost constantly." He looked at the cigarette smoking between his fingers. "Though now that the great work of my life is finished, perhaps I'll give the stinking things up." He ground it out in the dirt beside him, swept some gravel over the butt to cover it. As he dusted off his hands, he looked at Emily.

"We have completed our diggings in the ruins of the Temple," Perun said. "You might be surprised at what we have found."

He reached into his pocket and withdrew the hair sticks—battered and bent. He handed them to Emily, and she took them in trembling hands. She'd never expected to see them again.

"Now, it must be decided what is to be done with them."

"We're going to decide?" Emily said.

"No, Goddess," Perun said. "Not we. You."

Emily looked down at them, feeling sudden weight press down on her shoulders.

"We have deciphered them," Perun said. "It turns out they contain one more secret that we never guessed at. They do indeed contain the formula for Volos' Anodyne—a very powerful poison that would make magic unpracticeable for humans. Morozovich completed it before your father ever left Russia."

"But that was in 1851!" Emily said. "If Morozovich completed the poison twenty-five years ago, why was it never implemented?"

"Your father was bringing the poison to the Sini Mira when he met Catherine Kendall. Met her and fell in love with her. Your mother was cursed." Perun cast a sidelong glance at

Stanton. "Just like the burned, the cursed cannot control the magic that runs through their veins. Your father knew that if Volos' Anodyne was administered, she would die."

"As would many others," Emily said. "There are many people in the world who are cursed . . . or burned." Her voice caught on the last word. "Implementing the poison would be like sentencing them all to death."

"But My Divine," Perun said, flashing her a smile. "I haven't told you what else the hair sticks had on them."

"There was something else?"

"Another formula—a formula that your father developed independently of Morozovich. A compound that I believe we should call Lyakhov's Anodyne, in his honor."

"Why two?" Emily said, but understanding was already stirring in her—understanding that was far beyond her own human ken.

"Lyakhov's Anodyne is not a poison. It is very different. It is a readjustment of the very structure of the Mantic Anastomosis." Perun paused for a moment, choosing his words carefully. "Its effect is similar, in some ways, to the ability Mr. Stanton's body possesses. Mr. Stanton's burned blood gives his liver the ability to filter and purify Exunge, as you saw. That ability, on an infinitesimally small scale, will be woven into all living creatures born after the Anodyne's implementation. They will be able to assist the Mantic Anastomosis in processing Black Exunge. As this ability spreads over generations, the power to process Black Exunge will become widely distributed enough that Exunge will never again be able to build up in any quantity."

Emily didn't really understand the words, but she understood the idea in her gut, in her sensitive fingers. Lyakhov's Anodyne would not kill those who were burned or cursed. It would not kill Stanton. That was all she needed to understand, really.

"It is why he didn't contact us for so long," Perun said. "Why he didn't deliver the poison to us immediately. If we had known it was complete, we would have demanded it from him. We would have stopped at nothing to get it from him if he refused. And once we had it, we would have implemented it without a moment of hesitation." Perun looked a little ashamed. "He knew this. He spent the last years of his life looking for a way to save your mother from our impetuousness."

There was a long silence. Finally, slowly, Perun climbed to his knees. He bowed down before Emily, his forehead pressed against the soft fragrant earth of the conservatory. Emily's eyes found Stanton, widened questioningly, but Stanton put up both hands. The duties of a goddess, his upraised hands suggested, were not his to comment upon.

"We have come for your direction, *mat' syra zemliya,* Goddess of the Earth." Perun's voice was muffled from beneath his outstretched arms. "How shall we proceed?"

The silence hung for quite a long time as Emily tried to figure out exactly what kind of goddessing she was supposed to provide. Finally, sighing, she pressed her hands flat against the earth and closed her eyes.

Lyakhov's Anodyne, Emily said simply, her voice making all the leaves in the conservatory rustle.

Perun straightened and nodded. He brushed dirt from his trousers as he rose. Reflexively, he reached into his pocket for his cigarette case, then, thinking better of it, tucked it back down. But then he remembered something. Reaching inside his coat, he pulled out a golden ball.

"I almost forgot," he said, handing Komé's rooting ball down to Emily. "I believe you will want to get her into the ground soon. She's growing more quickly than anyone expected."

Emily took the golden ball and held it in her lap, feeling the truth of Perun's words with her new fingers. She smiled a greeting to Komé, but the baby oak tree within the ball had nothing to say to her at all.

Then Perun and Dmitri were gone, and Emily was left alone with Stanton, who sat looking at her, his eyes narrowed with glittering humor. She quirked him a smile, feeling ridiculous.

"Now you know how I feel," he said. She lifted an eyebrow at him, made her face into a serious frown.

"That's entirely different," she said loftily. "You're just a Sophos. I'm a goddess."

He smiled at her as he stood up.

"Indeed," he said. "But I knew that all along."

He reached down to give her a hand up, pulled her close to his side. Heat pounded from his body in waves, an unspoken point of a discussion she already knew they were about to have. But she wasn't quite ready for all that yet. First she had something to show him.

"Penelope's sent us a wedding present," Emily said, pulling at his hand. "Come see."

She led their steps toward a broad paddock where the Institute's horses were pastured. A pair of large black Morgans stood in the center of the field nipping at fresh green grass. Stanton's eyes widened with surprise and sudden joy.

"Romulus! Remus!"

He whistled to the horses, and they trotted over to the rail diffidently. He pressed his fingers to their velvety muzzles. They whuffled him a restrained greeting.

"Penelope had such a time getting them to New York," Emily said, as Stanton slicked his hand along Romulus' thick-muscled neck. "They're so all-fired lively."

"Hello, gentlemen," Stanton was saying softly. He looked at Emily. "I was always so fond of them."

That was an understatement, Emily thought. Stanton was fond of his horses like Nero had been fond of a nice tune. And seeing them again after a time away, Emily could suddenly understand the pride he took in the magnificent animals. They looked as if they could take vertical flight from a dead standstill.

Stanton's hand stilled on Romulus' neck, stayed there for longer than Romulus liked. The animal danced away. Stanton's hand fell to his side.

"What do you think?" Emily asked him. "How do they look?"

Stanton gave a whistle and a command and the horses went running. He stared after them as they cantered away. Then he turned, leaning back against the rail, giving her an appraising look.

"So, My Goddess," Stanton said, adopting the brusque tone of a Sophos, "it's time for that discussion you already knew we were going to have."

The statement was somewhat cryptic, but Emily knew exactly what it referred to—the heat pouring from Stanton's body. He was still burned. Even Ososolyeh had not been able to heal him of that. Or perhaps it had chosen not to, preferring to give him the choice. For the hundredth time, Emily felt both great appreciation for and great annoyance with the ancient consciousness of the earth.

"Lyakhov's Anodyne won't hurt you, won't impede your ability to work magic or run the Institute," Emily said. "There is nothing to discuss."

"But there is," Stanton said. "I can be cured. I had to preserve my ability to work magic so I could be Zeno's *desperatus,* but now that's over . . ." He paused. "I could give it all up, Emily. I could relinquish the power of the Institute and ask the blessing of the new Sophos. He could make me a silver touch-piece, and I could be healed. We could have a long and happy life. Together."

"We are together," she said. "Anything more than that isn't really up to us, is it?"

Stanton considered this. Emily squeezed his hand again.

"By the way, the answer is *the rope isn't tied to anything,*" she said.

Stanton looked at her, not comprehending.

"Horse has got a ten-foot rope around his neck, there's hay twenty-five feet away . . . remember? Well, I figured it out. The rope isn't tied to anything. Horse can eat all the damn hay he wants."

"Now, that's just not fair!" he protested. "You've got the whole consciousness of the earth on your side."

"The point isn't that I figured out your riddle, dear. The point is that you're free to choose," Emily said. "You've never been more powerful. You have a great future ahead of you. And I will be there for it, whether it's long or short or somewhere in between."

He looked at her.

"Even after everything?"

"Yes," Emily said. "Even after everything." She paused. "For better or for worse."

She said no more, but basked in the warm certainty of conviction. Nothing mattered except that she loved him. Not Black Glass Goddesses, not sadistic ex-mistresses, not even the Institute. He was decent. She knew it down to the bones of the earth that stretched far beneath them.

"We can have a huge wedding, and I'll make everyone love Dreadnought Stanton, Sophos of the Stanton Institute, as much as I do. Heck, I might even start an Admiration League."

Stanton's eyelids fluttered at the thought.

"And I'll sit in hot parlors and drink tea with tedious old women, and if they annoy me, I'll just wrap some roots around them. And even if I don't love every minute of it, I'll love you every minute."

"The roots idea sounds promising," he said, touching her face. "But even so, that's an awful lot to ask. You've already given up so much."

"I haven't given up anything," Emily said. "I've gained the world. Quite literally."

"Still," Stanton said. "Still—"

She put a finger over his lips.

"Not now," she said. "Tomorrow."

CHAPTER TWENTY-SIX

Gifts and Decisions

The next day, Stanton came for her early in the morning. He told her to fetch her hat and reticule, and put her into the Institute's carriage. They rode to the train station, where the Institute's private car was waiting for them, as overstuffed and elaborate as Emily remembered it. It was filled with flowers—masses of blush-colored peonies in heavy crystal vases. Emily settled herself onto a soft leather sofa; Stanton whuffed down beside her, dropping a silver and gold box onto her lap. It contained chocolates. He scooped out three for himself and held them in his hand.

"I've made three decisions and brought you three gifts. The chocolates are the first gift, but I mostly bought them because it didn't feel right not having three."

"Credomancers and their trines," she teased. She removed a silky chocolate from a gold foil shell. "All right then, let's have the decisions first. In order, so I can keep them all straight."

"First, I'm keeping the Institute. Second, we're eloping." He popped two chocolates into his mouth at once. "No big ridiculous wedding, no orange blossoms, no authority muttering a bunch of nonsense over our heads. Jump straight to the honeymoon. Seems better that way, don't you think?"

"Oh certainly. But I have to say, the second decision seems a bit at odds with the first." Emily bit into her chocolate, sucking at the sweet cherry at its center. "If there isn't a wedding, won't you be missing out on a huge credomantic opportunity? And who'll run the place while you're gone?"

"There's already been a wedding," Stanton grinned at her. "Mrs. Zeno is going to run the Institute."

"Mrs. Zeno?" Emily said. "I never knew there was a Mrs. Zeno!"

"There wasn't, until last night at midnight," he said. "Zeno married Miss Jesczenka in the conservatory. It was a beautiful ceremony. I wept."

"And how precisely did Miss Jesczenka go about marrying an orchid?" Emily said, not even bothering to imagine how such a union might be consummated.

"Well, actually it was more a kind of a credomantic swindle than an actual wedding," Stanton said. "By pledging herself to Benedictus Zeno, father of modern credomancy and founder of the Institute, she gains sufficient status to wield power on my behalf."

"So she can take care of things while we're off honeymooning and eating chocolate," Emily said. "That sounds like a wonderful arrangement. How long are we going to be gone?"

"That's the third decision," Stanton said, his eyes glittering. "We're never going back."

Emily looked at him.

"But you said you've decided to continue as Sophos. How can you do that if you're not in New York?"

"Another credomantic swindle," Stanton said. "It's not necessary to have Dreadnought Stanton running the Institute in the flesh, as long as the illusion of Dreadnought Stanton's mastery can be maintained and exploited."

"I don't get it," Emily said.

"It's an arcane concept known as Syndication," Stanton said. "'Dreadnought Stanton will still be Sophos—he just won't be me, and I won't be him. They've bought all the rights to my name, and will pay me licensing fees for it in perpetuity. They'll use it as they see fit."

"They bought your name? But I was just starting to get used to it!"

"For the Institute's purposes, Dreadnought Stanton will always be shrouded in mystery, never seen, always off on some grand adventure or another. Mystic Truth Publishers will keep putting out books about him. But Mrs. Zeno will run the show."

"What about the Stanton Agency?" Emily asked. "Don't tell me she's going to run the Institute and the Agency at the same time? What a lot of work!"

"I'm sure she can handle it all with briskness and dispatch." Stanton smiled. "She's the finest credomancer I've ever met."

Emily nodded at the assessment and took another chocolate.

"I'll have to pick an entirely new name, of course," Stanton said. "Which brings us back to the gifts. Gift number two, to be precise. I'm leaving the choice of my new name up to you, since you seem to be so particular about it."

"You're going to let me choose your name? My stars, what's gotten into you?"

"I'm in love," he said. "Madly and unquestionably."

"And no more secrets?" she said softly. "No more evil ex-lovers? No more bloated malevolent chunks of you hidden in remote locations around the world? No more Black Glass Goddesses who want to claim you for their own?"

"No more secrets," he promised.

"All right, then," she said. "What's your middle name?"

Stanton, seeing how neatly he had been trapped, frowned at her. He took three more chocolates and chewed them vehemently, arms crossed. He steeled himself, but then abruptly lost his courage.

"I can't," he said. "I just can't."

"No more secrets," she reminded him firmly. "And really, how much worse can it be? Aloysious? Percy? Lucifer?"

"Wordsworth," he finally muttered.

"Wordsworth?" Emily drew her brows together. "Dreadnought *Wordsworth* Stanton?"

"After William Wordsworth, the tooth-squeakingly pretentious English poet who wanders lonely as a cloud. I must say, it doesn't suit me at all."

Emily refrained from commenting on that.

"William," she said ponderingly. Then inspiration lit her eyes. "Will. That suits you perfectly!"

"Will Edwards," Stanton spoke the name experimentally. "Sounds very matter-of-fact. I shall endeavor to acquire a sunburned neck to go with it."

"Oh, stop it," she said.

"Should I adopt the custom of chewing on a straw, or should I carry a plug of tobacco in my jeans pocket?"

"Edwards is a perfectly decent name," Emily said frostily. "But, come to think of it, it's not really my name, is it?"

"We could always use my mother's maiden name, if you'd prefer."

"Which was?"

"Van Breeschoten," Stanton said.

"Edwards it is, then," Emily said. "And the third gift?"

"You do like getting gifts, don't you?"

"Who doesn't?" She tumbled over him, feeling in his pockets. Empty candy wrappers scattered like jeweled petals. "Now give! What is it?"

Stanton wrestled with her, laughing. He pulled her down onto his lap, then reached into his pocket. He pressed a silver dollar into her hand.

"What's this?"

"A silver touch-piece," he said.

She turned it over in her hand.

"My last act as Dreadnought Stanton, Sophos of the Stanton Institute, was to create a touch-piece with the power to heal any decent, loyal servant who craves the blessings of his Sophos, even if he be the lowliest of peasant."

"But I thought you couldn't heal yourself."

"I couldn't, not until I relinquished my name. It was put to a magical trust. And this physical being you see before you ceased to be Dreadnought Stanton. Dreadnought Stanton still exists, but this person before you is not him. This person before you is the lowliest of peasants, craving the blessing of his Sophos."

He took the silver dollar from her hand and touched it to his lips, closing his eyes with surprising reverence. Then he opened his eyes again and looked at it.

"Did it work?" Emily said breathlessly.

"I don't know," Stanton said. "I don't feel any different."

He snapped his fingers.

"Flamma," he said.

Nothing happened. He looked at his fingers for a moment, then let his hand catch Emily's.

"It worked," he said softly.

"Then you are—"

"Cured," Stanton said, nuzzling her neck behind her ear. "Completely and utterly unable to channel magic in any form."

Emily twisted to look back at him, her heart trembling. She pressed her hand to his face and realized that indeed he was no longer hot. His cheek felt warm and pleasant.

"It's done, Emily," Stanton said, as if he could feel how hard her heart was beating. "I'm just who I am—no more, no less." He was silent for a moment, and his face was slightly anxious. "Do you think it will be enough?"

Emily took his face between her hands and pressed her lips to his.

"It will be plenty," Emily said. "But you're sure you won't regret it?"

"I'll either regret it or I won't," he said.

The strange arrangement of words, the lack of utter conviction that she had come to expect from him, startled her. But then she realized that the uncertainty was one last gift—a gift he didn't even know he was giving. Any other answer would be a credomantic gloss, a promise he didn't know if he could keep. She flung her arms around his neck and hugged him tight.

"Thank you," she whispered in his ear. "For taking the chance."

When he looked at her again, his face had taken on a familiar polish. "I can tell you one thing with complete certainty. I won't miss Rose Hibble running around after me all the time."

"She was the first on my list for the root treatment," Emily confided in a low voice, sliding her hands along his chest. She loosened his tie, slid it from around his throat, let it drop to the floor among the shining candy wrappers.

"That might have been satisfying," Stanton said, his voice low. She unbuttoned his collar. Then she moved her fingers down the front of his shirt, one button at a time. "Miss Edwards, it appears that you're unbuttoning my shirt."

"I have some etchings to show you," she murmured. She pulled the fabric free and ran her hands over his smooth chest. Her new right hand had such delicacy of feeling that she could feel the edges of the red birthmark, the mark of an outstretched hand. She pulled back curiously, stretching out her fingers to cover it.

"It matches perfectly," she breathed, staring at it.

"I was born to be the consort of a goddess," Stanton said, his chest rising and falling beneath her hand. "I'm just glad it turned out not to be one of black glass." He pulled her close, his hands smoothing along her back.

"No corset," he said, squeezing, his words a teasing whisper. "Skycladdische."

"You'd better believe it," she said, pressing her chest against his and covering his mouth with a kiss that tasted of chocolate.

"Wait," he said, pushing her up a bit. "We can't."

She sat back, looked down at him, her eyes wide.

"You said we could jump straight to the honeymoon!" she protested. "Don't you dare tell me you've changed your mind, and you're going to get all persnickety now just because we haven't had some goddamn authority say a bunch of nonsense over our heads!"

"Not at all," he said, standing and sweeping her up into his arms. It was a rather undignified move, given the closeness of the car and the clutter of the decor, but he managed to accomplish it nonetheless. "It's just that this railcar happens to have a bed. A very large and proper bed. That would be nicer, don't you think?"

"Yes," Emily said, as Stanton bumped her head against a vase full of peonies, sending pink petals fluttering to the floor.

Epilogue

Several weeks later, each astride a frisking black Morgan that was displeased at having been pulled up to stand, Emily and Stanton sat looking down over a valley south of Sacramento. In the purpling summer twilight, with a gentle warm breeze stirring poppies and lupines, Stanton was moved to quote Wordsworth:

> *"It is a beauteous evening, calm and free,*
> *The holy time is quiet as a Nun*
> *Breathless with adoration; the broad sun*
> *Is sinking down in its tranquillity;*
> *The gentleness of heaven broods o'er the Sea:*
> *Listen! the mighty Being is awake,*
> *And doth with his eternal motion make*
> *A sound like thunder—everlastingly.*
> *Dear Child! dear Girl! that walkest with me here,*
> *If thou appear untouched by solemn thought,*
> *Thy nature is not therefore less divine:*
> *Thou liest in Abraham's bosom all the year;*
> *And worship'st at the Temple's inner shrine,*
> *God being with thee when we know it not."*

They were both silent for a moment, admiring the beauty of the valley and the resonance of the words. Finally Emily spoke.

"Didn't think much of the girl walking with him, did he?" she said.

"Apparently not," Stanton admitted. He directed her attention to a distant cluster of buildings. Barns, corrals, and other outbuildings stood scattered around a very large, pleasant-looking house with broad shaded porches. There were spreading oaks and flower beds and a vast kitchen garden plot that, even viewed from a distance, made Emily ache to plant something.

"Built by a cattle baron who went bust in the panic of '73," Stanton said. "Completely furnished, probably horribly. But there's six hundred and forty acres with good pasturage and water—perfect for horses. It's bordered on the west by the Sacramento River, very near Komé's tribal settlement. We can bring her home to her daughter." He allowed Emily to absorb the scene in a long silence before speaking again. "So, what do you think? Will it assuage the anguish of living in sin?"

Having engaged in vigorous and passionate debate while on their honeymoon trip from New York, they had arrived at the startling—and rather liberating—conclusion that the marriage itself was not at all necessary. Stanton no longer had a name to give, and taking Emily's would have involved all the tedium of authority and nonsense they'd hoped to avoid. So, in the end, he had returned to her the simple gold band she had worn for so long, sliding it onto the ring finger of her new right hand. And she had given him a slow soft kiss. They were the only vows required.

"It's perfect," Emily breathed. She reached down to pat Romulus on the neck. "Do you hear that, boy? We're going to start a legacy."

"Emily, they're geldings," Stanton reminded her. "You're going to have to learn a few things if we're going to breed horses."

"I may not know about breeding horses, *Will*," Emily said, "but I know all about creating legacies. Now, before the broad sun sinks down any farther in its tranquillity, I suggest we ride down and get started."

Stanton arched an eyebrow. "Unless I'm pleasantly mistaken, we've already done that, haven't we?"

Emily smiled secretly, the sensitive fingers of her right hand tingling over her belly. Her fingers felt the future, the roar of muddy boy-feet, the promises there.

"Indeed we have," she said, clucking to Romulus and urging him down the hill in a joyful, flying canter.